Also by Kathy Leveno Stackpole

A Bump at Pinnacle Flats

KA$H REUNION

KA$H REUNION

※ ※

KATHY LEVENO STACKPOLE

SENSE OF WONDER PRESS
JAMES A. ROCK & COMPANY, PUBLISHERS
ROCKVILLE • MARYLAND

KA$H REUNION by Kathy Leveno Stackpole

SENSE OF WONDER PRESS
is an imprint of JAMES A. ROCK & CO., PUBLISHERS

KA$H REUNION copyright ©2008 by Kathy Leveno Stackpole

Special contents of this edition copyright ©2008
by James A. Rock & Co., Publishers

All applicable copyrights and other rights reserved worldwide. No part of this publication may be reproduced, in any form or by any means, for any purpose, except as provided by the U.S. Copyright Law, without the express, written permission of the publisher.

This book is a work of fiction. Any resemblance of the characters in this book to actual persons, living or dead, is coincidental and beyond the intent of either the author or the publisher.

Note: Product names, logos, brands, and other trademarks occurring or referred to within this work are the property of their respective trademark holders.

Address comments and inquiries to:
SENSE OF WONDER PRESS
James A. Rock & Company, Publishers
9710 Traville Gateway Drive, #305
Rockville, MD 20850

E-mail:
jrock@rockpublishing.com   lrock@rockpublishing.com
Internet URL: www.rockpublishing.com

ISBN-13/EAN: 978-1-59663-602-6

Library of Congress Control Number: 2008920081

Printed in the United States of America

First Edition: 2008

Also by Kathy Leveno Stackpole
A Bump at Pinnacle Flats

This book is

dedicated

to all the

"Vogini" sisters

ACKNOWLEDGMENTS

I would like to take this time to give my thanks and gratitude to six people. Without their help this book would have never been finished.

To Patti Stewert for her advise about medical matters; to Michael Steidley for his technical support; to Jenny Secerto for correcting my poor spelling and punctuation; to Lisa Horowitz for helping with the proof; to Whinston Antion for the awesome cover design; and to my husband, Gary for putting up with me through the intense process of writing a novel.

PART ONE

AT FIRST
THERE WERE TWO ...

CHAPTER ONE

Without Order There Will be Darkness

1

Sam Kashette, or Kash as he was known to most, was escorted down the prison hallway to the visiting room. The guard's heals clicked behind him, keeping rhythm with the jingle of keys bouncing off his rather large hip. Each step they took echoed against the high, concrete hallway. That weak flat echo sounded awful to Kash, like the shrill of metal against the track of a slowing train. The facility reeked from the odor of stale urine, the damp air chilled Kash to the bone. He could not wait to get out of here.

The guard took his place at the door, after getting Kash seated in the tiny six by six cubical within the visiting room. Even though partitions provided visual privacy, Kash could clearly hear the hushed conversations in the other cubicles. In one cubical, a mother blamed a court system which had unjustly jailed her son. In another cubical, a nagging wife expressed her frustration to her husband who had stuck her with two kids and a bunch of unpaid bills. The conversation Kash found most enticing, however, was the one going on in the cubical directly behind his. Although he could see no faces, he had a good idea what the talking woman looked like. Because she cracked her chewing gum while she talked, he pictured her to be blond and busty. From the repulsive sounds she made while chewing, Kash had no doubt that the wad of gum in her mouth had to be as big as the wad of chew tobacco used by those old timers who sat outside the corner barber shop, talking, and chewing, and spitting the excess juice into a central spittoon (and sometimes directly on the sidewalk). He listened while the woman reassured her incarcerated husband that she had missed him and couldn't wait until he returned home. The conversation amused him; Kash snickered out loud. He figured this broad was doing every guy in town while her husband was inside, yet he was amazed at the way she was able to convince him of her sincerity. By Kash's standards, this woman, and others of her same breed, was considered to be an insignificant part of the human race, a mediocre species, which he regularly referred to as "Inferiors." Prissy, dizzy, stuck-up, snotty, or trashy women wore the brand of Inferiors. Kash had this particular Inferior figured from the start. She was quite a piece of work. He pitied the man in the cubical directly behind his. Obviously, this guy had no clue about the things Kash already knew. Kash had been there. He would never trust another Inferior again.

He checked his watch for the second time in the last three minutes, becoming instantly annoyed. *Where the hell is Carlos?* Kash had no room in his tidy little life for tardiness nor did he appreciate wasting time. Not many Saturday afternoons had been spent in this visiting room. He was a private person, basically friendless; therefore, he had few callers. He certainly had no tolerance for visitors who were late.

It was now April 1993, and Sam Kashette had been a guest of this Kentucky prison for 18 months. It seemed as if those months had taken forever to pass. Had it not been for an argument with another prisoner that ended in a fistfight, he would have been out six months ago. Now he had only 17 hours left of his sentence.

He thought back to that night, the night so long ago, the night when his life changed.

The Country Heaven Band—Tonight—8PM, the neon sign flashed against the darkness on the old back road. Sam Kashette had pulled his rig over for a late dinner and a little music. He had chosen a seat at the bar. A cute perky redhead had caught his eye at once. He bought her a drink. He stayed much longer than he had anticipated, and he quenched his thirst with a vodka and tonic after each dance. Because he worked hard and drove hard all day, every day, he had no problem justifying the long dinner break. Of all the women he had done, (and over the years Kash had had sex with plenty) he had never done a redhead. This was one mountain he had yet to climb. Even today, he still had not reached the top because when that night had come to an end, Kash found his rig smashed into the side of a Volvo on I-64 and by the time Kash regained consciousness, the redhead was nowhere near the scene. Police were everywhere. The driver of the Volvo had been pinned inside. He was a 17-year-old boy who died three days later. Kash had then been charged with DUI causing death. He served 18 months in prison—now he had but 17 hours to go.

Much of the time Sam Kashette spent in the minimum-security penitentiary in northern Kentucky, he worried about how he would earn a living without the use of his rig when he got out. His attorney assured him that his driver license would be suspended for a minimum of five years, thus giving the state the right to impound his rig for that time period. So his rig would have to stay parked. That would mean for five years he would be left with no way to support himself—five years with no money. He knew no other trade. He had spent four years in college but that was fifteen years ago and besides, he never graduated. He had only gone for the party anyway, knowing full well that he was going to drive truck over the road when the time came for him to grow up and get a real life. It took a long time, but the rig in the impound yard was his—free and clear.

At last, Kash's visitor entered the cubical, startling him. He had been jumpy since the day he arrived at this awful hellhole. Carlos sat down in the chair across the table. "How you holding up Kash?"

Kash pecked his finger against his watch again. "You're late. Where the hell have you been?"

"Yeah good to see you too, Kash," he replied in a sarcastic tone and then lit a Camel non-filter. Carlos was a washed up PI who was terrified of Sam Kashette. Carlos owed Kash a favor, and he would sure be glad when the debt was squared. "I got stuck in traffic. What's the big deal?"

"You know how I hate to wait. All I've done for the last 18 months is wait, and I'm tired of it."

"Okay, Okay!"

"Did you get what I needed?"

"I got everything I could from my people. I used the same source that I used to get the records on the other woman, Suzy."

Carlos puffed nervously on the cigarette, exhaling smoke over Kash's head. He was very intimated by Kash; the hand holding the cigarette shook. "You know, Kash, you're asking me to dig up things that happened damn near twenty years ago. It takes time."

Kash slapped the table, attracting looks from the guard. His voice remained just above a whisper. "Time is something I had 18 months ago. I'm running out of time now. And let's be clear, just for the record, I'm not *asking* you anything. You owe me pal, or have you forgotten already?"

"No, no Kash, I ain't forgot. Just lower your voice, don't get crazy," Carlos whispered.

He knew what Sam Kashette was capable of doing. He had just this morning described Kash to his wife by saying he was a bona fide coconut. He could think of no better way to say it, although the description certainly was accurate.

"Here's what I found—it's just the way you figured it. The good doctor wasn't always on the up and up. It looks like she had been skimming off the top of the drug vault while she was working as a pharmacy technician in medical school. She got pretty good at it too. Never did get caught. She made herself a comfortable nest egg and when she came back home to do her internship in Boston, she started mingling with the rich people. That's where she met her husband, Alex. He's an executive in a Boston bank."

"Man, I can't believe she actually became a doctor. She always swore she would make it. What is Dr. Cooper's married name?"

"Jordan and she's not just doctor anymore. She got herself promoted to Chief of Neurology."

"Well." Kash smiled and tapped his fingertips together while taking in this bit of unexpected news. "You have proof to back up all this stuff about the drugs?"

"Yeah," Carlos said. "I put all the information I scraped up on Lora Jordan and Suzy Whitmore in a manila envelope and mailed it this afternoon to the address you gave me."

"Good. That's very good Carlos," Kash said, pinching the cheek of his visitor.

"Look Kash, I know this is none of my business but …"

"You're right. It is none of your business."

"Yeah I know that, but what do you want with all this dirt on some old girlfriends you ain't seen in almost twenty years?"

"Let's just call it supplemental income. Now get out of my face, and I don't ever want to see you again. Got it?"

Carlos threw up his hands and shrugged his shoulders. He had no problem accommodating this man's request, no problem at all. It would be too soon if he ever saw Sam Kashette again. He nodded when he passed the guard and walked through the double doors out of the visiting area.

Kash was taken back to his cell to wait out the one remaining night he was forced to spend in this hellhole. He thought it ironic how he would be getting released from prison on Easter Sunday while at the same time, in another era, Jesus would be rising from the dead. If you believed in Jesus, that is. At one time, Kash did believe in a "Supreme Being" but he never could accept this *Virgin Mary conceived by God* thing. Who in their right mind would believe that a woman could get knocked up by some kind of Holy Ghost? And if not by the ghost, then she would expect people to believe she had done it all by herself? What Kash believed was simple: she had conceived this so-called Savior in the same manner every other woman ultimately did—with the help of a man. After all, wasn't that woman's lot in life, the primary purpose women were put on this earth? To serve man's needs.

At this stage of his life, Kash had no use for God or for church. He viewed everything he had been taught about faith in God and about religion as one colossal joke. How could a single entity in heaven be responsible for creating all living things?—and in six days, no less. Kash believed the earth and the universe were evolved by a perfectly normal scientific process. There had been no interaction by any superior entity. How could a God possibly track the lifestyles of every human being to determine his or her destiny? heaven and hell were the only two choices. No way ... ashes to ashes, dust to dust was what Kash believed. Death was an end, not a beginning.

His parents had no use for any form of organized religion either, but that never stopped Gabby, a long time family friend, from trying to save Kash's soul. She saw to it that Kash was baptized when he was five, and she gave him a proper Catholic upbringing. Kash's parents made no objections to Gabby's stepping in. Why should they care about Kash's spiritual well-being when they never cared about any other aspect of Kash's childhood? But even Gabby's influence could not sway Kash when he got older. By the time he was in high school, he frequented church less and less until finally he got away from it altogether. Kash was tired of living his life based on Ten Commandments written by someone he no longer accepted. He was tired of playing by the rules with the promise that if he did, his soul would return to heaven for eternity. There was no heaven, there was no hell, there was no final destination for his soul to reach, and so, what difference did it make how he lived? We live and then we die. Period. The end. Ashes to ashes dust to dust. Sam Kashette was numero uno, and he had to look out for number one. No spirit from heaven was going to do that for him any more than a spirit from heaven had knocked up Mary, queen of the virgins. His destiny was his own, whatever he made of it.

Kash sat down on the cot that had served as his bed for the last year and a half. This cell was the neatest and tidiest cell on the whole block. The cot had not merely been made but fixed in a fashion that would have made a 20-year military officer awaiting inspection, proud. Books were aligned on the shelf by size all fronted evenly to the edge of the board; the towel and matching washcloth were folded perfectly over the sink basin. His toiletries were neatly placed side by side, again by size, on the shelf above the sink. The Q-Tips and soap were the same color as the washcloth and towel. On the desk, things were arranged the way Kash preferred them, and they had not been rearranged for the past 18 months. Once Kash found a comfortable place for his things these days, he rarely moved them. It made it easier to take a quick inventory. Prisons (even minimum-security ones) were full of thieves. Everything had to be familiar for Kash, and nothing could be cluttered. It was part of *The Order*. He glanced at the nicotine stained walls encircling his cell room. Nothing he could do about that. The inmates were not permitted to use chemical cleaning solutions. Maybe the guards were afraid an angry inmate would use the cleaner as a weapon. Maybe they were right to be afraid.

He could not wait to sleep in his own room again. The confinement here was almost more than he could manage. He needed to relax. The constant noise at the prison caused him to be vigilant at all times. He learned to look over his shoulder regularly. One thing was certain: he would never come back here again.

Kash longed for a time when he could wear his own clothes again. He missed the comfortable feeling of his old blue jeans. The scratchy prison uniforms should have been punishment enough. He had come to appreciate the comfort of his soft, worn jeans, and his Stetson hat, which allowed just a trace of sandy blond hair to brush again his forehead.

Kash was 38-years-old. He stood over six feet tall and had a medium build. He had once been a nice looking boy who had grown into a strikingly handsome man. His eyes were the color of chestnuts, his chin square. His face was gentle yet rugged, and he had a strong Roman nose. Kash followed a regular work out routine these days. There was nothing else to do in the hellhole. He had built up what used to be bony arms and a flat chest into an impressive form. He was sure none of the shirts waiting for him in the dresser at home would fit. However, a shopping spree was far from his primary business. First, he would check the prearranged Post Office box, with the hope of finding a manila envelope from Carlos. The package had better be there, or Carlos would be as dead as Jesus by tomorrow night. Sam Kashette thought about Judas' betrayal of Jesus before His death, and he smiled. Ashes to ashes dust to dust.

2

Heavenly organ music seeped outside to the churchyard where Sister Rosa DeLucci sat on a bench in front a beautifully lit statue of Our Lady. The church was beginning to fill up for the Easter Vigil Mass, but Rosa made no notice. Couples and families walked by the statue to enter the church's side entrance. While a few of them smiled or nodded, most passed by without so much as a single glance. Rosa's heart had never held much envy, but at times she could not help but wonder what family life would have been like—having children, keeping house, holiday cooking, entertaining, sharing a bed. Some days these thoughts obsessed her, especially days like today. Holidays were always so empty.

Rosalee's legs were crossed; her hands were folded in her lap, and gathered within them were mother-of-pearl Rosary beads. Tonight, she prayed the Rosary as she did most nights. Even though the air was chilly, Sister Rosa's fingers were sweaty when they slid over the beads. Lately, she had begun her rosary by dedicating the first three Hail Marys to rain. Hey, Indians do rain dances; Catholics do Hail Marys. Either way was okay, as long as the good Lord heard and opened up the sky to relieve itself of some moisture. The limp, drooping plants and coffee colored grass made Rosa a little sad inside. She never had much of a green thumb and never considered herself a great admirer of flowers and plants, but she had no desire to see things die either. A row of hedges created a pathway between the school, the church, the playground, the convent, and the parish house. They were russet in color and sagged badly. It would have taken hundreds of stakes to prop up all the slack of hedge that curved toward the ground. It amazed Rosa how those same hedges remained rigid and healthy throughout many winters blanketed in deep snow for months at a time in subzero weather but had been defeated by a couple of months without rain.

Sister Rosa was near the end of a fifty-four day Novena in honor of the Blessed Mother. She prayed in petition for a particular favor and she gave thanks that the favor would be granted.

The word Rosary is defined "crown of roses." It was written by Saint Dominic, who had been given the Rosary by Our Blessed Lady through an apparition in 1214, that every Rosary prayed placed 153 white roses and 16 red roses on the heads of Jesus and Mary. St. Dominic promoted and preached the Rosary throughout his life. The Mother also told Dominic that a completed Rosary made a large crown of roses and each chaplet of five decades made a little wreath of flowers or a little crown of heavenly roses. Rosa figured heaven must be a never-ending field of flowers just from her prayers alone over the years. The Rosary had been given to Dominic as a tool, a powerful weapon, to convert sinners.

Rosa could relate to the power of converting sinners through the Rosary. It was her one and only reason for praying. She knew all about the magnitude of prayers it took to convert someone who was filled with sin, someone who was in dire need of redemption.

Rosa loved everything she had learned about Saint Dominic and the history of the Rosary. She had been fascinated by the Virgin Mary and everything associated with her since she was an adolescent in Catholic school.

Sister Rosa's devotion to Mary began one Saturday afternoon in the spring of Rosa's teen years. She and her mother had been preparing the church for Sunday Mass by placing flower arrangements around the altar.

Rosa had placed a small bouquet of daisies at the foot of the Blessed Mary's statue. At first the daisies seemed to pale against the other arrangements of red and white roses, carnations, and mums that filled other parts of the altar. The daisies were so small and so simple by contrast. She stepped back to make sure the daisy bouquet was centered on the pedestal when something happened. The vase seemed to shine, and she saw intricate markings along the vase that she had never noticed before. The leaves of the daisies seemed to be reaching out to the statue, and the delicate white pedals glowed. The yellow center appeared to cast illumination along the bare feet of the Madonna. Rosa stared in awe at the spectacular sight. Here was a beautiful woman smiling down on the congregation day after day giving hope and joy to everyone she touched. Here a woman smiled, even though her only Son had been beaten, ridiculed, and crucified, yet she held no ill-will toward His oppressors. Mary had been guided purely by faith. She had no proof that her Son was the Son of God, that He had died to open the gates of heaven for all man. Even in the beginning, when she first conceived, she was looked upon as an adulteress, or a whore, because she was with child before she had been wed. She had only loyalty to God and her faith to confirm her belief. Rosa truly believed the bouquet of daisies had been the loveliest in the whole church.

When they had finished decorating that day, Rosa knelt in front of the statue for the first time to pray to Mary. She had been praying ever since, in hope that her prayers would be answered.

Today and every day, she prayed for Kash, a man in great need of her prayers, a man whom she was incapable of forgetting. The bonds that united her heart to his were powerful. She could feel the ominous draw pulling on her heart everyday. Like a magnet to steel, she was lured to his heart. She knew instinctively when he needed her. She strongly believed in the mysteries of prayer and the power of the Holy Rosary. She had seen too many prayers answered not to believe. She knew the prayers for Kash would be answered in due time. Tonight, as she concluded the Novena, she appealed to Our Lady of Fatima.

"Queen of the Holy Rosary, inspire my heart with a sincere love of this devotion, in order that by meditating on the mysteries of our redemption I may be enriched with the fruits and the favor which I ask of you in this Rosary. Dear Mary, watch over Kash, as you have watched over and cared for your Son, Jesus Christ. Kash has had many crosses to bear in his life; his soul is weak and frail, but I believe that with your help he will be able to cope with the cross he carries. I ask this in the name of Christ our Lord. Amen."

Making the sign of the cross, Rosa tucked the pearly beads into the pocket of her skirt and walked to Mass.

3

Lora Jordan woke up still sleepy at 6AM sharp. She thought it was funny how a person's biological clock worked. Even without the alarm, she woke at her usual workday time. From the poster bed in the tastefully decorated room, she glanced out the window to find a new day just beginning. The weather was still chilly in Boston this time of year, but at least the snow had melted—what little snow there had been. It had not rained yet this year either, and the last snowfall had been in late February. The people who study these things said that the winter snow total had been dangerously below normal. While it was impossible to predict a drought, they said there could be real trouble if the sky didn't open up for a rainy spring. It was already April. So far, no April showers and probably no May flowers.

Today was Easter Sunday, and since Lora and her husband Alex were not church-going people, there was no need to get up just yet. With her fist, she fluffed the pillow and fell back off to sleep. She had been rising at 6AM for almost a year now, ever since she began a new position at Boston General as the Chief of Neurology. She found that she needed an extra hour or so at the hospital each day in order to complete the duties that came along with the title.

Alex slept soundly in the fetal position next to her. Lora adored him. She never really knew how wonderful it was to be in love until she fell in love with Alex.

She had been born Lora Denise Cooper on a cold morning in February to parents who spent more time at odds with each other than not. Her mother had been thrilled finally to have a little girl after giving birth to two boys. Lora's mother loved all three of her children equally, but she had saved a secret little space in her heart for Lora, and only Lora. She knew how a woman growing up in a man's world could be difficult, so she tried to prepare her daughter early in life to become her own person by instilling in Lora the development of a strong constitution and the quality of becoming a survivor. She did not want her only daughter to end up in the same spiritless role she had been in since birth. She wanted Lora to be independent and self-ruling, and by the time Lora was finishing elementary school, her mother could see that she had succeeded. Lora was becoming a leader. She was never afraid to face a problem or a complicated predicament head on. She was growing into the assertive youngster her mother had patterned her to become.

Lora's mother had not been a working mother when her children were young and in school. Her father, dear ole dad, was a mill worker who earned a decent wage, but between the horses, and the dogs, and the poker games, there was little left to bring home. Unless, of course, you count the good days he had at the track and at the table. When that happened, all the bills got paid to the current balance, everyone was treated to a new outfit, and the family made a trip to the grocery store where whatever was put into cart that day, miraculously made it through the checkout counter and eventually home. Most of the time, when the kids had put something in the cart that dear ole dad didn't deem a necessity, the item would end up in whatever aisle they happened to be going down at the time. Lora often wondered who went through the store after they left and put everything back where it belonged. The store people probably hated to see them walk in the door. *Here comes the Cooper Clan again; follow them,* she imagined they would say. When dear ole dad had bad days at the track and table, it had to be counted too. On those days, he gave nothing, and the only thing her mother gave was the cold shoulder to dear ole dad for spending everything he had earned. It was either feast or famine at the Cooper house, or maybe Cooper trailer would be more appropriate.

They had lived in a used mobile home, still on loan from the bank. Lora found it hard to believe she was living in a tin can on wheels. Whoever had heard of such a thing? The trailer sat on a lot in Majestic Oaks Trailer Park. The only problem was not a single oak tree grew from the grounds, and there was nothing majestic about any of it. A single gravel road took you in and out of the park (yeah right, park), and two dirt roads served to separate the twenty-one trailers into three rows of seven. At no time did Lora suspect she was poor until she realized that she was living among them, so naturally she figured she must be poor too. She came to call her home place Pathetic Jokes. As an adult, Lora tried to forget her childhood. She honestly had no fond memories of her days as a child.

Lora had not been raised in a family setting where love played a critical key role. Dear ole dad was an obsessive gambler who spent little time at home and even less time with his family. He had never been abusive; he had simply been absent. He would give his children's head an occasional pat on his way out the door, and on special occasions, (usually when his luck had been exceptionally good on the pool table), he would bring them home treats, mostly candy that was smashed or cracked from spending too much time in his pocket. This was the only affection Lora had ever received from dear ole dad.

Her mother on the other hand had much affection to give but felt it was inapt to show love to her children until much later in their lives. Her mother was the one who had the job of disciplining the family; therefore, she believed she had to display a rugged exterior for fear if she showed any real compassion, her children would no longer respect her authority. It was not very often that she hugged or kissed Lora or her brothers. Her mother's love had been mostly portrayed in the form of teaching, correcting, and molding her children to be the best persons they could be. Although Lora was the youngest, she understood better than her older brothers did why their mother had to be the way she was.

Lora's parents argued frequently. When they weren't fighting, they were separated. On the whole, they had parted company five times before finally divorcing. It happened just as Lora started high school. Her oldest brother, who was out on his own by this time, was spared the adversity of the family transition. Only Lora and her middle brother were left at home with their mother to carry on family life. Since the day dear ole dad left, Lora had never seen him or heard from him again.

Within days of their divorce, Lora's mom found a job. She still had two children at home to support. Never having worked outside the home, she was terrified to be in the workforce. A local restaurant needed a cook so Lora's mom took the job. The work was hard and the hours were long, hence she had little time left to spend with her son and daughter, but the money was decent and the tips were excellent. Lora had assumed most of the chores at home. She prepared meals, took care of the house, and did the laundry. When she found some spare time for herself, she would curl up on the couch and read romantic adventure novels that took her far away from her own pitiful world. Her mother tried to encourage her to get out more, visit with girlfriends or maybe go places with her brother, but he had friends of his own and did not want to be bothered by his little sister. Consequently, Lora spent most of her adolescence on her own. Because of this, she became a very independent teenager. She made a promise to herself one day after she had finished the last page of a very intriguing novel. She vowed to have whatever she wanted in her adult life, despite the manner used to get it.

With the approach of Lora's junior year in high school, came some good ideas about what she wanted to do with her life; she wanted to become a doctor. Grades would be a non-issue because Lora had carried a 3.5 GPA or better throughout high school. Money, on the other hand would be a major issue. She was nervous when she told her mother about her plans, but her mother was totally supportive. She told her they would get the money somehow. With Lora's other brother now married and also gone from the house, only Lora had been left at home. This gave Lora a bigger cut of her mother's paycheck. Her mother had scrimped and saved and had denied Lora a great deal of extras to put a few dollars away each week for her daughter's education.

In Lora's senior year of high school, her mother took on a second job in the evenings to try to build up the college fund. She cleaned offices in a building located not far from the restaurant where she worked during the day. After only a few days on the cleaning staff, another vacancy had become available, and Lora took the job. She and her mother enjoyed being together, and they worked well as a team. Mother and daughter used this time to refresh their bond—this time as adults. Lora's mom relaxed her rigid exterior, and she and Lora had become fast friends.

By the time Lora was ready to graduate high school, she almost hated leaving her mother alone. For months, she and her mother had looked at pamphlets and researched various colleges, until finally an excited Lora Cooper began her first semester at Kanawha State in West Virginia. She did a superb job academically retaining a 3.7 GPA through four years of college, but financially she was struggling. Her mother's meager savings was quickly dwindling, and Lora was maxed out on financial aid, so before Lora started medical school she got a job in the pharmacy of a hospital near the campus. After graduating from medical school, she had returned to her home state to do her internship at Boston General.

Lora moved into a townhouse in the suburb of a prosperous neighborhood. She budgeted her money carefully, always reserving something to send home to her mother each payday. She rarely spent money lavishly, but when she decided it was time to become active—in a social sense, that is, to start entertaining—she needed to have new furniture. Her taste had become more refined and as a result, she found herself at the bank applying for a personal loan to purchase five rooms of elegant furniture.

Alex Jordan had been the loan officer taking her application that day. The sparks between them were immediate. They began to date and within a year, they were engaged to be married. The engagement was short, only three months. The day Lora said *I do* in front of a few close friends and family members was the happiest day of her life. Now ten years later, Mrs. Lora Jordan was still as happy as she had been on that first day.

So far, Lora had met most of the goals she had laid out in her girlish youth: she had married a wonderful man that loved her very much, and she had made it through medical school, which gave her the cushy career she had always wanted. She and Alex were successful in their respective fields so she had all the money she needed. The only goal she had not fulfilled was the dream of having children. She wanted desperately to fill the house with children and raise them in a completely different manner from the way in which she had been brought up. She wanted to spoil her children, give them everything their little hearts desired. She wanted to lavish them with love and smother them with affection. She was convinced if she could do this, it would nullify the memories of her own deplorable childhood. However, after endless efforts and even some medical assistance, Lora was unable to conceive. They looked into adoption, but the agencies said that they were not good candidates. The Jordans' schedules were too full for a child and Lora was too selfish to sacrifice her career for motherhood. The agencies turned them down twice. Now, she accepted the fact that there would be no children in her life.

After an hour or so, Lora woke up again. This time she chose not to fight it. She quietly slipped out of bed and made her way to the bathroom. As she removed her nightgown in preparation for a shower, she glimpsed at her reflection in the mirror. *Not bad for thirty-eight*, she considered. Her long brown hair had yet to be hindered by gray, and she still maintained a flat tummy and hourglass figure because she chose to follow an exercise program when she could fit it in and she had healthy eating habits. Lora was five foot four and weighed about 110 pounds.

She glanced through the cracked door to find Alex still sleeping soundly. Alex was five years older than Lora. He had a large frame and carried way too much weight. Lora worried daily about his health. His cholesterol level was off the charts, and she knew all too well the consequences of clogged arteries. He could have a heart attack, or a stroke, or worse, he could die. Lora didn't want to think those thoughts. She was determined to do something to help him. Today was the day she would get him back on a diet. Being an officer of a bank branch, Alex got little exercise sitting behind a desk all day. His other problem was a really persistent sweet tooth. A dozen donuts was nothing to fill up his large, 6'2" frame. It was no wonder so many college scouts had recruited heavily to have him catch the football at their school.

She watched him sleep for a little while longer. His chest heaved up and down ever so slightly. A teeny snore sounded from his mouth. She felt the little butterflies in her stomach that reminded her of the love she felt for him. She grinned, knowing she simply had to think about him and all those feelings of young love were reanimated. After all these years, but still she worried. What if… no, Alex will never die. She will help him and make him better. But what about … no, she would not let herself think about that again either. Alex will never find out about the drugs or the money. How could he? She had covered her tracks cleverly. Hadn't she? Still, what if someday the truth were to be revealed? He would never forgive her—she would loose him for sure. She could not imagine life without him.

Getting quietly back into bed, she kissed her husband's neck and chest tenderly thus waking him. The shower could wait.

4

Kash roamed the streets of the small Kentucky suburb. The air was chilly. He walked swiftly to keep warm. The neighborhood was quiet and still. All the shops along Main Street were dark and empty. Apparently, not many establishments were open for business in this small berg on an Easter Sunday morning. He would have to stay in this crummy town until tomorrow so he could pick up his package at the Post Office. He had no idea how he would amuse himself in the interim, but hey, at least he was free—finally free to control his own actions again. Eighteen months of other people telling him what to do was over at last.

He had spent a big part of the morning in an all-night coffee shop along with a prison guard he had befriended. Even though the two men had little in common, they had managed to keep conversation going for several hours. The guard had seen Kash hitchhiking while on his way home from the graveyard shift, so he picked him up, and dropped him off downtown. Kash told the guard he wanted to locate the bus station. When he walked out of the Kentucky prison last night, his only possessions were the clothes on his back (including a shirt that was obviously too tight), $30.00 cash, and a bus pass home. He determined that he had enough money for three or four cheap meals and maybe a beer or two but not enough for a room tonight. He would worry about that problem later.

Still in search of the bus station, Kash made a left off Main Street and now walked along Logan Avenue. Coming upon a church, he crossed over to the other side of the street as to avoid walking directly in front of it. He had to cross—it was part of The Order. This particular church was a Catholic Church. Usually, he walked passed Catholic churches as swiftly as possible, but today he stopped for a moment, in the mood to watch people going to Mass. He was safe, though, since he was on the other side of the street. Entire families emerged from their vehicles in the parking lot. They were all dressed in their Sunday best. Parents clutched their youngsters by the hand as they strolled down the sidewalk. Little girls wore Easter bonnets and carried tiny pocketbooks while little boys wore creased shorts and oxford shirts with bowties and those awful knee high socks. Kash remembered wearing those as a child. He hated it because he felt like a sissy, but Gabby insisted that he look like a perfect little gentleman on holidays.

One particular woman strolling toward the church in a playful jaunt caught his attention. She arrived in a red sports car, and she was hot—maybe thirty or so, very tall and lean, short brown hair and an equally short brown skirt. Her full lips were pursed. She had legs that seemed to go on forever. Kash figured her to be a real bitch. Never again would an Inferior like this one capture his heart. Kash mentally undressed the woman. Oh, what she could do for him. Inferiors were not good for much else. Their sheer existence was of no importance. Kash commonly referred to women as Inferiors, which was exactly what he thought they were. Women were simply put on this earth to serve man's needs. Kash was a man, and he had important needs.

The more Kash undressed the woman, the more cynical he became. Underneath her clothes, he visualized not the perfect body that he had anticipated, but instead a used up body—one that had been around the block more than a few times. He threw his head back in disgust. His pulse quickened; his palms were clammy. The music sounded softly in his head at first, but Kash knew it would get louder; it always did. That ghastly organ music—not organ music coming from the church across the street, but organ music coming from the little organ keeper in his mind—always in minor cords like music out of a cheap horror flick; music which usually paved the way for the *Bad Thoughts*. The Bad Thoughts were starting. The little pictures only Kash could see. Mini movies that wanted him to do whatever he saw. His mind's eye had cast him the lead role. The thoughts flooded in much the same way water gushed through an open lock at a dam. Then the light in his mind dimmed, just like the overhead lights were turned down in a movie theater before the film started. He saw only darkness and the pictures—pictures which he called the Bad Thoughts for lack of a better term.

When Kash had been a child, naughty thoughts entered his mind. There was nothing odd about that. Kash was no different from any other kid his age. All preteens, both boys and girls, had eclectic thoughts. It was part of the maturing process, part of the learning process. But Gabby saw it differently. If she found out Kash had something on his mind that she believed had no place being there, Gabby would tell him, *"Kash, you just whisk those bad thoughts out of your mind. You don't want to be the kind of boy who has impure ideas. Just tell the bad thoughts to go away right now."*

At the time, a nine-year-old Kash assumed Gabby knew what he **was** thinking. It was only after he became older did he understand the only **bad** thoughts Gabby knew about were thoughts that existed in every young **boy's** head—catching a peek under Jane's skirt, smoking cigarettes, kissing **little** Sally (tongue kissing, of course) under the porch, and saying bad **words**.

Those had been youthful thoughts. The thoughts Kash witnessed as an adult were evil, but he called these occurrences the Bad Thoughts just the same.

Currently, things were happening inside of Kash's head—things that Kash would rather not have happen.

The Bad Thoughts showed up whenever Kash was overloaded by any one emotion. It could be any emotion: anger, lust, love, shame, greed, pain. There was not enough room within his mind for too much of any one thing. Kash had subconsciously divided his mind into different sections—just so. Every emotion had its own little compartment. Everything was balanced with just enough room for a certain amount of an emotion to fit in its assigned compartment. When Kash received too much of any one emotion, it spilled out of its compartment and created a domino effect, rushing out and flooding everything in the other compartments. All his emotions mixed together. The overflow jumbled his whole thought process and Kash could not handle it. The problem with Kash was that everything inside his head had to be nice, and neat, and organized, just like his physical actions on the outside. When all this confusion went on inside, his mind allowed the Bad Thoughts to sneak in the same way a diversion might allow extra kids to sneak into a movie theater. The Order had been disturbed and Kash was not capable of controlling it. If he could break up the one particular emotion—in this case, anger, brought on by the realization that the hot girl in the short skirt was not as perfect underneath—and restore The Order, everything would go back to its original compartment and the Bad Thoughts would usually go away.

Concentration on another level generally put his mind back to normal, or at least as normal as Sam Kashette's mind could get. Mentally, he created a crosshair over the center of his darkness, more specifically over the Bad Thoughts, and fired, using words as his bullets. With his eyes closed, he concentrated on the rhyme now and tried to suppress the thoughts:

> *One, two, three, four,*
> *Mary's at the cottage door,*
> *Five, six, seven, eight,*
> *Eating cherries off a plate.*

Kash repeated the Healing Rhyme again, and then again. Finally, his pulse returned to a normal tempo, and his palms had dried. His darkness passed. He was calm enough to resume his walk up town.

Kash found the bus station with no problem. It was located in a small building on busy Crook Street—the only street that showed signs of life at this hour on Easter morning. There were a few run down benches outside and a few not so run down benches inside. The clerk looked tired. From the way he shuffled papers and watched the clock, Kash figured it must be close to his quitting time.

"May I help you?" the man inquired.

"Yeah. I need to have this ticket validated for the next bus to Huntington."

The clerk adjusted his spectacles and stamped the perforated ticket Kash had handed him. "Bus departs from this station at 10:15 tomorrow morning. Will that be all right?"

"Yeah, fine. Do you know where a guy without a whole lot of money could get a decent meal?"

The man named off two places while he returned the ticket to Kash. Kash put the ticket into his wallet and bid the clerk good day.

5

Clayton Whitmore pulled into the car dealership. The gentleman he was going to meet had not yet arrived, so he took a few minutes to look over the cars in the lot. As he browsed through the rows of vehicles, he picked up a scent, not the new car scent he should have smelled, but a soiled smell. The air was lacking that clean crisp scent that should be eminent at this time of the year. There was no healthy plant life to perfume the air. It was stale and smelled off, somehow. Massachusetts sure could use some rain. Springtime was supposed to be full of life, bright with colored flowers and shiny green trees and shrubs. There was no indication of hearty foliage for as far as Clayton could see. What had grown was pale and dirty from the dust that blew up on occasion.

He spotted the black BMW parked inside the showcase window. Cupping his hands around his eyes to get a better view, Clayton admired the beauty of the vehicle. He was certain his son's sixteenth birthday would be one he would never forget.

Clayton looked away from the showcase window when he noticed another vehicle pulling in. He walked over to meet Anthony, who opened the door to the showroom and led Clayton to his office inside.

"Thanks for coming out this morning, Anthony. I feel bad about dragging you away from your family on Easter morning." Clayton clapped the elderly gentleman on the back.

"No problem, Mr. Whitmore. Anytime I can help out, I will."

Anthony owned the local BMW dealership in the small Massachusetts town of Dalton. The intrusion was easy for him to overlook when he thought about the commission he would be getting from this sale.

"I had every intention of getting all these papers signed yesterday, but I was detained at the University," Clayton Whitmore explained, signing the purchase agreement that Anthony had placed in front of him. "Suzy reminded me several times this week that Tommy's birthday happened to be on Easter Sunday this year, so I would have to take care of this business before the weekend. I guess I have too much on my mind."

"Being an important man like you, Mr. Whitmore, I can understand how easily you could forget something."

"Will you still be able to bring the car to the house today?"

"Absolutely, Clayton. I have a boy coming by in just a few minutes to clean her up and get her detailed for you. Does Tommy know he's getting a Bimmer for his birthday?"

"No, it's going to be a surprise. Our family will be attending Easter service at St. Joe's this morning. Would it be possible to bring the car by the house while we're in church?"

"Should take no more than an hour to get the car ready, so I don't see a problem. Do you want me to put her in the driveway or pull her around back?" Anthony asked visualizing the elegant manor on the hill.

Pull it around back. I don't want Tommy to see it when we get back from church."

Clayton Whitmore was a short man of forty-eight years. Being one of the youngest presidents of Hinsdale University in Dalton, Massachusetts, Clayton felt very blessed. He had a good job that he did well. He considered himself an honest, well-educated man. He had had a bout with death a few years back, so he regarded himself as fortunate to even be alive. He also had the woman of his dreams and a fine son who turned sixteen today.

"All right, Clayton. I'll have the car waiting there when you get back from church."

"Again, Anthony, I'm sorry for not taking care of this yesterday. I apologize to you and your family for interrupting your Easter morning," Clayton said sincerely.

"It's all part of the business, Clayton."

The two men shook hands and Clayton Whitmore departed in his University issued Lincoln.

6

Mrs. Suzy Whitmore stood at the full-length mirror in her bedroom applying a light coat of make-up. She used only a trace of mascara to accentuate her huge dark brown eyes but never any shadow or eyeliner. Her eyes were naturally beautiful. Suzy was a thin, tall woman, five feet eleven inches, to be exact. In the words of her father, Suzy was all legs.

Suzy Whitmore was born into a very wealthy New England family. Her name may have been Suzy Shaffer back then, but she was known as Prentis Shaffer's little angel. Because she was an only child, Suzy had been the center of her mother and father's life. She was truly fortunate to be part of such a loving family.

Prentis Shaffer had been a stockbroker and a rather shrewd businessman. He worked very hard after the birth of his daughter and in ten short years, he had become a multi-millionaire. He wanted only the best of everything for his family, especially for his little angel.

By the time Suzy was a youngster, her mother had begun to nurture and cultivate her in the ways of behavior, etiquette, and manners. Most weekends were spent learning the proper ways to sit, walk, talk, eat; even the proper way for a young lady to use a handkerchief. At first, Suzy thought all this training was a complete waste of time. She would have been much happier outside playing with the neighborhood kids rather than staying inside taking dancing lessons and piano lessons. But as she matured into teenhood and began to put to use all that she had learned, she was very grateful her mother had pushed her to be educated in the social graces.

Suzy had many gentlemen callers through her teen years. All her suitors were hand picked by her father. She was happy with the boys her father had chosen for her, but Suzy was approaching her senior year of high school, and she wanted to pick her own dates. Her father had every aspect of his little girl's life planned out for her. Next year she would go off to Harvard and major in law. After her formal education was completed, she would go into practice as a partner with Prentis' brother, Max, and in time, when Max was ready to retire, Suzy would be established, and the law practice would be handed down to her. Marriage would be considered only if Prentis Shaffer could find a suitable husband for his little angel, and the chances of that happening were slim to none.

One evening after supper, Suzy tapped on the door of her father's study and asked if she could talk to him. She explained how she was seventeen now, and that she would like a bit more freedom to govern her life. Her father's heart flinched a little because he knew his little angel was becoming a woman. He feared she would no longer need him one day. He and Suzy had sat in his study that night and talked into the wee hours of the morning. He had learned more about his daughter, and Suzy about her father, in those few hours than either of them could have shared in another seventeen years. Their bond was even more unbreakable now.

The year passed quickly and with her high school days behind her, Suzy was soon ready to pick a college. Prentis was disappointed that his daughter decided not to pursue a law career, but he stood by her decision to attend Kanawha State in West Virginia. She had chosen this university because of its outstanding Journalism Department. Suzy Shaffer wanted to be a journalist and maybe one day, become a writer. More importantly, she chose this school because of its reputation as a party school. Suzy was growing bored with prim and proper behavior being shoved down her throat day and night. While she would never forget how to act like a lady, she wanted to let her hair down and live a bit.

During summer vacation between her freshman and sophomore years at Kanawha State, Suzy received some tragic news: her father was diagnosed with lung cancer. *Those damn cigars*, she had told her mother, *it was those damn cigars*. Suzy told Prentis that she was not going back to school. She said she wanted to stay home and take care of him, but her father would not hear of it. Abiding by her father's wish, Suzy returned to West Virginia and college in the fall. She called to check on her father two or three times a week and made as many trips home as her schedule allowed. Then in December, only eight months after his diagnosis, Prentis took a turn for the worst. The family was called in, but by the time Suzy arrived, her daddy was gone. Suzy had a hard time dealing with her father's death. She had been cheated, not only by her father being taken away from her but also because she never had the chance to say goodbye; she should have set out a semester. She never forgave herself for going back to college that year. Suzy longed for her father daily. He had always been there to take care of her and help her along life's road, and now he was gone. Suzy was lost without his guidance.

After she graduated and went out on her own, she realized she knew nothing about life. She didn't know how to take care of her finances nor did she know how to make responsible decisions on her own. Her mother tried to help, but it simply was not the same as her daddy. She had made a lot of mistakes in those days, both out of ignorance and by trial and error, but one mistake she had not made was her marriage to Clayton Whitmore. From the day they became husband and wife, Clayton made sure Suzy was taken care of in every way. He became Suzy's supporter and protector.

Prentis Shaffer would have approved.

Now, at 38, Suzy was still dependent on Clayton for virtually everything. He didn't mind the role even though he grew angry with her at times, because she would not make an attempt to stand on her own two feet. Many a night they had spent debating the issue of Suzy's insecurity.

"What if I hadn't pulled through the surgery back then, Suz?" Clayton would say. "You don't even know how to fill your own damn car. You've got to learn to be more independent."

"You're much better than I am at taking care of all the little things. Besides, there will always be full-service gasoline stations. The attendant can pump it. Why do I have to learn to be independent darling, when I've got a service station attendant and you?"

"Because I may not always be here to look after you."

"Oh Clayton," Suzy would reply, running her hands over her husband's chest and through his hair. "You're strong and healthy, so you're not going to die any time soon if that's what's bothering you."

Then they would kiss and Suzy's insecurity would be forgotten for the time being.

Most of their quarrels, though, were over her tardiness. For the last three years, it seemed Suzy was always running late. She never dreamed being the wife of a prominent figure in the University would demand so much of her time.

She hurriedly applied a light touch of blush to her cheeks before returning the make-up to its case. Her beautiful deep eyes stared back at her in the mirror. Suzy remembered what her father had said to her in his study that sacred night years ago.

"Suzy, my little angel, you've got stars in your eyes. Someday you'll grow up to be somebody."

As usual, Prentis Shaffer was right.

There was a gentle rap on the door. "Mom, you almost ready?" Tommy pronounced sharply. "It's getting on 9:30!"

Tommy knew Mass would be starting at 10:00 and considering the twenty-minute drive to the church, he knew they would be late—again.

"I'm almost finished. I'll only be another minute."

Tommy rolled his eyes.

Thomas Allen Whitmore was the son of Suzy and Clayton Whitmore. His sullen attitude was due to the fact that today was his sixteenth birthday. Actually, turning another year older wasn't what bothered him. Why should it? At sixteen, his life was just beginning. What needled him was his mother's total disregard for the occasion. For as long as he could remember his mom and dad always made a big fuss over his birthday. Today though, no one had said a word—not even a simple happy birthday. Tommy figured it was because today was Easter Sunday. He was sure one of them would remember soon.

"Your dad's going to meet us in front of the church at fifteen 'till, so we've got plenty of time," Suzy said, brushing her short strawberry blond hair.

"Where did he go this morning?" Tommy pried, trying to get any indication that his dad might be out buying him a birthday present.

"Somewhere downtown. He really didn't specify." Suzy could not help but grin at the thought of Tommy's reaction when he saw the new car. She just prayed that Anthony could get it to the house while they were at church. She was a little concerned about the type of car Clayton had chosen. A BMW was a sporty, fast car. She only hoped Tommy would respect the vehicle. Suzy had used up her share of tragedy and tragic events for the time being after getting through Clayton's surgery. (An aneurysm had formed at the stem of his brain and needed to be corrected.) She did not want to go through another catastrophe from a car accident involving Tommy. She worshipped her husband and her son. She loved them both with all her heart, and she thanked God every day for keeping them a happy, healthy family.

"Okay, I'm ready. Let's hit it."

7

Due to the holiday, Mass ran a little longer than normal this morning. The digital clock on his dad's dashboard showed 11:00. Tommy decided to ride home from church with his dad to see if he would mention his birthday. He had ridden to church with his mom who said nothing about it, so Tommy hoped his dad would at least wish him happy birthday—he didn't. Instead, Clayton filled the conversation with small talk about school and about Dalton High's basketball season. The team had finished the regular season 12 and 1. The coach put Tommy in for a short series of plays during the state finals. He played the forward position. Clayton hoped his son would get more playing time next year, maybe even start, since he would be a junior.

Tommy inherited his height from his mother and a stocky build, much like that of his father. He was six feet three inches tall and still growing. Because of his coordination, height, and athletic ability, his chances for first string next year were quite good. Tommy wanted to be a starter. He liked being in a top position but did not like the struggle, and the sacrifices it took to get there. Simply, he lacked the incentive. Much like his mother, he didn't know how. Things had been handed to him all his life, so he was ignorant to the ways of working for whatever he wanted. Basketball came naturally, though, so it would be easy for him to reach the top.

Tommy was a far cry from the most popular kid in school. The girls had a problem with his attitude because he boasted regularly about his material possessions, and this sort of bragging didn't sit well with your typical 16-year-old girls. For the most part, boys his age dodged his company too because Tommy could be very domineering. He wanted to do whatever he wanted to do, whenever he wanted to do it. There was no comprising or conceding in Tommy's nature. In the rare event things didn't go his way, he would first pout, then get testy, and eventually snub his buddies or simply go home mad. His peers found him to be cocky and arrogant when in reality, it was far from the truth—he was simply shy and somewhat backwards. When in the company of girls or boys his own age, he had no idea how to blend in conversation, so he talked about all the things he had at home in lieu of saying nothing at all.

If you walked into Tommy's bedroom, you could easily mistake it for a downsized version of the local Radio Shack. Suzy had set up the room with a computer and printer, the latest video equipment, the newest electronic games and other things that provided entertainment to teenagers. He had his own television set and VCR, his own telephone, complete with an answering machine and the most technically advanced stereo system money could buy. Books, for both reading and research, lined the walls, and a desk with a comfortable executive chair filled the corner between his bed and the window. There was no reason for this kid to make bad marks in school. Running the length of his room (about twenty feet give or take) was a walk-in closet which housed rows and rows of neatly arranged pants and shirts, both dress and casual, each and every one of the highest fashion from the best designer labels. Suzy went to great lengths to provide her Tommy with the best of everything. Tommy's roomed changed with time as Tommy aged, but from boyhood to teen-hood, Suzy provided him with everything he needed—and some things he didn't need—to make his life comfortable. All of the luxuries his mother made available may sound like bragging to 16-year-old kids, even if those kids received the same luxuries at their houses, yet Tommy made few friends. If asked, he would have to say he had but one good friend, Jeff Baker. Jeff lived a few blocks down the street, and he knew how to handle Tommy. They got along famously. First thing this morning, Jeff had called Tommy to wish him happy birthday. At least somebody had remembered.

While stopped at a traffic light downtown, Clayton lit his pipe. As he puffed, the car filled with vanilla tobacco aroma. He glanced at his son, noticing how much Tommy's looks resembled Suzy's with each passing year. Oh, to be sweet sixteen again. He only now realized that Suzy had been just two years older than Tommy was now when Clayton had first met her.

He had been Professor Whitmore then, teaching at Kanawha State in Charleston, West Virginia, and Suzy Shaffer was one of his students. He had always had an eye for her but then as now, it was inappropriate for professors to date their students. Fate brought them together again four years later in Massachusetts. He had just changed jobs and was in charge of the History Department at Hinsdale University in Dalton. A fire had broken out in the

History of Learning building. Flames quickly filled the halls and branched out to engulf the rooms. The entire structure had been evacuated. After everything settled down, the press and television reporters had been permitted on site to interview some of the students and teachers as they sorted through the rubble. There in a bright red dress covered with suet was Suzy Shaffer frantically trying to get an interview with anybody who would talk to her. Suzy Shaffer had begun her career at the bottom with the Dalton Tribune as a reporter. Clayton had never lost his feelings for her. He gave her an interview that day, and their romance began with a date that evening. After just one year, they were married. Now seventeen years later, they were still happily married and had a 16-year-old son. *My God*, Clayton thought, *where did the time go?*

Suzy's car was already in the garage when Clayton pulled in with Tommy. Tommy pushed the button on the remote control to close the garage door behind them, and the Whitmore family walked into the house together.

After they had changed into more comfortable clothes, Suzy and Clayton went into the posh cherry kitchen to have a cup of coffee. Clayton checked the ham in the oven.

"How are we going to get Tommy out back?"

"Piece a cake." Suzy replied getting two coffee mugs down from the cupboard. "Leave it to mom."

She poured the coffee, set the mugs on the kitchen table, and walked to the foot of the steps leading upstairs. The second floor was filled with music coming from the stereo in Tommy's room.

"Tommy," she yelled, trying to overpower the tunes.

"What?" Tommy yelled back equally as loud.

"Could you take this bag of garbage out to the can for me?"

Tommy turned down the stereo. "Can't dad take it?"

"I'd like you to take it, please. And turn down the volume on the stereo a bit. Your dad and I would like to have our coffee without the company of Guns 'N Roses."

"Yes ma'am." Tommy uttered sarcastically, still annoyed. His birthday and all she had to say was take out the garbage.

Suzy jaunted back to the kitchen and tied up the nearly full bag of garbage. As she did, she felt her husband's arms around her waist. He looked into her deep dark, almost black eyes and said, "You're an inspiration. I love you so much."

"And I love you, too."

Tommy stomped through the kitchen, grabbing the garbage bag with one hand as he passed by, never speaking to either of his parents. Clayton and Suzy followed close behind Tommy through the door and out to the back yard. When Tommy finally spotted the jet black BMW, he stopped dead in his tracks. Anthony had put a huge yellow bow on the roof with streamers that flowed around both sides, over the front, and down to the bumper. Tommy turned around and saw his parents standing there arm in arm.

"Happy birthday, sweetheart!" Suzy and Clayton called as one voice.

Tommy dropped the garbage bag, his mouth hung open wide. He trotted toward his parents, laid one hand on his mom's shoulder, the other on his dad's and shook them both wildly.

"Is it really for me? Mom, Dad, it is great! I can't believe you bought me a car—I can't believe you bought me *this* car! I thought you forgot my birthday. I love it! And I love you both!"

Tommy ran back to the car, around the car, got in the car, got out of the car, walked around the car again, and called for Clayton. "Dad, please come with me. I just have to take it for a ride. I have to show Jeff, he'll just die."

As Suzy watched her husband and son, she thought of all the joy she and Clayton had brought to Tommy. She was fortunate to be able to raise her son so extravagantly. She waved as Tommy and Clayton drove out of the alley behind their home.

She grabbed the bag of garbage that never made it to the can and dropped it in. Walking through the yard, Suzy's mood quickly changed. She hung her head in shame mulling over the secret she had carried in her heart now on the verge of 20 years. She knew guilt was the reason she had indulged Tommy from the day he was born. She had drowned Tommy with love, attention, and affection. It was the reason she had bought him extravagant presents, and lavish gifts for no particular reason, and the reason she frequently threw money his way. Guilt could make you do funny things; make you act excessive and impulsive. Suzy Whitmore tried to sort it all out in her head. What she had done many years ago was something that had to be done. At the time, there was no other way out. Today it was more accepted, but not then.

Suddenly she was depressed. She realized the truth would destroy her family. She had to put it out of her mind. She must not dwell on the past. There was neither room nor time for it in this life.

She went through the backdoor to the kitchen and finished preparing Easter dinner.

CHAPTER TWO

Young Rosalee

1

The day after Easter began much the same way any other Monday did at St. Christopher's convent. It was laundry day. Most of chores around the convent were divided up between the six nuns: the dusting, floor scrubbing, vacuuming, kitchen and bathroom cleaning. The only two things each sister was solely responsible for was the care of her own bedroom and doing her own laundry. Sister Rosalee DeLucci had made Monday her designated washday ever since she first became a nun.

One would think a nun should have little laundry but clothing for the sisters had changed considerably over the years. The old bulky habits were relics now. Most of the time, it was hard to tell a nun from a layperson. Sister Rosalee had come back down to the laundry room because she thought her first wash load would be ready for the dryer. Her timing must have been off because she found the machine just starting the spin cycle when she arrived. So she waited and she wondered. She wondered what sort of trouble Kash had gotten himself into now.

Yesterday was Easter Sunday, the holiest and most joyous holiday on the Catholic calendar yet Sister Rosa felt anything but joyous. The little intuition hub buried deep within her heart, had sent out some major signals on Kash's behalf. She just knew he was in trouble and needed more of her prayers—massive prayers like the ones she had been saying so devoutly for the past 15 years. Sometimes she wondered, like she did today, if she could have helped Kash more by being with him, or at least near him, on a daily basis instead of sheltering herself here in convent. Perhaps if she had stayed at the bus station that day so long ago and played just one more game of pinball, she would have simply gotten back on the bus and gone home.

2

It was May in 1978, 15 years ago, when Rosalee had gotten off the bus. She laid her valise under the pinball machine and inserted a quarter into the slot. The ball ejected and music began to play. She took a long look around the bus station. The place was virtually empty except for a few people who waited to board the bus from which Rosalee had just disembarked. They looked her way, she supposed, because of all the noise the machine was making. She had racked up plenty of points on the "One Star" pinball machine. A few weeks ago, she had tried playing one of the new digital pinball machines, but she still preferred the older ones; the ones that continued to use meter counters. The old machines were not as quick as the new ones, but she liked that. She liked working the machine, shaking it to prevent loosing the ball. The new pinball machines were simply too easy to tilt.

Her stance was loose—feet 18 inches apart, arms bent at the elbow cradling the machine, middle fingers working the flipper buttons on each side—her body stood a good foot away from the machine itself. Rosa's aim was on today. Using skillful maneuvers to control the ball, she had hit all the ramps so far, causing the machine to make quite a bit of racket. After bouncing off the bumpers a few times, the metal ball shot directly between the flippers and down the hole.

The first ball was played and so too was the first part of Rosalee's young life.

She needed to kill time because even now it was too early to leave for her appointment. To some extent, she was nervous about the meeting, while at the same time she was excited. It seemed Rosalee had a hard time making up her mind about everything these days. A quick game of pinball was the best way she knew to clear her head and calm her nerves. It was a pretty good way to pass time too. So she turned her focus to the game.

Placing her fingers on the flippers once more, Rosa put the second ball into play. Deep concentration was the key to playing any pinball machine and right now, she wanted nothing more than to get her mind off her problems. Twenty-two-year-old Rosalee DeLucci had mastered the game with accuracy. She played pinball well, and she liked the challenge. This being one of the few things in which she excelled. She had learned about the game as a child by tagging along with her older brother Frankie to the bowling alley or arcade. He was only two years older than she was, but still he was older. They had spent a great deal of time together growing up. He never minded taking his little sister with him wherever he went.

The five-hour bus ride was beginning to take a toll on Rosalee even though she had taken a nap. Her back was sore, and she fought heavy eyelids. Ball number two buzzed past Rosalee's foggy target into the machine's belly. If only she had learned to drive. She could have slept an extra hour this morning, maybe even two, instead of taking a bus that made several stops along the way—not to mention, out of the way—only to drop her at her destination well before the meeting. Frankie had tried to teach her how to drive once when she was sixteen, but after several weeks of lessons and arguments, Rosa decided that she did not belong behind the wheel of a car. So now, she depended on public transportation and the kindness of friends to make her way from one place to another. Rosa loved her brother very much, even more so for trying to get her on wheels.

Frankie was more than a brother; he was her friend, sometimes her only friend. She would really miss him now that she was going away, but he had made it clear that he would always be there for her, no matter what. It helped, too, knowing that her family supported her plans for the future even if they failed to understand it. Sometimes Rosalee was unsure if she understood it too, but she had made the only choice—of that, she was sure.

Rosa was special. Her Mama and Papa told her that she was special, her *Nonna* told her she was special, and Frankie told her she was special. She knew she was special, but not in the same way her family thought. They believed Rosa touched people in a unique way. While that may have been true, Rosa only strived to touch one person. It was that one person to whom she was connected, that one person whose soul was joined with hers as surely as if they had been Siamese Twins. It was Sam Kashette whom she yearned to touch.

This attachment, this weird feeling toward him, was deep, sometimes too deep for Rosa's comfort. Some days the weird feelings were strong. Rosa could feel them tugging and pulling at her soul. Most days though they were weak, feeling like nothing more than a flip-flop in her stomach, as if she had just plummeted down a steep incline on a rollercoaster at the local amusement park. Only she wouldn't be at the amusement park. She would be in class, or in the shower, or in church, or making dinner, or sitting on the shitter, for God's sake. Where she was when the feeling hit was not important. The important part was the fact that he needed her. The weird feelings conveyed this important message to her.

Ching-ching, ching-ching-ching, was the only sound Rosa focused on now. The last of three balls bounced from bumper to bumper. The meter clicked as it accumulated points earned. Lights flashed and bells rang. Rosa continued to shake the machine taking care not to tilt. She worked the controls like a pro, jerking her body and lifting her shoulder with each tap of the flippers that kept the silver ball from going astray. If only growing up were that simple: keep the ball in sight, get around as many obstacles as possible, rack up points as you go, advance to the highest level, and maybe when it was all over, you end up with a bonus. Things were not that simple for Rosalee DeLucci. She had been struggling frequently with her conscience over the past five years, but now she was ready to put her life in order. She was finally ready to put Rosalee DeLucci first. She looked at her watch; it was time to go.

3

Young Rosalee walked the short distance to her meeting at the convent in a daze that day 15 years ago. Before she was able to change her mind, she could see the large white complex approaching. It sat atop a hill in the mountains of northern West Virginia.

Maybe I'm not here at all, she thought. *Maybe I'm really at home asleep and this is nothing more than a dream.* In reality, she knew this was not the case. She was here all right; this was the real thing—real life. She just wasn't sure this was the place where she belonged.

The building itself was quite lovely, painted a taupe color with green shutters. The windows sparkled in the morning sun. The lawn was perfectly manicured; shrubs and flowers landscaped the grounds as if a celebrity or a dignitary took residence here. To another person the view would be breathtaking, but to Rosa it looked like Hotel Hell, or a haunted house, or some other such nonsense. She felt like she was approaching a spooky castle complete with a moat and a dungeon where men, dressed in steel armor with funny looking weapons, would torture twenty-two-year-old girls who made poor decisions. To her the building looked ominous and cold. Very uninviting. Although no one forced her to be here—she could walk away if she wanted—she truly believed she had run out of options. The part of her brain responsible for making decisions was tired. This place was her destiny; in her heart, she knew she was supposed to be here. All the second thoughts were used up. So were the thirds and fourths, and fifths, for that matter. There was no more time for thinking.

She glanced over her shoulder, reluctant to climb the five steps toward the door. She checked the ground around the building and saw no moat (that was a good thing) so she took the steps slowly and cautiously. The warm breeze blew her waist-length hair into her face. She gathered the mane at the nap of her neck and fastened it with a clip from her pocket. It was ten o'clock in the morning. The sun peaked over the horizon with great energy. It was to be unseasonably warm today. She cleared a few stray hairs away from her eyes and then asked herself one more time if this was really what she wanted. She answered the question by ringing the bell. The door was answered quickly.

"Ms. DeLucci. Please come in. Let me take your bag," the tall woman said in a deep, course voice. Rosalee believed she was the tallest woman she had ever seen.

Rosa wondered if she was the only one who the nuns were expecting. If others had been scheduled, how did sister know with such certainty which one she was? Of course, she could have been the last to arrive, which would have given the sister her name by process of elimination. Surely, she was not to be the only new one here.

She stepped inside and laid her baggage at the foot of the steps. Once she stepped over the threshold, she knew it would be too late to turn back. Her formal application had been processed, and her candidacy had been accepted.

Sister Helen, who was to be her vocation director, led Rosa through a long narrow hallway and into a large dining room where eight other sisters sat around a huge table.

Rosa looked around the room and into the adjoining rooms on either side of the dining area. The rooms were tastefully decorated in soft pastel colors, accented with silk flower arrangements and religious and scenic pictures. Some of the groupings included sconces complete with lit candles that created a homey glow. Swags hung above some of the other prints. It was really very charming.

Introductions were made around the dining table; Rosa's mind raced. Had the decision she made only six months ago been made in haste? After all, she was only 22-years old and entering the convent scared her terribly. It was a lifelong vocation, and she was not sure she was ready for such commitment.

Rosa had a notion about her life. She had mapped it all out. She would go to college, get a good job, fall in love, get married, buy a house, have beautiful children, and live happily ever after. She did finished college, but somewhere between that time and happily ever after, she fell in love and was never able to climb back out. Unfortunately, the love she felt was unrequited love.

Rosalee had been drawn to Sam Kashette, a young boy who lived in her hometown, since she was the tender age of fifteen years, a very impressionable age, an age of new emotions and unvisited feelings, an age of dreams. The family had called it a crush or puppy love, but the energy that pulled Rosa toward Kash was more. It was real and it was forever; it was unforgettable. She adored Kash, idolized him, even chased him through their high school days and then through college. Sometimes she caught him, but nothing serious ever developed. Despite this, she never gave up. The force that steered her toward him never tapered. For as long as she had known Kash, she had accepted these weird feelings about him. Of course, everything about her feelings for Kash was weird. For the life of her, she could not understand why she felt the way she did about a man, who in all honesty, had not paid much attention to her. But still, she had a need to take care of him, an urgent summons that said without her attention, he was a doomed man.

By the time they had gone to college, Sam Kashette had become the center of Rosa's life. He consumed her totally. Kash, however, did not share Rosa's enthusiasm. It wasn't enough for Kash to be the center of Rosa's attention; he needed to be the center of *everyone's* attention. They attended many of the same parties, and it was at those parties that Rosa had begun to binge drink in an attempt to get closer to Kash. He stayed stoned throughout much of his young adult years so Rosa did the same—she needed to be near him. Rosa did eventually succeed in getting Kash's attention, but nothing more than a short-term relationship ever developed.

During her last year in college, she realized she was unable to neither start the day, or end the day, nor handle any kind of stressful situation without turning to alcohol. It was time for Alcoholics Anonymous; she was powerless over alcohol. After a few meetings, Rosa realized that most of the 12 steps in the "12 Step Recovery Program" required faith in God or God's help to get well. It was after 50 weeks of AA that Rosa discovered God was full of surprises. After many months of prayer and soul searching, she decided that God had been calling, and it was time to pick up the phone. She came to a point where she had to make a choice between chasing Sam Kashette, smoking pot, and getting drunk or a vocation of religious life serving God. Quite a lifestyle contrast Jesus had handed her, but she believed God never gave His children more than they could handle, so she had accepted His challenge.

Rosa took the cup of herb tea offered by one of the sisters. While she sipped the brew, she checked out each of the other women at the table. They seemed to be having such a good time laughing, and talking, and cutting up. She expected everyone here to be solemn and pious, maybe even afraid to smile much less laugh. Most of the nuns were middle-aged, except for one who was very old, and two others who were very young. The latter wore pure white habits donned by those who had not yet taken their vows. Rosa thought one of the white habits looked to be even younger than she was.

Rosa had graduated from Kanawha State in Charleston, West Virginia merely three weeks ago. Her degree was in elementary education. She loved children and the thought of molding their young minds enticed her. She told this to her family when she moved back home after graduation. They were excited about her teaching career. Rosa never revealed her drinking problem to her family, although her brother Frankie suspected. She never told them about the AA meetings or about the 12 Step Program either, but she did reveal the mental and emotional outcome from that period of her life.

One morning after breakfast about a week before Rosa left for the convent, Rosa had told the members of her family that her candidacy to become a novice had been accepted. They had been stunned by her sudden career change. It surprised them because Rosa had been neither energetic about taking part in church activities nor had she been passionate about religion, for that matter. Yes, she had attended Catholic school—grades one through eight—and yes, she had gone to Mass every Sunday and most Catholic holy days; she had even done some volunteer work once in a while, but nothing to the extreme that would have made them believe she was considering the convent. She had told her *Nonna* later that day, "For many years I dreamed about a fairy tale wedding where Papa would give me away to Kash. Kash would be my partner for life, but I didn't think I could give my heart over to him when I had not given it to Jesus first. As I pondered on that theory I found Jesus to be a true gentleman, and I accepted his invitation to a life with him."

Nonna and Frankie said they understood, but her parents were a little disappointed and more than a little confused by her impulsive, overwhelming devotion.

For Rosa, devotion had not been the only motive. First, she needed to get into an environment where drinking was not accepted. She was sure nothing stronger than herb tea was stored in this place. She had to stay sober to prove to herself that she could. And second, she had been rejected by the man she loved. Other men would have probably entered her life, but she would never feel the same way about them as she did about Kash. She would never find that connection, that utter electricity like she had found with Kash. She wanted his love in return, and being denied that, she made herself available to serve the Lord. She had been hurt too many times to remember. Being away from him was the only answer, and moving to another town was not enough. She could move a thousand miles away, and he would still be there. Their souls were connected. The invisible thread attached her heart to his. Distance was not the issue, but solitude and time were, for she knew that with both those things on her side she could overrun these feelings of defeat and failure. However, she had to go far enough away to a place where her heart could heal. She could not bear to spend another night in the same town where he lived, in the same town where he drank and carried on with other women, in the same town where Rosa carried the heavy burden of being the only person who knew his secret. She had to go away to a place where he could never touch her heart again.

The convent was that place, not only because her heart was safe from hurt, but also because she could use her life's work to pray for him. She could have taken her teaching degree, joined the working class, and still made time to pray for Kash, but she believed the kind of prayers he needed—the magnitude he needed—had to come from someone who could devote a lifetime to pray for him. She believed earnestly in the power of prayer, and she was sure that with enough prayers, his life would turn around, and she would be able to spare him the fateful pain that surely awaited him.

When their tea was finished, Sister LaSalle, who was to be Rosa's spiritual director, accompanied her to a room on the second floor of the convent. Rosa peaked into the other rooms as she walked by. This floor too was beautifully decorated. Each bedroom was painted in rich colors with matching bedspread and curtains in different prints. On the floor, plush carpet stretched out full. It looked so fluffy and inviting it made Rosa want to slip out of her shoes and socks, and let the carpet squish up between her toes as she walked across it.

The room to which she was finally escorted was small, but it contained all the essentials: a bed, dresser, nightstand, and a tiny writing desk with a built-in reading lamp. This one had a bedspread and curtains done in a pale floral print of peach and coral. The walls and carpet were beige. The color scheme appealed to Rosa—nothing too bright or colorful—just something plain and simple, much like Rosalee. A two-foot high kneeler stood in the corner near the door. Above it hung an oversized crucifix of Jesus Christ. She gazed at the empty shelf below the crucifix and knew immediately what would look perfect there. She was beginning to get comfortable. This was to be Rosa's room; this was to be Rosa's home.

In a plastic cleaner's bag lying on the bed, was a white habit identical to the ones worn by the two younger novices. Sister Helen appeared at the door and asked Rosa to sit in the chair by the desk. Sister LaSalle then took a pair of scissors from the middle drawer.

"I find it's better if we do this now, without delay," Sister Helen explained to Rosa. "It seems this is the hardest part for some of the young girls."

Rosa's eyes drifted from the shiny silver of the scissors' blades to the jolly-looking nun holding them. She had not taken into account this tiny sacrifice.

Sister Helen was still talking, "If it's any consolation, Sister LaSalle is a very good barber. I think you'll be pleased with the outcome."

She removed the tie that held Rosa long black hair. Sister LaSalle began by brushing the glossy strands. When Rosa heard the first snip of the scissors, she flinched as though the strands of hair had feeling, as though each strand would bleed when severed, yet the soothing voices of the two nuns calmed her at once. The ebony locks fell to the floor. When the task was complete, Sister Helen told Rosa to change into the habit which had been laid out for her.

Before the two nuns exited the room, Sister Helen said, "We are consecrated to God through the vows of chastity, poverty and obedience." She smiled compassionately, then asked, "Are you sure you're willing to accept these vows Rosalee?"

"Yes Sister, I am."

"You'll be included in a program of prayer, study, and community living. We will prepare you for your perpetual vows."

Then she told Rosa to come downstairs, after she had dressed, and get acquainted with the other sisters. She said they would help her to become familiar with the tight schedule on which the convent was run.

When she was finally alone, she looked at her image in the mirror. Her waist length hair which had not been cut in eleven years (aside from an occasional trim) was now cropped above her ears. As promised, the style was attractive, but what did it matter? She would be the only one who would see it. She felt as though her femininity, as well as her childhood, had been sheared away with the mane. Tears spilled down her cheeks cleansing a soul that was so confused. She was frightened and alone and mixed up in a strange place with strange people. She wanted her family and the security they provided. She wanted to go back home. She wanted to help *Nonna* with supper, she wanted to give Frankie a back rub, she wanted to play gin rummy with her Mama and Papa, but she was here, in a convent, and she had to stand by her decision. Change was inevitable; it was too late now.

She wiped away the tears and quietly unpacked the small valise she had brought with her. On the shelf below the crucifix, she placed a ceramic Madonna given to her by Father Bump when she had been a child. She prayed to the Blessed Mother every day. This little corner, with its shelf and kneeler, will be a peaceful place to pray.

Doing as Sister Helen instructed, she removed the habit from the plastic bag and slipped the outfit over her head. The material was soft against her youthful skin, leaving her with a sense of comfort. The headpiece fit snugly along her scalp; only a tiny whisper of hair feathered around her young face.

She was about to put her valise in the closet when she realized it wasn't empty. She pulled out a cedar lock box that held Rosa's own secrets. She brushed her hand over the smooth top, inhaling deeply the strong smell of cedar. She placed the box on top of the dresser. Studying the room, Rosa started to feel good about her decision. Maybe this was the ideal place for her.

Before she left her room, she looked at the image in the mirror again. What she saw this time was favorable. It was not a frightened child running from herself who looked back from the mirror, but instead a grown woman who was willing to make a sacrifice in her life in order to protect a man she loved, knowing if she prayed long and hard God would find it in His mercy to let this man be whole. She would ask God through His mother to spare Kash the torment passed down through his blood. God was forgiving, and God was compassionate; therefore, Rosa was certain her only wish would be granted.

She closed the door behind her. The habit made little swishing sounds as she walked softly through the hall. She was surprised how easily she had adjusted to wearing the new habit, and she was warming to her new surroundings as well. She walked slowly down each of the steps, careful not to trip on the habit. The closer she got to the bottom of the steps, the more intense the smell of baked pastries became. It was banana bread to be exact. Yes, maybe she would fit in here just fine after all.

When Rosa entered the main floor, she paused at the French doors adjoining the dining room. The other Sisters in there were talking and laughing. They were waiting for her. Clutching the brass door handles, she hesitated knowing that beyond the door was a new life, one from which she could not turn back, one which she would spend alone, without the man she so deeply loved. The door handle squeaked a bit when she turned it. There was an unseen, unspoken boundary that lay just beyond the doorway. Rosalee understood that when she crossed over the threshold, she would be doing more than simply entering a room. She would be entering a new life as well. One she would share with Jesus Christ.

4

That seemed like an eternity ago to Sister Rosa. She shifted one load of wet clothes to the dryer and packed the second load into the washer. Fifteen years of praying for Kash and she would pray for fifteen more if that's what it took to get rid of his darkness. She was totally committed to restoring his sanity.

CHAPTER THREE

*Paving
the Way*

1

Sam Kashette had spent Easter night in the small Kentucky town. A concession stand at the high school football field provided him shelter from the weather. The small wooden building was in dire need of painting. He had chosen this spot for two reasons: the football field was located only two blocks from the post office where he needed to visit in the morning, and more importantly, the padlock on the door was easy to pry open. The location was also ideal because the surrounding area was virtually abandoned. The few houses within sight of the field were nowhere near close enough to reveal that Kash had taken up temporary residence inside.

The interior of the concession stand was larger than it appeared to be from the outside, but because several rows of baseball and football equipment lined the floor around all four walls, Kash had been left with a closed-in, frightening feeling. Judging from the size of the equipment, the field must be used for small children, maybe between the ages of six and ten. Assembled along two of the walls were shelves, one of which held #10 cans of hot dog chili, nacho cheese, ketchup, mustard, relish, while the other held paper products like french-fry cups, hot dog boats, napkins, straws, cups, and lids. On the two remaining walls hung cabinets, which looked like something that had been discarded from someone's 1950ish kitchen, after the completion of a major remodel project. Kash had snooped around in there but found nothing useful to him. In one of the floor cabinets, he had found a cloth bag stuffed with rags, which he now used for a pillow.

The chilly April night was in the fifties. Kash kept warm by using a thermal blanket he found wrapped around some glass coffeepots.

Kash's eyes fluttered in his REM sleep. He was having an intense dream. He began to thrash his body from side to side on the wooden floor, slamming into anything in his path. With a sudden jolt, he woke up, covered with sweat and feeling terribly alone and scared. Slices of daylight peaked through the cracks between the boards of the old structure. He was relieved to see it, more so than he cared to admit.

Kash had dreamed this same dream when he first arrived at the Kentucky hellhole. At the time, he was convinced he'd had the nightmare because of the confines of his cell. He was a free man now, so why had the dream come to him again? Was it because of the cramped closeness of the concession stand? Could the little boy in the dream be him? What was the blob in the dream, and why was the little boy so scared? Kash picked up a scent of something musty. Yes, that had been in the dream too. In addition, he was thirsty as was the little boy in the dream.

Once fully awake, Kash felt better. He gathered up his things and started walking to the post office. He pushed the nightmare to the back of his mind. He only wanted to go home.

Kash found the post office with no trouble. The postmaster was just opening up.

"Good morning," Kash greeted the man. "I had a box rented for me by a second party a few weeks ago. The number is 627. I need the key to get my mail."

The gray-haired postmaster looked through his file of index cards. "Are you Samuel Kirkland?"

"That's correct,"

The man removed a key from the small pegboard hook. "Here you go. Six twenty-seven is near the corner over there, see?" the postmaster pointed. "Your box is paid up until April first of next year."

"Okay, thanks," Kash said as he walked toward the little box in the wall.

Just as Carlos promised, the manila envelope was propped upright in the box. Kash pulled it out, locked the box again, and left the post office. He checked his wristwatch and discovered he still had two hours to kill before he had to meet his bus. He decided to go back to the diner where he ate lunch yesterday. The food was not bad for the price, and besides, there was a bar next door that Kash was certain would be open today. He had not had a beer in 18 months. It would sure taste good.

The walk from the post office to the restaurant was only a short hike. He passed a western shop on his way. He snickered at the name of the business—Lora's Leathers. Kash wondered how Lora (Cooper) Jordan would react to seeing him again after all these years. She had always been a beautiful woman, a bit on the feisty side, but Kash liked that. The harder they fought the more it excited him.

He was curious about her life since their college days, remembering how the Cooper's had little money and how each semester at old K State had been a financial struggle for Lora. When Lora's parents had divorced, there was hardly enough money for her and her mother to live on, much less to send her to college. Kash recalled Lora telling him that. He also remembered how, with the help of grants, school loans, and work programs, Lora had single-handedly put herself through college.

When Kash's own parents had died, Lora had encouraged him to do the same, but at that point, he was done with the higher education scene. He had had enough of the professors' bullshit and enough of their political correctness for one lifetime. Kash never returned to classes after mid-terms that year. Without his parents' income to support him, he would have little money to party away. His parents had not yet been 40 when a malfunction in their car's brakes hurled them over a West Virginia hillside to their death. His parents like many people their age, carried very little life insurance, so the policy left Kash with enough money to bury them and only a few thousand left over after paying all the bills. There was practically nothing to spare. Back then, he had been a real spender who resented being without cash in his pocket, so he went to work. Lora broke off the relationship when Kash announced he was quitting school to take a truck-driving job. She claimed they no longer had anything in common. *Lose the dough; lose the dame*, Kash thought. Then an afterthought, *screw that Inferior*. At any rate, Kash knew the real reason Lora had severed the relationship: so long as Kash was a college preppie, he was good enough for Lora, but once he became part of the working class, he was no longer suitable for her. Just imagine ... a truck driver not good enough for Lora Cooper, pure trailer trash. He still carried bitter feelings that the break-up caused. *That's okay*, Kash thought. *She'll pay her debt to me in full before I'm finished with her*. He despised Lora and all the other *stuck-up, I'm-better-than-you* Inferiors that made him feel common.

He approached the diner and was close enough to read the sign hanging above the door. Breakfast was served until 11AM. Good ... because he was hungry for bacon and eggs. Then he would go next door and have some beers. The papers in the package would not be inspected until he was alone on the bus.

2

Kash was comfortable in the seat on the bus. He selected one near the back, and since the bus was only partially full, no one sat next to him, thankfully. When the driver started the coach, the smell of diesel fuel perfumed the interior. Kash was right at home. He missed the sound of grinding gears and the odor of diesel fuel. He missed the tires humming under his feet, and most of all he missed the easy pickups at the truck stops. Those wenches would do just about anything for a meal, a couple drinks, and a few bucks. Damn, he was going to miss his rig.

When he and his rig had been on the road, he was in total control. He decided when he ate, when he slept, which way to go, when to leave. He was in complete control of his destination. If he wanted to, he could get in his rig on the east coast on a Tuesday and get out of his rig on the west coast before the weekend. He could go anyplace the highways took him, spending hours, even days, chasing sunshine from one state to the next. He was free when he was in his rig; no ties to any one place. The whole country was at his disposal, there for the drive.

The rig had been his office, his living room, and his bedroom all on 18 wheels rolling down the freeway—everything nice and tidy in one large package. His truck had been kept as meticulously neat as his cell room in Kentucky and his house in West Virginia. He could blindly reach for anything in his rig and find it because it was right where it was supposed to be.

Now, on the bus taking him home, Kash reached into the manila envelope. He pulled out a folder filled with several pieces of paper. He leafed through it. He also found a cassette tape. He knew whose voices would be on the tape, and he anticipated hearing the details of the interview.

Carlos had told Kash, during one of his visits to the prison, how he had found an old coworker of Dr. Lora Jordan's who was willing to talk to him. Carlos posed as a police lieutenant when he had visited the home of Rob Parker, Lora's co-worker. Parker had been arrested for possession of a controlled substance but was now out on bail. Carlos, playing the role of lieutenant, offered Rob a plea in return for information on Dr. Jordan. Parker had bought into the bit of trickery and agreed to a tape-recorded interview with Carlos. Kash would have to wait until he was home to listen to the audio, since a tape player was unavailable.

Digging deeper into the envelope, he found an ID that Carlos had assured him would be there. Using a bogus birth certificate, Carlos applied for and acquired a driver's license in the name of Samuel Kirkland. He was amazed at how much the man in the picture looked like him. He wondered where Carlos had found him and how much of the man's appearance was made up or touched up by the forger. Kash understood that this license would only allow him to drive his pickup truck—not a commercial vehicle. Since the Federal Government started regulating Commercial Driver Licenses (CDL's), Kash felt it too risky to attempt getting another one in Sam

Kirkland's name. Even if he could pull it off, he would have to take a job with a trucking company because the state still had his rig. If he could not drive as an owner-operator using his own rig, he would not drive at all. Anyway, working for someone else would mean he'd have a boss, and Kash had no use for a boss other than himself.

Kash had a genuine problem with authority. He let no one tell him what he could or could not do. It was from that premise that he had formed his opinion and denial of any religious deity. After all, wasn't God the ultimate boss, the premier authority figure?

Kash put the new driver's license in his wallet, thankful at least for the freedom to get around in his personal vehicle. He neatly arranged the rest of the papers and the cassette before he put the contents back into the envelope.

Carlos had certainly done his homework. His debt to Kash had indeed been squared.

He laid his head against the back of the bus seat. He was getting tired. He watched out the window for a while. Everything outside was dried up. The Crown Vetch that flowed along the banks and in the medium of the interstate should be in full bloom. The vines should be loaded with beautiful rich purple cups that would invite you to run through them in your bare feet, but instead the vines were scarcely populated and the plant seemed to huff and puff to blow out the faintest color of purple. The grass along the banks had not turned brown yet. It looked to be the colors of gold and tan, but soon, it too would die like everything else that could not live without moisture. The appearance of withering plants and dying vegetation was not unappealing to Kash. Everything in his world was black and dead anyway. If Mother Nature wanted to have a bad day, that was fine with him. Everyone would have to wait for her darkness to pass just like Kash sometimes had to wait for his own darkness to pass. It was not something that could be rushed.

Sam Kashette was grateful that the ride across the West Virginia state line taking him home would only be a little more than an hour. He dozed off thinking of his home, the house where he had been raised.

3

Lora Jordan arrived home from the hospital at her usual time today, about one hour ahead of Alex. She liked getting home first so she would have time to start dinner. Walking into her country kitchen, she thought about the news she had received today. She could hardly wait to tell Alex about it.

Dr. Jordan had met with the Foundation Board at the hospital this morning, and she was given approval to raise funds for a new scanning machine.

As she seasoned some salmon she picked up at a local fish market on her way home, she thought about all the work ahead of her. After putting the fish in the oven to bake, she sat down at the window seat to put her fund raising ideas on paper. The kitchen was Lora's favorite place to think. When she and Alex had bought the large old New England style house eight years ago, it had been pretty run down. They remodeled each of the seven rooms one by one. With Alex's architectural knowledge and Lora's keen eye for design, the remodeling efforts resulted in a truly spectacular home.

Lora loved brass and her home was full of brass things—brass lamps, brass figurines, brass candlesticks, brass fixtures, brass vases, brass tables. Everything brassy, just like Lora. She liked the gloss of the polished metal.

All of the rooms in the Jordan's house were full of beautiful posh furniture and accents. Lora preferred the rich look of cherry and walnut, which made up most of the furniture. The wall groupings throughout the house were made from the very best wood. And only prints done by artists who excelled in their trade were displayed. The flooring varied from room to room but whether it was hardwood, carpet, or slate, only the best that money could buy went into the house. She had come a long way from the tin can on wheels at Pathetic Jokes. The kitchen, done in colonial blue décor with chestnut cabinets and stainless steel appliances (top of the line, of course) was the first room they had remodeled. It was still Lora's favorite.

She had only recently been appointed to her current position as Chief of Neurology by the Chief of Staff at Boston General. Alex had been so proud. She wished her mother could have been there, but she passed away the year after Lora had married Alex.

Lora's oldest brother had contacted their father back then, to let him know that she died, but dear ole dad had not seen fit to show up for the funeral. It was probably a good thing he didn't because Lora would have made a scene; she was sure of it. Her two brothers picked up the phone every once in a while to check in, but it seemed to Lora that the calls got more intermittent each time.

Since her new appointment, she had never had the opportunity to purchase additional equipment for her department. The PET scan would be fundamental in detecting abnormalities in the brain.

After its purchase, she hoped a newspaper article or two about the PET scan would get around to the people at Pathetic Jokes. It would be gratifying to rub the title, Chief of Neurology, in the noses of those bullies who really were no better off than she was at the time. In the daydream, she could see huge headline: *Local Girl Makes Good—Raises Money Single-handedly for New Lifesaving Equipment*. There would be a picture of her—probably her medical school photo, or better yet, the shot taken of her shaking hands with the Chief of Staff on the day she was promoted—and a detailed story about her life. That would show them all.

Using the computer printout she brought home from the hospital, she started jotting down names. One of her plans to raise money was to solicit ex-patients for donations. She looked to contact those patients whose lives had been made better by the neurology department at the hospital.

A short while later, she took a break from the names to peel potatoes for dinner. By the time she put the potatoes on the stove to boil and the broccoli in the steamer, Alex had come home. She went to the living room to greet him. He kissed her lightly on the cheek and said, "Hi babe. You have a good day?"

"I had a wonderful day," she said. "How was yours?"

"Hectic, like most Mondays."

"Alex, I got my grant!" Lora blurted excitedly.

"For your new machine?"

"Yes. I met with the Foundation Board this morning, and they told me if I could raise one half of the endowment, they could match it with a federal grant."

"That's great Lora. I know how eager you are to get the PET scan. How are you going to raise the money?"

"Well, that's what I was working on in the kitchen. First, I'm going to put together a mailing list asking for donations from ex-patients. Then I thought about an auction of some sort, maybe ask some of the local businesses to donate merchandise or services."

"That's a good idea. Let me talk to George down at the bank. His brother owns an appliance store at the mall, and I'm sure we could get him to donate a microwave or a portable TV set or something."

"Oh honey, that would be a big help." Lora hugged her husband.

Alex took Lora's face in his hands. He loved to look at his wife when she was this happy, this full of enthusiasm. In a tone that still made Lora melt he said, "I'm so proud of you, Lora. You've done so much good with your life, not only at the hospital, but at home as well. You've worked hard for everything you wanted and struggled for everything you have, but in the end, it all paid off. You're the most decent person I know Lora Jordan. The way you always do for everyone else; you're as close to perfect as anyone can get."

Lora looked into Alex's eyes. She smiled on the outside, but on the inside, she wondered if she would ever live up to her husband's expectations.

Lightening the mood, Alex asked, "What's for dinner? It smells good." He removed his jacket and tie, and draped them over the back of the lounge chair.

"Salmon steaks, parsley potatoes, and steamed broccoli with just a drizzle of cheese sauce,"

Alex turned his nose up. "None for me thanks. I think I'll fry a pork chop."

"Alex! I'm really worried about you. I want those cholesterol numbers to be reasonable before your next doctor's appointment. How much did you weigh on your last visit?"

Alex made no attempt to answer.

"All right, case closed. Tomorrow I'm going to start packing your lunch again, and I don't want you sneaking out to the fast food joints downtown this time. Got it, buster?"

"Yes Doc."

They went into the kitchen. Lora put two place settings on the oak table. Alex looked over her mailing list. He whistled, "There are some pretty prominent people on this list."

"Yeah, I know. Even rich people need the services of a doctor at one time or another. Sickness and disease know no status."

"Hey babe ... why not assemble the names of all the well-to-do patients and maybe include some notable people in the community, and throw a party. You know people will always give more face-to-face especially if 'Mr. Smith' finds out that 'Mr. Jones' gave more than he did. You know what I mean?"

"Oh Alex, that's a great idea. I could still mail solicitation letters to the rest of the people on the list and mail invitations to the more prominent ones."

"Yeah," Alex pondered the idea. "You should call that lady from the newspaper, Denise somebody. The one who does the society page. I'll bet she'd do a write up on your party."

Lora kissed her husband's cheek. "You're so creative, honey. I knew there was a reason why I married you."

Alex smacked his wife's fanny.

During dinner, neither Lora nor Alex talked much. The wheels in Lora's mind turned wildly. She thought about what she would serve at the party. Should she cook or should she have the party catered? Of course, it would be at their house. She loved to show it off. Some people would say Lora liked to brag, but she didn't brag. She simply had nice things, and she wanted everyone to see them.

Alex shoveled food into his mouth as if eating briskly would somehow improve the taste of the fish. He tried thinking of the salmon as a big greasy pork chop. It didn't work.

After dinner, they cleared the dishes and loaded the dishwasher together. Lora wiped off the table, and Alex went to the den to read today's newspaper. Lora turned on the radio—a Bose Wave radio, which she kept on kitchen counter—to a classical station and sat back down at the window seat to continue composing her list. After separating the names she had already written, she resumed browsing down the computer printout. The list was compiled alphabetically. When she got to the W's and saw the name *Whitmore, Clayton*, she seemed somewhat surprised at first, but then she vaguely remembered something about Suzy's husband having an aneurysm several years ago. She and Lora had been roommates in college at Kanawha State in West Virginia.

She put the Whitmores' name on the party list.

4

The bus arrived at the Huntington Station on schedule. The walk to the modest neighborhood, which had been Sam Kashette's home for years, took very little time. He had only a few dollars left in his pocket. He stopped at a mom and pop store along the way to buy a six-pack of beer and to see if any new marbles had come in since he'd been gone. His obsession with the round gems had been put on hold since he'd been inside.

As he neared the Emanuel Baptist Church, he again crossed over to the other side of the street. Passing a house of the Lord always gave Kash the heebie-jeebies. To say why he harbored these feelings would be of no use, seeing as he held no loyalty to any god nor did he feel any guilt about the way he chose to live. It made no sense that he would be so jumpy whenever he was in close proximity to a church. He was a freethinker—plain and simple. Kash saw no evidence of God during his life, so where was it written that he had to believe in the entity when no one could prove to him that one even existed? Yet he maintained a need to walk on the opposite side. Besides, he had to cross the street. It was part of The Order.

As Kash approached the white two-story house, he noticed it looked different in some way. From inside the confinement of his small cell room, Kash had remembered the house being bigger—bigger and brighter. Looking at the house now, it seemed dull. It was not dirty, and it was not in need of painting, yet it looked faded—as faded as white could get, anyway.

Letting himself inside through the back door, the musty smell hit him at once. He immediately opened a few windows to let in some fresh air. The kitchen was very small. Not even a tiny table and chair set would have fit. A breakfast nook and two stools served as his kitchenette. The dining room was off the kitchen to the left and had plenty of room for a full size dining table, six chairs, china closet and hutch; however, the only furniture currently occupying the room was a small desk. Kash rarely used this area since he had no cause to do much entertaining these days.

Touring the house, room by room, he found that nothing had been disturbed while he was away. Everything was exactly as he had left it 18 months ago. Gabby insisted on dusting and sweeping from time to time, but Kash knew everything would be put back in its exact place. It was part of The Order—Gabby understood about these things.

He unpacked the beer and the marbles he had bought at the store. A set of steps at the far end of the kitchen led to the basement. Taking the marbles, he went to the stairs and descended to the sub-floor where he grabbed a fresh jar from the shelf and added this newest selection. In all, there were 30 shelves in the basement and each shelf held approximately 15 jars. Each jar was filled with different colors and patterns of children's marbles. Kash had been fascinated by the swirls and bright colors of marbles since his childhood—colors that ran altogether but at the same time, colors that were coordinated and appealing to the eye.

Jackson marbles were the most colorful and Kash believed the most beautiful. Each member of the Jackson family designed his own marble. Kash owned three Jacksons. They were his favorite shooters.

The game of marbles is an ancient one, more than 4000 years old. The Romans played with marbles made from clay and stone. Much, much later, Brittany brought the game to America. When Kash was a child, the game of marbles had been as big as baseball. Once, when he was ten, Gabby took him to Wildwood, New Jersey to watch the national marbles tournament. It was there that his need originated to save the little round gems. Kash preferred the British version of the game. It was played with 49 marbles placed in a ring. Each successful shot merited the player another turn. The player who could knock out the most marbles won. Since Kash played alone, he always won. It had been a long time since he actually played the game; mostly he just admired his collection and cleaned the jars.

Back in the kitchen now, he put the six-pack of beer in the refrigerator. His cupboards were virtually empty, and there was nothing in the fridge except for a few condiments and a box of baking soda that must have been left there by Gabby. He made a mental note to do some grocery shopping today before the markets closed.

Gabby appeared at the kitchen door. "Hello Kash." She held her arms out for a hug. "I'm so glad you're home."

"Gabby," Kash said caressing the undersized, overweight old lady, "I'm glad to be home."

Sarah Gabbert was a sweet, seventy-something silver-haired woman who lived next door. Only a narrow strip of yard separated her house from Kash's. She had taught fifth grade for 27 years before retiring. She had been Kash's teacher and a close friend of the Kashette family ever since Kash could remember. Gabby (as Kash had affectionately called her since his childhood) had always been around. After the accident that killed Kash's parents, Gabby took Kash under her wing. She had six kids of her own; what was one more?

"Thank you for keeping the house cleaned up for me. And thank you for the visits, as well as the care packages you sent down. You have no idea how much those visits meant to me. Did things go well here while I was gone? Any new gossip to tell me?"

"Oh a few things happened, I reckon. Let me see: Sally Wallace finally got someone to marry her—a fellow from upstate New York. Ellen Snyder had a baby boy a few months back. You know her; she's married to Ed Snyder. Benson's Grocery was robbed while you were away. Oh, and the little community building burned down, too. Some kind of wiring problem, they said. That's about it."

Just the way Kash preferred things. Eighteen months of information all summed up into a few short sentences. Gabby really understood Kash, and she knew better than anyone did what was going on in Huntington. She rarely forgot anything, either.

One time when Kash was in high school, he had introduced Gabby to a girlfriend. That particular day happened to be his girlfriend's birthday. The next year his girlfriend—who had not been his girlfriend for several months—got a birthday card from Gabby. When Kash asked her how she had remembered the girl's birthday, Gabby replied, "My dogwoods were just starting to bloom the day I met her, and they've bloomed the same time every year for the last three decades. So when they bloomed this year, I sent a card." Kash was amazed. Almost like word association, he figured.

Gabby handed Kash his checkbook and an extra book of checks.

"Thanks for paying out my utilities while I was gone. I could have had everything turned off before I left, but I couldn't see paying all the reconnect fees."

Kash spent his money wisely. He never wasted anything for that matter—money, food, time, beer, energy, shampoo, toilet paper, water, love—especially love. Gabby was an honest woman. Kash knew every penny in his checkbook would be accounted for. She handed him some mail she figured might be important. The junk mail, she had discarded.

Looking through Kash's cupboards and in his refrigerator, Gabby said, "My heavens, boy ... you've not a thing to fix for your supper tonight." Then, using that tone she took with her six children and her elementary students, she said, "I want you at my house at five o'clock for dinner. Understood?"

"Sure Gabby. You don't have to threaten me to come over and have supper with you." Kash was actually hoping she would ask. "A home-cooked meal will be a real treat for me after a year and a half of eating prison food."

The meals at the Kentucky hellhole were probably the worst part of his time spent there. The food was essentially very tasty. The inmates were served well-balanced meals with good cuts of meat and real potatoes. It was the presentation of the meal that bothered Kash the most—the careless way with which the cooks slopped the food on the plate. The meat touched the vegetables, the vegetables mixed in with the potatoes; the bread was on the side of the dinner plate instead of on a plate by itself. Kash would have to separate the foods before eating each food group one at a time, taking care not to eat any of the pieces that touched the others. If the bread had become soggy from lying against the other foods, he would forfeit his ration with that meal.

Kash bet nothing would be touching anything at Gabby's dinner. She understood it was part of The Order.

As if reading Kash's mind, Gabby inquired about his time inside, but Kash politely cut her off, telling her he'd rather not talk about it right now. She confirmed the mealtime with Kash and then excused herself.

Kash took a quick shower and changed his clothes, after finding a tee shirt big enough to fit his now stocky chest and shoulders. He chose black denim pants, a maroon tee, and his maroon Stetson hat. It was important that his shirt and hat always match, this being part of The Order. Next, he searched for his walkman. He remembered using it last when he had cut the grass, so he assumed it would be outside in the shed. That was exactly where he found it.

Taking the tape from the manila envelope, Kash tried the tape player. He feared the batteries would be dead; they were good. Grabbing a beer on his way, he perched himself into his favorite old chair in the living room. He popped the top on the can, took a drink, and placed the beer on a coaster being careful not to drip condensation on the end table. After situating the headpiece to fit his head, he turned on the walkman and listened:

Carlos: For the record sir, would you state your full name?
Parker: Robert Darell Parker.

Carlos: Mr. Parker, do you agree to have this interview tape-recorded?
Parker: Yes.
Carlos: In 1974, where were you employed?
Parker: Charleston Memorial Hospital.
Carlos: And where is that located?
Parker: Charleston, West Virginia.
Carlos: What did you do there?
Parker: I worked in the pharmacy as a technician.
Carlos: What were your job duties?
Parker: Let's see. Picking up orders from the floor, writing up dispensing tickets, filling orders, and putting data into the computer.
Carlos: Mr. Parker, were you acquainted with Lora Cooper?
Parker: Yes.
Carlos: How well did you know her?
Parker: Pretty well, I guess.
Carlos: Are you still in contact with Miss Cooper?
Parker: No.
Carlos: Were you aware that she's married now and that her name is Dr. Lora Jordan?
Parker: No. Did she marry a rich doctor?
Carlos: No, she married a banker. Why do you ask?
Parker: Well, it's just that she always said she was going to find her a rich doctor to marry after she graduated. She said she was never going to be poor again.
Carlos: What were Dr. Jordan's job duties at the pharmacy?
Parker: She was an Order Technician. She kept track of all the inventory through the computer, ordered the drug supply, unpacked and counted it, and put the supply in the vault.
Carlos: Did she have a key to the vault?
Parker: No. The pharmacist opened it and supervised anyone who went in the vault.
Carlos: Did Lora ever take any drugs from the vault?
Parker: No.
Carlos: Did she ever take any drugs from the pharmacy at Charleston Memorial?

Kash heard a slight hesitation on the tape then a click, indicating the recorder had been turned off momentarily. "Damn it. The creep is gonna to back out," Kash said slamming his fist hard against the arm of the chair. Another click and now the tape resumed:

Carlos: I ask again, Mr. Parker ... did she ever take any drugs from the pharmacy?
Parker: Yes.
Carlos: How did she do that?
Parker: Using false dispensing tickets.
Carlos: Explain please, Mr. Parker, exactly what did she do?
Parker: She wrote up a dispensing ticket for an order that did not exist.
Carlos: What did Dr. Jordan ask you to do to help her?
Parker: She asked me to fill the order and put the data from the dispensing ticket into the computer.
Carlos: What was the purpose of putting the data into the computer? It seems to me she'd want to keep it out of the computer.
Parker: Oh no. She wanted me to enter the drugs on the dispensing ticket against the inventory in the computer, so it wouldn't show anything short. See?
Carlos: Yes, I see. What did you do with the false dispensing tickets?
Parker: After the weekly physical count was done, she told me to destroy them.
Carlos: What kind of pills did she steal?
Parker: Uppers, downs. Mostly Perocet, Darvocet, Dexedrine, Ritalin.
Carlos: What did you get for doing all this?
Parker: Money. Fifty dollars a week, sometimes seventy-five, depending on how much we lifted that week. It doesn't seem like it now, but that was a lot of extra money to an 18-year-old in 1974.
Carlos: How many times a week did you do this?
Parker: Anywhere from twice a week to every day.
Carlos: How much do you think Dr. Jordan brought in on a good week?
Parker: Oh, about three or four hundred I guess, not counting what she made on the vials.
Carlos: What vials?
Parker: When a doctor or an anesthesiologist checks out a vial from the pharmacy, say a 10cc vial of Morphine, and only uses 2cc, he returns it to the pharmacy where Lora was suppose to mark it on a dump sheet and squirt it down the drain.
Carlos: She didn't do that?
Parker: Hell no. She took it home.
Carlos: What kind of drugs would be in those vials?
Parker: Mostly narcotics. She liked Demerol and Valium 'cause she could get rid of it quickly.

> Carlos: How long did you work with Lora?
> Parker: Over four years.
> Carlos: How long did Lora Jordan rip off the hospital Pharmacy?
> Parker: Over four years.

Kash lifted his beer can—it was empty. He crushed it effortlessly. The headpiece slipped easily from his ears when he released a burst of laughter. With this evidence, she was putty in his hands now.

He had to admit, it was really very clever of Carlos to tip the police that Parker had drugs in his house. If Parker had not been arrested then the phony plea bargain could not have been arranged. Parker would have been less likely to talk had it not been for him thinking he was getting something in return.

Going to the fridge for another beer, he looked through the papers in the file folder. He had Lora right where he wanted her. The clock on the kitchen wall showed close to five. He had to get to Gabby's house. The thought of her cooking made Kash's mouth water. It was sure to be some dinner.

5

Kash took the next few weeks to get his house in order. He got the grass cutting caught up and painted the trim on the house in the slim hope that the dull, dreary look would go away. It didn't, so he concluded that the reason he remembered the house as being a big bright place was because anything outside of that 5' x 8' hellhole looked bigger and brighter. It took Kash two days to clean the rooms inside thoroughly. He washed walls, scrubbed carpets and floors, laundered curtains, and cleaned windows. He also stocked the kitchen. One entire day was spent in the converted basement tending to his marbles. As if handling containers of plutonium, he removed each of the 450 jars from the shelves, wiping them one by one before rearranging the jars according to size. Kash's collection (not really a collection, more like a hoarding) of marbles dated back to his adolescence.

With his chores at home complete, he withdrew several hundred dollars from his savings account to do some shopping for new clothes. His final chore, his worst chore, was saved for last. He hated going to the mall. Malls were full of Inferiors spending all of her husband's hard-earned money on petty things for themselves—perfumes scented to lure men, tease them; sexy clothing designed to draw the male's attention toward seduction; high-healed shoes that strapped around the ankle and made the legs look enticing. Inferiors did these things to men—the taunting and the vexing—then when men act on that behavior, it's the men who get the bad rap. Those whores should be home taking care of their husband needs: cooking the man's dinner, cleaning the man's house, raising the man's children, and waiting for the man to come home so she could satisfy the man's needs. She should not be spending all her time at the mall flaunting herself in public, glancing at other men as they pass by with her flirty little smiles and hellos. The very existence of women was one huge mistake—most women anyway. Nonetheless, Kash needed new clothes, so he made the sacrifice.

He had bought several shirts and two new Stetson hats in new colors that were not found in his wardrobe. His shirt and hat must always match. It was part of The Order.

With the trip to the mall behind him, he had a few dollars remaining in his pocket, and he was pleased with the fact that he still had a decent balance in his savings account. A decent balance, yes, but not enough to hold him over for five years. Saving for a rainy day had been a good thing to do. It would help him get by until the time was right for him to make his move.

Since returning home, Kash had subscribed to *The Boston Times* so he could stay abreast of any happenings in that city. The paper was delivered to his house by mail each day. After all, Boston, Massachusetts was where Lora lived. He had to protect his investment.

He checked the mailbox on this cool but clear May morning on his way home from the mall. When he saw the headline on the society page, Kash knew that the time to make his move had come. He would go today and get his plane ticket to Massachusetts.

CHAPTER FOUR

Let the Games Begin

1

Mrs. Suzy Whitmore shuffled through the neatly hung clothes in the walk-in closet of the master bedroom. She wanted to look her best for the speaking engagement this morning, so she chose the beige two-piece suit which her husband had bought for her last Christmas. Being a university president's wife, she had been a guest speaker at many functions. Today, however, she was more nervous than usual. She had the strangest feeling something was going to go wrong. Maybe the feeling was due to the location of her speaking engagement or maybe it was just good old-fashioned gut instinct. She would rather have turned down this invitation, but her conscience told her she should do it.

Clayton had gone down to the campus and Tommy was visiting with Jeff, so the house was empty when she came downstairs. She quickly poured herself another cup of coffee—again she was running late. She hoped the coffee would satisfy her appetite until after the speech. By then brunch would be served. There never seemed to be enough time to eat.

She checked her wristwatch, chugged the remaining coffee in her cup, and put her earrings on as she darted for the door. Once outside, she was pleased to feel the unusual warm air for an early May morning in Dalton, Massachusetts. The cloudless sky most likely meant there would be no rain again today.

She grabbed the mail from the mailbox on her way to the car. Sorting through the sale papers and bills, she handled a silky satin envelope. The address was beautifully written in calligraphy. Not being able to wait until later, she settled herself inside the car and opened it. Reading the raised letter invitation, she smiled and said, "Lora."

Lora and Suzy had been roommates in college along with Rosalee DeLucci. Lora's invitation requested her presences at a fund raising dinner party at Lora's house in a few weeks. She was trying to get donations for a new piece of equipment for the hospital—the same hospital that had saved Clayton's life. Suzy would send money and try to make the party.

She checked the car's gas gauge—full. She knew it would be. Clayton always made sure her car had a full tank of gas. She started the engine and pulled out of the driveway.

Once on the highway with the cruse set to 70mph, Suzy reviewed her speech from memory. Her first instinct was to turn down this engagement when Mrs. Sullivan, the Pregnancy Crisis Center's Director, approached her, but Clayton thought it was a good idea, and she did not want him to become suspicious or ask her why she would rather not talk to a few pregnant girls. She was unclear as to the reason why she had been chosen in the first place. This was an issue Clayton heavily endorsed, not her. Who was she to tell anybody about right to life? She was certainly no expert, but she worked hard on the speech, at any rate, and thought it was pretty good. She started to feel better about the significance of the speech. Maybe she would make a difference in one or two of the girls' lives. Her nervousness subsided, and she relaxed.

At this speed, she expected to arrive at the Crisis Center with barely a minute to spare. Too bad Lora's promptness had never rubbed off on her. She passed by the rest of the drive with memories of her younger days at Kanawha State.

The seventies were a confusing time to be a young adult in college, especially for someone of Suzy's naiveté. The sixties left many innovations and new technologies unfinished. Change was inevitable—some good and some bad. American astronauts had walked on the moon, pulling them ahead of the Soviet Union in the space race. Computers were making their debut in large businesses. Satellites were being launched into space for military spying and also for better television reception. The Vietnam conflict was in full swing.

Another sign of the change in society was the rise of rock bands. Their music was new and raw, and most people who enjoyed it, or even listened to it, were considered by many to be hippies. Four-hundred-thousand young people attended a music fair on Max Yagur's farm in Woodstock, NY. Drugs were commonly used, and the youth of the day didn't seem to fear anyone or anything. The young adults of the seventies had the task of securing their future in a time when everything seemed to be running wild. A time of peace, free love, and flower power. The world was turned upside down.

By the time Lora, Suzy, and Rosalee were finishing high school, the antiwar movement was the cause of protests at many colleges and universities bringing about the killing of four students by National Guardsmen at Kent State in the spring of '70. Rosalee was bothered most by the shootings. She watched every available newscast. Although she was not personally acquainted with any of the students, it never stopped her heart from going out to the victims and their families. That was Rosalee—she always cheered for the underdog and was always the most sympathetic in a crisis.

By 1972 when the threesome entered college, President Nixon had withdrawn 90% of the troops from Vietnam, which disappointed Suzy, considering Nixon's campaign pledge that he would end the war. Suzy had planned to vote for him, should he seek re-election, but by reneging on his promise, she felt distrust in his leadership. When someone said he would do something, the young Suzy Shaffer expected it to be done.

By the mid 70s, when Suzy and Rosalee were about to graduate and Lora was readying herself for medical school, American woman had invaded many fields: politics, law, the military, literature, and religion. So welcomed were their presence that TIME magazine gave "Women" the title of "Man of the Year" in 1976. Suzy remembered Lora's gratification when women were finally recognized for their accomplishments. She knew of Lora's struggle, and that of her mother's, to be independent. She admired the Cooper women but sadly knew she would never mature into a self-sufficient adult. Lora was smart, strong, and self-assured. Suzy was grateful for this because Lora became Suzy's guardian and protector from the first day they met in the dorm room at Kanawha State.

Lora had been sitting cross-legged on the bed balancing her checkbook that day when Suzy arrived carrying her over-stuffed designer luggage. Outfitted in bell-bottomed jeans with the word *love* stenciled down one leg and a bandanna twined around her forehead, Lora looked in disbelief at her newest roommate. Rosalee had already moved in and was checking out the campus with her boyfriend. Suzy unpacked her clothes, and then pulled out a calculator from the bottom of her bag. She handed it to Lora.

"Will this be of some help with your figuring?"

Lora looked at the gadget, "Yes, very much so. I've seen these in the store and have wanted one, but they're priced way out of my budget. Where did you get it?"

"My dad bought it for me, but I don't know how to use it, so you can have it if you want."

"You're giving it to me? Do you know how much these cost?"

"No, but you can have it anyway if you'll balance my checkbook when you're done with yours," Suzy said somewhat ashamed. "My dad tried to show me how to do it before I left, but I couldn't get the hang of it. Daddy's been taking care of my checkbook since I was ten."

"You had a checking account when you were ten?"

"I've had an account at the bank since I was born, but Mother didn't allow me to have the checks until my tenth birthday. I had no trouble at all learning how to a write check, but I have a hard time making sure there's enough money in there to make it good."

Lora wasn't sure where this newest roommate had come from, but she knew it wasn't from her side of the track.

Suzy said, "I don't know what I'm going to do when my car gets low on gas. Daddy always took care of filling the tank for me."

It seemed daddy took care of everything, Lora thought but didn't say.

"Well I guess you'll have to go to the station and put gas in it," Lora replied poking fun at Suzy.

The joke seemed to slide by Suzy, but she rambled on just the same, "As long as it's full-service. So many of the filling stations have become self-serve these days. I hope it's just a passing fad, because I haven't a clue how to work the manual pumps."

From that moment, Lora played the role of Suzy's caretaker. She performed the tasks at school which Suzy's daddy had taken care of when Suzy was at home.

After their sophomore year, Lora, Suzy, and Rosalee moved from the dorm to a roomier place. The apartment was still on campus, but there were none of the restrictions that applied to dorm living. The trio had become very close over the past year. They often visited each other's hometown on weekends. Suzy recalled one such visit when she and Lora had gone home with Rosalee to her parent's house. They returned to their apartment on a Sunday evening, to discover that someone had broken into their apartment. Nothing was missing; however, the intruders had fixed themselves something to eat and had taken a shower. The three roommates were terrified. For almost a week, they slept together on the living room floor—there was power in numbers—with a pellet rifle at Lora's side. Neither Suzy nor Rosalee knew how to use the gun, and the funny thing was, neither did Lora, but she never let on. Two months later, they found out they should have first pumped the rifle in order to make it work.

Good old Lora, always ready to take control of the situation, even if she didn't know what she was doing. But this situation and ones like it only proved to make Lora stronger. She became more assured of herself and of her future with each passing year. On the other hand, daily circumstances only made Suzy more dependent on her friends. After the passing of her father, Suzy relied on Lora more and more. Sometimes they would fight, because Lora wanted to show Suzy how to do things instead of doing it for her, but Suzy was resistant to learn—she simply wanted someone else to do it. Finally, Lora gave up and accepted the fact that she would not only have to take care of herself for the next four years, but she would have to take care of Suzy as well.

The partnership between the two women brought togetherness and a bond that Suzy believed would never fade. They were inseparable then, yet she had not seen her old roommates for many years.

Suzy had gone to Lora's wedding ten years ago and that was the last time she had seen her. She felt guilty about that too, because Dalton and Boston were less than a hundred miles apart, yet they never visited each other.

Suzy pulled into the lot at the Pregnancy Crisis Center. The large three story house was old and in need of new siding. The existing panels were warped in some places and curled in others—the whole building was badly discolored. The porch was rickety, and the windows were outdated. Taking the first available parking space, Suzy pledged to drop a check in the mail for the center as soon as possible.

She killed the car's ignition and again checked the digital clock on the dash—not a minute to spare. Suzy looked at Lora's card one more time. Not knowing about the promotion, Suzy was proud to see the title Chief of Neurology under Lora's name at the bottom of the invitation. She put the envelope along with the other mail above the sun visor and jogged toward the building. The old memories of Lora calmed Suzy. The cycle was now complete—Lora had taken her daddy's place, and now Clayton had taken Lora's. Those she had depended on had not let her down. In return, she would not let Lora down. She would make it a point to be free the weekend of Lora's fundraiser reception.

2

Sam Kashette bounced up and down on the bed in the small motel. He knew the bed would be hard. It always was in a cheap motel. At least the room was clean and so far, he saw no signs of any bugs ready to scurry across the floor. He reserved the room for a whole week because he didn't think he could finish his business in less time. The motel was located in the middle of the small state of Massachusetts. This was possibly the best location he could have wished for—forty-five miles to Dalton and forty-five miles to Boston. It was perfect for Kash's needs.

He unpacked his clothes and prepared to take a shower. The iron he had brought along could remain in the suitcase. All his clothes had been packed in such a way that nothing inside was the least bit wrinkled. He neatly placed the toiletries on the counter in the bathroom. His razor and shaving cream could stay in the case as well; he decided not to shave. He would have to wear a five o'clock shadow for a few days, but soon his sandy beard would grow in thick and full. He had been denied the privilege of growing a beard in prison, but he was out now. He could do whatever he pleased. Sometimes he had to remind himself of that fact. Eighteen months of solitude took a real toll on him psychologically, but he was truly free now. Not free like before the accident, (he had taken freedom for granted), but free like the war was over, and he had been named the victor.

After showering, he chose something a little dressy for today's affair: baggy tan cords, a black tee shirt, and a black Stetson hat. His shirt and hat must always match—it was part of The Order. After drying and combing his hair at the bathroom sink, he turned to the full-length mirror on the wall. He looked sharp. Removing *The Boston Times* from the suitcase, he double-checked the address but could not resist reading the entire article again.

He was ready to go. He did not want to be late.

3

"Life is the most wonderful gift a man and a woman can give to each other. Unfortunately, 28% of all babies born in the United States are born without fathers. Since 1960, this percentage has increased more than 400%. Today nearly one unmarried teen girl in ten will get pregnant ..."

Suzy straightened her paper at the podium in the large living room which today served as a meeting room in the old house. She restlessly shifted her weight from one foot to the other. The nervousness was back.

"... you twenty five young women here today are not alone. I was both honored and delighted when Mrs. Sullivan, your director, asked me to speak to you at the Pregnancy Crisis Center. I'm sure the timing was intentional, as tomorrow is Mother's Day."

The audience of pregnant girls giggled.

Kash stood in the doorway toward the back of the room. *You two-faced little bitch.* His brain registered what his ears were hearing; he just had trouble believing the words he heard. The audience consisted of mostly young pregnant girls, however, there were a few men scattered about here and there, so he blended in without notice.

"... so you see experiencing a crisis pregnancy, as it is called, doesn't have to be a crisis at all. The counselors here understand the emotional trauma you're going through. They know the doubts, the fears, and the feelings of shame. They know you're scared—no, it's not enough to say you're scared; you're terrified. But these good people are here to help you through all the nightmares and frustrations. They can and will help you with the agonizing decisions you face and the pressures you feel."

Kash was filled with disgust. He could barely listen any longer. How could she say these things? How could she stand there so righteous when her words were nothing but empty sounds—totally insincere? Disgust turned to hunger as he watched Suzy.

To Kash's eyes, she had remained as attractive as he remembered. Suzy Shaffer had been the most seductive woman Kash had ever done. She could sexually excite him in ways that nobody else ever could. She'd had an erotic power over him, one of an almost animalistic quality, that he had not been able to control nor had he ever been able to find again. At one time, he had loved her as much as he could bring himself to love. Now those old sensations of lust sent signals of urgency to his throbbing groin. He noticed she had preserved her lovely figure which he had so fondly touched and caressed back then. She wore her hair differently these days, but her eyes were still the same—oh those eyes. Even at thirty feet, (Kash's approximated distance), he could still see those beautiful sable eyes. He saw in his mind's eye the single bed where Suzy lay naked waiting for him, ready to do all the things Kash desired. He had wants and needs, and they had to be satisfied.

The Bad Thoughts were creeping into the recesses of his conscious mind again. He had to make them go away. He could ill-afford to let himself be noticed—not yet.

While in the Kentucky prison, Kash had told the resident shrink about the Bad Thoughts. He described how the Bad Thoughts came in flashes much like the old silent movies from the twenties. The pictures were jerky and rough, like shutter clicks of a photographer camera, but Kash knew what he saw. Kash knew the flashes were a preview of the act his mind urged him to carry out. Most of the time, the Bad Thoughts were preceded by music. Awful organ music hammered out by the little organ keeper in Kash's mind. Some days he thought the music and the visions would drive him mad, but then the Kentucky doctor prescribed the Healing Rhymes in an attempt to bring order to Kash's thoughts. He explained in layman's terms that when Kash was overwhelmed by emotion, his mind became muddled, his thoughts were unorganized and the Bad Thoughts were then allowed to take over. He taught Kash how to concentrate on the Healing Rhymes much the same way one would silently sing a song to oneself when trying to block out what someone else was saying. Kash preferred rhymes containing numbers because he maintained that counting brought additional order to his mind. So now he started,

> *One, two, three, four,*
> *Mary's at the cottage door,*
> *Five, six, seven, eight,*
> *Eating cherries off a plate.*

It was not going away. The little organ keeper shrilled music in Kash's ears. His darkness forced itself into his mind like liquid forced itself through a crack in a drinking glass. He tried reciting another one.

> *One, two, three, four, five,*
> *Once I caught a fish alive.*

Better—his darkness was turning to light, but the Bad Thoughts were still there.

> *Six, seven, eight, nine, ten,*
> *Then I let it go again.*

His darkness had passed—he was better now. The Kentucky doctor's Healing Rhymes had worked.

"I promise not to bore you with anymore statistics," Suzy continued. "It won't always be easy for you girls. All of you are unmarried; many of you have yet to finish high school. You will have to find a way to support yourself and your baby, and you will have to do this alone. There will be nobody to help you with the middle-of-the-night feedings and diaper changes; nobody to give you a break from the baby. But when you look into that child's face and realize that he or she is a part of you, you'll know in your heart that you made the right decision. You'll know that your child has life because of you.

"I would like to tell you a story about a woman who was taking a trip. She couldn't decide whether to get on the interstate or take the country roads. You see the interstate was paved. It would be much easier on her car. It was also faster so she would have more time for herself when she arrived at her destination. The paved road also provided fast food restaurants and bathrooms if she needed to use them. The country road, on the other hand, was not paved. Only dirt and gravel made up the surface; therefore, it was much slower. She'd have to dodge many potholes; she may even have to stop and wait for a deer or some other wildlife to cross the road. But then, she thought about the beauty of the countryside that she would miss if she took the interstate. She would let pass by all the little streams and creeks, all the scenery, the mountains and fields, all the splendid wonders of nature. She could still get something to eat even though it may take her a bit out of her way. But the food would be home cooked, not processed, and the people there wouldn't be rushing. They'd take the time to say hello and be friendly.

"The point I'm trying to make is that your decision to bring your child into this world and raise it alone is not so unlike the woman's decision whether to take the interstate or the country roads. You chose the country road, too. You've been riding on the dirt road for years—it's called life. It will take you where you need to go, but it won't always be easy. There will be times when you'll think you can't possibly dodge another pothole or wait another second for a deer to cross, and there'll be times when your life is entirely consumed by the ride. But you'll be there to see all the beauty, to see your child take its first steps, to hear it utter its first word. When you hold the little baby in your arms, you'll know you've made the right decision."

Kash grinned. *Is she for real?* He wondered if her husband spit this kind of quackery in his speeches too. He knew Clayton was heavily into the pro-life movement on campus, but be had no idea Suzy was so involved. Kash had never met Clayton, which left a lot of unanswered questions about Suzy's husband. Kash was curious to know what he looked like. What kind of a person he was? He knew Clayton was Suzy's elder by ten years. He had read somewhere that women who marry older men usually do so because she needs someone to replace her father. He could easily see Suzy latching onto a husband as a replacement for Prentis. He remembered from his days in college how Suzy Shaffer had a constant need for someone to look after her. Unlike Lora, Suzy was not the strong-minded, or daring, or independent one, which is why Kash chose to take on Suzy first.

He resumed watching as she concluded.

"In closing, I would just like to say that you young ladies in this room are to be commended. It takes courage and bravery to decide to keep your babies when the paved road was directly in your path. I'm talking about abortion. You are the most unselfish group of girls I have ever known. I am so proud of you, and I thank you, from your 25 unborn children. Happy Mother's Day."

"Bullshit!" Kash muttered discreetly.

As Suzy stepped away from the podium, the audience applauded. Kash wanted to remain unseen for now. His plan was to wait outside until she came out. Only then would he show himself. What he came to say could wait another 30 minutes; he had waited 18 years already. He wanted to confront her alone so there would be no witnesses.

When Suzy heard the applause, she knew it was over, and she was relieved. For a while, she was sure she would begin to cry. Of course, she could always blame the tears on the pride she claimed to feel for the girls. She stepped away from the podium and started to mingle with the group of teens. Several of them volunteered reasons why they could not abort their unborn child. This weighed heavily on Suzy's heart because her own reasons for the decision she had made were those of a selfish nature. She wanted to finish college. She wanted a prestigious career. She wanted a big house with the white picket fence. She, she, she. Never once did she think about her own unborn child. She only thought of herself and of her own selfish goals. The girls here today were not afraid to tough it out. Some were turned out by their parents, some were dumped by their boyfriends when the pregnancy was discovered, and others were alone to begin with, but none of them chose to have an abortion. Eighteen years ago, Suzy took the paved road.

The house director moved toward Suzy.

"Mrs. Whitmore, thank you so much for speaking to my girls. The speech was very motivating. It will give the girls a lot of encouragement. I'm sure at times they wonder if they've done the right thing."

"Yes, I'm sure."

"I feel certain your talk today has removed any doubt. You did a wonderful job presenting it."

"Thank you," Suzy said feeling a bit like a hypocrite.

"I heard your husband speak once at a pro-life rally on campus. He was inspiring, as well. Have you ever spoken on this issue before?"

"Yes, but mostly at rallies. I've never talked to girls on a personal level and never as one-on-one as today. I picked up the research material used for today's speech from my husband's participation over the years."

"I thought so. You seem very informed on the topic. Please Mrs. Whitmore, come have something to eat."

Suzy was grateful for the change of subject. She was all talked out about abortion and unborn babies. Besides, she was very hungry. She ate two finger sandwiches, some Swedish meatballs, a pickle, and drank another cup of coffee. She thanked Mrs. Sullivan for her hospitality and for the opportunity to speak, and then she excused herself. She could no longer continue this crazy charade.

As she walked toward the door, a young girl, about the same age as Tommy, approached her.

"Mrs. Whitmore?" the girl called.

Suzy stopped and turned. The girl appeared to be neither pregnant nor poorly dressed, unlike the other young mothers here. She looked to be about sixteen; her hair was fashionably styled; she wore only a little make-up. An elegant gold chain coiled around her neck and ended in a pea-sized sapphire, which lay at the midpoint of her chest, just below her collarbone. Matching post earrings peaked out from her earlobes, covered by hair. This girl came from money, Suzy could tell.

"Mrs. Whitmore, I wanted to thank you."

"For what?"

"When I came to this home a week ago, I wasn't sure I was going to stay. I had already looked into the cost of an abortion and my boyfriend, who has a good job, was willing to pay for it. But after listening to you talk this morning I know for sure what I want to do now. I'm going to keep my baby!"

Suzy was dazed—she could have been this girl. "How far along are you? You don't even look pregnant."

"Eight weeks," she replied.

Eight weeks! Suzy thought. Eight weeks was exactly how far along Suzy had been when she terminated the pregnancy; eight weeks was the amount of time she had agonized over the decision; eight weeks was how long the torment lasted—torment that she assumed would go away after the procedure but had instead, turned into 18 years of guilt and remorse.

"I was living with my boyfriend." The girl was still talking. Suzy barely noticed. "He's twenty-four, but as soon as I told him about the baby, he threw me out. My parents wanted nothing more to do with me, so I came here. Until this morning, I was still undecided which way to go; now I know what to do. I'm going to have my baby and try to be a good mother. Thank you again." The girl threw herself at Suzy giving her a huge bear hug.

Suzy stared at the clinging girl. Pending tears threatened to dump from her eyes. She pulled herself away from the girl's embrace. The lump in her throat grew, and the dizziness in her head increased. She shot a final glance at the girl who had hurt her, the girl who had genuinely pierced her heart as surly as if she had used a scalpel. Suzy ran down the hallway and out of the old house. Her high heels clop, clop, clopped on the hardwood floor.

When she arrived in the parking lot, she wiped her nose and eyes with a tissue while she searched her purse for car keys. Finding them, she tried to regain her composure. As she neared her car, she thought she saw someone lurking. She wiped tears away from her eyes again to get a clearer look. She hoped that she was seeing things, but she wasn't.

Then she spotted him.

"Is that really you?" she said. "What are you doing here?"

4

St. Christopher's school and church were situated in a village-like complex in West Virginia, only a short drive from the town where Sister Rosa was raised. The schoolhouse was old but well kept. The two-story building housed grades one through eight. The convent, parish house, church, and playground were located at close proximity, with shrubbery-lined walkways connecting all the facilities. The community it served was small, about 5,000 residences, but the people were very generous when it came to supporting its church and school.

The seventh grade students at St. Christopher's wanted to start a school newsletter. Although it was May and the school year was about to end, three of the interested students asked Sister Rosa to meet with them and help them get some topics organized so they could begin work on articles over summer vacation. Rosa was truly surprised when she was selected to head up the operation. Dealing with third grade children Rosa knew about, but working with teenagers was a new ball game. As she waited in the school library, she grew a bit apprehensive.

She tried to recall herself at that age, her teen years. Her mother insisted she was boy crazy and often threatened to send her off to the convent. How ironic. She reflected her own high school days. Sister Rosa had grown up in a very Italian family. You might say being very Italian is like being a little bit pregnant; either you were or you weren't. Rosa's family was truly a traditional old-world Italian family. Her mother was the first generation to be born in the United States. Her girlfriends enjoyed coming to visit at the DeLucci home. They thought it was neat how everybody tended to talk at the same time. (You know, all Italians have so much to say and everyone wants to say it first.) Nobody could understand what anybody else was saying, but the house had been filled with excitement. Rosa missed the closeness provided by family. When she was there, she felt loved and wanted and very much a part of her family.

The other thing she missed about home was the food. She could still see her *Nonna* getting up at the crack of dawn on a Sunday morning to knead dough for *Ravioli* or *Gnocchi* for dinner. After Mass, the whole family would come to *Nonna's*. The entire house was filled with the aroma of simmering marinara sauce. *Nonna* would put water on to boil as everyone anticipated the taste of the homemade pasta. Her favorite memory included her older brother, Frankie. She remembered the two of them drawing pictures or playing tic-tac-toe on the windows steamed up by boiling water on the stove in *Nonna's* kitchen. These days, *Nonna* was confined to a wheelchair and lived with Sister Rosa's parents. Everyone had been so happy and carefree back then. She wished she could be a little girl again. Everything was so simple. Nothing was complicated. Those days were the best days of her life.

After fifteen years in the convent, she still was unsure about where she belonged—whether or not the convent was the place she wanted to fulfill her existence. She walked the fence on this topic daily, sometimes changing her opinion twice in the same day.

Sister Rosa was a short woman, only five feet tall, and a little on the chubby side. She wore her dark black hair in a shoulder length, conservative cut, although the short veil-like habit concealed most of it. She wore no make-up, even though the church accepted a light application in soft colors. She was perfectly happy with her plain appearance. She had been plain and simple all her life.

When the three seventh grade girls arrived, Rosa motioned them in. Rosa was sitting in front of a computer screen ready to open up a publishing program on the school's PC. Jeanne and Joann entered the room and took a seat across the table from where she sat. A third young girl—Tina, sporting blond curls and an attitude—leaned in the doorway. Rosa motioned for her to come in and join the others.

"Come Tina, have a seat."

Tina answered, "I don't know Sister … maybe this isn't such a good idea."

Tina was a new student to the school, beginning the first of her classes this year after the Christmas break. She had been a very defiant child. Her parents pulled her from the public school system and enrolled her at St. Christopher's with the hope that some religious teaching and discipline from the nuns would settle her down. So far, little progress had been made. Jeanne and Joann had asked Tina to accompany them in this project hoping that if Tina got involved in a school activity, it might sweeten her sour disposition. The two girls invited Tina again to come in and help.

"Why don't you think this is a good idea, Tina?" Sister Rosa asked. "Do you not have any time to spare for the school newsletter, or are you afraid you won't be able to write the articles?"

"Hey sister, I ain't afraid of nothin'."

"Hey sister, I am not afraid of anything," Rosa corrected, "and if you're not afraid of anything, then what is the problem?"

Tina thought for a few minutes, never taking her eyes off of the tiny nun. "I just don't see myself as an inspiring writer. I mean, I'm still not sure I believe all this Catholic stuff I'm being taught."

Rosa took the opportunity to open the doors to this child's mind. "What is it you don't believe?"

"Well, for starters, I don't believe in things without proof. Everything you teach here is either from the bible or from the so-called scriptures. How do I know for sure those people ever existed?"

"You don't know for sure. That's why it's called faith," Sister Rosa said, and then she asked, "Can you prove to me that the world is round?"

"No, but Christopher Columbus did."

"How do you know that?"

"Hell Sister, it's in every history book. Are you a real teacher or what?"

"You believe what you read in your history book. You accept the fact that Christopher Columbus proved the world is round on the authority of someone else, yet you don't believe what you read in the Bible, stories told by people who lived with Jesus. If you think about it, most of what you know you haven't personally experienced or proved. Why can't you accept religion the same way?"

"I don't know ... I just can't. What you're saying could explain some of it, but if God is so great and giving, why did He create the devil to tempt us?"

"When the devil was created he wasn't bad. The devil is actually an outcast angel, who had gone against God's will. He tried to dethrone God and rule God's kingdom. He was made a serpent to crawl forever on his belly, and then he was sent to the fiery pit of hell. The devil tempts us because he's angry with God for what He did to him. He tries to make us do things against God to get back at Him."

"Then why doesn't God just banish him?"

"Because God never goes back on His word. It's like I told you the other day in class: the devil was once an angel; therefore, God had accepted him into heaven at one time. He sent him to hell as a means of punishment, but now the devil has his own reign, and he doesn't want back into heaven. Do you understand?"

"Yeah, in a way. I guess life would be kind of boring if there were no bad guys."

Everyone laughed and Sister Rosa agreed with Tina's theory.

Tina joined Jeanne and Joann at the table. Sister Rosa turned the computer's monitor around so everyone could see it.

"Well girls," she said, "it seems we have the topic for our first article." Rosa typed the title in large points on the screen: *Teens and Their Faith*.

Faith was something of which Rosa had plenty. Fifteen years ago, she had put her entire life in the hands of her faith even though she still had lingering reservations about her present life and taking her vows. She wondered if things could have worked out with Kash. When she had entered the convent, she was certain that a drastic lifestyle change would whisk away any residual feelings she kept tucked away deep inside herself for him. Whatever pain she felt, she tried to put behind her, but she had been unsuccessful thus far. She continued to pray for him, just as she had done when she first entered the convent, because she knew he had no one to guide him, and she wanted the best for him. She knew she was influencing his life with her prayers, even though she had no solid proof. Again, it was faith that confirmed this—faith and a whole-hearted connection to his soul. Sister Rosa remained bound by instinct, or a sixth sense, if you will, when it came to Sam Kashette. She seemed to know when he needed her. She envisioned a transparent thread hooking Kash's soul to hers. Much the same way two children used string to attach two tin cans together so they could talk to each another, she made her connection to Kash. Sister Rosa still loved Kash, but she had an interesting ideology when it came to this quandary: her heart was big enough to both love him and serve God as well.

When the meeting adjourned, Sister Rosa packed up her things and proceeded to the convent by way of the winding sidewalk. During the course of the walk, she thought about the man she had loved for so many years.

5

"Kash, what are you doing here?" Suzy Whitmore repeated.

Kash leaned against the trunk of her car. "Hello Suzy, what's the matter? Not happy to see me?"

"It's not that. I'm just shocked to see you, is all. You didn't answer my question. What are you doing here?"

"To be perfectly honest, I couldn't pass up the opportunity to hear your speech today. When I saw the headline: *University President's Wife to Speak at Home for Unwed Mothers*, I just had to come. You see, I was curious about how you would defend a bunch of knocked up girls choosing life over abortion when you never gave our baby a chance at life."

"Please Kash, don't bring that up. You may not believe this, but I still have a hard time dealing with the miscarriage," Suzy lied, on the verge of tears again.

"Let's talk about that miscarriage. Shall we? I think it would do us both some good. The timing was rather convenient, don't you think? The timing of the miscarriage, I mean."

"What are you talking about? You act like I could have controlled when it happened."

"It's almost as if you did control it. Let's check the sequence of events. First, you tell me you're pregnant and then when I ask you to marry me, you tell me you'll have to think about it. Second, I ask you to take a fishing trip with me, and much to my surprise, you say you'll go. You hate to fish. You once told me you could think of nothing more boring than sticking a pole in the water and waiting for something to take the bait."

"I went to get you off my back Kash, nothing more."

"Third, when it was time to get on the boat and go fishing, you suddenly become sick."

Suzy cut in, "My God Kash, I was pregnant. Pregnant ladies get sick."

"Fourth, I find it a bit coincidental that the day after we returned from our trip you are no longer pregnant. You had a miscarriage, so you say, and then you wait two days to tell me about it."

"I wasn't up to telling anybody. I was mourning the loss of my baby."

"Our baby Suz. It was my baby, too. And I know what happened to it. I know about Kentucky."

"What's to know about Kentucky? I've never been there before."

"The hell you haven't. I know about the clinic, the appointment, and the abortion. You deceived me from the start; from the first day you knew you were pregnant. You had no intention of accepting my marriage proposal or keeping our baby."

"You're crazy Kash. This whole idea of yours is crazy! I told you, I had a miscarriage. I didn't plan it—it just happened."

"Yeah Suz, you had a miscarriage at the hands of a knife-bearing doctor. It's too late to deny it. I've got the papers from the clinic, Suzy. There's no need to deceive me anymore. I can tell you what day you had it done, what time, even how much it cost you."

"You'll never know what it cost me," Suzy said speaking metaphorically. "That abortion has cost me plenty every single day of my life. I wake up to it. I go to bed with it. I hear the sounds of that damn vacuum buzzing in my head almost every waking minute of the day. So don't act like you're the victim here. *You* were the problem. I have you to blame for my conscience. The whole thing was your fault."

"I hate to be the one to tell you this, but where I come from it takes two to make a baby," Kash straightened his hat.

"How dare you make light of this issue. You don't know the hell you've caused me."

"I caused you? I didn't do anything, except maybe love you, but that wasn't enough. You did this to yourself, and if you're going through hell, then maybe you should ask yourself why you did it, Suzy? If it's been so hard on you, why did you murder our baby?"

"I had no other choice. It was the only answer. You know that."

"No, I don't know that. What gives you the right? You snuck off and had it done without ever asking me how I felt."

He stared at her through eyes that had a weird, glassy look. Suzy became frightened. She glanced around the parking lot, looking for someone to rescue her if she needed help. Nobody was around.

Kash could feel his emotions slipping away. The Bad Thoughts were trying to come back. Not wanting to loose control, he tried to cut it off before it started. Now his darkness was only a gray hue. Soon it would be pitch black. He still had business with Suzy Whitmore. He began to silently count, using extra concentration as he had been taught.

> *One potato, two potato, three potato, four,*
> *Five potato, six potato, seven potato, more.*

He recited the Healing Rhyme again and a third time. He was finally able to cut off the Bad Thoughts at the pass. His darkness had passed.

Suzy watched Kash close his eyes and move his lips. At first, she wondered what he was doing. It sounded like he was whispering some kind of children's rhyme. Was he talking to himself? Then she began to see the transformation. A face, which had been full of tension, changed right before her eyes into a docile face, one full of only contentment. She watched as the lines that were etched in his face disappeared on the spot. His shoulders slacked and his mouth dropped open, only a little. When he opened his lids again, she saw before her a pair of eyes—eyes that only an instant ago had been glassy and full of stress—were now calm, almost serine. A short period of silence followed before he finally spoke.

"I'll never forgive you for what you did … for taking my child away from me."

Suzy felt uneasy with him in light of the makeover she had just witnessed. She had run out of things to say. "I have to go now," she announced inching toward the car door.

Kash stepped in her path—he smiled.

"Don't you want to know why I came to see you Suzy?"

"I assume you've fulfilled the purpose for your visit. You've let me know everything that you know, and you've humiliated me most successfully. That *was* your purpose, wasn't it?"

"Well darlin', not entirely. You see I've run into a little lapse in my career. Due to some circumstances beyond my control, I won't be able to work for a while, so I have a small cash flow problem. I was wondering if you could help me out with that."

Suzy looked at him. He gazed deeply into her dark eyes.

His voice became hard. "I need money, Suzy dear. I thought you'd be kind enough give me some. After all, you and your hubby have enough for all of us. You snagged a rich one this time, didn't you Suz?"

"I'm not the corner bank. If you need money I suggest you get a loan."

Agitation swept Kash. He found it hard to control his temper. "I'm not looking for a loan," he said angrily. "I need a steady supplemental income. I think a thousand a week ought to do it. Just until I get back on my feet."

"You must be crazy if you think I can come up with that kind of money."

"Suit yourself, but I'll be forced to tell the sad saga of little baby Kashette and how he never made it into this world. Wouldn't that be an upsetting story for your husband to hear? He's real big in this pro-life thing, isn't he? I bet you'd be a big embarrassment to him, huh? He'd be smart to cut his losses and distance himself from you. He might even divorce you." Kash laughed then added, "Oh, I saw your son this morning. Tommy isn't it? Fine young boy, nice car, too. He told me it was a birthday present from his parents. Must be nice."

"You stay away from my son. Where did you see him?" Now it was Suzy who found it hard to control her temper.

"At the 7-Eleven this morning. By the way, did you know he smokes?" Kash snickered. "You really should make him quit. It's a nasty habit and it's not good for his health either." Again, he snickered. "Now, are you going to help me or not?"

"No!" Suzy said firmly. "It's my word against yours."

"Don't be stupid Suzy. Do you think I'd come around here asking for money if I didn't have something to back me up? I've already told you I know which abortion clinic did your little procedure. It's amazing how careless those baby stabbing doctors are with their patient records."

"You're lying. You don't have any records." Suzy prayed she was correct.

"You want to try me. The media and press will be all over a story like this one." He handed her a piece of paper with a name and address on it. "Here, this is in case you change your mind, which I strongly suggest you do. I want the check made payable to Samuel Kirkland and mail it to the address on the paper. Four thousand dollars. Payment will be due on the fifteenth of each month. We can start next month. I'll give you a thirty day grace period, just like the corner bank."

Kash tipped his hat to her and walked away never turning to look back.

Suzy froze in fear. The soles of her shoes seemingly melted to the asphalt surface of the parking lot; she could only sway because her knees were locked in place. Nothing else could move, only her eyes, as she fixed them on Kash departing the crisis center.

Suzy's nerves were on the verge of snapping. She was not sure if she said the right things. She had no way of knowing whether Kash was telling truth. She had no way of knowing if Kash really had anything to show Clayton. Kash was right about one thing, though: even if he had no proof—if it was his word against hers—the press would jump at the story. Her husband's reputation would be ruined.

Suzy did what she always did when faced with a dilemma: she cried. Normally she would turn to Clayton for support or advice, but this time she was on her own. Sobbing, she weighed her options. She could either pay him or not pay him. There wasn't much to weigh. She felt a headache coming on. When she finally induced movement, she inserted the key to unlock the car door but found it already opened.

She could have sworn she locked the door.

CHAPTER FIVE

Lora
Plans a Party

1

Dr. Jordan sat at the desk in her office on the fourth floor of Boston General Hospital. Whether in her office or in her home, Lora surrounded herself with beautiful things. She needed a constant reminder that she could afford almost anything she desired. The rich mahogany furniture in her office was highlighted by chrome accents. She liked the glossy look of it, but chrome also added a sense of sterility that Lora thought should be abundant in a hospital setting. The carpet was a dark Berber and the office was bursting with live plants and flowers.

She was extremely busy today. The budget reports were due this afternoon, yet she had completed only half of them. The scheduling was based on a two-week period, and tomorrow was the last day, so the new one would have to be created, too. She was grateful, however, that she had to see only three patients today. That would give her the time she needed to get caught up on her administrative duties.

So far, approximately ten RSVPs for the fundraiser had come in. She was dying to open the new ones that had just arrived with today's mail. For the last two weeks, all Lora had been able to think about was planning the gala. She knew what food she was going to serve, and she had a theme in mind, but she had no idea what she was going to wear. Being as it was a formal affair, she considered buying a new gown. She had to look her best, and she dared not wear something from her closet for fear one of the wives may have seen her in it before. A woman of her status in the community was expected to have a new dress for every new occasion.

As the date of the party drew near, Lora became more excited. She wanted to prove herself worthy of her position. She knew she could handle it, but she still felt the need to prove herself to the rest of her colleagues. She remembered another party a long time ago—a party that took place in another life, or so it seemed to Lora.

One evening, (it must have been summertime Lora remembered, because it was hot in the tin can on wheels and all the windows had been opened up) dear ole dad had come home from the track in an extra good mood. Lora had been about ten or so. In his hand was a shopping bag filled with party fixings: chips, pop, frozen pizzas, and Dixie cup ice cream in chocolate. When Lora looked in the bag, she asked, "What's all this stuff for?"

"A party," had been his response.

He explained how it had been a good day at the track, and how a horse named Maxwell Smart had pulled in a shitload of money for dear ole dad. "Get Smart" was dear ole dad's favorite TV show. Sometimes he would laugh so hard at the shenanigans of Smart and Agent 99, that a coughing fit would fester up from his lungs. Maxwell Smart was his hero—some hero, huh?

Anyway, when she inquired further about the party, he told her that the party was for her. She could not imagine why he would want to throw a party for her.

"I thought you could call up your girlfriends and invite them for a sleepover. They could bring their sleeping bags, and you girls could talk and giggle all night."

The last thing Lora wanted to do was have a party. There was nobody she wanted to invite to her house. On the contrary, she tried to hide Pathetic Jokes from her friends at school. She certainly would not ask them to come for a sleepover.

"Please daddy, don't make me do this."

"I'm not forcing you. I thought it would make you happy. I don't know of any little girl who didn't want to have a slumber party."

Well he was sure out of touch when it came to knowing his daughter, Lora, but the party had taken place anyway. If Lora had turned down dear ole dad's generosity this time, she knew there would be no next time. She had to grab whatever he was willing to give and be thankful for it. It wasn't that she had no friends; it was more that she lacked a certain breed of friends. She wanted to be in the company of girls from the south side—the wealthy section of town—but she had yet to figured out how to get into that clique. So she had invited four girls from Pathetic Jokes just to keep dear ole dad from thinking she was an ingrate. Lora had no interest nor did she enjoy the sleepover in the least. These girls were hardly the kind of company she wanted to keep.

Now her friends and colleagues were pillars of the community, all of the very highest standards, and it was these people whom she would be entertaining at the fundraiser. She knew the reception was an extra-curricular function so her duties as Chief of Neurology would have to come first. She got to work, as hard as that was.

By the time the noon hour arrived, Lora had finished most of her executive jobs. Since she was packing a nutritious lunch for Alex every day, she decided to pack the same for herself. She had two patients to see this afternoon, the first one in half an hour, so she pulled her brown bag out of the dorm size refrigerator to eat lunch. It was now or never. While eating her low-cal turkey ham sandwich with fat free mayo, she could no longer resist the temptation to open the other four RSVPs from today's mail. The first one she opened was from the Whitmores. Lora was so pleased to see that the *will be attending* box was checked. She had not seen Suzy and Clayton since her wedding. She felt badly about that too, because they lived less than an hour away. Of all the friends she had made in college at Kanawha State, Lora was the closest to Suzy. Suzy had admired Lora's confident attitude, and this touched Lora. She was glad somebody finally noticed she could hold her own. Besides, they all had lived together. She got along well with Rosalee too, and considered her a good friend, but Suzy and Lora shared a lot of things and a lot of thoughts. Once, they even shared a boyfriend. She wondered whatever happened to Sam "Kash" Kashette.

Looking over the card, she noticed a phone number written in one of the bottom corners. The handwriting was Suzy's, she could tell, because an *XXOO* took the place of the signature. Suzy always signed her notes in this fashion. The note said, please call. She could kill two birds with one stone— eat lunch and make the call—so she picked up the phone along with her sugar free Jell-O and started to dial.

It had been many years since she had thought about Suzy. She would never tell her this in a million years, but Lora had been jealous of Suzy back then—not so much jealous of her, as of her money. Lora had worked hard for everything at good old Kanawha State and along came Suzy, who had things handed to her left and right. She never had to work for spending cash. Hell, she never even had to ask for it. Daddy made sure that she had cash in her pocket at all times and backup money in her bank account. Suzy had shown up in August of 1972 with a 1973 Corvette convertible. Candy Apple red, it had been with black leather interior. Only the best for Prentis Shaffer's little angel. It should have mattered, but it didn't, that Suzy was incapable of putting gas in the car her father spoiled her with or that she hadn't a clue about balancing the checkbook he padded for her. Yet she had a great car to drive and lots of money to spend. Where was the responsibility factor in this family? Suzy's tuition had been paid in full on the first day of each semester, while Lora and her mother had worked their butts off for years to supplement what financial aid and student loans did not cover.

There was a flip side, though, to having a spoiled rich girl for a roommate—the clothes. Suzy dressed in only designer duds, and Lora swore she had never seen her in the same outfit twice. She always looked like she had just stepped out of a Saks Fifth Avenue catalog or off the showroom window of the local Kaufmanns or Lazarus. Lora would borrow something, a sweater or a pair of jeans or a dress, and when she would return it, Suzy would say in her sweet but dizzy voice, "Oh why don't you just keep it Lora. It looks better on you than on me anyway."

At first Lora took offense, thinking that perhaps Suzy didn't want it back simply because Lora had worn it. After all, she didn't have cooties or any other bugs for that matter, and Lora's personal hygiene was good. Then she realized Suzy had felt sorry for her, even though Suzy never said it, and Lora hated that even more. She despised it when someone pitied her or looked down upon her because she had less than they had. She did appreciate the new clothes, just the same. Most of her own wardrobe had come from the discount stores and then only if they had been marked down in a big way.

Suzy may have had all the money in the two-some, but it was Lora who had all the will. Her determination was something to be admired. When she wanted something, she went for it. It mattered not how hard she had to work or whom she had to run over in order to get it (and she had run over more than a few in her day). Medical school was academically challenging and Lora had the added burden of working practically full time in a pharmacy, but not once did she regret what she had to do to make it. She moved forward every day, stayed focused, and never looked back.

The phone rang three times before Suzy picked up.

"Hello?"

"Suzy? Hi honey, this is Lora."

"My God Lora, it's so good to hear your voice. How are you?"

Suzy and Lora got the formalities out of the way first: all of the "How is such and such, and have you seen so and so, and wonder what ever happened to this one and that one?" Suzy finally divulged the reason she wanted Lora to call her.

"Lora, I was wondering," Suzy asked awkwardly. "Do you think Clayton and I could come out for the fundraiser a day early? I know you'll be busy preparing, but I could help. I've thrown a few socials myself for the University, and I'd really like to have some extra time alone to talk to you."

"Of course you can come early. You don't need to be invited. Do you have something in particular you want to talk about?"

"My life. My life is falling apart, and I don't know what to do or where to turn."

"What is it Suzy? Is it Clayton's health?"

"No, thank God. Nothing like that. Everyone's in good health."

"Please Suzy, don't make me worry. What's wrong?"

"Something happened a couple weeks ago, and I'm terribly upset about it," Suzy said solemnly. "I feel just awful about dumping my problems on you when I haven't seen you for so many years, but I know you'll know what to do. I think we should wait until this weekend, though. I'll explain everything to you then."

"All right, if you're sure you'll be okay."

"I'm sure. I'll be able to make it a few more days."

"So you'll be at our house on Friday. What time should I expect you?"

"Is five o'clock too early? Clayton should be done at the University about three, and by the time he comes home and we get on the road it should put us in Boston around five."

"That's fine. I want to warn you, though. I put Alex on a strict diet, so you guys will be eating healthy Friday night. But we'll make up for it Saturday at the party. Did you have any trouble interpreting the map to the house I sent along with the invitation?"

"No, it looked pretty simple."

"Well then, I guess we'll see you on Friday."

"Yes, thanks for having us the extra day. And Lora, I can't wait to see you again."

"Me neither."

"See you then. Bye-bye." Lora hung up the phone.

As she put the containers from her lunch back into the paper bag, Lora felt tears in her eyes. She had loved Suzy so much back then. It would be great to see her again. She thought about calling Rosalee and trying to set up a reunion, but she knew she would have her hands full with the fundraiser. She barely had time to spend with Alex. Anyway, she had no clue where to begin looking for Rosa. She and Rosalee had lost touch a good eight years ago. Maybe they could all get together another time.

As she was pulling her thoughts back to the present, Annie barged in to announce her 1:30 appointment.

Annie Crane was a young woman, of 25 years with a bubbly personality. She was not only Lora's receptionist, nurse, and right arm, she was also a good friend. Due to a birth imperfection, Annie was born with only one full leg. She wore a prosthetic on the other. She walked quite normally, but on some days, especially when she was tired, she tended to drag the fake leg a little. Lora admired Annie. She was not so sure she would be able to cope if she were in Annie's shoes.

Annie ran a tight ship, so she did not take kindly to it when Lora ignored her announcement. "Dr. Jordan, your 1:30 appointment is here," she said a little louder.

"I'm sorry Annie; I was daydreaming. I guess Friday will come soon enough."

"Huh?" Annie said.

"Never mind. Would you send in Mrs. Bell, please," Lora said smiling.

2

Suzy hung up the phone. Her hands trembled considerably. How would she bring up the subject of Kash and the blackmail to Lora when there had been so many years missing in between? It never occurred to her that she would have to talk to someone about this. The last week of May was already here, so she would have to make up her mind soon whether or not to pay Sam Kashette the money. It wasn't that she didn't have the money. She controlled a checking account in her name solely that was used for her own indulgence. It was made up mostly from interest on CD's she had bought, and dividends from a good chunk of company stock left to her by her father. She also had money in a trust fund from her father's estate. Clayton would never have to know about the 4000 dollars a month. She was certain he had no idea as to how much money she had. His accountant took care of the finances from their joint account, but the firm Suzy's father had used handled all of her personal money affairs.

She had been dusting the living room furniture when Lora Jordan called. Suzy tried to resume her work. Even though she had a cleaning lady come in every Saturday, she liked to keep her house looking nice in between. Dusting the coffee table with a feather duster, her hand still shaky, she knocked over a vase of fresh cut flowers. Water spilled everywhere. She went to the kitchen to tear off a few paper towels, and in doing so, bumped her arm against the canisters on the counter top, spilling the one marked sugar. She looked at the mess she had created and started to cry. She was falling apart, a total nervous wreck.

Because she was in a position to do so, she had invariably let someone else take charge of problem issues. She never handled these things herself, and she sure had no experience in dealing with a situation of this nature. If Kash made good on his threats, it could destroy her family. She had no comprehension of how to fix this one. She would have to pay him until she figured out what to do. Suzy sat down at the kitchen table, cupped her hand over her face, and burst into tears again.

Tommy came in from school via the kitchen door. When he saw his mother's frail condition, he became alarmed. Laying his books on the counter top, he asked, "Mom, what's wrong?"

Suzy sniffled and wiped her eyes. "Nothing, honey. I'm just having a bad day." Using the messes in the kitchen and living room as an excuse, Suzy explained to her son why she was crying.

He gave her a big hug and while he embraced his mother Tommy said, "Gee mom. It's not like it's something you can't clean up."

Suzy looked into her son's eyes and said, "Oh Tommy, I hope so. I really hope so."

CHAPTER SIX

That's What Friends Are For

1

Lora Jordan strolled along the sidewalks of downtown Somerville. Not wanting to fight the traffic and crowds of Boston's business district, she chose the neighboring village of Somerville to do her shopping. Besides, this neighborhood was a hot spot for Boston's rich and famous. It was like an obsession with Lora: she wanted—no, she needed—to be around wealthy people, to be seen in the places where they gathered, to shop where they shopped, to buy the things they bought.

She parked the car and walked a couple of blocks to a quaint dress shop where she planned to buy her dress. She stopped to look at the window displays in the other shops along the way. The clothes were all so beautiful. When she was a child, sometimes she and her mother would go into town where they would window shop and dream about buying entire outfits right off the mannequins in the window. Today, she could afford to do just that.

Lora dressed modestly for the most part, but she wanted to look extra special while assuming the role of hostess at the reception. She had a dress style in mind and upon entering the store, she saw something to her liking immediately. The ensemble she spied was a black spaghetti strap cocktail gown, accented with delicate iridescent beading. The front had a modified v-neckline and a white Bolero jacket, accented with black swirled beading, accompanied it. She checked the garment with the sales clerk and went into the dressing room. The minute she put it on, she knew it was perfect. The a-line bodice looked lovely against her smart figure, and the fit was flawless. No alternations would be necessary. Never once looking at the price tag—the cost was immaterial; she could afford even the most expensive dress in the store—she took the gown to the counter and paid for it. She would never again be denied something she wanted.

In her car during the 10-mile drive home, she listened to her favorite radio station. Classical music always helped, somehow, to put her thoughts in perspective. She ran down a mental checklist of her party preparations. There was only two days to go; Suzy and Clayton would be there tomorrow. She was so excited to see them. She decided to do chicken and baked potatoes on the grill Friday night, and later she and Suzy could catch up. Lora wanted to know about everything that Suzy had been doing. She wanted to know about Clayton's presidential promotion, too. He must have shown a lot of ambition and potential to be appointed to such a high rank in the University at his young age. She also wanted to hear about Tommy. During their phone conversation a few days ago, Suzy told Lora that Tommy had just turned sixteen. Lora was shocked. She could hardly believe it. He was only a little boy the last time she had seen him. Where had the years gone?

Pulling into the driveway, Lora was surprised to find Alex home. When she checked her watch, she saw that he wasn't early; she was late. She had taken so much time shopping, she must have lost track of time. When she entered the living room, packages in hand, Alex was waiting for her.

"I see there's no need to ask where you've been," Alex grinned.

"Stop teasing, I didn't buy that much."

"Did you leave anything for the other women in town?"

"Alex ... I only bought a new dress and shoes. You want me to look good on Saturday, don't you?"

"You would look beautiful if you were wearing nothing but a burlap sack," Alex said lovingly.

"How sweet. What's in the envelope?" she questioned after seeing it on the coffee table.

"Tickets. Do you know if Clayton likes hockey?"

"I don't know," Lora admitted.

"Someone, down at the bank, gave George two tickets to the Bruins playoff game for tomorrow night. George doesn't like hockey, so he asked me if I wanted them," Alex explained. "I thought maybe Clayton and I could get out of the house tomorrow evening and leave you women to your reminiscing."

"I'm sure Clayton will enjoy going even if he doesn't like hockey. I don't figure he'll want to stay around here and listen to Suzy and I relive old times."

"I looked at the seating chart, and it appears our seats are in a good location for being complementary tickets," Alex said. "I think he'll have a good time."

"I do too," Lora said. "Are you hungry?"

"Starved." Alex held his stomach. "Can we have pork chops tonight?"

"Not on your life, buster. We're having tuna surprise," Lora replied, hurrying into the kitchen.

"Yeah, and I'll bet the surprise is peas and carrots. Damn!" Alex mumbled to himself.

"What'd you say, honey?" Lora yelled from the kitchen.

"I said yum dear. Yum."

2

The days passed quickly for Suzy since she had talked to Lora on the telephone. She was relieved, in a strange sort of way, knowing she would soon have Lora to lean on. Somehow, she knew everything would be all right—Lora would make it so; she always did.

She and Clayton were currently on their way to Boston, even though a mix-up in Suzy's schedule put them on the road an hour late. No matter, Clayton was used to it by now. Suzy was always late.

Suzy had been quiet for most of the hour-long trip. She was thinking of a way to tell Lora about her problem.

Clayton lit his pipe. The vanilla aroma filled the Lincoln. Suzy gazed at her husband. She loved him so much, and she was irate to think something she'd done two decades ago could hurt him or his career. He smiled at her and said, "You're awfully quiet today. Are you nervous about seeing Lora after all these years?"

"Yeah, I guess I am." Suzy lied, looking at the map Lora had mailed with her party invitation. "You need to make a right at the next intersection. That puts us on Kelsey Circle. Her house is the last house on the left."

"Okay, we're almost there," Clayton said.

3

By the time the Whitmores pulled into the Jordan's driveway, Lora was already coming out to meet them. Suzy got out of the car first, and Lora welcomed her with a big hug. Alex had come out too. He was shaking Clayton's hand.

"Good to see you again, Clayton," Alex said. "It's been a long time."

"Good to see you, too," Clayton returned. "You've got a nice place here, Alex."

"You should have seen it when we bought it. We had to replace this whole side here ..." Alex rambled on, walking Clayton around to the side of the house.

While she escorted Suzy through the front door, Lora laughed, "He'll have Clayton bored to death before he's finished with his remodeling stories."

"That's okay, he's proud of the work you've done. It is a lovely home, Lora," Suzy said looking around the charming foyer and the exquisite living room. Lora had sure come a long way from Pathetic Jokes.

"Thank you. So how have you been, Suz?"

"Pretty good," Suzy was not sure if it was the right time to begin. After all, they had only arrived five minutes ago, but she needed help. "Until two weeks ago." She hated being in such a big mess.

"What happened two weeks ago?"

"Well, I was giving a speech to a group of unwed mothers at a pregnancy crisis center, and you'll never guess who I ran into."

"Who?" Lora questioned. The guys were just coming in from their tour around the house.

"I'll finish later. We have all evening," Suzy said somewhat relieved. She really didn't think it was the best time.

Lora directed her guests to their room, showed them where she kept the necessities in the bathroom and told them she was going to start dinner. If they wanted to clean up, they should feel free.

Lora went to the kitchen and removed the chicken pieces from the refrigerator as Alex told her Clayton was indeed a hockey fan.

"He seemed really excited when I told him about the two tickets I had for the playoff game tonight," Alex said.

"Good, because Suzy is acting really weird. I think something very heavy is weighing on her mind. I don't know what's wrong, but I'm sure Clayton's not in on it. She quickly changed the subject as soon as you two came in the room earlier. So don't say anything to him, okay?"

"I won't. Do you have any idea what it's all about?"

"Not a clue. At first, I was concerned about Clayton's health. But when I asked her about it on the phone the other day, she said everyone was fine. Something happened two weeks ago. I don't know what, but it sure has upset her."

"I don't think it's a good idea for you to get too involved in her personal problems."

"She's a friend."

"Yes, a friend you haven't seen in years. People do change, you know."

"Not Suzy. She's still just as helpless today as she was the first day I met her."

"That's my point. All I'm saying is, don't get yourself in the middle."

"Trust me Alex ... I know how to take care of Suzy. I've done it for years."

Lora smiled, as she took the chicken already par boiled and arranged on aluminum foil, out back to the patio.

Suzy and Clayton came out a few minutes later. Suzy asked if there was anything she could do to help. Lora told her everything was in order. Alex brought out the last of the condiments for dinner. While the chicken was cooking, the four of them chatted about everything that had been going on in their respective lives. Clayton talked about the University, Suzy talked about Tommy, Lora talked about the fundraiser, and Alex talked about his diet.

"I actually carried butter out here today. I honestly thought they quit making the stuff," Alex teased licking his lips.

The three laughed. Lora announced that dinner was ready. She said, shaking her finger at Alex, "The butter is for our company. You and I get the lo-cal sour cream on our potatoes."

Alex glared at her, pouting like a little boy whose candy had been taken away.

They continued to shoot the breeze through dinner. When they were finished eating, Clayton lit his pipe, and Alex offered him a drink.

"I'll have bourbon, if you have it." Clayton said politely.

"I have that. Do you want it straight up, or on the rocks, or with a mixer?"

"A water chaser will be good."

Alex went to the bar to fix his guest a drink. On his way, he passed through the kitchen. He asked Lora, "Does my doctor permit me to have a drink with Clayton?"

Lora smiled at him. "Oh, I suppose there's no harm in one drink. Suzy, would you like a glass of wine?"

"Sure."

"Honey?" Lora called. "Fix us two glasses of Zinfandel, please?"

"Coming up." Alex answered heading for the bar in the den.

After returning with the beverages, Alex and Clayton talked about local politics. With the kitchen cleaned up and the dishwasher running, Lora and Suzy returned to the patio to join their husbands.

Suzy asked nervously, "What time does the hockey game start? Shouldn't you two be going?"

Lora looked awkwardly at her. She had the impression Suzy was trying to get rid of the fellows. When it came to Suzy, her instincts were rarely wrong.

"Yeah, we probably should get going." Alex explained that the Boston Gardens, where the Bruins played their games, was only a fifteen-minute drive; however, with the traffic delay they should leave a bit earlier. The two men rose and kissed their wives good-bye. After a short lecture from Lora to Alex concerning junk foods at the Gardens, the men left the two gals alone.

Lora offered Suzy another glass of wine. She accepted and while Lora was off getting the refills, Suzy wondered how telling Lora about her problems with Kash was going to solve anything. For almost 20 years, she had kept this secret to herself, and now she questioned whether she should be sharing it with anyone, even with her oldest friend.

The spring evening air was cool but not uncomfortable. The Jordan's neighborhood was silent, save for a pair of croaking toads making conversation back and forth.

Lora came back to the patio carrying a plate of fruit and cheese and the opened bottle of Zinfandel. She poured more wine into Suzy's glass.

"I thought I'd bring the bottle. I have the feeling this is going to be a long talk." Lora stared seriously into Suzy's beautiful dark eyes. "Now, tell me what happened two weeks ago that has you so upset."

Suzy took a drink from her glass, sighed heavily, and started to tell her story again. "Well, it's like I was saying before. I was speaking at a home for unwed mothers, and I ran into somebody from our past."

"Our past? Who?"

"Kash."

"Sam Kashette from Kanawha State?" She remembered thinking about him just the other day, the same day she called Suzy.

"Yes. Sam Kashette."

"What was he doing there? Don't tell me he's running a home for unwed mothers?" Lora said jokingly, but she saw that Suzy's emotion was cold sober. "Seriously, what was he doing there?"

"He was looking for me."

"What? Why?"

"Oh Lora, where do I begin?"

"How about at the beginning? I had no idea you were still in contact with Kash."

"I'm not."

"Then why was he looking for you?"

"He wants something from me. Lora, I want to tell you about it, but I'm just not sure I can. I did something when we were in college. Something I never told anyone."

"What did you do? It can't be that bad."

Suzy ran her fingers through her hair. "Have you ever done something that you were ashamed of?"

"Yeah, I guess we all have."

"No, I mean something so deplorable that after 20 years it still makes your blood run cold when you think about it?"

"Suzy, you're scaring me. What are you talking about? Maybe you'll feel better if you get it off your chest."

"Maybe, but I'm not sure I'll ever feel better even if I get it off my chest. You see, I have an emptiness inside of me that can never be filled, a chill that has never quite been warmed; a grief that will never end."

"What grief? Who died?"

"Nobody died but nevertheless I grieve. Try to think back, way back. Do you remember when Kash and I went away for a weekend between summer sessions? We went on a weekend fishing trip to Kentucky."

Lora thought. "Yeah, I do remember. I thought it odd that you went since you never liked to fish. You broke up with him right after you came back, didn't you? I tried to tell you he was a jerk."

"Yeah, well I should have listened. Maybe I would have spared myself a great deal of sadness, depression, and shame if I had."

"Why are you consumed by all these emotions over Sam Kashette? You said you haven't been in contact with him. He's not been in your life since college."

"Oh you are so wrong, Lora. Indirectly Sam Kashette is in my life almost every day. You see I didn't go fishing that weekend," she hesitated before continuing. "I went away to take care of a problem. I was pregnant, and I chose not to have the baby." She started to cry.

"Suzy, are you telling me you had an abortion?"

"Yes."

Lora laid her head back against the lawn chair. "I can't believe it. How could you terminate a pregnancy? How far along were you?"

"Eight weeks."

"Eight weeks! Do you have any idea how developed a baby is at eight weeks? It had all of its fingers and toes. It had a good strong heartbeat and brainwaves that sent signals to the other organs. The stomach was developed, and the kidneys were beginning to function. The jaw was formed, and it had little teeth buds in its gums. The tiny fetus responds to touch. Do you know what fetus means? It's a Latin word meaning young one. Your *young one*, Suzy, had its own fingerprints by the time you aborted it. It exercised its tiny muscles by turning its head and curling its toes, and opening and closing its mouth. At eight weeks, it even had the capability to suck its thumb. How could you?"

Suzy darted to a standing position, knocking over the chair in the process. "Do you think I don't have a conscience? I have been awakened from my sleep many times over the years by silent screams, by nightmares you know nothing about. I envision my baby begging me not to go through with it. Some nights when I'm alone I have to block out the sickening sounds of the suction that took the baby from within me."

"That suction didn't just take the baby. The technique is called Suction-Aspiration and the baby didn't come out whole. It pulled the baby's body into pieces."

"Don't lecture me with your fancy medical-school talk. You weren't in my shoes back then Lora. You don't know how you would have reacted in a similar situation." To defend her actions, she continued, "I didn't know what else to do. My family would have disowned me, and I really was not ready for motherhood, and I wanted to finish college, and I didn't—dear God—I didn't want to marry Sam Kashette. I knew I could do better. What other options did I have?"

"How about adoption, for starters?"

"I was too scared to consider the alternatives."

"You really should have Suzy. There are thousands of couples who can't have children. They would have jumped at the chance to adopt a newborn. Every year two million requests for adoption go unsatisfied."

"No it never would have worked. Kash never would have gone for the idea."

"Really ... but he was okay with the idea of killing your unborn child," Lora added with a hint of sarcasm.

"No, Kash wanted the baby. He was crazy about the fact that I was pregnant. He wanted me to marry him. I had to sneak away to have the abortion. He didn't know anything about it. I told him I had miscarried. You see, that weekend we were supposed to go out on a fishing boat with Kash's friend. I already had an appointment set up for Saturday at the clinic. I told Kash I wasn't feeling well, and he should go on without me ..."

"And while he was gone, you went to the clinic," Lora finished for her.

"Yes."

Suddenly Lora felt sympathy for her old friend. Suzy had handled the situation all by herself, even if she had made a poor decision. Knowing Suzy's innocence, Lora realized this must have been a hard thing for her to take on alone. Perhaps Lora had been a bit harsh by scolding her and humiliating her. There was a lot of truth to the words Suzy spoke: Lora had not been in her shoes, Lora had not been carrying the baby of a man she didn't love or a man with whom she would rather not spend the rest of her life. Suzy had been vulnerable back then—it was hardly Lora's place to judge. She could see her friend was still tortured by guilt.

She righted the overturned patio chair and patted the seat to signal Suzy, "Come on Suzy. Sit down. I'm sorry for being so judgmental."

Lora moved her chair closer and took her old roommate by the hand. "Why didn't you tell me? Honey, I could have helped you deal with it. My God, what you must have gone through."

Suzy looked up at her. "I couldn't tell you. Damn it Lora, you were heading off to med school soon. You were going to be a doctor. You were going to save lives. How in the world could I tell you that your best friend was going to kill her baby?"

"Maybe you were afraid to tell me. Maybe you were afraid I would talk you out of it?"

"Maybe."

Lora reached inside the kitchen door and pulled out a box of tissues from the counter top. Suzy was still crying—more like being on the verge of hysteria.

"Oh Suzy," Lora said, "You've carried this around all these years. Have you ever told Clayton?"

"No!" Suzy said. "And I don't ever want him to know. That's what this thing with Kash is all about."

"What? Are you saying that the reason he was looking for you has something to do with the abortion?"

"Yes. He wants me to give him money. He's trying to blackmail me, Lora."

"What's his intention? Is he threatening to tell Clayton about the abortion if you don't pay up?"

"Yes."

Lora was shocked, but only a little. Her memories of Kash led her to believe he had a dark side—a haunting of demons—which had been the primary reason why she had gotten away from him. Back then, she had tried to tell Suzy to steer clear of him too, but it seemed, to Lora anyway, that it was essential for Suzy to date Kash simply because Lora had. Oddly, Lora was touched by the memory, by the fact that Suzy had looked up to her, had tried to emulate her.

"Look Suzy, I don't approve of what you did, and I'll admit I don't know Clayton very well, but I know Clayton loves you enough to understand that you made a poor decision some 18 years ago. He's not going to be troubled by it, I'm sure."

"Lora, there's something you don't understand." Suzy tried to pull herself together. Her lip was shivering and her voice quivered when she spoke. "My husband is an avid pro-life advocate. He speaks out every chance he gets on the abortion issue. He has for the last 11 years. Hell he was even arrested once for protesting in front of an abortion clinic. The press was all over it. We have both made public statements about our stand on abortion. If this ever got out, he would be the laughing stock. I've always suspected his upstanding character was one of the main reasons he'd been promoted within the University at such a young age. My God, Lora, I was thanking a bunch of pregnant girls for *not* having an abortion, when Kash confronted me with all this. Don't you see the mockery? It would cause so much embarrassment to myself and to Clayton—even jeopardize his career—if this matter ever got out."

"And Kash knows this," Lora said finishing her wine. "Well it's your word against his."

"That's what I told him. He said he has proof. He said he has my records from the clinic."

"That's easily checked. We just call the clinic and see if they have them."

"I've already done that." Suzy said bewildered. "Records dating back that far are kept in a storage house, and unless I can prove a life or death situation, they won't look for them. Lora, what am I going to do? Even if he doesn't have the records, the press and the media will run crazy with a story like this. I can see the headlines now: *Pro-life University President Discovers His Wife's 18-Year-Old Secret Abortion!* If Kash doesn't have my records, the reporters would most likely dig up the records for him. I can't tell Clayton. I've been a bundle of nerves since the day Kash came back into my life." Suzy started crying hard again.

"Is it because of the abortion that you got involved in the pro-life movement?

"It was a healing process, a way to repent for the life I took away. I talk to youth groups and pregnant teens and adults. I try to convince them to have their babies. I've never shared my testimony with them, and I'm anxious before those engagements but after each speech, I somehow feel better. I feel like my baby has forgiven me a little more each time, even if I have never been able to forgive myself."

"And now Kash wants to profit from your guilt. That scum. You can't pay him." She looked at Suzy. "You aren't planning to pay him, are you?"

"What else am I supposed to do? I can't let him tell Clayton or anyone else."

Suzy opened her purse and took out the piece of paper Kash had given her. She handed it to Lora. "He wants four thousand dollars a month. Until he gets back on his feet, he said." Suzy laughed. "Sometimes I think I'm going out of my mind."

Lora read the note. "Is this the name he wants the check made payable to?"

"Yes and the address is where he wants me to mail it."

"Why doesn't he want cash?"

"I guess he doesn't want to deal with facing me every month."

"Oh Suzy, please don't pay him?"

"I have to, for now anyway."

"What happens later? What do you plan to do then?"

"I could always kill him!" Suzy said, her lips pressed together tightly. Her beautiful dark eyes watered. They gawked straight ahead, cold and hard in appearance.

4

Lora woke at her regular workday time, six o'clock. Today was the big day; today was the fundraiser reception. She wanted to be up and about early in order to prepare a nice breakfast for Suzy and Clayton. She jumped in the shower, and upon finishing, felt alive enough to start her day. She quietly set the alarm on Alex's nightstand for eight o'clock. She did not want him to sleep the day away when there was company to entertain. Lora went to the kitchen to start breakfast.

Meanwhile, in the guest room of the Jordan's seven-room house, Suzy stirred restlessly. Sleep had not come easily these past few weeks; however, with the half bottle of wine she'd consumed last night, she was finally able to get five hours of peaceful rest. Now she was wide-awake. She rolled over, closer to Clayton, and snuggled her husband firmly. Clayton woke and smiled at his wife. "Good morning, sweetheart."

Suzy wiggled in even closer, if that was possible, and told her husband the same. Still clinging tightly to him she said, "I love you so much, Clayton."

"I love you too Suz. You've been acting strange lately, is something bothering you?"

"No, honey, I'm fine." Suzy lied. "I'm just feeling a little insecure these days. Hold me tight Clayton."

Clayton did as he was asked and wondered out loud, "Are you going through the change of life?"

Suzy made no attempt to answer. Instead, she kissed her husband passionately on the lips. The love she felt for him flowed through her body as unmistakably as blood flowed through her veins. Her heart overflowed. It spilled out through her kiss. Clayton became erect at once. He removed his wife's nightclothes, and kissed her large breasts tenderly. When she assumed the position on top of him, he entered her gently. His compassionate hands ran over her large breasts and stoked her waist wildly, guiding her in passion. She knew at this moment of her lovemaking, that she would never let anybody take this feeling away from her. She would do whatever was necessary to prevent her family from ruin.

5

The party was scheduled to begin at 6PM. There had been so much to do, and as promised, Suzy had been a big help. The menu had been planned out weeks ago, but after Lora showed it to Suzy last night, Suzy persuaded her to make a few last minute changes. Suzy always had a knack for throwing a good party. The women had gone to the fisheries and picked up most of the food: sea sticks, crab claws, shrimp and bay oysters. Stopping at a local bakery, they picked up several different kinds of baked goods. When they returned Suzy stuffed mushroom caps. Lora had never eaten a stuffed mushroom before, but after sampling one, she found the morsel quite tasty. She whipped up a clam dip to be served with seasoned bread squares and cheese. Alex and Clayton had helped out too. They sampled the food as it was being arranged on serving trays. In all honesty, they did make a trip to the grocery store to pick up a prepared vegetable tray.

With the stage set to receive her guests, Lora dressed for the fundraiser. She hoped to raise a plentiful amount of money to put toward the new PET scan. In conjunction with this evening's affair, she planned to announce that a date for the auction had been set. She would wait until after her guests had made their donations before making the announcement so they would not lessen their original contribution.

The people who would be attending tonight's gala were very wealthy. All of Boston's movers and shakers would be there. Lora had met some of the high society crowd during Alex's business conventions, and she liked the way she felt while in the company of classy people.

Coming down the steps now, she saw Suzy and Clayton were already in the living room waiting for their hostess.

"That red silk looks stunning on you," Lora commented to Suzy.

"Thank you, Lora. You look absolutely gorgeous yourself."

Lora spun around to show off her new dress. Clayton cleared his throat. The two women made a little fuss over how wonderful Clayton looked as well.

Lora had arranged for Charlie Cotter, a nurse at Boston General, to act as bartender for this evening's affair. He had arrived at 5:45 and was just about finished setting up the portable bar Alex had wheeled into the living room from the den. At 6:05, the doorbell rang bringing the first of Lora's guests. She looked the room over, and after finding everything satisfactory, she welcomed Dr. and Mrs. Peter Hoskins.

Dr. Hoskins was the Chief of Staff who had appointed Lora to her new position just over a year ago. By 6:20, all 32 guests had arrived.

Lora watched her husband holding a captive conversation with Mr. Holden, President of the Board of Directors at the bank where Alex worked. She saw two cream horns and an éclair on his plate. She figured she had better go tend to Boston's version of Fat Albert before he put on the sixteen pounds he had taken off thus far.

Alex noticed her approaching and tried to conceal the plate.

"Mr. Holden, I'm so glad you could make the time to help us out tonight," Lora said, turning on all the charm.

"I wouldn't have missed it Lora. You know, since the Missus passed away, I grab any chance to get out of the house, and I've always been a sucker for a good cause."

"Did you bring your checkbook?" Alex said jokingly.

"Sure did," he said, patting the breast pocket of his jacket.

"Good," said Lora laughing. Turning more seriously to Alex, she whispered, "Take it easy on the goodies, buster. I don't want you going into sugar shock."

"I only had a few."

"A few plates maybe."

Lora excused herself so she could talk with her other guests. She was pleased to see Suzy mingling with some of the women. It was never a problem for Suzy to make friends. She was the queen of small talk. Lora knew Suzy had a lot on her mind; although, today she seemed less edgy than she was yesterday. Maybe she just needed to talk with someone, open up, and let someone else share her burden. She also assumed being busy with the party preparations all day helped take her mind off things too. Suzy seemed to be having a good time, despite the circumstances; still she worried about her. It had been awhile, but that was her job.

Lora was talking to Mrs. Kent, one of her wealthier patients, when the doorbell rang again. She checked her wristwatch and saw that it was close to seven. "Who could that could be?" she asked, sending a puzzled look Mrs. Kent way. "Everyone who responded is already here."

Mrs. Kent took a nibble of her mushroom cap and said, "You know Dr. Jordan, sometimes people are so careless about sending back the return cards—not me, of course, but some people. It's probably just one of those irresponsible late comers."

"Yes, I'm sure you're right. Excuse me, while I get that."

When Lora opened the door, she saw a well-built man leaning against one of the white columns on the porch. He used his elbow as a prop. He was dressed in faded jeans, a gray cotton shirt, gray tweed jacket and a gray Stetson hat which hid most of his face.

(*Shirt and hat must always match—it was part of The Order.*)

"May I help you?" she asked.

The man raised his hat just enough so that Lora could see his face. She vaguely recognized him but could not put a name to the face. Then he spoke.

"Hey darlin', I'm hurt. You throwin' a big shindig like this and didn't bother to invite me."

When she heard the voice, Lora knew immediately to whom the face belonged. She turned to see if anyone was watching her. Finding that no one was, she slipped outside onto the porch and closed the door behind her. "I can't believe you had the nerve to show up here. I want you to leave at once," she said with a bitter tone of authority.

"Awe, but Lora darlin', I so wanted us to chat a bit. We have lots to catch up on," Sam Kashette said with equal contempt.

"I have nothing to say to you. Now get out!"

"But you don't understand, Lora. You see, we have this mutual friend …"

"How dare you come here to harass Suzy. Don't you think you've put her through enough?"

"I didn't come here to harass Suzy." Kash said grinning. "I came here to see you." He pulled a Walkman from his jacket pocket. "The mutual friend I'm talking about is Rob Parker. You remember him, don't you Lora?"

6

"Hail Mary, full of grace, the Lord is with Thee …"

Sister Rosa sat in front of the Madonna statue and prayed her rosary. The churchyard sat atop a hill that looked across the mountains of West Virginia. She loved to come here and pray. She enjoyed looking at the mountains. Usually the view appealed to her, although tonight she took little notice. She found it hard to put the nagging thoughts of the two women out of her mind. Sister Rosa kept seeing their distant faces. She had not seen either of them in years, so this sudden prediction troubled her. She always knew in her heart when Kash was in trouble, so she prayed intensely now, because she sensed the two women were somehow connected with him again.

Her summer sabbatical would be coming up soon. Sister Rosa wanted very badly to see her family, but she felt that in view of the recent premonitions, she would also have to make time to visit Kash. Having not seen him in nearly two decades, she was unsure about how to approach him with the fact that she had become a nun. After college, the few friends who had stayed in touch with her were shocked to discover her plans for a religious life. Even her parents didn't accept it at first. She was quite sure this would take Kash completely by surprise. She wondered if he still lived in the same house, even the same state for that matter. She would make a point to get some answers to these questions as soon as she arrived home. If she could talk to him, maybe she could help him. She was sure he needed her support. He was into something bad. She could sense it.

"Holy Mary Mother of God, pray for us sinners, now and at the hour of our death, Amen."

She hoped it wasn't too late.

7

"Rob Parker?" Lora asked in surprise. "What does he have to do with this?"

"Here, would you like to listen?" Kash shoved the headpiece of the Walkman close to Lora's ear. She pushed it away. He said, "I'm sure you'll be interested, darlin'."

"I'm not interested in anything you have to say. Now, please leave."

"Didn't I see Doctor Hoskins arrive a little while ago? I'll bet he'd be interested in hearing what your old buddy Rob has to say."

Lora knees suddenly became weak, her head spun with dizziness, her face flushed with anger; frustration bubbled in her blood. He was going to do the same thing to her that he had done to Suzy. Walking off the porch toward the side of the house, she motioned for Kash to follow her. When they reached a discrete destination where Lora felt that they would not be overheard, she said, "Okay ... what does Mr. Parker have to say?"

"Well darlin', I'm glad you changed your mind." Kash again forced the headpiece to Lora's ear. This time she refrained from pushing it away. He had recorded parts of the original tape onto another tape, retrieving only the vital portions.

As Lora listened to Rob Parker's testimony indicting her with over four years of stealing drugs from Charleston Memorial's Pharmacy, a combination of fear and anger smothered her—anger for Sam Kashette and fear for herself, for what she might do. Her lower lip began to quiver; her knees noticeably shook. "You can't prove this is Rob Parker's voice."

"Lora, I can produce Mr. Parker if you like."

"How much did you pay him to say this? I'll pay him more to say he's lying."

"Not everything is about money, Lora. He was more than happy to volunteer the information. Maybe you should have cut him in on a bigger piece of the action. Did you know the whole time Rob was helping you to build your little enterprise he was also thinking about what a greedy little bitch you were?"

Kash started to laugh. A laugh that shot chills through Lora's backbone causing a rash of goose bumps to surface up and down her arms. Her stomach churned, and her head spun faster. Lora was out of control; she was furious. She grabbed for the Walkman and fought to remove the cartridge from it. She pulled the tape from its casing and ripped it to shreds. Kash laughed even harder aggravating the anger that had been bubbling in her veins to begin to boil.

"Darlin', that's not the only one I've got."

Now Lora was frustrated. She feared what she would do. For the first time in her life, she believed she could kill another human being, if Sam Kashette could be considered a human being. She was quickly becoming unraveled. She had to regain her composure. She refused to let Kash win.

Amassing some effective words to combat this terrible situation, she managed to calm herself and finally said, "You still can't prove anything. I knew what I was doing back then. It's still my word against his. I covered my track entirely."

"Not entirely Lora. I have copies of the dispensing tickets."

"Now I know you're lying. Rob destroyed those tickets after the inventory was taken each week."

"Are you sure about that? Did you ever see him shred the tickets or throw the tickets in the garbage, or burn the tick …"

"Okay. You've made your point. No, I never saw him get rid of the tickets, but why would he hold on to them after all these years? What did he think he could gain from bringing this up now?"

"I told you darlin', he didn't think he was being paid enough for all the risk involved. He was going to hold those dispensing tickets over your head one day, but I've got them now. And honestly, it wasn't that difficult to get them from him."

Again Kash laughed. The more he laughed the more peeved Lora became.

She lunged toward Kash throwing herself against him. She violently pounded his chest with her fist as she cried out. "You're not going to do this to me. I won't let you," she said, still jabbing at his chest and face with her fists. Sobs threatened now; she didn't know how much longer she could hold back the tears.

He expected Lora to be feisty—even anticipated their encounter—but this was even better than he ever could have imagined. He touched his crouch and discovered that he was aroused.

Kash wrapped his arms around her in an attempt to stifle her punches. The tighter he wedged her toward him the harder she squirmed. The blows didn't hurt Kash in the least, but the woman was becoming uncontrollable. He grabbed her by the shoulders, shook her, and whispered coldly in her ear, "Since Suzy is here, I suspect you know what I want from you." He handed her a piece of paper, just as he had done with his other victim. "Same deal as Suzy's, only you don't get the grace period. She didn't give me as hard a time as you did. Four thousand dollars a month, first payment is due the fifteenth of this month, just like Suzy. Oh, and by the way, I'm not bluffing about having the proof on either of you. If the checks aren't in my hand by the fifteenth, I'll be showing my proof, but it won't be to the two of you. I'll be showing the documents to your husbands," then he added, "for openers."

He brushed himself off and straightened his hat. As he walked away, he glanced back for one more look at Lora, usually strong and fiery, now weak and broken. He rubbed his crouch again. The hardness he found there, along with the little tingles in his groin and stomach, revealed how much he enjoyed afflicting pain on her. The Bad Thoughts were coming again. He considered saying the Healing Rhymes but then decided he would find a whore tonight. Women were put here to serve man's needs, and tonight Kash needed to have a whore. He walked away leaving Lora standing against the side of her house quietly whimpering.

8

Lora watched Kash glance back at her over his shoulder. She could no longer hold down the appetizers she had eaten earlier. Doubling over, she vomited all over the side of her beautiful house. How symbolic. If Alex were to find out what she had done, she would be throwing up her marriage as well. She was still crying. On the ground close to the place where she and Kash had struggled, lay a piece of paper. When her vision cleared a bit, Lora saw it and picked it up. There was still sufficient light outside, thanks to daylight savings time, for Lora to identify the piece of paper once she picked it up. She could see a handwritten map leading to her home. It was similar to the ones she had mailed out with the invitations to those people who were not familiar with her neighborhood. The only difference being: this was not her handwriting. The routes were written the same way, and the landmarks named were the same, but the writing was different. She assumed it had fallen out of Kash's pocket when they were wrestling.

After allowing herself a few more minutes to let it all out, Lora pulled herself together and continued walking around the side of the house. She figured she could go into the house through the kitchen door and return to the party without being missed. Lora tucked the map into the pocket of her dress and made her way to the back door. Upon entering the kitchen, she smoothed her hair and checked her reflection in the toaster. She ripped off a paper towel to wipe under her eyes where mascara had smeared from her crying and being sick. Her stomach was empty but not because she had thrown up; it was empty from the pit that lay there awaiting the tragedy which had yet to come. She put on a big happy face and entered the living room. She wanted desperately to find Suzy. Glancing over the room, she came up empty, but she did spot Alex bending over the pastry tray.

"Alex, have you seen Suzy?"

"Yeah, she took Donna Evans upstairs to show her where the other bathroom is. The one down here always seems to be full."

Lora headed for the stairs, never responding to her husband's reply. Alex knew something was wrong. He had literally been caught with his fingers in the notorious cookie jar, yet Lora spared him a reprimand. He kicked around the idea of going after her, but he figured it must have something to do with whatever Suzy wanted to talk to Lora about, so he decided to keep his nose out of it. Besides, Lora would tell him about it later. She told him everything. They had no secrets from each other. He took a sip of his Tanqueray and tonic and popped another nut roll into his mouth. He was going to take full advantage of his wife's absence.

"Suzy," Lora called as she neared the top of the stairs. She found Suzy and Donna Evans standing in front of the bathroom door.

"Lora," Suzy said, "I was just showing Donna where ..."

"Yes, I know," Lora said. "Donna, how wonderful to see you. So glad you could attend."

"Wouldn't have missed it," Donna returned. "We just must do lunch sometime soon, Lora."

"Yes, we must. Suzy, could I talk to you?"

"Sure."

Suzy followed Lora into the master bedroom. Lora sat on the bed and Suzy pulled out the vanity chair.

Whispering, Lora said, "He was here. Can you believe he had the balls to show up here?"

"Who?" Suzy asked.

"Sam Kashette."

"Was he looking for me? How did he know where I was? He didn't talk to Clayton, did he? What did he want?" Suzy threw the questions at Lora.

"He didn't want you, he wanted me. Suzy, he's trying to blackmail me now."

"You!" Suzy was alarmed. "What does he have on you?"

"Oh Suzy, you're not the only one with skeletons in your closet." Lora stood up and paced the bedroom floor. "Do you remember back at Kanawha State when I took a job in Charleston with the hospital pharmacy department?

"Yes, that was just before I graduated. The same time you were getting ready to begin graduate studies. You worked there the whole time you were in medical school, didn't you?"

"Yes," she said and then Lora told Suzy the story of how she stole drugs and sold them while she worked there. She also told her about Rob Parker's involvement in the scam and about all the things Sam Kashette promised to do. "I banked almost a hundred and fifty thousand dollars in that four year period. I could loose everything—my licenses to practice, my husband, not to mention Kash could have me locked up. I still have most of that money in a bank account in Somerville. Alex doesn't know anything about the account, or the money, or where the money came from. He's always based our marriage on honesty and trust. This will crush him. He will never be able to forgive me for being so deceitful."

"Why did you do it? You were making a decent salary at the pharmacy, weren't you?"

"Yes, but it wasn't enough. I wanted money, Suzy—not a salary or pocket money—big money. I was so sick and tired of doing without things I wanted and having to live on a poverty budget. I wanted new clothes, like you had, not somebody else's hand-me-downs. I wanted cash in my pocket if I wanted to see a movie. How many times did I pay when you and I went out somewhere?"

"I don't remember, nor do I care."

"I cared Suz. Twice, that's how many. I remember those times, and I hate the memories. All my life, money has made me second best, and I was not about to go through my adult life like that too. I had a plan. When I went out to do my internship, my intention was to get acquainted with groups of well-to-do people. You see, it takes money to know money. You have to have money to fit in with those kinds of people. You have to have money even to meet people with money. The plan was to join a country club and to become a regular patron of fancy restaurants. I was going to dress nice and shop at all the ritzy stores, so I could meet other rich people. All that took money. That's why I did it."

Suzy was shocked. She had no idea how important material things had been to Lora. While Suzy no more approved of what Lora did than Lora approved of Suzy's abortion, Suzy was not going to make the mistake of judging Lora or belittling her. Suzy had been on the other side of that fence last night. When Lora criticized Suzy for having the abortion, it hurt Suzy tremendously. She would not put her old friend through something like that. So now, she would suck it up and be there for Lora just as Lora had eventually come around for her last night.

"Kash said he had the dispensing tickets. Did he show them to you?"

"No. He said that if he didn't receive both of our checks by the fifteenth he would show the papers—both the dispensing tickets and your medical records—to Alex and Clayton. Suzy, he sounded like he meant it."

"Well, I think we should pay him on the fifteenth and buy ourselves some time."

"No ... no way. I don't think we should pay him anything."

"But what if ..."

"He won't." Lora anticipated Suzy's question. "Look, don't you think if Rob really had those tickets, he would have done something with them by now. He wouldn't have waited 20 years, and he wouldn't have just given them to Sam Kashette, a total stranger, either. He would have used them himself. He never would have cashed them in."

"Let's assume he doesn't have the dispensing tickets; he still may have my medical records. What then?"

"Look, you called the clinic yourself. It would take an act of congress to get a minimum wage receptionist to dig out those records. Kash doesn't have those kinds of connections. He doesn't have the records either, Suz."

"You're probably right, but I still think we're making a big mistake. I'm really scared."

"I am too Suz. We've got to stick together on this, or we will hang separately. He wouldn't dare go up against both of us!"

"I'm still not convinced." Suzy rubbed her fingers against her temples. "Do you think he followed me? How else did he know where I was or that we were even together, for that matter?"

Lora pulled out the folded piece of paper.

"This fell out of his pocket when I was fighting him."

Suzy looked it over and smacked her fists on her lap. "I knew I locked that door. I just knew I did!"

"What are you talking about?"

"At the Crisis Center, the day when this all started, I told you that Kash was leaning against my car waiting for me. After he left, I put my key in the car door to open it, and it was already opened. I knew I locked it; I always lock my doors. You see, Lora, I picked up the mail that morning on my way to give the speech. Your invitation was in the car. I read it and tucked it under the sun visor until I got home that afternoon. He must have broken into the car, found it, and copied it down for himself." Suzy felt even more violated now. "My God Lora I led him here—I led him right here to you."

"You did not. If he wanted to find me, he would have found me another way, so it doesn't matter."

There was a knock on the door. Both women flinched.

"Honey, are you in there?" It was Alex. "People are asking for you."

"I'll be right there, babe," Lora said.

Suzy spoke out to protect her friend, "Lora spilled wine on her dress, and I'm helping her get it out before it sets. Please, keep everyone occupied. We'll be right down."

Again, Lora's hands shook; her knees trembled. She clung to Suzy's arm as if the big bad wolf were at the door.

When Alex left, Suzy said, "He's right, Lora. We have to go back downstairs. We've been up here over half an hour. We can't let Kash interfere with our lives anymore. We have to get our priorities in order. Right now, you have a PET scan to raise money for, so let's get down there and charm the checkbooks off those people."

"Suzy, you always could make me laugh, even when I didn't want to."

"Hey what about you? Last night, when I was sure I was drowning, you threw me a lifeline just like you've always done. I thought I was going out of my mind until I talked to you."

Lora smiled. If only for a minute, it was as if their roles had been reversed. Lora was the one who was shaken and falling apart, while it was Suzy who was prioritizing, using her head, and keeping it all together. Lora was truly impressed. The two women hugged, and Lora asked Suzy if she could spend one more night so they could talk again in the morning.

"I'll have to call the Bakers and let them know. Tommy is spending nights with their son Jeff while we've been here. Anyway, I don't think it's a good idea for Clayton to be driving home tonight. He's had a bit too much to drink. It wouldn't look good if the president of a major university got a DUI, now would it?"

Suzy dabbed some water on Lora's dress so it would at least look like they had been trying to remove a stain. Getting caught up in a little fib was the last thing they wanted to do.

The women rejoined the party, apologizing for their absence. The remainder of the fundraiser went well. There were no more interruptions from the past.

Lora had taken a picture of the machine for which she was raising money and displayed it along with some documentation about its uses and function. Below the display, a table was set up housing a cardboard replica of a piggy bank. Envelopes had been laid out beside it, so people could write their checks, seal it in an envelope, and then drop it into the piggy. Lora noticed that the piggy bank was getting full. Everyone was having a good time. Despite her own problems, she believed the fundraiser was a complete success. As the evening started to wind down, Lora announced when and where the next fundraising auction would be held.

At about 8:45, some of the guests started to leave. The invitations stated 6:00PM to 9:00PM, so shortly thereafter, others followed suit. Lora thanked each guest for coming and for their contribution, and by 9:20, the Whitmores were the only couple remaining. Charlie Cotter stayed around to help clean up. Before he left, Lora took fifty dollars from her purse and gave it to him.

"Hey, Dr. Jordan," Charlie said, "I didn't expect to be paid tonight. I did this because you asked me. I wanted to help out."

Lora stuffed the money into his shirt pocket. "You did a wonderful job, and I want you to have this. You gave me your time this evening. I appreciate it. I'm sure a good looking fellow like you probably had to cancel a date or something tonight."

"No date tonight. My girl's going to medical school, so she studies most nights. I'm so proud of her, you know. I guess it's not so bad to give up a date every now and then so she can make good grades."

She could only hope Charlie's girl would not make the mistakes she had made. Lora thanked Charlie again and saw him to the door. She surveyed the grounds outside her house one more time before she locked the door for the night.

There was no sign of Kash.

With the Jordan's home somewhat back to its original condition, Clayton was the first to excuse himself to go to bed.

"I guess I drank a bit more than I thought. My head feels a little woozy." Turning to Suzy he said, "Are you coming up, too. I was hoping you could put me to sleep tonight the same way you woke me up this morning!"

"Clayton!" Suzy screamed.

"Well, we're all adults here—we're among friends." Clayton was slurring his words together.

The three friends giggled at Suzy's embarrassment. Suzy hugged Lora, thanking her for putting up with them for another night. Alex was also sleepy from gorging himself on all the pastries. He went up shortly after the Whitmores had retired.

Alone on the living room couch, Lora was left to think. She found it hard to believe all the events that had transpired over the past two days. What started out to be a reunion between a few of old friends turned out to be a nightmare staring Sam Kashette as the boogieman from hell. He had to be bluffing. Kash was no threat to either of them. She would try to contact that backstabbing Rob Parker and ask him about the situation. If she could locate him, that is. Lora finally finished the drink she had been nursing for the last hour. She turned out the lights wanting only to join her husband in bed.

On her way upstairs, she could not help wondering if Suzy would be able to hold up her end of the arrangement. She feared Suzy would become frightened and yield to Kash's demands. If this happened, it would be over. No, she would have to straighten this thing out for both of them. Just like old times, she would take care of herself as well as Suzy. She would deal with Kash in her own way. Rage stewed and churned in the pit of her empty stomach. The frenzy returned. She knew about death; she was doctor. There were all kinds of ways for people to die. She was bound to protect human life—only human life. That being said, she was convinced that Sam Kashette was not entirely human; he was some kind of monster. Where was it written she was bound to protect a monster's life? It was at this point that she knew she could kill to protect her marriage.

Lora opened the bedroom door to find Alex already sound asleep.

9

The next morning, after a good breakfast, both Suzy and Lora appeared to be much better. Maybe purging their souls this weekend of the terrible secrets that had been locked inside there for so long, had done the pair some good. A night of restful sleep was beneficial as well. The two women were in good spirits. While they were left alone to clean up the kitchen, they used the opportunity to talk freely. Both Lora and Suzy decided to take an indifferent approach concerning Kash's blackmail threats. They would contact each other on the fifteenth of each month to make sure nothing was happening on either end. They vowed again that they would not pay Kash one red cent for his intimidations.

Shortly after breakfast, Suzy excused herself in order to pack her and Clayton's clothes and toiletries for the trip home. Now in the cozy room where she and Clayton had spent the last two nights, Suzy conjured thanks for Lora's return to her life. She was happy to have been reunited with her old friend; however, she wished it had been under different circumstances. She was glad, just the same, to get back to Dalton and to her beloved son Tommy.

The Jordan's guest bedroom door was open. Lora tapped gently on the doorframe before walking in.

"Oh Suz, I'm going miss you so much. It seems as though we've just gotten to know each other again."

"Yeah, I feel the same way, too."

"Now listen, we're not going to worry about this Kash thing, right?"

"Right," Suzy said. "I did some thinking last night, and I believe you're absolutely right. He's not going to try to take us both on. He's got to be bluffing, just like you said."

Lora picked up the Whitmore's overnight bag and started for the door. Suzy called to her, "Lora."

Lora turned to face her old friend.

"Friday night when we talked about the abortion," Suzy began, "you said I should have considered putting the baby up for adoption. You said there were couples who would have jumped at the chance to adopt a newborn. Are you and Alex one of those couples?"

Lora put down the Whitmore's bags and leaned against the doorframe. This was a touchy subject, but Lora opened up in the end.

"Yes we are," she said nodding her head gently. "We've tried for eight years. I can't seem to conceive."

"Oh Lora, I'm so sorry. I didn't know. My actions must have felt like a slap in the face. It must have been devastating for you to hear what I had done."

"It's okay, Suzy. It all happened a long time ago."

Lora helped Suzy downstairs with her things. The four friends said their goodbyes. As she watched the Whitmore's car depart Kelsey Circle, Lora felt a sudden sensation of emptiness. It was hard to believe so much time had passed since she and Suzy had been roommates. Her sensation of emptiness went deeper than just missing Suzy though. Kash had taken a part of Lora's decency when he re-entered her life. She had forgotten what life was like back then: an era when she had spent so much of her time alone at Pathetic Jokes for lack of friends who had yet to welcome her. Kash launched in her an air of hostility, and mistrust, and loneliness, and seclusion that had been sleeping for many years. She would wait until the middle of the month and if need be, she would take matters into her own hands. As hard as she tried, she could not get the spiteful image out of her mind—the image of Sam Kashette standing around the side of the house laughing at her.

CHAPTER SEVEN

In Search of Inner-Peace

1

The Whitmores were back in Dalton before lunchtime. Clayton took their overnight bag upstairs. He had a terrible hangover from the party last night. As he ascended the steps, little squeaks made by the riser's boards sounded like giant claws running over a chalkboard to Clayton's tender ears. He had to take something for his head.

Tommy was already home from the Bakers. Suzy found him in the kitchen preparing a sandwich. As she watched her son, she was finally able to grasp onto reality again. She was back in the familiar surroundings of her home with her family. It was as if Sam Kashette and his threats never existed.

"Hi mom," Tommy said. "How was Boston? Did your friend raise all the money she needed for her machine?"

"Yes, she did. It was a lovely party." Suzy gave Tommy a peck on the cheek. "Were you and Jeff well behaved for Mrs. Baker?"

"Of course. You know Jeff and I would never dream of misbehaving."

"Of course not!" Suzy said sarcastically.

Clayton entered the kitchen. He hoped the three aspirin in his hand would soothe his thumping head. He reached into the fridge and poured himself a glass of water from the pitcher. As he downed the pills, he moaned.

Suzy laughed and explained to Tommy, "Your dad has a bit of a hangover today. He put quite a dent in the Jordan's vodka supply last night."

Tommy laughed and gave his dad a few pats on the arm. The taps felt like blows from a professional boxer. His entire body hurt.

"So, you're not feeling up to par, ah dad? I don't understand what you adults get out of drinking. You always suffer for it the next day."

"Don't worry about me. The last thing I need is a lecture from a 16-

year-old, okay?" Becoming irritated by his son's know-it-all attitude but more so because of his nasty headache, Clayton added, "You're not perfect, Tom. I'm sure, even at your age, you've got a few vices of your own."

Tommy started to eat his sandwich. The snap and fizz from the pop can he had just opened was the only sound in the kitchen. Tommy hated it when he didn't get the last word, but he remained quiet, nonetheless.

Clayton told Suzy he was going upstairs to lie down. He asked her to wake him in a couple hours.

Suzy had wanted to talk to Tommy about a few things but was not quite sure how to bring up the subject. Her husband's comment gave her an opening, so she ran with it. Tommy, your father mentioned vices. I want to ask you something, and I want you to be honest when you answer. I've heard that you've been smoking. Is this true?"

Tommy looked at his mother. The question took him by surprise. Not that is wasn't true because it was. The question bothered him because he was puzzled how she knew. He always used mints or gum for his breath and always washed his hands afterwards to get rid of the nicotine scent, and he only smoked outside, so no odor would linger on his cloths. He could think of only one thing to say, "Who told you that?"

"It doesn't matter who. Do you? And please don't lie to me. You've never lied before. Don't start now."

Tommy's face became flushed. "Yeah, I smoke every once in a while. How did you find out? Did Mrs. Baker tell you that Jeff and I were smoking cigarettes?"

"No, she didn't." Suzy rubbed her temples with her fingers. She was disappointed in her son. First Kash, now this. "How many cigarettes do you consider every once in a while?"

"Just four or five, maybe six."

"A day!" Suzy shrieked. "Tommy, you know smoking is very addictive, not to mention bad for your health. I want you to stop immediately. Do you have a problem with that?"

"No ma'am." Tommy hung his head. He was getting it from both ends. First, his dad complained about Tommy voicing his opinion, and now his mother caught him up in a fib. He wished they had stayed in Boston a few more days. He liked having the house to himself with no one to boss him around. "Are you going to tell dad?"

"No I'm not. However, if you chose not to quit, I will be forced to tell him then. Do you understand?"

"Yes." Tommy took the last bite of his lunch and washed it down with the pop. He put his dish in the sink and threw the pop can in the garbage.

"Good." Suzy was glad to get that resolved. "Now honey, I'd like to talk to you about something else."

"What else did I do?"

"Nothing. You didn't do anything wrong. I want to ask you about a man you saw a few weeks ago. It would have been when you and Jeff were at the 7-Eleven. The man would have been tall, blond, well built, and he was probably wearing a big cowboy hat. He asked you about your car. Do you remember seeing him?"

"Yeah, I think so. Was it around Mother's Day?"

"Yes, that would be around the time."

"Do you know him?"

"No … not personally." Suzy lied. "Did he say anything else to you that day?"

"No. He just said I had a nice car. I think he called it 'a fine ride.' I told him it was a present from you and dad."

"Okay, that's fine. Did you and Jeff spend any time here, at the house while your dad and I were away this weekend?"

"Yeah, a little. We played some video games. What's with all the questions? Don't you guys trust me?

"Of course we do, Tommy. This has nothing to do with trust. I need to know if you saw that man around the house."

"No. What is he, some kind of pervert or something?"

"No honey, nothing like that." Suzy said. "Have you ever seen him again after the day at 7-Eleven?"

"No. Mom, what's going on?"

"Tommy, I can't get into it with you, but I want you to make me a promise. Stay away from this man. If you ever see him again, or if he ever comes around you, do not talk to him. I want you to tell me about it right away, okay?"

"Okay. But mom, if you don't know this guy, how do you know I should stay away from him?"

"I said I don't know him personally. The things I do know about him are not good. He's a very wicked man, and I don't want him anywhere near you."

"All right, I'll tell you if I see him again."

"And Tommy? I would appreciate it if we could keep this between the two of us. I don't want your father to know about this. I'll keep the cigarette issue to myself if you'll keep our conversion to yourself. Deal?"

"Sure, but I still don't see what the big deal is."

"There is no big deal, honey. It's just that I can take care of this myself, that's all. Your dad has enough worries down on campus. Fair enough?"

"Fair enough." Tommy replied as he looked at the clock. "If there's nothing else, I'd like to be excused. I'm supposed to meet Jeff at the park. We're going to shoot some hoops."

"There's nothing else." Suzy hugged Tommy. "Don't forget, no smoking, and tell Jeff, the same goes for him."

"Mom, you wouldn't tell Mrs. Baker that Jeff smoked, would you? He'd think I ratted him out."

"No Tommy, I won't tell her. I would never put you in a compromising position."

"Good. And thanks mom. I'll see you at dinner."

Tommy went out; the screen door banged behind him. Suzy was alone. Over the hum of the refrigerator motor and the ticking of the kitchen clock, she heard her own voice echoing repeatedly, *I would never put you in a compromising position!* My God, she had just bribed her son. You keep my secret, and I'll keep your secret. Was it possible she was putting her son in a comprising position without ever realizing it?

2

Tommy reached the park five minutes before he was supposed to meet Jeff. Near the basketball court was a tree under which Tommy sat thinking about his mother's peculiar behavior and the stranger who caused this behavior. The slight breeze blew his hair, tickling his neck. He wondered why his mother was so concerned about a man whom she admitted not to know. Why was she so secretive about him, and why did she want to keep all of it from his father? Tommy was in such deep thought, trying to piece it all together, he neither saw Jeff's approach, nor heard the orange basketball bouncing against the pavement.

"Hey Tommy, what are you thinking about?"

"My mom and dad. They can be a real drag sometimes."

"No shit. What happened now?"

"Oh, my mother found out I was smoking cigarettes and she got on my case about it."

"No way! Does my mom know too?"

"No and she said she promised not to tell her."

Jeff was relieved. "Did you get grounded or beat or anything like that?"

"Nah, she just lectured me."

"How'd she find out?"

"I don't know, but she's acting really weird. She's asking all kinds of questions."

"What kind of questions?" Jeff was curious now.

Tommy told his buddy about everything him and his mother had discussed. Tommy didn't figure he was breaking any confidence because his mother had made it clear that the person she wanted to keep this from was his father. He was sure he was doing nothing wrong by telling Jeff. When he finished explaining, he asked his friend, "What do you think?"

"Well Tom, I think this mystery man with the cowboy hat is the one who ratted us out. If you remember, we were sitting on the hood of your car that day smoking a cigarette when he talked to you. He saw us smoking. Now that I think about it, it seemed like maybe he was trying to make conversation. I'll bet he knew who you were all along."

"Well maybe, but why?"

"Got me," Jeff started, "but a few things don't make sense here. First off, if your mom says she doesn't know this man personally, she's lying. She must know him pretty well if he knew that you were her son, and she must have talked to him in order for him to tell her you were smoking. Right? So she *does* know him."

"But why would she lie?"

"Can't help you with that one, but you said she doesn't want your father to know, right?"

"Yeah."

"Well, maybe she's having an affair with this guy. She doesn't want him to get too close to you because she's afraid if he talks to you, you'll figure it out. That's why she doesn't want him around you. That's also why she doesn't want your dad to know." Jeff was proud of his assessment.

"That's crazy Jeff." Tommy laughed. "My mom would never run around on my dad. You've seen them together; they're nuts about each other. Always huggin' and kissin' like a couple of teenagers in love and not afraid to show it. Besides, my dad treats my mom like a queen. He gives her everything."

"Yes, but maybe what she wants, your dad can't give her anymore." Jeff dribbled the basketball and started laughing. "Maybe he's too old to get his pecker up these days!"

"Oh, shut up. You're gross!" Tommy said, disgusted by the thought of his mom and dad having sex.

"Well, you asked me what I thought and I told you. Are you ready to shoot some hoops now, or are we going to discuss your parents love life some more?"

"No, I'm ready for basketball."

"Good."

The boys stayed at the court and played ball for over an hour, but Tommy's mind was elsewhere. He was not satisfied with Jeff's explanation for his mom's behavior. He was disturbed by her strange actions, and he promised himself he would get to the bottom of the matter as soon as possible.

3

Back in West Virginia Kash stirred restlessly in his double bed. The warm air was still, just barely moving the curtains on the window near the bed. Kash hated these kinds of nights—the restless nights when he tossed and turned, fighting sleep, when actually he was fully exhausted. When his head hit the pillow, he was supposed to fall asleep. It takes the average person twelve minutes to fall asleep. Kash expected to fall asleep in the average time. It was part of The Order; it was the way it was supposed to work. Now his covers were a mess, and the sheets were wrinkled, and he was not able to get comfortable. His neck and shoulders ached; they were knotted with stress. If he could see his face, he would see how worry had caused tiny creases and folds around his eyes and on his forehead. He had much on his mind tonight. The problems of the world were in the bed with him.

He rolled from one side of the bed to the other without disturbing anyone in the process. Tonight Kash wished he were not alone. He wasn't afraid of the dark, nor was he afraid to be alone; he was simply lonely. Deep inside, he longed for a companion—someone whom he could love and someone who could love him in return. It was on nights like these that Kash wished he had gotten married. While he believed that women were put on this earth to serve man's needs, he did not disbelieve in marriage. Sex was not the only need by which women could serve man, but it was a biggie. A woman could also cook for him, clean his house, do his shopping, and wash his clothes. She could keep him company when he desired company, and she could be there to answer him when he spoke. She could act as a personal assistant of sorts, and a maid, in addition to her primary duty of satisfying his sexual needs. His would have to be a courthouse wedding, of course—no church wedding for Kash.

He ran his hand over the vacant side of the bed and hugged his pillow. His life may have turned out differently, if only he had found the right woman. He craved a good woman, one who understood what was part of The Order and what was not, one who could help him make the Bad Thoughts go away and make it stay away forever. He was becoming restless with whores and one-night stands. His aim was to have a woman long term, one who could take care of him as he grew old, and one who truly loved him in every way. He had a girl like that in his life, once, but at the time, he had no interest in her offer. Back then, she had been crazy for him, or so the buzz around campus alleged, but that had been many years ago. Even so, he wondered about her tonight. He wondered if *she* had ever gotten married, and he wondered how she had turned out. Her name was Rosalee. He struggled for a last name—she was Italian, he remembered. DeLucci came to mind. Yes, that was her name, Rosalee DeLucci. She would have been a perfect addition to The Order. It seemed like forever since he had thought about her. Then he concluded that she was probably married and had a dozen kids by now. He remembered that she liked children, too. She would have been a good wife and a good mother.

The Inferior Suzy had killed his child. She took away Kash's opportunity at fatherhood. If she hadn't, Kash would have had somebody to love and somebody would have loved him back. His child would have been about 18 years old now, give or take a few months. If the child had been a boy, it would have pleased Kash very much to be able raise a son to be part of The Order, to bring him up with Kash's own beliefs and attitudes. His boy would have taken care of him and devoted his life to him. It would have been part of his son's order, his duty. He would have been a part of Kash; therefore, he would not have existed without Kash. Kash's life would then have meaning. Kash loved himself very much but sometimes, like tonight, he wished he could share just a little of that love with another.

He turned on the radio with the hope that some music would relax him. An all-night country station played classic country from the 60's, 70's, and 80's. Country music was real music. It was man's music. The lyrics in country songs dealt with things like drinking, fighting, hangovers, and truck driving. Some songs were written in the form of stories while others dealt with single topics like fast cars, and dogs, and truckers rolling down the highway—man things. Kash noticed, every now and then, a deejay having a bad day would slip in an old sappy love song about a woman breaking a man's heart. Kash could live with that because overall, the man in those love songs always landed on his feet. No woman could knock down a real man— not for long anyway. There were no county music songs that told stories about women leisurely strolling the malls spending all her husbands' money. The women in country songs were home where she belonged, taking care of her man, fighting for her man, standing by her man.

Even though it was almost midnight, sleep still evaded Kash. He thought about the sequence of events which occurred since he had been released from the hellhole. He was pleased with his accomplishments. So far, the whole program was going as planned.

Kash had been moving around freely with the driver's licenses in Sam Kirkland's name. He had purchased his plane tickets, and made his motel reservations as well, in the name of his alias. For this reason, he felt in no way threatened by his parole officer. With the exception of a bi-monthly visit to the courthouse, he never saw the man anyway, but still, there was always a first time. The slightest parole violation would be enough to lock him up again, this time for ten years. Under no circumstances could he ever cope with that again. The thought of prison made his whole body tense up much like his neck and shoulders had been earlier. He could feel the cold dampness of his prison cot. It made him shiver although the night was muggy. Kash pulled the sheet clear up to his neck now. No, he would have to protect his freedom at all cost. There was no way he was going back to the hellhole.

Kash had flown back to West Virginia the day after Lora's fundraiser. He knew he was taking a risk each time he traveled, because he was breaking his parole agreement every time he left West Virginia. This was the second trip he'd made to Massachusetts. Both times, he had come home no better off than when he left; however, the trips would be profitable in the long run. He hoped the Inferiors would be obedient, even enthusiastic, when it came time to pay their debt to him. Suzy and Lora were users. Users deserved whatever they got. If they chose to defy him, he was prepared to show evidence that he was sure would make the Inferiors or their spouses pay up in the end. It really didn't matter whether Mr. or Mrs. signed the bottom right corner, just so long as it was signed. There was only one week until the fifteenth.

His plan for the fifteenth of each month was relatively simple. He would drive into Kentucky, pick up his checks, open a bank account in the bogus name, deposit the money, drive back into West Virginia, and spend it. Round trip would take less than four hours. Two thousand bucks an hour sounded like a fair wage to Sam Kashette. He would have to avoid the local police in any event, (there were only four of them), because they knew his record. They knew about the DUI, and about the rescinded driving privileges. Driving with a suspended license was also a parole violation. He would have to be cautious, but he believed he could pull it off.

He had spent these past two weeks at home relaxing, with the exception of a few visits to the local whorehouse. But he soon grew bored of trading flesh with empty Inferiors. He needed a change of scenery, so he decided to take a ride up to the northern part of West Virginia in search of some new marbles.

Kash loved his marbles and he loved hoarding them. In many ways, marbles were like women. Marbles were nice to look at; they came in all different colors and had many different designs. Yet, all marbles were the same; they were marble—small colorful glass orbs. By that same token, women were easy on the eye; they were all built differently and had varying personalities. Yet, all women were the same; they were women—inferior nobodies. Marbles actually served no real purpose except to provide pleasure to the person who was shooting them. Also, they remained idle without man's assistance. Women were much like marbles, in that women provided pleasure to man but were not good for much else, and they certainly would be helpless without man's support. Kash liked the way a marble felt in his hands, too. They were made of glass, so they were breakable, but at the same time, they were tough enough to bang into other marbles without cracking. A woman felt good in Kash's hand as well. They were fragile and delicate, yet they were resilient when knocked around a little.

The furnace marbles, made in Paden City, West Virginia, were Kash's favorite because every marble made there had a small imperfection, a tiny internal fracture. Kash knew all about little imperfections and tiny internal fractures. He was fractured inside too, just like the furnace marbles. Also like him, the furnace marbles were rare; only six thousand or so were made.

During his ride up to the northern panhandle, he bought one gray marble with black symmetrical swirls and one gold marble with a bright yellow design. His prize gem, however, was found when he impetuously stopped off at a flea market on his way home. It was a handsome handmade glass shooter, 2½" in diameter. Technically, it was impossible to produce a handmade glass marble greater than 2½," so Kash figured this marble would bring a high resale value. (Not that he ever intended to sell it.) It was nearly perfect except for a slight chip and a couple of subsurface moons from knocking into other marbles. Still the condition was close to mint. Kash was very proud of his marbles—all five thousand of them.

Kash and Gabby had spent some time together this week, as well. He really enjoyed the old woman's company. When Kash was a youngster, he had spent much of his time at Gabby's house. His parents, Katy and Howard Kashette, conceived and birthed Kash at a very young age. The two teens had been mere children themselves, so how could they be expected to bring up a child? They knew little about child rearing and worse yet, they didn't care. Gabby tried to run interference where she could, but the recently wed Kashettes allowed only a small amount of intrusion where advice was concerned. When Kash was a baby he had been provided the essentials in that he had been fed, bathed, and his clothes had been kept clean, but that was the extent of it. The shine had quickly worn off the chandelier. Katy and Howard had more important things to do than to be tied down with a child. They had parties to throw and parties to attend. They had beer to drink and drugs to take. They had concerts to see and bars to visit. There had been little or no time to spend with their baby Kash. When Kash was too young to take care of himself, they took the child most places with them (to the bars and to parties), but they saw him as nothing more than a nuisance.

As he grew to boyhood, maybe the age of seven or eight, Katy and Howard believed Kash was old enough to stay alone. When that time came, his parents did exactly that, they left him alone. They would put him in his room at bedtime and wait until he fell asleep and when he did, they would leave him to go to the parties or the bars. Gabby tried to provide Kash with companionship on these occasions, but it was no replacement for his parents' love. Gabby had scolded Katy and Howard for their rash treatment of young Kash, so they started to stay home more. Only the problem became further aggravated because now the parties and the bar patrons came to Katy and Howard's house instead. By the time Kash was ten or so, he had been drinking almost every night, pilfering beer, or wine, or sometimes whisky from the guests of the Kashette house. He was smoking cigarettes before he turned 11 and once even, he stole a pinch of somebody's pot, mixed it in with the cigarette tobacco and smoked it too. He liked the buzz from the pot and booze. It made his childhood more manageable.

As an unsupervised teenager, Kash had become a major hell-raiser. By this time, his parents believed he should be able to take care of himself, so they never asked him what he was doing or where he was going. They were too busy doing their own thing. Their wild lifestyle was still their top priority. They were getting tired of the child cramping their style. On rare occasions, Howard would take his family on a vacation or a trip. Kash was taken along but was never really included. His mother would load him up with money hoping he would find something to do elsewhere. He rarely let her down. Even though he was still being ignored, at least he had money in his pocket while it was happening. Money and unattended teens was a harmful mix. Kash could find trouble easy enough without being weighted down with a wad of cash. He'd had a couple of scrapes with the law too but nothing of a serious nature. Some nights he would stay out and drink all night, never once having been missed at home.

His life was heading down the path of alcoholism and drug abuse and perhaps even suicide. He never would have survived those years without Gabby. Her door had always been open for him. At least when the things at home got tough to handle, he had the option to go to Gabby's house.

Sarah Gabbert was a real piece of work. She could do everything from reciting Shakespeare, to clearing a billiards table in three shots or less, to creating a five-tier wedding cake. She was an excellent cook, a good handyman, a competent mechanic, and she could chug beer with the best of them. She had become a master of many things in her 75 years. Kash really admired her.

While he was in the hellhole, Gabby had written to him every week. Sometimes she would send a package containing toiletries, books, and treats. She always included a tin filled with Kash's favorite cookies. She had visited him in Kentucky on occasion, but her letters and packages were more frequent than her visits. If he ever lost track of the days, which he often did, he always knew when Wednesday had rolled around, because Gabby's letter would be there. He looked forward to the little piece of home she had brought in each correspondence. At a time when everyone in town had been calling him a drunk and a murderer, he was sure glad to have Gabby in his corner.

The thoughts of the sweet old lady eased his mind enough to let him drift off to sleep.

He dreamed about cashing the first of his checks in one week.

4

"Bye Sister. See you next year," one child waved.

"Have a good summer, Sister Rosa," another yelled.

"I'll miss you Sister." The third youngster hugged his teacher. His family would be leaving West Virginia this summer; consequently, he would not be returning next year.

"I'll miss you, too, Scotty," Sister Rosa said as she held the boy tightly. At nine years old, Scotty was very mature for his age. I guess you could say he was one of the few *pets* she had. She tried always to be equal when it came to the kids, but every now and again, a special, extremely bright student such as Scotty came along. Sister Rosa could not help giving these students extra attention. She believed that not only the message of Jesus Christ, but love as well, must permeate in the school curriculum in order to help each student grow to his full potential as a child of God. She strived to provide an education that enabled her children to advance as Christians along with their academic growth. She took her teaching very seriously.

Each year, when the children left for the summer, she felt a certain loss. She had been teaching the children of St. Christopher's for almost five years. She understood now why the Bishop preferred that the nuns—and the priests too, for that matter—not stay in one parish for a long tour. It was so easy to become attached to the people. The parishioners of St. Christopher's were easy to become fond of because they were very kind and good people. She would miss it if she were asked to go to another school.

With all the children gone from the schoolhouse, Sister Rosa packed her belongings into a cardboard box. She looked up from her packing when the smell of homemade cinnamon sticky buns reached her nostrils. Gazella, the school's middle-aged head cook, stood at the door with a tray and two cups of coffee.

Gazella was a little round woman with thick salt and pepper hair bundled loosely into a hairnet. She had the considerate heart a good Christian woman and the trash mouth of a sailor. You never had to wonder what was on Gazella's mind because she told you straightaway, never holding anything back.

"I thought you might enjoy one more sticky-bun before we leave for the summer. I know how much you like them."

"You are so right, Gazella. I love them. But if you don't quit feeding them to me, I'm going to look like a blimp."

"Nah Sister Ro, you're not big. Anyway, I always believed nuns were supposed to be a little on the chubby side. Now take me for example, my husband is always bitching at me because of my weight. Did you know he put diet pills in my Christmas stocking last year?"

Sister Rosa giggled like a schoolgirl who was privy to a private joke.

Gazella continued, "Just those cheap over-the-counter pills, mind you. The least he could have done was get me the good stuff from the doctor. You know … the ones that leave you with a nice speed buzz. Maybe it would have made it easier to move this 200-pound body a tad faster. You, on the other hand, don't have anybody to bitch at you. You married Jesus, which is who I should've married too. Jesus is a very silent husband, so you've got nothing to worry about."

"Good point," Rosa replied, but at the same time, she was thinking about Kash. What if things had worked out with him? She certainly didn't feel very attractive these days. Maybe it would have been better if someone had been bitching at her all along. She would have taken more pride in her appearance.

By the time they had finished their rolls and coffee, Rosa had put all her belongings into a small cardboard box. She thanked the cook, before Gazella went back to the chore of cleaning up the kitchen. Rosa left her school room behind for another year and went back to her room at the convent.

Rosa's sabbatical was drawing near. After a few days of spring-cleaning at the convent, she and three other nuns would make a trip to the Mother House. A total of six sisters shared the convent at St. Chris.' She was fortunate because at least two sisters had to remain in the convent for the summer vacation, and she was the last one to ask for a sabbatical. She would probably spend two weeks at the Mother House before asking for a forty-day leave. She would explain to Mother Superior that she wanted to see her family, but the trip would also include a visit to see her old friend, Kash. A visit she would not explain to Mother Superior. All in all, she was sure Mother Superior would have no objections.

In her room at the convent, Rosa unpacked the contents of the cardboard box. The books, she placed on the shelf, the box of tissues, she laid on top the nightstand, the paper, pens, and such, she placed in the drawer of her writing table, the tube of hand cream and spare brush and comb, she put in her valise to take with her on her vacation. While the valise was out, she decided to go ahead and pack a few pieces of clothing. Opening her underwear drawer, she ran across the cedar box. She picked it up with both hands, as if it were a delicate bomb. Many times before, she had removed the key from her purse, tempted to open it and relive the memories locked within, but every time she did, her heart jumped telling her that those memories should stay where they belonged: locked in the past. She carefully set the box in her valise. She would take it home with her as well.

Sister Rosa had never had a problem with her vow of chastity over the past 15 years. However, with the recent, not to mention overpowering, thoughts of her old love, some long forgotten feelings have found their way back into her heart. Some nights, lying in bed, she would long for the touch of a man, not *a* man, but the *one* man with whom she had never had the opportunity to love in that special way. She was torn between the life she created at the convent and the life she yearned for with the man she loved. She was taught to pray for courage when these feeling occurred, but sometimes they were paralyzing. She moved quickly to the statue in the corner and fell to her knees.

In a voice just above a whisper, she begged, "Oh sweet Mother Mary, I need you now as I've never needed you before. I'm haunted by anxiety over Kash. I know you're watching over him like you promised, but now I feel that it's me you should be looking out for. The absence of Kash in my life is becoming more intolerable by the day. Celibacy is possible, even gratifying, when you are satisfied with the tasks you're performing for the Lord, but I'm not as happy with the Lord's work as I was when I first entered into this life. I'm 38 years old; I'm not getting any younger, and I'm not sure I want to spend my golden years cooped up in a convent for over-the-hill nuns. I'll never have a family of my own, I'll never experience the day-to-day routine of married life, and I want to see what I'm missing.

"I don't mean to sound ungrateful. God knows you've done plenty for me, but I feel like my teaching career has peaked and that I have nothing left to offer. I know what you're thinking: what about Tina and little Scotty? Yes, they both presented two very different challenges. Scotty needed me because he was so very bright and in need of acceleration academically, and Tina needed me as a spiritual pilot, but those cases won't be here every day. I need something more daring. I need Sam Kashette.

"God made us the way we are, so why do I feel so damn guilty wanting a more traditional life. Please Holy Queen, I need help! I need to get my priorities back in order. Don't let me down on this one. Please!"

Sister Rosa had good faith, but was faith enough to whisk the thoughts from her mind and the sensations from her body?

5

"Good morning, Dr. Jordan," Annie greeted her boss.

"Good morning," Lora replied with no emotion.

Annie noticed how Dr. Jordan's nature had been different these past few days. Lora had always been chipper and pleasant, and now she seemed cold and mistrusting. She rarely talked, except about hospital business, and she was acting rather secretive about matters in her personal life. Annie saw the change in Lora after the fundraiser, and she wondered what had happened that night to distract her this way.

She handed Dr. Jordan some messages and reminded her about her appointment with Dr. Hoskins this morning, then she handed Lora a folder.

"This came over the fax last night after you'd gone."

Lora opened the folder and saw the records from Charleston Memorial. "I've been waiting several days for these papers. Why didn't you tell me about this earlier?"

"I told you the fax just came in last night. It's only a personnel file on an employee. I didn't see the urgency to bother you at home." Annie defended her actions.

Lora was angry, not so much with Annie, but just the same, she was angry. "You should have called me about this. I needed to see these papers as soon as ... I'm sorry, Annie. You had no way of knowing these records were important. Please accept my apology for being so abrupt. I've got a lot on my mind."

"Apology accepted. You know, Lora, you've not exactly been yourself lately. I hate seeing you upset all the time. If you ever want to talk, I've been told I'm a good listener."

"Thank you," she said and squeezed the hand of her co-worker, "maybe some other time. I've got to figure this one out on my own."

Lora made her way into her office. The light pecking of Annie's keyboard could be heard through the closed door. She sat at her desk and took a good, long look at Rob Parker's personnel records from Charleston Memorial. She had to pull some strings to get the records, and the staff at Charleston Memorial took several days to get them to her. There was precious little time left. The fifteenth was only a week away. If only she could talk with Rob, she would know what to do next. Maybe she could pay him to keep his mouth shut. On the other hand, maybe she could persuade him to make himself scarce or something. She had to find out if he did indeed have those tickets. First, she had to locate Rob Parker, and she had to work fast.

She started with the termination slip, glancing at the column labeled potential employer. As she read the name of the pharmaceutical company, she picked up the phone and dialed directory assistance for Lakeland, Florida. There was no listing under that name in Lakeland; in fact, there were no pharmaceutical companies listed in Lakeland. She called the in-house pharmacy and found that Boston General had dealt with Jasper Pharmaceutical in Lakeland, but the company had been out of business for quite a few years. Next, she looked over the application for a phone number. The space was empty. Lora remembered that when she worked at Charleston Memorial, Rob had lived at home with his parents. She thought it probable that the address listed in the file would be that of his parents. She had no idea of his parent's first name, and she was sure there would be dozens of Parkers listed in Charleston, West Virginia, so she ruled out calling directory assistance.

Lora was becoming more frustrated by the minute. Although she felt strongly that Kash's threats were empty, Lora was not willing to risk an encounter between Kash and Alex. The little part of her mind that told her not to trust anybody except herself was not totally convinced. She was still fighting her conscience about the truth. If Alex were to find out, he would lose all faith and respect for her, and she was sure she would never be able to earn it back. He had always told her how much he admired her honesty and frankness about things. This 20-year-old lie would make him suspicious, would make him question whether she had kept other things from him as well. She had to talk to Rob Parker. She had to do something to wake up from this nightmare. She had to make Kash go away.

"The library," Lora said as she jumped up from her desk. She would go to the library and look through the city directory for Charleston, West Virginia. The directory would be listed by street address, and she would have access to the telephone listing for that residence.

She came out of the office to find Annie still busy at the computer. Lora told her she was going to run an errand, but Annie reminded her again that she was to meet with Dr. Hoskins in thirty minutes. He wanted to look over the figures from the funds she had raised for the PET scan. It would be impossible to make a trip to the library in that length of time, so she returned to her office. As soon as she sat down, her eyes were drawn to the picture of Alex sitting on her desk. She was more determined than ever to put this *Kash business* behind her. There had to be a way to track down Rob quickly. Then another idea came to her: call the library and hope she could convince the clerk to look up the address for her.

The pleasant librarian, whom Lora pictured to be a plump, jolly, middle-aged woman, answered in a cheery voice. After identifying herself as a doctor, Lora made an excuse about having to locate the family of a patient in West Virginia. She said it was an emergency, and that time was of the essence. The librarian was checking the directory.

"Did you say Maple Grove?"

"Yes, that's correct, 109 Maple Grove," Lora answered in anticipation.

The librarian gave Dr. Jordan the telephone number listed, and Lora thanked her for her cooperation.

She hung up and quickly dialed the eleven-digit phone number in Charleston. After three rings, a man answered the phone. "Hello?"

"Hello, is this the Parker residence?"

"No, it's not."

Lora verified the number. After finding she made no mistake in dialing, she explained to the man that she was trying to locate the family who lived in his house before him.

"Well ma'am, I'm afraid I can't be much help. We bought this house from the Parkers in 1984, but I don't know where they moved to. Only thing I can tell you is Mr. Parker was in the military, and he was being transferred. I'm getting on in years, so my memory isn't so good. If he did tell us where he was being transferred to, I don't remember."

"Oh no," Lora said with disappointment. "How about your wife? Do you think she would remember?"

"My wife passed away seven months ago."

"I'm sorry, sir. Thank you for your time, and I apologize for disturbing you this morning."

"That's okay. Sorry I couldn't be more help. Good luck finding the Parkers."

"Thank you, good-bye."

Lora stretched out in her chair and ran her fingers through her long hair. Another dead end. She was even more perplexed now. If only she knew someone in the IRS or the Social Security office or the DMV. She had all the necessary numbers from his application at Charleston Memorial to track him down but no one to help her.

Looking at the clock on her desk, she grabbed the reports for her meeting with Dr. Hoskins. She put Rob Parker's records in her briefcase and headed for the conference room, one floor up. In the elevator, she almost cried thinking about her situation. How was she going to handle day-to-day life and still act as if nothing were wrong? She decided she would have to put it out of her mind, pending the outcome of events on the fifteenth. If nothing happened then, she would know Sam Kashette was just bluffing. But what if ...

The elevator stopped at the next floor.

CHAPTER EIGHT

Off the Deep End

1

Kash arrived at the small Kentucky post office just before noon. The Kentucky address was only used for the checks from the Inferiors, so he was surprised to see his box, box 627, jammed full of papers. Leafing through the mail, he found outdated sale papers, pamphlets from several politicians wanting his vote, contest packages, all addressed to the current box holder, but nothing from the Inferiors.

"Damn them!" he cursed in a low voice.

He discarded the junk mail and left the post office in a mood.

While driving back to the West Virginia state line, he contemplated what his next move should be. At first he thought about getting a flight out tonight to Massachusetts, but then decided he would have to give more thought about how best to handle the situation. His tentative plan was to methodically create a line up and pursue each individual in an orderly fashion. Order was part of life. He did not want to make any speedy decisions or go there half-cocked. He knew if he were to get anything from the Inferiors, he would have to convince them that he meant business. If force was necessary, that was okay too, because those uppity broads needed to be taught a lesson. For a couple of college-educated women, they were acting pretty damn dense. This only confirmed what Kash already knew: street-smart people were actually smarter than book-smart people.

Sam Kashette was not misleading anybody about his threat. He would hold true to his word. Nobody played him for a fool, and nobody messed with The Order.

With each passing mile he drove, his thoughts dug deeper—deeper into that part of his mind run by the little organ keeper—until finally he was fuming. The two-lane road on which he was driving was straight for the most part, (an oddity in itself, since most West Virginia state roads were winding) so Kash paid relatively no attention to his driving skills. His teeth were clenched tightly, and his eyes gave off a glassy shine. He pushed heavily on the gas pedal. The speedometer registered 70mph. His heart raced; he could hear it pounding in his ears. His fingers were slippery from perspiration. Slamming his fist against the steering wheel of the truck only made the rage inside of him grow. Hairs on his arms and neck stood at attention. The little organ keeper hammered out those awful cords in D minor, slowly at first, then faster and louder like music written to climax a scene in a Stephen King movie. He was tired of pissing around with them. If the Inferiors wanted to play hardball, he would gladly oblige.

The ugly Bad Thoughts poured into his mind two by two; his darkness surrounded them. He approached a four-way intersection, never slowed, and rambled straight through it. He didn't care if he died; it really didn't matter any more. His existence had no meaning anyway. Adrenalin replaced the blood in his veins. The heart that should beat around 90 beats per minute raced out of control. It now sounded like a jackhammer working on a stubborn plot of concrete. His eyes focused on the road. Even though he was speeding along at 70mph, his innersole was in slow motion. He was experiencing the rush—the high—of living on the edge, and he remembered it. There was a long period of time that had passed by since he had lived this way.

The broken lines painted in the center of the roadway appeared to be a continuous single stroke, like a flowing ribbon that followed the slight curves of the road. The truck kicked into overdrive when he accelerated to 80mph. Its engine screamed in protest of the speed. From Kash's peripheral vision, dead trees and foliage along both sides of the moving vehicle looked like nothing more than stick people dancing in some sort of crazy animation. The truck's tachometer registered five. It redlined at six. Rattles and squalling commotion cried from the truck's interior.

He began the Healing Rhymes, trying to bring about order.

> *One, two, buckle my shoe,*
> *Three, four, shut the door,*

Just ahead was a pothole big enough to swallow a Volkswagen Bug. Kash was concentrating so hard on the rhyme that by the time he saw the hole he had to jerk the steering wheel instead of gently guiding it, in an attempt to miss the hole. The effort only half worked. The right front tire caught about a quarter of the crater causing the truck to bounce to the left. The impact was too great for the shocks to absorb. Thumping sounds and ear splitting metal scraping against metal, shrilled from both the cab and the bed.

> *Five, six, pick up sticks,*
> *Seven, eight, lay 'em straight*

Kash stomped the brake petal with both feet just as the Ranger went off the road and into an empty field, or a field at least that appeared to be empty. Making matters worse, the Bad Thoughts were not going away, either. This reckless action, this unorganized activity, was out of character for Kash. Maybe the Kash of 20 years ago would have gotten off on this hasty behavior but not the Kash of today. At this moment, he allowed his actions to be ruled by the Bad Thoughts. He really had no say in the matter.

> *Nine, ten, a big fat hen.*

Actually, it was a big fat deer—a large buck judging from the spikes that were producing this year's rack. When the truck plowed through the field, it surprised the deer as much as the deer surprised Kash. Dirt flung around the back tires as he tried to slow the speeding truck enough to avoid hitting the animal. The left quarter panel collided with the buck and kicked out the truck's back end to the right. In a single split second, the truck had done a 180 and was heading back in the direction from which it had just come. The deer got back to his unsteady feet and scampered back into the safety of a thicket. Kash tromped the gas pedal and a second or two later he was back on the two-lane hardtop gaining momentum again as if the miscue and collision were nothing more than a minor detour.

The speedometer registered 85mph now. The truck was quickly catching up to a car traveling in the same lane as Kash. He laid on the horn and passed the car without ever checking the other lane for oncoming traffic. The Bad Thoughts were still alive, and the awful organ music was blasting in his ears, so he said the Healing Rhymes louder.

> *Eleven, twelve, dig and delve,*
> *Thirteen, fourteen, maids a-courting,*

And louder,

Fifteen, sixteen, maids a-kissing,
Seventeen, eighteen, maids a-waiting,

And even louder,

Nineteen, twenty, I've had plenty.

And Kash did have plenty. In fact, his plate was overflowing. By the time the Bad Thoughts were completely gone and his darkness had passed, he was screaming so loudly he could feel the heat from his lungs and smell the odor of his breath. He wondered if this was how it felt to go mad.

He didn't bother to reduce his speed until he crossed the West Virginia state line. There, he spotted a sporting good store, pulled into the parking lot, and went into the shop. The manager was very happy to help Kash select a .44 caliber pistol that was suitable for his needs.

2

Suzy Whitmore was as jumpy as the spooked deer from Kash's field, because she was mindful that today could bring demise to the family she so dearly loved. It was seven o'clock in the evening, and so far, all was well. In the back of her mind, she hoped Kash was just trying to make a quick buck and would do nothing when he discovered there was no money from her or from Lora.

She was in the kitchen taking a meatloaf out of the oven for dinner. She tried to act naturally. If you were unfamiliar with Suzy's ways, you would think everything was fine. But Tommy, who knew his mother inside out, was sure she still was not acting like herself. He looked for that zip in her walk, or that glow in her face when she smiled, or that sparkle in her eyes when she was doing something she enjoyed, but he found none of these traits. Instead, he saw a woman who was extremely distracted, one who was trying to put on a front, one who showed little emotion at all.

Clayton had a meeting this evening, so Tommy and his mother dined alone. After they were finished eating, Tommy volunteered to help his mother with the dishes. The phone rang, and Tommy, being a normal teenager, ran to answer it. Suzy headed him off just before he picked up the receiver.

"I'll get it Tommy."

Tommy had never seen his mother act like this. She was hiding something. There was no doubt about it. The phone was located in the kitchen near an archway that led out to the living room. Tommy walked through the archway and ducked around the corner. He hated eavesdropping on his mom, but it was the only way for him to find out what was going on with her.

"Hello?" Suzy said suspiciously, until she heard Lora's voice on the other end of the line. "Oh, thank God it's you!" Suzy responded. She casually glanced around the room to see if she was alone. "I thought maybe he was calling."

Tommy's ears perked up. He was sure both the phone conversation and his mother's strange behavior had something to do with the mystery man in the cowboy hat. He could only hear Suzy's end of the conversation, but Tommy assumed whomever his mother was talking to knew about the mystery man. He stayed out of sight and continued listening.

"No, everything's been quiet over here. I'm sure if he was going to make a move he would have done it today." There was a pause in Suzy's end of the conversation. "Yes, I know, but I don't think it will come down to that," Suzy said. "I had a talk with Tommy, and he promised me if he ever saw him again, he would come to me immediately." Another pause. "No, Tommy understands. I'm sure he won't tell Clayton what we talked about." Suzy shifted nervously from one foot to the other while Lora talked. "NO! I won't let that happen." Tommy heard his mother's tone change from scared to furious. "He doesn't want to play games with me when it comes to my family. I'll kill him; so help me God, I'll kill him. I refuse to let him ruin my life because he can't get over something that happened a long time ago."

Tommy quietly slipped upstairs once his mother's phone conversation had ended. He went to his room and sat on the bed. He considered Jeff's theory. Could his friend's estimation be accurate? Could his mother be having an affair with the mystery man in the cowboy hat? No, Tommy thought, not having an affair, but perhaps *had* an affair with him and now that it was over, he refused to let her go. Yes, he thought, that summed up nicely. Tommy was certain he had the answer. Because of the promise he'd made to his mother, he would not tell his father about the things he and his mother had discussed. Tommy reckoned the solution would fall solely on his shoulders. He must find the mystery man in the cowboy hat who had talked to him at 7-Eleven and put a stop to this craziness at once. He would have to assume responsibility and protect his mother's reputation.

3

Two days later an alarm clock sounded in the Jordan's bedroom at 7:15. After Alex turned it off, he closed his eyes and mentally reviewed his agenda for a few seconds before climbing out of bed. Today's date was the 17th, and he recalled an important meeting this morning that could mean a lot of new business for the bank and maybe a bonus for him. He needed some extra time this morning because he wanted to pay special attention to his appearance while dressing for work so he would look his absolute best. As he pulled himself out of the bed, he was startled to see Lora there, still sleeping. Taking for granted that she had slept in, he shook her gently to wake her.

"Alex, I'm not going to the hospital this morning," Lora said still half asleep. "I have a nasty migraine. It's so bad my stomach is queasy from it. Could you please call Annie and ask her to reroute my morning patients to Dr. Ludwig. He owes me one. Tell her I'll be in for my afternoon appointments, okay?"

"Sure babe." Alex placed the back of his palm on his wife's forehead checking her temperature. He didn't know why he'd done it because a fever was not something that customarily accompanied a migraine. Besides, he wasn't the doctor; nevertheless, his diagnosis was favorable—no fever. "You take anything for that headache?"

"Yes, when my alarm went off at six."

"That's good. Can I get you anything before I go? How about something to eat?"

"No, nothing right now. I'll fix something later. And Alex, please keep out of the donuts this morning. I know you already snuck two of them. Your lunch is in the fridge. I fixed you a plate of leftovers from last night's dinner."

Great ... round two of boiled chicken, brown rice, and steamed carrots, Alex thought but was hesitant to say.

Instead, he said, "Okay dear, you go back to sleep now. I'll give you a call around noon to check on you."

Lora smiled at her husband. "Goodbye sweetheart, I love you."

"I love you, too."

Alex wore his best suit. He double-checked his tie in the mirror to make certain it was perfect before leaving the bedroom. His wore his special-occasion cologne and even gave his hair a little squirt of Lora's hairspray.

In the kitchen, he filled a large mixing bowl with Kellogg's Fruit Loops, sprinkled the already-sweetened cereal with several spoonfuls of sugar, and began eating the biggest breakfast he had eaten in six weeks. He fixed himself four pieces of toast, heavily buttered, then dumped a whole can of Yoder's Country Sausage Gravy—he had the gravy stashed in the back of the cupboard for just such an occasion—over the toast. He had two cups of coffee with real sugar, not a sweetener and real Half-n-Half, not skim milk. For dessert, he scarfed down two more donuts that were like the forbidden apple in the Garden of Eden. He was in his glory. While he ate, he called Annie and explained that Lora was not feeling well, and then he looked over some figures for his meeting.

When he had finished the mega-breakfast, he felt like he could take on the world. His conscience, however, had caught up with him. He felt guilty about the binge, but there was nothing he could do about it now—short of purging, that is. He put the milk back into the refrigerator and reached for the lunch Lora had packed, but then decided he would skip lunch today to make up for the major pig-out this morning. He left the house whistling, as content as a baby who had just finished a bottle.

Lora slept soundly for nearly three hours. When she woke, her migraine was just barely noticeable, and her stomach was back to normal. When she walked downstairs, she felt well-rested and hungry. Ready for some breakfast, she fixed herself a cup of black coffee, some non-fat yogurt, topped with fresh strawberries and bananas and two graham cracker squares. When she opened the fridge, she spotted the microwave plate containing Alex's lunch. Lora assumed that Alex had been in a hurry and simply forgot it. The clock put the time at 11:15. She calculated that she had enough time to get ready, run the leftovers by the bank, and still get to the hospital before her afternoon patients.

Lora had been persistent in her mission to track down Rob Parker, but every time she thought of something or someone who could help, she ran into another dead end. After about two weeks of unsuccessful searching, she finally gave up. Lora felt more confident about her secret with each passing day after the 15th. For two days now, nothing out of the ordinary had happened. At this point, she was confident that Kash was still the all-talk-and-no-action ass he had always been. She showered, dressed for work, and was on her way to the bank before she realized her headache had completely gone away. She took this to be a good omen. Things would be getting back to normal real soon.

4

The men with whom Alex had met this morning were impressed with the proposal they were presented. It appeared that things were going to go in Alex's favor. He was satisfied with the results, as were two of the bank's board members when they called to see how the meeting had gone. Smugly seated at his cherry desk, Alex realized that it was almost lunchtime. He didn't want to forget to check on Lora. Now he wished he had grabbed the lunch this morning. He was getting hungry.

Kristin was Alex's secretary. She tapped lightly on the door before walking in.

"Alex, there's a fellow out here wanting to see you. He doesn't have an appointment, and he won't give his name, but he said he was good friends with your wife, and he needs to talk to you about some kind of financial arrangement. Do you have some time to see him, or shall I have him make an appointment?"

"No, I'll see him, but I'll be another ten or fifteen minutes. I want to finish reviewing the changes we made this morning while they're still fresh in my mind."

"I'll tell him sir," Kristin continued. "I have a lunch date today, so if you wouldn't mind letting the gentleman know when you're ready for him, I'll be going now."

"I don't mind at all, Kristin. Enjoy your lunch, and if you're not hungry, enjoy you're date." Alex chuckled.

"Oh, Mr. Jordan." Kristin smiled and blushed as she left.

In the outer office, she told the mysterious man to be seated and that Mr. Jordan would call for him directly. She excused herself, locked her desk, picked up her purse, and left the office. In the main lobby, she passed Mrs. Jordan, Mr. Jordan's wife, carrying a microwave plate. The two women exchanged pleasantries, and Kristin hurried off explaining that she was meeting someone for lunch.

When Lora reached the foyer adjoining Alex's office, she saw a bearded man leafing through a magazine evidently waiting to see Alex. She was about to enter Alex's office when something about the man struck her as familiar. It took another quick glance before she realized it was Sam Kashette. He had grown a beard all right, but it was unmistakably him. The cavalier smirk gave him away. Her heart began to pump in extreme pulses, and her stomach did a little flip-flop. Her headache was back. She could feel her face heating up as she ardently gazed around the room. With no one paying any attention to her, she approached Kash and took the chair next to his.

Kash raised his face from the magazine, "Hello, darlin'. Fancy meeting you here."

"What are you doing here?" Lora tried to whisper, for fear Alex would here her voice and come out.

"Well darlin', it's like I told you, if the checks weren't in my hands by the fifteenth, I'd be paying a call to your husbands." Kash's voice took on a sarcastic tone. "I didn't think you would be surprised to see me. You should have been expecting me. I decided to see Alex first when I couldn't get in to see President Whitmore this morning. Do you know how difficult it is to get an appointment with that man? I hear bankers are always ready to talk. I guess they assume you want to either give them money or borrow money. Either way it's profitable for them, but a university president only gets grief from unscheduled appointments."

"Look Kash, could we go some place and talk about this?" Lora kept an eye on her husband's office door. "I'm sure there's been a mix up. We mailed our checks just like you told us."

"Shame, shame Lora. First stealing and now lying. I guess I had your number from the start. You were nothing but trailer trash then, and you're nothing but trailer trash now. How do you except to fit in with the prim and proper, to mingle with the high society crowd when your word can't be trusted? You should know these people expect honesty from their own. Your husband will thank me one day for exposing you for what you really are: common trailer trash."

Lora may have been staring into Kash's eyes, but what she saw was something deeper than a mere eyeball.

She was there again, at Pathetic Jokes, in the front yard of the trailer—if you considered a six-foot square of crab grass, weeds, and dandelions a yard. She was dressed in a badly faded cotton sleeveless dress; she wore no shoes. It was the summer of her tenth year. She had cut a piece of her mother's clothesline and had tied big knots in both ends to make a jump rope. She sang the songs that little girls sang in those days and skipped rope to the melody.

Three, six, nine, the goose drank wine. The monkey chewed tobacco on the streetcar line. The line broke, the monkey got choked, and they all went to heaven in a little rowboat.

Life was good, until she saw the boys coming down the gravel road toward her trailer.

"Look guys, it's Pooper Cooper," one of them had said.

"Yeah we're among royalty," another had chimed in. "It's the queen of trailer trash."

"If I'm the queen, Bobby, you must be the king. I didn't see a truck haulin' your trailer out'a here today," Lora had responded.

"Oh, I'm not goin' anywhere. I'm the king. You're nothing but a girl—my humble servant. Even a queen must bow down to a king." Then he added, "Don't you have anything better to play with than an old, raggedy clothesline?"

They all had a good laugh at Lora expense but she was not about to let it ride. Kids could be so cruel.

She yelled back to them, "At least I have something. I don't see a shiny new bicycle under any of your asses, either. Wouldn't be walking if you did. Seems to me like you boys won't get any farther than your feet can take you."

That wiped the smile off of their faces. Bobby Jones was the ringleader.

He spit a hawker the size of a quarter on the ground to prove he was cool. The other two followed suit. Monkey see, monkey do.

Monkey got choked, and they all went to heaven in a little rowboat.

"Hey Bobby, I think we could use that rope. Don't you?" Chad Billings said.

"You can't have it," Lora answered and tightened her grip on the rope.

"I can have anything I want."

"If you think you can take it, you can have it."

Just then, Bobby grabbed the rope at a point near Lora's left hand and jerked one end free. His hand sliced down the rope and stopped abruptly at the end when it met the knot Lora had made. Lora pulled her half, and the tug-of-war commenced.

Bobby outweighed Lora by a good 25 pounds, nevertheless, Lora moved him around the yard. Chad coupled with his leader. He said, "You know what we could make out of this rope, Bobby? A hangman's noose, that's what. I heard my dad say that Lora's old man got hung real good on a long shot in the third race last week. We could slip a noose around his neck and finish what the long shot started."

The two boys tried to giggle but had a difficult time of it, considering all their energy was used trying to keep their end up. They tugged with all their might. Could she really be holding down both of them? She was just a girl, for God's sake. Bobby and Chad gave each other puzzled looks.

Lora was like a powerhouse. Even though both boys were pulling on the other end, Lora still moved them around with ease.

The last boy, Tony "Tubbs" Toochie, joined in to help the team. Tubbs was literally a tub and Lora feared with his added weight, she would not be able to hold her end much longer. Tubbs whispered something to Bobby and Chad. They laughed like mad, then Tubbs hollered, "Three," and the boys let go of their half causing Lora to land smack on her butt in the grass.

The three bullies huddled up in hysterical laughter and then Lora took off after them, chasing the boys for five lots down the gravel road in her bare feet. Needless to say, Tubbs was the slowest, and Lora finally caught him by the back of his worn out, torn tee shirt. She could not believe they'd had the nerve to make fun of her clothes only a few days ago.

As she raised her hand to slap the boy at Pathetic Jokes 28 years ago, she realized she was raising her hand to slap Sam Kashette's face today.

Kash grabbed her arm and jerked it back into her lap.

"Don't provoke me Lora. I'm not in a good mood today." Kash's attitude was brutal. "Now I'm going in to talk to your husband and let him hear what Mr. Parker has to say and when he defends you—which I'm sure he will—I'm going to show him these dispensing tickets with your signature. If you have a problem with that, I suggest you get the hell out of here, understand?"

"Please, Kash." Lora found herself pleading. My God, how had this gotten so far out of hand? "Come outside and we'll talk. I have my checkbook. I'll write you a check right now, but you have to come outside with me. Please!"

Lora could hear movement in Alex's office. She knew he was coming out. With tear-filled eyes, she pulled her personal checkbook from her purse and showed Kash the balance. *"PLEASE!"* she begged.

"All right, let's go."

Kash and Lora were in the main lobby heading out when Lora turned to see Alex searching for the man who Kristin had said would be waiting. Kash had a hold of Lora's elbow, guiding her out the door. She prayed nobody would notice her.

Outside, on the main street, they sat on a bench used as a bus stop a few blocks down from the bank. Lora wrote the check, as she had promised, but when she handed it to Kash, he tore it up and gave the pieces back to her. "You didn't figure in the interest. With the rate of inflation, I'll need five thousand now."

"You're crazy!"

"When did anyone ever accuse me of being sane?"

"So now, you think you can just change the amount anytime the spirit moves you?"

"No Lora, you pay me on time every month until I get back on my feet, and you'll never see me or hear from me again. When this is all over, you can have your damn dispensing tickets and Rob Parker's tape, and I'll be out of your life forever."

"I thought you were out of my life 16 years ago."

Kash smiled.

Lora wrote another check, this time for $5000, and handed it to Kash. With her hands still shaking, she stuffed the checkbook into her purse and stood up to leave.

"Woo darlin', were not finished yet." Kash started. "What about Suzy's money? You know you two are in this together. If one doesn't pay, I'll show my stuff to both of your husbands."

Lora was outraged. "You're disgusting, Sam Kashette. You're a sickening, arrogant, horrible excuse for a human being."

"I see your vocabulary has improved over the years. If we're going to get into name calling, I'll stick with a simple one ... bitch!"

"Okay, enough," Lora said, shocked to find she had stooped to such a childish level. "What do you expect me to do about Suzy?"

"Well, it would be in your best interest to get her here with a check wouldn't you think?"

"Couldn't I write you another check for her money?"

"No dice darlin'. You can't pay Suzy's debt. This is her blood money, her debt to me. I want her here. Now."

Lora was full of hatred for this man. "I'll call her and let her know what you want. Where can we reach you?"

"Nice try darlin'. I'm not telling you where I'm staying. I'll contact you in a few hours, and we can arrange to meet then. Does that sound fair to you?"

"None of this sounds fair to me, but I'll do as you ask, and I'll try to convince Suzy to do the same."

"Tell my lovely Suzy that I have also brought with me a copy of her records from the clinic. I'll be more than happy to show them to Clayton if she doesn't believe me." Kash's smile was stern.

"I'll tell her." Lora said, ashamed to be backing down. Pathetic Jokes all over again.

Kash stood up, tipped his hat, and walked down the street and away from the bank. Lora stayed on the bench a moment longer to regain control of her temper. In her heart, she knew if she had a gun, she would shoot him in the back. She watched Kash enter a downtown bar as if he had not a care in the world.

5

Suzy sat on the couch completely engrossed in an afternoon movie on the TV. It was a love story, and as she watched it, she was able to relate to so many of the emotions that were exposed by the lovers. For example, when the two characters first met, she was reminded how thrilled she had been when Clayton entered her life, and when the TV lovers had a fight, she recalled how relieved she was to finally make up with Clayton after they'd quarreled. She also related to the joy the actress felt on her wedding day, as Suzy was so high on her day, she didn't ever want to come down from it. Somehow, she thought, the moviemakers always made life so simple. In the end, they always lived happily ever after.

During a commercial break, Suzy switched the station to the Weather Channel. Everyone up and down the east coast tuned in to your local weather on the 8's, hoping to find a glimmer of green on the radar screen indicating precipitation for his or her area. They would watch as a system from the

Gulf colored the radar in Florida, Louisiana, Georgia, South Carolina, then slam into an invisible wall at the Virginia and Kentucky border. On other occasions they would watch a system from the west creep green from Kansas and Indiana, only to fizzle out somewhere in Ohio or Michigan. But like Suzy, they watched anyway. Nothing promising showed on the radar in Dalton, Mass. today.

With the passing of June 15, Suzy viewed her life as peaceful and placid as Dalton's radar picture. Yesterday, she was less panicky than the day before, and today she was even calmer than yesterday. She had made up her mind to put Kash's threat behind her and to start each day with a new appreciation for the wonderful family with which she was blessed.

Before the movie returned, Suzy went to the kitchen to get a glass of iced tea. The phone rang. In a pleasant tone she answered, "Hello?"

"Hi Suz … it's me, Lora. We've got trouble."

Suzy's behavior changed instantly. The tremors in her legs returned, the pink blotches caused by her nerves cropped up again around her neck and chest, and the queasiness bounced back in her abdomen. She listened intently as Lora explained the events that had transpired this afternoon. She was frantic to keep Kash from coming to Dalton before she got her check to him.

"Suzy, don't go hysterical on me." Lora tried to calm her friend. "Kash is going to call here in a few hours to let me know where you can meet him. How soon can you be here?"

"If I leave right now, I can be in Boston in a little over an hour. Will that give us enough time?"

"It should."

"Please, whatever you do, don't let Kash come to Dalton. I have to see him there. This is such a small town, and everybody knows me. Do you understand? It would be too risky."

"I'll hold him off, but get here as fast as you can."

Suzy repeated from memory the directions to Lora's house before the women hung up their respective receivers. When Suzy turned around after hanging up her end, she saw Tommy standing in the doorway. She had to pull herself together, for she did not want her son to know she was a wreck again.

"Hi honey," Suzy tried to sound like her cheerful self, "will you be okay for a few hours? I have to go out for a while."

She kissed Tommy on the cheek and wondered how much of the conversation he had overheard. She ran to the den, pulled open the middle drawer that housed her personal checkbook, and trotted through the front door. Once outside, she realized she had left her car keys behind. She re-entered the house, snatched the keys from a hook on the wall, and made her way outside again.

Tommy was dumbfounded by his mother's conduct. He watched her from the bay window in the living room. His mother never left the house without first freshening her make-up and running a comb though her hair. She didn't care if she was just going to the mailbox; these two acts of personal hygiene were always performed. Suzy was wearing old faded jeans and a tee shirt that had been laundered so many times, the business logo was hard to make out. Unless it was a terrible emergency, she would have changed her clothes before leaving the house. Today, she did none of these things. Tommy watched as she dropped her keys twice trying to get the car door opened, and then after succeeding, she knocked her head on the doorframe. But Tommy was most amazed by the fact that his mother wore no shoes, and he believed she was truly oblivious to it. He watched her pull out of the driveway squealing tires as she went.

Tommy grabbed the pencil and pad which always sat on the countertop beside the phone. He started to write the directions the way he remembered hearing his mother say it. He felt comfortable that his directions were accurate, and he knew he had the right street name, Kelsey Circle, because he had a crush on a girl named Kelsey in school. He was confident he could follow his mother's directions. He was certain, too, that she was going to meet the mystery man in the cowboy hat from the 7-Eleven. He overheard his mother call the man Kash, so now the mystery man had a name. He went to his room, took fifty dollars from his sock drawer, and proceeded toward his car in search of his mother's lover.

6

Kash called Lora exactly two hours from the time they had parted company downtown. When he ended the phone conversation, Lora slammed down the receiver, heavy with bitterness for Sam Kashette. She wondered how one man could be so arrogant. To be blackmailing them was bad enough, but to be so brash about it just proved what Lora always suspected: the man was a pompous ass—a real son-of-a-bitch. She knew shortly after they had started dating that he was a jerk, but she had no idea how big a jerk he really was, until now.

She opened the front door and sat down in a chair that gave her a full view of Kelsey Circle. She waited patiently for Suzy's car to pull in the driveway. She looked intently out the door through dazed eyes. To her, this seemed like a bad dream, like she would wake up at any moment and life would be back to the way it was a few weeks ago. She hated to admit it, but perhaps if she had not been reunited with Suzy, none of this would have happened. Her life had been perfectly peaceful before Suzy came back into it. It's as if Suzy had brought nothing but an abundance of confusion and bad luck. Then after giving it a second thought, she realized Suzy should not be blamed for what was happening to Lora. Suzy had her skeletons, and Lora's closet was far from empty. Kash would have tracked her down in the end anyway. It was simply a coincidence that she and Suzy had been together.

She heard a car pull in. Dashing for the door, she watched Suzy emerge from her vehicle. Lora looked at her friend and did not recognize her as the same person whom she had seen just two weeks ago. Suzy had been crying, Lora could tell by looking at her red swollen eyes. Her hair was a mess and her face was pale. She looked scared to death. She appeared to have dropped a few pounds too, so the clothes which always fit her to a tee seemed to hang limply on her body. And …

"Suzy," Lora squealed, opening the door, "where are your shoes?"

"I was halfway here before I realized I wasn't wearing any. I left as soon as I hung up with you," Suzy clarified. "Am I too late? Has he called yet?"

"No, you're not too late and yes, he called. He wants to meet you at Sadler Park at 3:30. There's still plenty of time. You've got to pull yourself together; straighten up. You look a mess. You can't let him know he's upsetting you. This is exactly what he wants to do."

"You talked to him today. How did you manage to keep your cool?"

"I didn't manage it very well, but I didn't allow him to break me either. I lost my temper and tried to slap him."

"My God, did he hit you back?"

"No, I only tried to slap him. He grabbed my arm before I made contact. I'm certain, though, if I had hit him he would have decked me on the spot. He had this weird look in his eyes."

"Oh Lora, I'm scared." Suzy began to tremble all over. She was crying again, too.

Lora took Suzy by the shoulder and shook her gently until she calmed down. "Pull yourself together, girl. We've got to get through this until we figure out what to do next. Now go upstairs and fix your face while I find a pair of shoes for you to wear."

"Lora?" Suzy asked, "Were you planning on going with me?"

"I wasn't planning on it, but if you'd feel better with me there, I'll go."

"No, I'd rather you didn't. I'd like to have a chance to talk to him alone. You see, I have this idea. It's all I thought about on the way up here. Maybe I can talk some sense into him. I used to have a way with Kash. I know all his sex games. I know how to perform all the unpleasant little acts that satisfy him. Lora, I'd be willing to be unfaithful to Clayton if I knew he would leave us alone afterwards."

"Are you suggesting you'd sleep with him?"

"That's exactly what I'm saying. I'll give him the damn four thousand dollars and do all the dirty little things I used to do to him if he'll give me the papers and the tape."

"Oh Suzy, I don't think this is a good idea. He's not the same Sam Kashette we knew at Kanawha State. He's turned into some kind of evil, sinister thug. A monster, if you will. I think he's capable of truly hurting anybody who'd try to stand in the way of him and his money."

"I'll be careful, but I've got to try something to stop him. I don't know how much more I can take. I find myself looking around corners in my own house, and I'm not imagining the way my son looks at me differently. It's as though he's disappointed in me, or he suspects that I'm hiding something." She started to pace. "Hell, I am hiding something. I can't take it anymore."

"I know how you feel. When I saw Kash sitting in the waiting room outside Alex's office, I thought I was going to faint. For right now, we have no choice except to pay him. I should have listened to you from the beginning. He told me today that if he doesn't get a check from both of us every month, he'll show the papers to both Alex and Clayton, regardless of who missed the payment."

"That son-of-a-bitch! Do you see what he's doing? He is pitting us against each other. He's relying on you and me to keep the other in line, so the money keeps flowing."

"I know, and I hate it. I saw his proof, too. I saw the dispensing tickets. He waved them in my face today." Lora waited for Suzy to stop pacing before she finished. "Here's the biggest blow: we now owe him five thousand dollars. Interest, he called it. He says he'll leave us alone as long as we keep paying him."

Suzy was loosing her temper at a rapid rate. "Fine, if that bastard wants a fight, a fight is what he'll get."

Lora tried once more to calm her. "Now settle down, Suzy. You can't become reckless. You've got be very calm with him; don't set him off. I'm telling you, he's on the edge of the deep end, and it won't take much to push him over. If that happens, I do believe he will hurt you. Now, go on and get ready."

Suzy made her way to the upstairs bathroom. Lora rummaged through the hall closet to find a pair of shoes for Suzy to wear. She was reminded of her college days, ironically, and how often she and Suzy had swapped clothes and shoes and jewelry. Lora, of course, borrowed more of Suzy's things than the other way around. They were so close back then.

When Suzy returned from the bathroom, she looked much, much better than when she had first arrived. She told Lora she had gotten a handle on her inner-demons and that she was simply going to talk to Kash. She promised not to provoke him in any way. Lora gave Suzy the shoes, and as Lora watched her put them on, she too was convinced that Suzy was in command of her emotions again. She checked her directions to the park, and then walked Suzy to the car. She prayed Suzy would be able to maintain control. After all, Lora felt as though she was sending her to meet with the devil himself.

7

Kelsey Circle, as the name implied, was a group of a half dozen homes constructed in a large semi-circle with one path for both entering and exiting. It was located in a ritzy section of town. Tommy pulled his Bimmer along the side of some bushes at the entrance to the circle. The shrubbery provided ample camouflage, nearly covering his entire car. He was about to get out and walk closer to the Jordan's house when he saw his mother on the porch embracing another woman whom he assumed to be Lora Jordan. He watched Suzy get into her car and pull out of the driveway. Tommy ducked down in the seat as his mother passed by the entrance. He pulled out behind her, determined to find out where she was off to now.

Following at a safe distance, the six-mile drive took him into downtown Boston. He was at a stop light when he watched his mother's silver Mercury pull into the parking spot near a recreational area.

Tommy circled the block, in order to canvass the park, but found it rather lifeless. People were hustling and bustling on the street and sidewalk, but no one took the time to sit down and enjoy the beauty of the park. With the exception of a few children playing on the swings and the mothers who watched over them, Tommy saw only one other man sitting on a bench near the fountain. He observed Suzy approach the man. As Tommy continued to circle, he squinted, straining his eyes to get a better look at the individual. After focusing in, he verified that this man and the mystery man in the cowboy hat from the 7-Eleven were one in the same, except now the man, Kash, sported a beard. Tommy still had reservations about the theory of his mother and Kash having an affair. There had to be another logical explanation for all of this queer behavior surrounding his mother and this Kash person.

He parked the BMW in a place where he could watch the meeting and still remain inconspicuous. The encounter appeared to be that of a business-like nature, as he saw Kash handling papers in a folder. They talked for a few minutes before his mother pulled out her checkbook and wrote the man a check. Looking on intently, Tommy watched Kash scan the check and put it into his pocket. As the two continued to converse, Tommy wondered for what reason his mother possibly could be paying this man. Maybe she was having a gift made for his father. After all, their anniversary was coming up. On one hand, it would explain why she wanted to keep it a secret from his dad; on the other hand, it supplied no answer for her warning to stay away from this supposedly evil man. He noted Suzy moving closer to Kash. She removed his hat and ran her fingers through his hair as she spoke to him. He watched Suzy straddle her leg around Kash and sit on his lap facing him. His first impression was that of a stripper performing a lap dance. The color drained from Tommy face. The pain he felt in his stomach was intense—so much so that it would have hurt less if he had been kicked there. His eyes filled with tears, one sliding down his cheek at a snail's pace to drip off his chin finally. He would give anything to hear what they were saying.

He watched his mother kiss the neck and ear of a man other than his father. He found it rather peculiar that Kash seemed to be unreceptive to her actions. If this was an affair, it sure didn't appear as though his mother had called it off. Kash didn't seem to be pressuring her at all. If anything, *she* was seducing him. Suzy cupped Kash's face around her hands and kissed him full on the mouth. The kiss was extremely aggressive but still, Kash made no reaction. His arms and hands hung limply at his side. As she stroked his face and hair, she continued to talk to him, but Tommy noticed the conversation appeared one-sided, too. Kash never responded in any way.

Suddenly, yet gently, Kash took her by the arms, turned her upper body away from his and said something that infuriated Suzy. Tommy noticed his mother's smile morph into the sullen lips of an angry, hurt woman. Kash was laughing at her now. Suzy wildly grabbed her purse, pointing her finger at him repeatedly as she talked. Then she walked away with her head held high never once looking back.

Tommy considered confronting Kash about the situation right here and now but then decided against it. He felt certain neither Kash nor his mother knew he had been watching, and this was a plus for him. He needed more time to acquire facts, sort out the confusion, and fill the holes in his theory so that when he did finally confront one of them, he would be able to conclude whether or not he or she was lying.

Kash picked up his folder and put his hat back on his head. He walked toward a small burgundy rental car, perhaps a Geo or a Chevette. Tommy started his car and proceeded to tail the car through town and onto the interstate. They were traveling west. Tommy wanted to find out where Kash lived.

8

Suzy remained agitated by the encounter with Kash as she drove east on the interstate, speeding to get home. Clayton would surely be there by now, however, when she opened the garage door, she was stunned to see that Clayton's car was not in the garage. She wasted no time getting her car into the garage and getting herself into the house.

"Clayton!" she yelled. No one answered. What if he started to worry and took off in search of her? How would she explain her whereabouts? All of a sudden, she realized she should have left a note or something. "Tommy!" she shrieked heading for the kitchen.

Someone had been home and made spaghetti. The remaining dinner was still in the pot on the stovetop. Suzy spotted a Post-a-Note on the refrigerator. After reading it, she learned that Clayton had gone to the gym to meet the guys and play some racquetball.

She looked out the back door to the carport they had built for Tommy's car. It too, was empty. Feeling confident about being alone, she picked up the phone and dialed Lora's number. Suzy filled Lora in on what took place at the park.

"I tried to reason with him, tried to make him see that what he's doing to us is wrong, not to mention illegal, but he didn't want to hear it. I tried offering myself to him. I put my lips on that horrible man and whispered the filthy things I would do to make him feel good. I told him I would be willing to exchange sex for the papers. He told me those papers were worth more than a roll in the hay. He called me a slut. Can you believe it—a slut? At one time, my teasing drove him crazy. Do you remember?"

"Yes, I remember." Lora was sorry for her old friend.

"Well it doesn't work anymore. He grabbed my arms and pushed me away. He told me to stop playing college games. He said I was a big girl now, and I had big girl secrets, so I'd better hold up to my end of the bargain or my secret would be in all the papers. I was so pissed, I swear, if I had a gun, I would have shot him."

"I know. I felt the same way this afternoon."

"But I kept calm because I could smell the booze on him. I think he was drinking whiskey."

"He went to a bar after he left me at the bank," Lora said. "He probably stayed there until it was time to call. He never could hold his liquor. Whiskey always made him mean."

"Yeah, I remembered. That's why I backed off. I did try though. I gave it my best shot. I'm sorry Lora, he just wouldn't listen."

"It's not your fault, honey. If only there was someone Kash would listen to. Someone all three of us could trust."

Then, as if a light bulb lit up on both ends of the phone, they said in unison, *"ROSALEE!"*

PART TWO

... AND THEN THERE WERE THREE

CHAPTER NINE

Going Home

1

Sister Rosalee DeLucci enjoyed the view of the mountains while riding on the bus that took her from the Mother House to her parent's home. The bus was traveling off the interstate highway now on Route 12 toward her hometown. Rural Route 12 ran all the way from the Mother House, but buses never used it until they had to. The interstate was faster and more profitable for the bus line, so buses took the interstate to the closest exit. It seemed a shamed to Rosa that the beauty of her charming state would go unseen except for this short stretch.

If only she had learned to drive. She could have taken the roads she wanted and stopped anywhere she pleased along the way. It would have made the trips home more convenient, not to mention, more frequent.

To answer the question of why she had never learned to drive was easy: she was simply not built to sit behind the wheel of a car. Passive was the word Frankie had used, when she was sixteen and he had tried to teach her to drive. He said, "You're too passive Rosalee. To be a good driver you need to be aggressive but at the same time be watchful of the other drivers on the road. We sat at the 4-way intersection at Green Street and Maple for nearly ten minutes."

And they had, Rosa remembered. Car after car had gone through the intersection while Rosa sat patiently until no one could be seen for blocks down the other three roads. Then she drove through at a mere snail's pace. Being in control of a 3000-pound car was too much for Rosa to manage. She drove too slowly and always left at least three car lengths between herself and the car in front of her. People would pass her at every available opportunity, holding up the infamous middle finger that stood for so many things out there on the highway. Those who chose not to salute would lay on their horns as they jetted by.

No sir, sitting on the bus, leaving the driving to someone else was the only way for Rosa to go.

She watched out the bus window not looking at anything in particular. Every now and then, a house would pop up over a small hill or knoll. Nice houses, they were, with lots of land encompassing each property line. Good farmland was plentiful all over West Virginia—rich soil, decent climate. The only downfall was the many hills. Rosa pitied the poor people who had to work those hilly fields. One row of corn was one row, but a person would have to plow up the hill, down the other side, up another hill, and down the other side. These were not little hills either. Some of them could be as much as a 45-degree incline. Sometimes she wondered if it wouldn't have been easier to get a big piece of equipment in there and level off the whole field before the first seed had ever been planted in the ground. Then it occurred to her, if they had done that, there would be no difference between West Virginia and Iowa or Kansas. People loved West Virginia *because* of the hills and hollows. They found the mountains appealing.

Unfortunately, the view of the mountains today could not look more unappealing. Rosa saw nothing that looked lush and green. The color bronze came to mind. The mountains could have been an enormous bronze statue. The sun seemed to be baking on a bronze glaze and the brightness of the sun gave the mountains a glossy shine that only enhanced the image of a statue.

Rosalee wished it would rain; she prayed for rain. Three inches of snow had fallen at the end of February and since that time there had been no further precipitation, outside of a few sprinkles that wet the ground briefly before drying up five minutes later. The meteorologist's forecast could have been a repeat night after night and nobody would have been the wiser. Extremely hot days, they had said, below normal temperatures at night, humidity and dewpoints in the teens and twenties with a 0% to 10% chance of rain. A couple of times a week they would throw a wind advisory out there just to change things up a bit. The gusts would range from 30 to 40MPH and swirl the dry land around like dirt devils. She had no choice but to turn her attention elsewhere because the view from the window made her terribly sad.

She moved about in her seat. She was so eager to see her family again. After all, it had been three years since her last visit. She tried to imagine how everyone would look. She wondered if any of the older relatives had gotten grayer, or if the younger ones had a more mature look now, or if anyone had lost or gained weight. Then there were the babies … oh my, the babies she had seen three years ago would be walking and talking by now, no longer wearing diapers and no longer taking bottles, but eating at the table. She couldn't wait. Rosalee's heart flinched every now and again reminding her that she missed her family, but she had no idea just how much until she started home this afternoon. The feelings she harbored now were similar to the ones she felt when she would come home from college for the weekend. She was eager to visit, but happy to know she would only be there for a few days. Sometimes Lora, or Suzy, or both, would make the trip with her. Massachusetts was too far for Lora and Suzy to travel home every weekend, and Rosa hated leaving the girls behind, so the three of them would make the short drive to Rosa's hometown instead. The girls fit in very well at the DeLucci home, Rosa remembered.

Rosa remained puzzled when it came to the feeling of urgency she faced with regard to her two old friends. She was certain they were somehow tied into the troublesome urges she felt about Kash. She made a mental note to get in touch with one or both of them and find out if the premonitions were valid, even though she knew they would be. Her sixth sense about Sam Kashette was never wrong.

The bus entered the depot. She watched out the window, looking for a familiar face. Her mother's letter said someone from the family would meet her at the station, but it failed to specify which one. Sister Rosa was a little nervous. Because her street clothes were more relaxed than the clothes she wore at the Convent, she could not only feel, but also see the extra pounds she had recently put on. She looked pudgy, especially in the face, and was embarrassed by her appearance. The tone of her family was very open and most of them thought themselves comedians, so she prepared herself for some good-natured ribbing. She knew they would tease. It was in the blood, part of their nature. She was sensitive these days so she hoped the family would take it easy on her.

As she descended the bus, she spotted her very handsome brother. His dark, wavy hair blew gently against the hot, dry breeze, and his big beautiful smile could be seen a mile away.

"Eh, Rosalee," he said in his American-Italian accent. If you didn't know that Frankie had been born in West Virginia, you would swear he was born and raised in Brooklyn, New York. His speech was a combination of a rustic West Virginia drawl and an Italian New York twang. His dialect sounded much like a hit man in a mafia movie. The mobster hit man (probably a guy named Vinnie or Geno) would say, *"Hey boss, you want me to make this yo-yo go away permanently? I could fit him with a nice pair of cement shoes."* Rosa loved to listen to him talk.

Frankie waved his hands in the air to flag his presence. He watched passenger after passenger dismount the bus steps. Finally, his sister appeared.

"I'm glad you're home." He caressed his sister for a long time, then stepped back to look at her. "I can see you're eating well at the convent. Put on a few pounds, uh?"

"Yes Frankie, I put on a few pounds." It's not like she wasn't expecting to hear this. She had no choice but to grin and bear it.

"What? You thought nobody would notice. You still look good, though." Then he added, "You didn't think I'd let it slide just because you're a nun, did you?"

Rosalee knew that nothing would slide with her family. When she was in her mother's home, she was simply Rosalee DeLucci—not Rosa, the third grade teacher, or Sister Rosa, servant of the Lord, but instead plain old Rosalee. Her family regarded her with no deference. When she was home, her mother believed that God had loaned Rosa to the family; therefore, it was the family's time, not God's. She could be God's minion again when her vacation was over. Until then, she would be considered no differently from any other family member.

Rosalee squeezed her brother's large shoulders and arms. "You don't look like you've missed any meals either."

"Eh, that's muscle, little sister, muscle. Down at the station, they make us go to the gym three times a week. There are no flabby cops at our precinct."

"Is Aldo Carlotta still on the force?"

"Yep."

"How's he doing with this new rule? Last time I saw him, he was well over 250 pounds."

"He's doing great. He had 60 pounds to loose, and he's already taken off nearly half."

Frankie picked up Rosalee's luggage and guided her by the arm to his car. He acted like she was a little old lady using a walker. This was also something that was in his blood: to protect and look after his little sister.

On the way, they chatted about Frankie's precinct, and Rosa inquired about family members and friends.

The humidity that usually came along with a hot West Virginia summer day was nonexistent today. Rosalee was grateful for the car's air-conditioning at any rate. The outside air was 90 degrees, and she was hot. A pink tint covered her neck and arms. Her skin was itchy from the dry heat. She felt weighed down with exhaustion because of the sultry conditions. Once inside the vehicle, Rosa felt more comfortable from a physical standpoint but still distracted mentally. Frankie noticed her uneasiness.

"Okay Rosa, what's on your mind? You look like you're a hundred miles away."

"I'm fine Frankie," Rosalee tried to sound convincing, "I'm just enjoying the cool air. It's so hot outside. And I am a little tired from the bus ride. Don't worry about me."

"Hey, you're my sister, we're family. It's my job to worry about you." Frankie knew every aspect of his sister's character, and this one was definitely an act. "Now come on, out with it."

Rosalee remained silent. When they were kids, if she wanted to avoid answering his questions, she would merely say nothing and usually his questions would stop—but not now. Being a detective had improved his interrogation skills.

"Rosalee, what's up?" Frankie took a guess at the answer. "Hey, you're not thinking about that Kashette boy, are you?"

"I hardly think he's a boy, Frankie. He's the same age as me and that's almost 40," Rosalee said sarcastically.

"Uh huh, you were thinking about him."

Rosalee turned her head and rolled her eyes.

"Like I told you 20 years ago Rosa, the guy's a bum."

"He's not a bum, Frankie. You never liked him."

"I never like him because he was a bum—nothing but trouble. I didn't like him then, and I don't like him now. Mama was right you know. She said he'd never amount to anything, and he never did. He was in some trouble awhile back. Did you know that?"

"No, I didn't. What sort of trouble?"

"Big trouble."

Trying to sound casual, she said, "Knowing the way our family feels about him, I'm sure everyone made a big fuss about it."

"Christ Rosalee ... the guy killed someone. The whole town made a big fuss about it."

Rosalee swung her head around so fast, the clip in the back of her hair fell out. "What did you say? He killed someone? How?"

"One night he got all jigged up on booze—and probably dope too—and smashed his rig into a seventeen-year-old kid's car. The boy was only a senior in high school; his life was just starting until Kash creamed him. A day or two later the kid died."

"Oh my God. Why didn't someone tell me?"

"You mean Mama didn't write you about it? I can't believe she passed up the opportunity to say *I told you so*."

"Well she did. This is the first I've heard about it."

"He did time somewhere in Kentucky for DUI with death."

"When did it happen?"

"Couple years ago. One of the guys at the station heard he was supposed to get out around Easter time. I'm telling you Rosa, he's a looser."

She did not want to hear any more trash talk about her Kash. Rosalee sat silently for the rest of the ride home. She spent the remaining time in the passenger side of her brother's car deep in thought. She remembered midnight Mass on Easter, how she had stayed out in the yard to pray because she could sense Kash was in trouble. She tried to piece her thoughts together, create a timeline in her mind. If he had been about to get out around Easter, why had she felt he needed the prayers then? Why didn't she sense he was in trouble when the accident happened or when he went to prison? And how were her ex-roommates involved? She needed to get some answers.

Frankie pulled up in front of the DeLucci's modest home. It was an old two-story row house but one that had been well maintained over the years. The wooden fence encasing the house was painted charcoal gray, same as the house. The doors and windows had been upgraded, and a beautiful full deck had been added to the back, making it a lovely home.

After shutting down the motor, Frankie shot a stern look in the direction of his little sister. "Hey, don't go in there talking about Sam Kashette. You know how upset Mama gets when she thinks about how many times he broke your heart. Everyone's happy to see you, so please be happy for them, okay?"

"Frankie, I am happy. I'm upset about what's happened to Kash, is all. He has no one to look after him, no one to take care of him. I can't just shake him from my mind."

"Well, try Rosa. Stay away from him. He's trouble, I'm telling you."

"Please Frankie, not now, okay?"

"Look, we'll talk more about this later. All right?"

"Fine with me," she said as she emerged from the vehicle.

Strolling up the walkway, Rosalee looked around the yard at her mother's flowers. Her mother grew the most beautiful plants, but this year none of the bushes were budding nor were any of the plants, which dotted the yard, in bloom. It was already mid-June and all the plants' growth was stunted as if it were early April. Even her mother's touch had not been able to make them grow.

Frankie put his arm around her shoulder. She looked up at him, smiled, and said, "Oh Frankie, I *am* so very glad to be home."

2

Sam Kashette's plane landed at the Charleston, West Virginia airport a few minutes ahead of schedule. Because he kept his overnight bag with him on board, there was no need to wait at the luggage pick-up line. He went directly to the parking lot to retrieve his pickup truck. He was eager to take the short drive into Kentucky to deposit his checks. The money excited him—ten thousand dollars neatly tucked inside his shirt pocket. He was pleased with himself for forcing the Inferiors to make the larger payment. He wished he had thought of it earlier. Their debt to him was worth more than ten grand but by the time he was finished with them, the dollar value would be substantial.

He was happy he had thought of concocting this gambit. At first, he was doubtful that he could pull it off, but he did. Not only had everything gone as planned, he was sure the Inferiors were petrified now. They would never miss sending a payment. They had seen first hand what he intended to do if they disobeyed him. He had shown them a part of himself that he tried to keep buried. He wanted them to see this trait, and he wanted them to fear it. He intended to make a lasting impression so they would never want to see him again, and he was positive he had succeeded.

He thought of the fright in Lora's eyes at the bank when she realized Alex was ready to come out of his office. She was begging him to go outside with her. Begging—Kash liked that. And Suzy ... now Suzy was a piece of work. He chuckled to himself as he remembered the way she had thrown herself at him, offering him sex for her records. What nerve. He had been tempted for a short time to let her do all the dirty acts she had promised. The things she had bargained with were things that no other women had ever been able to duplicate. Kash would have reached total ecstasy. Even if he had given in to the temptress, there was still no way he would have given Suzy the papers. She must be clear crazy if she thought he would fall for such a foolish act. He remembered all the times they had had sex in college, and he believed she was more aggressive than ever yesterday. He enjoyed putting the prima donna in her place and even if he did become aroused, he never let her know it. The Healing Rhymes he had silently repeated made the Bad Thoughts go away. He did wish Clayton could have seen her performance, though. It would have been interesting to watch Suzy destroy the man of her dreams.

Once inside the National Bank of Kentucky, he opened an interest-paying checking account and applied for a money access card so he could go to an automated machine to withdraw any cash he would need in the future. Modern technology was wonderful. Just put the card in the machine, anytime day or night, and out comes your money. It sure simplified matters for Kash, since his money was now in another state. The new accounts officer told him his card would arrive in a few days. He would have to set aside some time to drive back to Kentucky and pick up his card. This should present no problem. He had nothing but time—time and ten thousand dollars.

While driving from Kentucky back to West Virginia, Kash unlocked the neatly arranged glove box to put his bank papers in a safe place. He pulled out the .44 caliber he had purchased a few weeks ago. Handling it, he thought it a shame he wasn't able to sneak it on the plane with him. He would have liked to show it off to the Inferiors. The thought of their reaction, should a gun be shoved in their faces, amused him. He laughed out loud at this daydream.

Before returning to his house, Kash made a stop at the local florist. He selected an arrangement of fresh cut yellow carnations garnished with green ferns. The cost was high due to the drought along the east coast. He assumed the flowers had been flown in from another part of the country. The cost didn't matter to him. He had money to splurge and besides, she was worth it. The finely detailed vase looked out of place in his beat-up old pickup.

When he arrived home, he pulled the truck around to the back of the house, gathered up the vase of flowers, and walked across the yard to Gabby's house. He dearly loved that little old woman.

3

Sister Rosalee DeLucci sat on the bed gazing around the room where she had slept for so many years. Her mother had left the room exactly the same as it had been all her life, aside from tucking away a few keepsakes that used to be proudly showcased on the dresser. The sight of the room left the impression it had been sealed off after Rosa had gone—as if it were somehow memorializing Rosa's honor.

Prior visits home had not affected Rosalee in this way. She never thought much about what living here had been like or for that matter, what it would be like to live here again. In the past, she concentrated only on getting together with the family for a short time, then returning home—home being the convent. Now she wondered if this was the place she should be calling home. She had had doubts about the convent before but never as strong as this. Looking around her old room, she felt as though she was looking at it through different eyes. She looked at everything now and saw it as she had 20 years ago. It was as if she never left. She regarded herself not as a visitor this time but instead as part of this family once more.

Rosa proceeded to unpack her suitcase. Opening one of the dresser drawers, she found the items her mother had removed from atop the dressers. She pulled out the whole drawer and sat it on the bed to look through it. She had never given this drawer a second glance on other visits. Carefully shuffling the contents, the first thing that caught her eye was the pom-poms which once upon a time had been fixed to the tongue of her roller skates. Nearly every Saturday night had been spent at the roller rink with her girlfriends. Even after her skating days were over, she hung the memento over the mirror in her room.

She saw something shining at the bottom of the drawer. Moving her yearbooks from both high school and college, she uncovered a POW bracelet from the Vietnam War era. She had worn the bracelet faithfully despite the fact that after six years there had been no word on Sergeant Michael Mitchell, the prisoner of war whose name had been etched on the bracelet. On one visit home from Kanawha State, she had taken off the POW bracelet and hung it on her jewelry tree. My God, the memories these things brought back.

Digging a little farther into the drawer, she found a gum wrapper chain she and Gina Bartoni had made in the fifth grade. The chain was thirty feet long. When completed, both she and Gina swore off chewing gum for a long time.

Next, Rosa picked up two stuffed animals. She held them close to her heart. Kash had won them for her at the county fair one year while they were still in high school. She couldn't lie to herself any longer; she still carried deep emotional feelings for her first love. Even though he may have hurt her several times, it did nothing to erase her feelings. If anything, it intensified them. If only she had waited. If only she had not closed the book on them so early. They were so young then, barely old enough to begin sewing all the wild oats. Maybe in a few years he would have been ready to settle down. She should have been there waiting for him. But she wasn't and now, especially these last few months, she regretted the rash decision she had made.

After hanging her clothes and arranging them in the closet, Rosa unpacked her unmentionables. There was only one item remaining in the valise: the cedar lock box. Why had she brought the box with her? The contents within were not something she wanted to deal with now. So why? Because she knew by nature what a very nosey lot nuns could be. Usually there was insufficient excitement in the lives of the sisters, so snooping into one another's personal belongings when they were not in house was one way to satisfy their curiosity and maybe start a little gossip at the same time. A locked box of any kind would certainly send a message to her fellow sisters that whatever was inside was supposed to be something private, and private only spiked their curiosity further. She knew they would try to open it; hence, she brought it with her.

Reaching into her purse, Rosa unzipped the compartment made for holding little objects such as hairpins and paper clips. She removed the key to the box and was just about to open it when she heard a cry from the first floor.

"Rosalee, *Mangiare!*"

Rosa put everything, including the cedar box, back in the drawer and reinserted the drawer into the frame of the dresser. It was not uncommon for Italian words to be thrown around in the DeLucci house. Her mother had called her for dinner.

The dining room was full, as was the norm for a DeLucci family dinner. The table, which was made for eight, held eleven adults and one high chair. Everyone packed in elbow-to-elbow, but nobody minded a bit. This was what being part of a family was all about. Not so much being stuffed around the dinner table, but more about everyone being together, enjoying one another's company, and sharing in both the joys and pains of each other's lives. The children were seated separately at the kitchen table. This was done, not to slight the children or outcast them from the family setting, but to give a little relief to the parents and maybe even provide a little sanity while they ate their meal. Mama DeLucci was bringing out the last of the spread she had prepared for her daughter's homecoming when Rosa joined them.

All attention was focused on Rosa when she squeezed into her usual seat at the dining room table. *Nonna* said blessings over the food and also thanked God for sharing Rosa with them for a few weeks, before the group began to dig into the wonderful Italian dinner. Between bites of ricotta/spinach stuffed ravioli, the family asked questions concerning Rosa's work at the convent, her teaching at St. Chris', and her plans for the rest of her sabbatical. Rosa munched on marinara short ribs and answered their questions one by one before asking a few of her own to catch up on all the family news. While biscotti, pizzelles, and coffee were being served, Rosa sat back in her chair and listened to the babble generating around the table. Just as she recalled in her fondest memories, everyone was talking simultaneously. From her best estimation, there were four different conversations going on. Some were in English, some were in Italian, and some conversations started in English with Italian words thrown in for good measure. She delighted in hearing the broken English spoken by her native Italian family. The love she felt in the dining room at that very moment was a love like no other. Yes, this was exactly what it was like to be part of a family, and this was *exactly* what Rosa wanted from life: love.

4

Although Tommy had slept very little last night, he still woke up early this morning. Birds chirped outside his open bedroom window. He rolled over and looked out. Upon further investigation, he found that a single tiny blue jay, perched atop the television cable, was the culprit of all the noise. The jay looked too small to be on its own. When Tommy walked to the window, the bird raised its wings as if to fly off but then, after giving him a more thorough inspection, it decided Tommy was no threat. He watched the bird watch him.

"Hey, little guy. How'd you get up here?"

The blue jay cocked its head to the left.

"I hope your mother's close by. You look too young to be out all by yourself."

The jay let out a screeching yelp then returned its attention to Tommy.

"I know just how you feel little one. I think I'm too young to be hanging from a line too, but I may be out there real soon to join you."

His mind battled a barrage of confusing thoughts. Attempting to sort it all out, he continued conversing with the fascinated bird.

"You see, my mom doesn't seem to be happy here anymore, and if mom's not happy at home, she'll probably be leaving. On the other hand, if dad finds out what my mom has been doing, he'll be leaving. Either way, I'll be left out, hanging on a line just like you. How could she do this to dad and me?"

With all the power in him, he tried to imagine what his life would be like without his parents together. It was impossible to fathom, and the very thought of it frightened him. Tommy was the kind of person who had trouble relating to conflicts. He would walk away from an argument rather than face it and work it out. But now, he had to grow up (and quickly) in order to face what was happening to his family and try to fix it before it was too late. This was one conflict he would not be able to walk away from.

The tiny blue jay chirped twice, picked a bug from its wing feathers before it reverted its curiosity back to Tommy.

"So far, I've found out what the other man's name is. It's Kash. I know what he looks like, and I know where he's staying. What I don't know is where Kash lives? I followed him last night to a motel about halfway between Dalton and Boston, but I didn't talk to him. It wasn't the right time."

Even if it had been, Tommy couldn't have faced him. He was no more able to handle confrontations than conflicts, but preferred not to pass this little piece of information on to the bird. He was ashamed of his weakness, even if it was just a bird to which he was confiding. Again, he tried to encourage himself.

"I've got to change; I must find a way to take control of this situation without my parents' help, and I need to find out more about Kash. You see, little bird, I always assumed I knew my mom—her likes and her dislikes. If I were asked to describe the kind of man my mother would go for, this guy would not be it. I figured she would be attracted to a businessman-type, a man who went to work in a three-piece suit, not a guy who wears faded blue jeans and a cowboy hat. I also figured she would like someone quiet, someone soft spoken, and serene. Kash doesn't appear to have any of these qualities either. And I thought she would want a man that was settled and secure financially. This guy doesn't give the impression that he has money. He drives an economy rental, and he hangs out in a motel, for Christ's sake."

Then Tommy realized that the man he had been describing was his father. He could not even consider his mother with another man.

"You know, I don't understand the motel, either," Tommy told the blue jay. He stooped at the window to get a little closer. "If mom and Kash have a love nest, why not go there last night? Why did they meet fifty miles away in a public park? I suppose it's possible mom could have gone to the motel after I left? When she kissed him, though, why wasn't he more receptive? Unless of course, they had a fight or something since I couldn't hear their conversation. My mom did have a really pissed look when she left. Then there's the question of the money. Why did my mother give him a check?"

He prayed to God that she was not keeping him financially, or worst, paying him for services rendered. He hoped to answer these questions first, then he could confront one of them with the facts he had learned.

The sun coming through the window was hot even at this early hour of the morning. The little blue jay's fascination had never once strayed throughout the conversation. Because of the lack of rainfall, Tommy wondered if the bird was finding enough food. He knew birds liked to eat worms, and worms made their home in the earth. He remembered gathering earthworms for fishing expeditions after a big rain, but he didn't know if worms could be coaxed out of the earth without their world being flooded by a big rain.

A very large blue jay arrived at the window and perched itself next to the smaller blue jay. Must be the mother by the way she squawked at the little one, almost as though she was scolding it. The baby blue jay gave Tommy one more happy chirp and then a quick wink before it flew away behind its mother. Tommy was almost jealous of the baby jay. At least its mom came for it while, Tommy, on the other hand, felt like he had been left alone to sink or swim.

Tommy heard someone walking around in the hallway. He looked at the alarm clock on the nightstand and was amazed to find that it was nine o'clock. He had been talking to the bird for almost two hours. His mother tapped lightly on the door before opening it.

"Good morning, honey."

"Morning," Tommy replied coldly. He was still stooped at the window where he had been chatting with the bird. He stood up now and busied himself with the bedding to keep from being mouthy with Suzy. It was hard to hold his tongue. He found it even more difficult to act like he knew nothing about what was going on with her.

"Hey, I'd like to know where you were last night. You were out pretty late, weren't you pal?"

"Don't call me pal." Tommy turned his back on her and said, "Pals don't keep secrets from each other."

5

Rosalee was the last of the female family members to wake. When she entered the kitchen, she found the others busily preparing various foods. Cousin Demi and Aunt Dominica (Minnie to the family) were fixing a traditional American breakfast of bacon, sausage, eggs, and toast, while her mother and Aunt Nina, worked at kneading dough for homemade bread. *Nonna* supervised the production from her wheelchair. With their male counterparts still asleep, the women made the best of their time by joking and cutting up. Rosalee stood in the kitchen doorway a few seconds before entering just to listen to the storytelling and laughter spouting from within. She missed living here very much.

"*Boun giorno*," Rosalee greeted the family, kissing her *Nonna* on the cheek.

"*Boun giorno!*" they replied.

"*Come sta?*" Nonna asked.

"*Bene, Nonna, bene,*" Rosa answered, telling her grandmother she was fine today.

She poured herself a cup of coffee and sat down at the table. Although she appeared to be listening to the conversation, her mind was on other things. She watched her Mama's face, as Aunt Minnie boasted about her grandbaby. Her mother seemed to be envious. The possibility of her Mama wanting grandchildren never occurred to Rosa. Suddenly she was overwhelmed with selfishness. When making the decision to give her life to the Lord, she never thought about the effect it could have on her Mama or Papa. Not once, until now, had she thought that maybe her mother would have liked a little one to brag about and spoil or that her father would have enjoyed a son-in-law to accompany him during his Friday night poker games at the Italian-American Citizen's Club. A sense of embarrassment rushed through Rosa. How could she have treated such an important decision so lightly without thinking of the rest of her family? Because the way the rest of her family felt was irrelevant. The only thing that mattered to her was the rejection she repeatedly sustained from Sam Kashette—that and her problem with the alcohol. In truth, she used the convent as a place to hide from herself. The drinking had become a real problem in her last year at Kanawha State. AA helped her to cope with day-to-day situations, but she continually turned to the bottle whenever she encountered rejection or trauma from Kash. She could not have Kash, and she knew that no other man could take his place in her heart. She went to the convent where she assumed she would feel at home, taking for granted that the women there had never experienced real love either. In the convent, she was equal to all the other sisters. There was no need to prove that she was better than anybody else, as she had to do with Kash. She would no longer be forced to battle for anybody's affection or fight for anybody's attention. She had run to the convent in a desperate attempt to forget about him and here she was, 15 years later, still thinking about him.

Rosalee poured another cup of coffee and took it to the picnic table on the back porch. Her mother followed her out carrying a cup for herself. As they sipped their morning coffee, they talked.

"Rosa, what's wrong?"

"Nothing Mama. I'm just doing some soul searching."

"Are things not going well at St. Chris'?"

"No, everything's fine at the parish and the school."

"Then why the long face?" her mother asked as she brushed a few stray hairs away from her daughter's eyes.

"Mama?" Rosa hesitated. "Do you ever regret it ... that I became a nun? I mean, would you have preferred it if I had gotten married instead?"

"No honey. I'm happy you chose a life of religion. I'll admit, though, it took us all by surprise back then. Your father and I are both very proud that you're our daughter and we're happy with the way your life turned out. Besides ... your life's vocation can't hurt come judgment day either, you know what I mean? We're not getting any younger." Her mother giggled.

"Please Mama, I'm serious."

"What's this all about Rosa? You've been a nun over ten years now. Why all the questions?"

"Well ... it's just ... I was wondering," she sighed heavily. "Do you ever wish you had grandkids?"

"Oh sure. But I'll have grandbabies, lots of them. One of these days, Frankie will find the right girl, get married, and our house will be full of kids."

"Yes Mama, I hope, but it's still not the same as your daughter giving you a grandchild. I mean, if Frankie did marry and if his wife did conceive, you and she would not have the same kind of close relationship a mother and a daughter would have. She'll turn to her mother for guidance, and you'll be left out. She'll call her mother when the baby kicks or when she starts feeling labor pains. And after the baby comes, she'll tell her mother when the baby takes its first step and when its first tooth pushes through. And what about babysitting? I'll bet you she'll ask her mother to watch the baby before she asks you. It's just not fair."

"Oh Rosalee," her mother said lovingly, "you worry too much for such a young woman. You have Frankie married off with children and already you don't like his wife. Don't worry about me. Everything will work out. God will see to it. And if He never blesses me with a grandbaby, I'll always know He blessed me with two very wonderful children who love me very much."

"Oh Mama," Rosa said enfolding her mother into her arms. "I do love you."

"I know you do, and I love you, too," she said using her finger to wipe away a single teardrop which gathered in the corner her eye. She straightened her posture at the picnic table, a bit ashamed to be caught crying in front of her daughter. "Why don't we change the subject?"

Rosa still had not found the answers she wanted to hear, but because her mother was visibly uncomfortable talking about it, she did not pursue the matter.

"What are you planning to do today?" her mother asked.

"Well, I thought after breakfast, I'd try to look up Suzy Shaffer. Do you remember her? She and Lora Cooper and I shared an apartment in college."

"Yes I remember both of them very well. They were lovely girls. What made you think about Suzy? It's been years since you've seen either of them."

"I know it has. We exchanged cards at Christmas time for a while, but I've not heard from them for several years. I guess I'd just like to see how everyone's doing. I saved the most recent address and phone number from Suzy's last card, so I thought I'd start with her. Maybe she could put me in touch with Lora."

"That's great. Come, let's go in and have breakfast then you can make your calls."

6

"Tommy!" Suzy said in a shocked tone. "What do you mean by pals don't keep secrets. I've never kept anything from you."

Tommy realized his heart had gotten ahead of his mouth again. He was not ready to reveal his theory. Not yet. He needed to come up with something fast to cover his tracks.

"Why didn't you tell me that dad was taking me camping this weekend? Do you know how embarrassed I was when Jeff told me last night that he and I and our dads were going camping this weekend? I felt like dad didn't bother to tell me because he didn't want to go."

"Is that all that's bothering you?" Suzy said somewhat relieved. "The truth is, your dad didn't find out if he could get away from the University until yesterday morning, and he didn't want to tell you until he was sure. You should have known better than to think he wouldn't want to spend time with you. If you had been home at a reasonable hour last night, your dad would have told you then. Now back to my original question ... where were you last night?"

Tommy made a weak excuse, saying he was at Jeff's house and fell asleep, but Suzy accepted it without question. He was just about to ask her to leave so he could get dressed when the phone rang. She scurried to the extension in the upstairs hallway. When she found out who it was, she took the call in the kitchen.

"Rosalee, I'm so glad you called. I take it Lora phoned you this morning."

"No," Rosalee replied, "I just thought I'd call and see how everyone was. It's been a long time?"

Suzy was dumbfounded by the call. She was hesitant to say anything to her. If Lora had not made contact with Rosa, which apparently she hadn't, then the responsibility would fall on Suzy to fill Rosa in on everything that had happened. She was skeptical about how to do this. She was certain of one thing: Rosa would never believe Kash was capable of doing any of the horrible things he had done.

"Well Rosalee," Suzy started, "you must have ESP. Lora was going to call you today. There's something the three of us need to talk about."

"This is really uncanny, because I've been thinking about the two of you for a couple of months. Is everything all right with both your families?"

"Yes, everything is fine." Suzy thought Rosa was fishing for some explanation. "Where are you now?"

"Right now I'm on leave from St. Christopher's. I'm calling from my parent's house in Huntington, West Virginia. You know, I've been having strange thoughts about Sam Kashette, as well. I think while I'm in town, I'll go over to his house and see how he's doing too."

"*NO!* You can't do that. Not until we talk to you." Suzy tried not to react, but this was all too weird: Rosa making a phone call out of the blue, not to mention expressing a desire to see Kash after all these years. The latter, however, did not take Suzy by surprise. It was no secret that Rosalee was in love with Kash, but she was a nun now, right? Didn't she take some kind of vow to love God and only God? Surely, she didn't still have feelings for the jerk.

The silence concerned Rosalee. "Suzy, are you still there? Are you okay?"

"Yes, I'm fine. Listen to me Rosalee. Don't go near Kash until the three of us get together. We've got to talk to you about what's happening with him. If I have a ticket waiting for you at the airport, can you come to Boston for a day or two?"

"When?"

"Tomorrow is Saturday ... could you come for the weekend?"

"Tomorrow? That's kind of short notice."

"I know, but it's really important. Lora lives less than an hour from here, and she doesn't work on the weekends, so she'll be free to drive up here. Clayton and Tommy are going camping tomorrow with Mr. Baker and his son, so the timing is great for the three of us to be alone. I don't mean to be so mysterious about this, but I think it would be better if we told you together, in person. Do you understand?"

"No, I don't. How am I supposed to understand if you won't give me a clue about what's going on? Does this have something to do with Kash's accident?"

"What accident?"

"My brother told me that Kash was involved in an auto accident a while back. I thought maybe your news had something to do with the accident."

Rosa felt she should have kept the bit of information about the mishap to herself, and she clearly wanted to refrain from saying anything about Kash being in prison. She had the distinct feeling she should not trust Suzy, at least not yet.

"How did the two of you get involved with Kash again after all these years, anyhow?"

"It's a long story. We'll talk everything out when you get here. Please say you'll come, Rosa?"

"I guess I have no choice if I want to know what's going on, now do I?"

"Oh thank you Rosalee. I knew you wouldn't let us down. I'll have the airline call you later to let you know what time your flight will be leaving. And please, I'm begging you, don't go anywhere near Kash. Will you promise me?"

"No I won't promise you, but I will give it some thought."

With that said, Rosalee hung up the phone.

CHAPTER TEN

To Buzz or Not to Buzz

1

The distant purring of the big jet engines rumbled outside like whistling thunder. Pittsfield airport in Massachusetts was busy this morning. People were hustling and bustling in all directions. Shrilled voices over the loud speaker announced flights and gate numbers.

Lora and Suzy were fidgety sitting on the hard row-chairs which made up the waiting area in the airport lobby. Their mood was nervous, their outlook, upbeat. Both women rose to their feet when flight 210 from Huntington was called. Gate 2 was directly in front of them.

About a dozen people came off the ramp before Rosalee finally made her way down. They were looking for a woman who was clad in a nun's habit but were surprised to find Rosa dressed in regular street clothes. In fact, she looked rather normal in the lightweight wind suit she was wearing. Although they had not seen her in 15 years, they recognized her immediately. She was a bit heavier now, but she was invariably sweet, plain Rosalee. Suzy waved her arms to get Rosa's attention.

Rosalee sized up her friends. Lora looked good, the same as she remembered but yet different. She had retained her lean lanky figure over the years. Her wholesome beauty remained noticeable. Even though she was dressed in jeans and a pullover shirt, Rosa could tell the outfit was of good quality. Her jeans had a sharp crease down the leg and the white shirt was crisp and snow-white. No more discount stores or hand-me-downs for Lora, Rosa was sure. Her posture was erect, her head held high and confident. She had become a true professional and an elegant woman. Rosa saw no evidence of aging in Lora's face.

Suzy, on the other hand, looked old in so many ways. Her hair was obviously touched up with color. Porcelain nails covered over the natural ones, probably bitten to the skin, underneath. Dyeing her hair and getting her nails done were things Suzy could easily cover up or fix, but the lines and wrinkles so evident in her face were not as easy to mask. Suzy's smile seemed to be fake, and she carried herself in a slack fashion. There was no make-up on the market that could cover up poor self-esteem and a frightened demeanor. Her eyes, however, were still the most beautiful Rosalee had ever seen, and they looked as young as the first day Rosa had met Suzy at their Kanawha State dorm room. Regardless of this beauty, the crow's feet and creases around her eyes revealed Suzy's inner worries. Dark circles showed despite the use of a cover stick. She apparently had been sleeping poorly.

Lora approached Rosa first. "Rosalee, how wonderful to see you again."

"I'm happy to see the both of you too."

Lora thought she detected something edgy in Rosalee's voice.

"How was your flight?" Suzy asked.

"I couldn't tell you. I slept through most of it. Which of you scheduled me on a flight that left at seven in the morning?"

Now Lora recognized the edgy tone: Rosalee was never much of a morning person, she remembered. "That would be Suzy," Lora said wanting to be off the hook quickly.

Rosalee directed the rest of her statement to Suzy. "I'm supposed to be on vacation, you know. Sleeping in is one of the few pleasures in life I have left."

"Sorry," Suzy said.

The three women exchanged pleasantries during the walk from the airport to the car. Once outside, away from the noisy crowd and the chatter of the airport's loud speakers, Rosalee inquired as to the importance of her visit.

"Okay guys … tell me what's so important that I had to come all the way up here. What's going on with Kash?"

"We'll talk in just a few minutes," Lora said as she waited for Suzy to open her side of the car door. "There's a little beanery not far from here. We can have something to eat and talk then. I'm sure you're hungry."

"Yes, I am a little." But then Rosa always seemed to be hungry. What other vise was a nun entitled to?

"Great," Suzy said, "it'll be like old times."

The seating arrangement, Rosa noticed, was not like old times. Suzy drove, Lora sat in front seat, and Rosalee sat in the back seat. She was not forced back there, nor was she coaxed into sitting there, it was merely implied that she would sit in the backseat. All nuns were supposed to sit by themselves in the back seat. If it had been like old times, as Suzy mentioned, they would have sat three in the front just as they had done when Suzy had her two-seat Corvette at Kanawha State. God knows there was room enough for three in the front seat of this luxury boat, but Rosa was alone in the back seat nonetheless. Suzy glanced at Rosa through the rear view mirror and smiled. Rosa rolled her eyes. She felt like sticking out her tongue to Suzy's reflection in the mirror but then resisted the temptation. It was going to be two against one this weekend, Rosa was certain.

The ride took just over ten minutes, but Rosalee felt as if it took forever to get there. It had been such a long time since she had been with real friends. Surprisingly, she was uncomfortable in their company. At the convent, the other sisters were simply roommates; in no way did it compare to the friendship she, and Lora, and Suzy had shared. After fifteen years, she found herself lost for something to talk about with them. She knew very little about their personal lives now, too little even to ask an intelligent question. She searched her memory for the name of Lora's husband but drew a blank. She was not sure what to tell them about herself either. She was certain that the boring life of a nun and the struggle she dealt with daily about whether or not to remain a nun was not something they wanted to hear about. She could only imagine what earth shattering news about Kash these two were going to drop in her lap.

At Lora's request, the hostess at Bubba's Beanery seated them at a table near the back. Rosa ordered breakfast, and Lora ordered lunch. Suzy just wanted a sweet roll and coffee. She didn't have much of an appetite these days. The waitress brought their drinks. The small talk continued. By the time the food arrived, Lora decided someone had to break the ice.

"So Rosalee, what are your plans for the rest of the summer?"

"Come on Lora. I know you didn't fly me clear up here just so I could give you my itinerary for the rest of my summer sabbatical."

"No we didn't, but we do want to thank you for coming up this weekend. I've wanted to put together a little reunion with the three of us for some time now, but I didn't want it to be under these circumstances."

"What circumstances?"

"I don't know how to tell you this, Rosa, but it's Kash."

Alarm showed in Rosa's face. "What about Kash? Is he ill? Has he been hurt?"

"No nothing like that. You see, Kash has some serious problems. He's out of control. I don't know how else to put it."

"What are you talking about? What do you mean he's out of control?"

Lora looked to Suzy for some assistance with the definition.

"Well Rosa, you see" Suzy stammered, "Kash is trying ... what I mean to say is, he's been ... well ..."

"Oh for God's sake Suzy spit it out," Rosa interrupted. The women could hear the agitation in Rosa's voice.

Rosa turned to Lora for some answers. "For the last time, what is going on with Kash, and what does it have to do with the two of you?"

"He's been harassing us," Lora explained. "For the last month or so, he's been interfering with our lives."

"Why?"

"He wants money from us."

"Money?"

"Yes, lots of money. He's pressuring us because he knows something about our past, something we never wanted anybody to know, not even each other."

"Are you saying he's blackmailing you?"

"Yes."

Rosalee smiled and shook her head. A little giggle escaped her mouth. "You guys have got to be kidding me."

"Please Rosa ... let me start at the beginning."

With that, Lora began to tell the story of how Sam Kashette had been extorting money from them. Without going into the details of her swindle and Suzy's procedure, she told Rosa about the terms of Kash's contract. She told Rosa how Kash had come to the bank to see Alex that day with the evidence in hand.

"He's invested plenty of time and effort into this, Rosa. He's dead set on getting what he wants."

Rosa was not too quick to accept the explanation. "Are you both crazy? Do you expect me to believe Kash is taking money from you to keep quiet about a secret? I can't believe that. I will never believe that. Granted, the two of you didn't part on good terms with Kash, but you'll never convince me he's been carrying around a 15-year-old vendetta. I'm sorry, but I won't believe that. Nothing you can say will make me believe that."

"I don't know whether or not he's carrying a vendetta," Suzy said, "but he was certainly out for blood when he came here to Dalton threatening me. It sure seemed like revenge was his motive. He told me what he wanted, then a few weeks later, he showed up in Boston to hit Lora with the same deal."

"What does he have on the two of you?"

"That's not important, Rosa," Lora said. The point I am trying to ..."

"Oh, I see." Rosa cut in. "We can't tell sweet innocent Rosalee what we did. It might be too much for her to handle. Is it something perverted? Maybe you're afraid it will embarrass me. Well let me fill you in on a little secret of my own. I can handle anything you two throw at me. My name may be Sister Rosa now, but I'm not the sweet, frail young girl you knew in college. I'm a grown woman who's trying to help her friends. You brought me here; let's not forget that. Is it my mission to pray you out of this mess? Is that why I'm here?" She glared at them, her eyes cold and hard, focus shifting back and forth from Lora to Suzy. They had never seen her like this before. "Damn you two. You bring me all the way out here, pour your hearts out to me, and then you won't tell me what fabrications you've come up with."

"They're not fabrications Rosa. They're real stories that affect real people and the less people who know about what happen back then, the better."

"We were only 22 years old back then. What terrible thing could either of you have done that would be worth money to keep it quiet? It was such a long time ago. How could it possibly affect your lives now?"

A pleasant waitress interrupted the conversation. Lora was never so glad to see anybody in her life. The server, Jill, judging from her nametag, inquired about refills of coffee. Lora and Suzy declined, but Rosalee accepted the refill then asked what time the bar opened.

"The bar's open now," Jill offered. "Can I get you something?"

"Yes," Rosalee answered. "I'd like a shot of Lord, please, straight up."

She wasn't being sarcastic. Lord Calvert was her whisky of choice. Rosa had only slipped off the wagon twice since going off to the convent. Her intent was only to shock these two into reality, not to drink the alcohol. She only wanted to show them the extent of her maturity. When it came to Kash, Rosa DeLucci could expose her claws and come out swinging.

Lora and Suzy were stunned by the odd request. Rosa shot a defiant stare in their direction. *Yep, here we go*, she thought, *two against one*.

"What's the problem? You two never see a nun order a drink before. I'm getting a little bored with the effects of the altar wine, so I thought I'd try something a bit more spirited. Hell Suzy, I'm surprised you didn't order a white wine spritzer. Isn't that what you high society women drink?"

"Rosa!" Suzy started.

"All right, enough." Lora tried to settle them down. "There's no need for all this sarcasm. Rosa, if I insulted you earlier, it wasn't intentional. It's just that whatever we did privately in the past doesn't really concern you."

"If what you did concerns Kash, then it concerns me, too."

To this day, Suzy could not comprehend Rosa's loyalty to this evil man, a man, who with the exception of a short-term fling in high school barely noticed her.

The waitress brought Rosa's shot. She downed it immediately, and then, before Jill could get away, ordered another one, on the rocks this time. The devil made her do it. At least that would be her defense tonight when she prayed for forgiveness to the Blessed Mother. Or maybe it was just force of habit as interpreted by the saying: *old habits die hard*. Anyway, it would be impolite not to partake when a drink was placed in front of you. For whatever reason, she had fallen off the wagon for a third time now.

The premonitions turned out to be true, just as she knew they would be. The magnetic force, which drew her to her beloved Kash, pulled with great energy. She was so angry with her old friends. She hated what they were saying even though she knew all the accusations were true. Still, it didn't make the truth any easier to accept. So she drank and maybe God would let her forget.

Suzy was outraged by Rosa's social graces or maybe her lack thereof. "Rosa, is this acceptable conduct for a woman of your esteem? I mean that's not altar wine, that's whiskey. You're going to get drunk."

"I can handle my liquor, Suzy. Don't blow a gasket." She giggled, not because she was drunk—any alcoholic will tell you they never get drunk, they merely get buzzed—but because she was tickled by the saying. "Blow a gasket … I've always wanted to say that you know. I hear my third graders say it all the time: 'don't blow a gasket Sister,'" she said in a whiney mocking voice. "As for my conduct Suzy, I don't know what's proper any more. For the last three months, I can't seem to get Sam Kashette off my mind. Now you tell me *that's* proper conduct for a woman of my esteem. My mind is all twisted. I'm riddled with self-doubt and insecurity. I'm not sure who I am or what I am. I'm not sure if I'm as happy as I can be. I'm not even sure what I want from my life, but there's one thing I'm damn sure of: I still have very deep feelings for Sam Kashette, and I don't appreciate you two making him out to be this vile terrible person that you say he's become. I've prayed for this man from the first day I entered the convent. I know my prayers have been answered too. I know our Blessed Mother has watched over him. She would never let me down, just as I would never let Kash down. I've never stopped loving him after all these years." With tears building in her eyes, she took a big gulp of the whiskey Jill had set in front of her.

"Oh Rosa, you can't be serious," Lora said.

"Oh yes, I'm very serious. I can't tell you how many times I wished I had given more thought to the way I chose to spend my life or how many times I wished I could restore what Kash and I once had."

"You didn't have anything Rosa." Suzy said, in a tone that suggested she was deeply sorry for her friend. "It was a high school crush, not love."

"I'd expect that from you, Suzy. You don't know what we had. You don't know anything about our connection, or about our inner energy, or about our attached souls."

Suzy rolled her eyes toward Lora, who shrugged her shoulders as if to say, *I have no idea what she's talking about.*

"You don't know anything about me. I was never happier than when I was with Kash. He made me feel special. Then you two came along and spoiled him. Do you know how hard it was for me to watch him take up with my two new roommates? When Lora finally broke it off with him, I thought maybe Kash and I could get back together again, but no, that didn't happen either because Suzy had to have her turn next. Whatever Lora did Suzy had to do too. You two gave him a taste of how the other half lived. You showed him what it was like on the other side of the fence. Suzy's side that had lots of money and fancy clothes and little sporty cars, and Lora's side that was smart and strong and independent. Then you both decided that he wasn't good enough for you anymore, so you threw him away. Well, he was and always will be good enough for me."

Jill passed by their table carrying three salads on a tray for the table next to theirs. Rosa threw her hand up and asked, not very politely or very quietly either, for another drink. Then on second thought, she ordered a double.

Tension built around the small table at the beanery. Suzy began a rebuttal, but Rosa threw up her hand again, this time to silence Suzy.

Rosa continued, "And now you two expect me to believe he's blackmailing you. I know him better than either of you, and he's not capable of doing something like that."

"Rosa, you don't know him anymore," Suzy cut in anyway. She would not let herself be silenced by a drunken nun. "He's not the same person he used to be. You only remember what he was like back then. It's as if you've been asleep for 15 years. You may not have changed nor have your feelings for him changed, but Kash is not the same Kash as he was back then. You have to stop living in the past. We are all grown up now; you have to grow up too."

There was some truth in the words Suzy spoke, but Rosalee pushed it aside not wanting to deal with it here, in a strange city in a public restaurant. Rosalee had never grown up because she never had to grow up. She had not experienced the circumstances that allowed young girls to mature into women. She was 22 when she entered the convent. Up to that time, she had never been loved by anyone other than family members. Jesus loved her as He loved all his children and the Blessed Mary loved her, she was sure of that, otherwise she would not have answered so many of her pleas for help. What

Rosa lacked was mortal love. Not necessarily love in a physical sense, but more an emotional nourishment that would allow her to grow and mature. She had never been married, never bore children, never had the responsibility of running a household, never really found it necessary to take care of herself. Her parents had taken care of her in her early life, and then later, the parish of St. Christopher's did everything for her. She didn't even know how to drive a car, for pity's sake. All she had left were dreams and memories, and she would be damned if Suzy or Lora were going to take either of those things away from her.

She polished off the whiskey remaining in her glass when Jill arrived with the double shot. Sipping on the new beverage, she allowed the alcohol to settle her a bit. Her eyelids sagged, but only slightly. She could feel the whiskey surge through her system; she missed the warm, calming effect of it.

In a composed even tone, she asked, "Why are you telling me this anyway? Just exactly what do you expect me to do if he is taking your money?"

"We want you to help," Lora replied. "Will you please help us, Rosalee?"

2

Wind ruffled the recently erected tents. It was suppertime at Deerfield Lake Park. Dan Baker and Clayton Whitmore selected a campsite that was close to the bathhouse but not so close to the firewood. This was the second load of wood Tommy and Jeff had carried. The boys wiped sweat from their brow; it gathered there after they walked a quarter mile twice with a bundle of wood under each arm both times. Although the sun was about to set, it still had plenty of power.

Deerfield Lake was known for its fishing; however, there were no fish in the pan at this campsite. After five hours with their lines in the water, both dads and sons had come up empty. The dads brought along other provisions for a situation like this one. They were having smoked sausage, fried potatoes, and green beans, if the black flies didn't get it first.

The boys asked to be excused while their fathers struggled to prepare supper at the primitive outdoor kitchen. Tommy and Jeff headed toward the woods. When they got to the other side, they were again near the water. They carried their shoes and socks and waded out about ten yards into the lake, where water barely reached the boys' knees. Normally if they had waded out this far into the lake, the water would have been over their heads or at least up to their necks.

Their destination was a large boulder that protruded from the water. Usually, only a foot or two of the rock would be visible, but today six feet or more stuck out. The lower portion, which was generally not exposed, was the color of rust and had a slimy feel when touched. The water level here, like most bodies of water along the east coast, was deficient in a big way.

"This is where my dad taught me to swim," Jeff explained as he and Tommy climbed on the massive slab to sit down.

"Really," Tommy said, not caring in the least where Jeff learned to swim. He had other things on his mind.

"I was about five when my dad and I started coming out here. He'd sit on this rock and I'd swim over to him."

Tommy said nothing. He was preoccupied by the sounds of nature. He listened to the chirping of the crickets, the water sloshing as it churned near the edge, and the pecking of a single woodpecker in a nearby tree. He challenged nature for an answer to one simple question: how can the rest of the world go on as usual when his whole life was crumbling around him?

"Hey Tommy, you ever smoked pot?"

Jeff's blunt question brought Tommy back to reality.

"Pot? No, I've never smoked the stuff."

Jeff reached into his pocket and produced a joint. "You wanna try some?"

"No."

"Okay, suit yourself." Jeff lit the sweet smelling cigarette. Tommy watched his friend inhale the smoke and hold it deep inside his lungs.

"What does that stuff do to you anyway?" Tommy questioned.

"It makes you feel good. It relaxes you. Sometimes when my mom's having one of her screaming fits, I like to catch a buzz. I can almost block out her voice. It sort of makes everything seem all right, you know what I'm saying?"

"Christ Jeff, how long have you been doing this shit?"

"A couple years."

"Man, I never knew. You always seemed the same to me."

"I'm not any different. When I'm high I just see things a little differently, that's all."

"You mean if I'm worried about something, getting high will make it seem better than it really is?"

"Yeah, something like that."

"Let me have a puff."

Although Tommy had seen people smoke marijuana on TV, he had never been exposed to it for real. Jeff explained how he should hit it and hold it down as long as he could. It made Tommy cough a little. After three tokes apiece, both boys were high. Tommy did feel relaxed, but the problems that plagued him were still there. The pair stared silently at the water, both wrapped up in their own buzzes.

"Hey Jeff … do you remember when we talked about my mom and the man with the cowboy hat? You said you thought my mom was having an affair with him. Did you mean that? Do you really think it could have happened?"

"Sure. I wouldn't be shocked if my mom has a booty call."

"Booty call?"

"Yeah … someone on the side, someone with no baggage. Stop and think about all the kids we know. Most of their parents are divorced which means they weren't happy together. Right? The only difference between their moms and ours is that our dads make a lot of money and our moms don't want to loose the big bucks, so they have their little booty calls on the side and stay with their husbands."

"Do you really think that's how it is?"

"Yeah, I do. Are you still bugged by that guy?"

With his mind impacted by the grass, Tommy felt as though he could take on the world. He felt strong and confident that he could resolve the problem with Kash.

"Yeah, I'm still bugged by him. His name is Kash."

"Wow man! How'd you find that out?"

Tommy entrusted his secret to Jeff. He told him the whole story from top to bottom: how he had followed his mother to Boston, how she had met with Kash, how she had made sexual advances toward him, and how he had followed Kash to the motel. He told Jeff how frightened he had been, not only frightened of this man coming between his parents, but also scared of having to handle it all on his own.

"But you know what Jeff? I think I can do it. I really think I can meet this Kash face to face and make him leave us alone."

"Is that what you plan to do?"

"Yes. I have to get more information first then wait for the right time."

Tommy wanted to hear once again that his secret was safe with Jeff, so Jeff reassured him one more time that he would tell no one. The sun was going down faster now, and dusk was quickly settling in. Tommy and Jeff decided it was time to get back to camp. They performed the task of wading through the water, this time in reverse. After getting back into their shoes, they started through the woods. With each step they took, little twigs, and leaves, and brush crackled under their feet. Without rain, the whole world was dry and dying just like Tommy's family would dry up and die if Kash was not stopped.

As they neared the campsites, Tommy could smell food being cooked from all directions. His mouth watered.

"Man, am I hungry," he said picking up his pace.

"Oh yeah, I forgot to tell you. Pot gives you the munchies. You're going to eat like this is your last meal."

When the two boys rejoined their fathers, they were told supper was ready. Jeff opened a bag of corn chips, but Tommy's hand was the first to dive in. He was famished. Both boys filled their plates with healthy portions and began to dig in at once.

"Tommy ... you're eating green beans," his father commented.

"Yeah, dad I know. They taste different out here."

"See Clayton," Dan Baker said, "I told you getting these boys out into the woods would be good for them."

"Hey, I guess you're right. It's certainly done something for Tommy's appetite."

Tommy and Jeff smiled at each other.

After they had eaten their fill, the boys went to the bathhouse to get a shower. When they returned, the men had built a small campfire in the same ring that had served to cook their supper. The fathers and sons pulled up chairs around the blaze. Tommy listened while Clayton and Dan talked about tomorrow's agenda.

The flickering orange fire devils mesmerized Tommy. He looked at his father then back to the fire. He had never realized how much he admired his dad. He wished Kash were dead. The false, pot-induced sense of courage was slowly dwindling away along with his buzz, but he knew that he could revive this same courage anytime he wanted now. With a good buzz on, he was confident he could get Kash for what he had done to his family.

Dan Baker reviewed the next day's events with the boys. They were going to get up just before daylight and fish the lake until noon. Then they would come back, fix lunch, and tear down camp. Clayton wanted to be back in Dalton around two o'clock. With tomorrow's schedule understood, the teenagers retired to their tent.

Settled in his sleeping bag, Tommy listened to the hushed breathing of his friend, already fast asleep. He rolled over on his back and propped his head up on his wrists. He thought about Kash, about how Kash was tearing his family apart, and he anticipated the face-off between himself and the meddler. Tommy had no idea as he fantasized about the meeting, that he would be the only one responsible for tearing his family apart.

3

Rosa sat stone-faced on the couch in Suzy's colorful peach living room. It had been over seven hours since they had left the beanery, and in that time, Rosalee had said only a few words. She drank three more drinks at the restaurant and four from Suzy's bar. A normal person would have been totally inebriated, yet Rosa's outcome was a bit different: she was angry. Lora could feel the tension between Rosa and Suzy. Suzy always seemed to know how to push Rosa's buttons. Since Rosa never did answered Lora's plea for help, Lora took the opportunity to ask Rosalee again, while Suzy was in the kitchen fixing a quick dinner.

"Rosa, will you help us?"

Rosa turned to Lora. Her lips were pursed. She asked, "Why should I help? Let's just assume I believe that Kash is blackmailing you. Maybe if I knew the whole story, then I would be willing to get involved. If I had some idea of what he's holding over you and why you did whatever it is you did, I would have a clearer picture of the situation. The two of you don't trust me with the whole story. If Kash is holding something that bad over your head, you need to seek help from the police, not me."

"All right, if we tell you exactly what we did that caused all of this to happened, will you help us then?"

"No promises, but your chances will be a lot better if I know the truth."

"Okay, let me talk to Suzy about it."

Lora found Suzy at the stove flipping grilled cheese sandwiches and warming tomato soup. She smiled when Lora entered the kitchen.

"I thought the soup would help warm us. Since the sun has gone down, the air's gotten a bit chilly."

"Soup's fine, Suzy."

"Any word out of our silent monk?"

"Suzy please, don't be a smartass."

"Well I can't believe the way she's acting. She's a nun. Nuns are supposed to be chaste, and pure, and kind, and loving. She's been nothing but cold and mean and drunk. She's supposed to be our friend, remember. We never should have asked her to come here. I was afraid she still had feelings for Kash, and I was afraid she wouldn't believe us, and now I'm certain she's not willing to help us."

"Actually, she is willing to give it some thought if ..."

"She is?"

"If we tell her what Kash is holding over us."

"Oh come on Lora. You're not suggesting ... yes you are suggesting. I can see it in your face. You want to tell her the rest of the story."

"Yes, I think we should."

"Well I'll have no part of it."

"She has a right to know. We should have told her from the start. I can't justify asking her to help us if she knows only half truths."

"Damn it Lora. Do you know how hard it was for me to tell you what I'd done? You're a doctor, a woman of science. Now you expect me to tell a nun, a woman of God, a woman of moral standards, even if she doesn't seem to be living up to them today. Have you given any thought to how you're going to tell her you were a drug dealer? And one who stole her drug supply, to boot. She's not just Rosalee our roommate anymore; she's Sister Rosa a nun."

"It won't be easy but it's our only choice. We don't have any proof to show her, and without letting her in on what we've done, we can't even tell her what evidence he has. The only thing she wants in return is to know why. Why he's doing this to us. We've got to tell her. I'll tell her for you if you'd rather not go through it again."

"Did it ever occur to you that once she knows what we did, she'll be less likely to help?"

"No, I don't think that's the case. I think if we lay our cards out on the table, she'll come around."

"Fine, you tell her, but prepare yourself for a good long lecture from *the holy one*."

"We're doing the right thing, Suz. You'll see."

"Okay, it's your ballgame," Suzy said while putting the soup and grilled cheese on the table. "These sandwiches are done. Call her, and we'll eat while *you* talk."

They assembled around Suzy's oak table in the kitchen. As they ate grilled cheese sandwiches and sipped cups of tomato soup, Lora went into the long scenario about the predicaments they had gotten into some two decades ago. She began with her story and ended with Suzy's

Rosalee, much to Suzy's surprise, listened without saying a word. By the time the threesome had finished their chocolate moose, the stories had been told.

Rosa shook her head when she finally spoke. "I can't believe the mess you two are tangled up in." Everything had happened right under her nose back then, and she never saw any of it. Maybe she really was simple and naïve like Suzy said. She sighed heavily. "What makes you think I can help?"

"Because Kash trusts you," Lora replied.

"What do you want me to do, talk him out of this?"

"Exactly." Again Lora spoke. "He'll listen to you. Make him see that what he's doing is wrong."

"Please Rosa," Suzy said, "my marriage depends on it."

"What kind of evidence does he have?" Rosa asked.

"The kind that will prove he's telling the truth." Suzy answered.

Rosa was quiet for a few seconds. In her mind, she weighed the pros and cons of the situation. The girls were telling the truth, of that much Rosa was sure, but Kash must have a good reason for doing what he was doing. Suzy and Lora were not telling her everything; they were still holding something back. There was more to the picture; she could feel it in her gut.

"What about coming clean with the truth? Tell your husbands. I'm sure they'll get over it," Rosa asked, fishing for more information.

"We considered that," Lora said, "but there are people other than our husbands involved. Kash could show the dispensing tickets to the authorities, and I could go to jail. If Suzy's abortion were to be announced, the press would have a free-for-all. She and Clayton would both be ruined."

"Do you really think people would react that way? Maybe they wouldn't even believe Kash."

Suzy smiled at Rosa, a genuine smile. She truly had no desire to fight with her anymore. "Oh honey, you are so naive. Don't ever underestimate the public's appetite for a good scandal. They'll eat it up. Take my word for it."

"I don't know about this, guys. I don't know if I can help. It's been a long time since I've seen Kash."

"Yes, it has been," Suzy started, "and again I want to warn you: he's not the same person you remember from school. He's totally different."

"Different how?"

"He's changed, Rosa. I don't know how to explain it. He has this evil look about him or something. He's a little bit off—a little on the wacky side. Here's a good example. We were in the middle of a conversation, the day he came to the Crisis Center, and all of a sudden, he starts to talk to himself. He was reciting some kind of nursery rhyme. He was whispering, but I could make out some of the words. It was definitely a nursery rhyme. He did the same thing at the park just the other day. He wasn't making any sense."

"Oh come now, Suzy. Saying a nursery rhyme doesn't make someone crazy. You've been watching too many horror movies. What do you mean by him having an evil look?"

Lora interceded. "It's not so much his look as it is his actions. He's become mean and manipulative. His attitude is cocky and egotistical. The way I remember it, Kash was a lover, a comedian, the life of the party. He loved being around women and getting attention from them. He may have been a jerk at times, but he was always a gentleman. He became violent with me on two different occasions since he's come back into our lives. Can you ever remember Kash being disrespectful to a woman?"

Rosa lowered her head. She was familiar with Kash's darkness—she had lived it. Embarrassment prevented her from looking into Lora's face.

"He's got a wicked air about him," Suzy picked up now where Lora left off. "He's smug and arrogant. He enjoys degrading other people. He scares the hell out of me. Evil is the best adjective I can think of to describe him."

Rosa shot up from her chair. Two against one was getting old. "I don't have to stay here and listen to this. You two make Kash sound like the devil himself. If there's a villain in this whole story, it's you and Lora. You're telling me I don't know Kash anymore. What about the two of you? I thought I knew you girls too. Dear God in Heaven I lived with you for four years, and I didn't have a clue that either of you were unhappy with yourselves. You would think in that length of time I would have known everything about you, but today I see I hardly knew who you were."

"You're blowing things all out of proportion," Lora said.

"Am I? I assured myself that if you confided in me I would not judge you no matter what you told me you had done. It's not my place to judge, but if you're going to be so quick to judge Kash, then let's take a look at your slates.

"My God Lora, I admired you so much for the way you helped your mother and the way you put yourself through school. I admired the sacrifices you made for your education. I was in awe of you. Now you tell me you were selling drugs because you didn't have enough money—not money for essentials: food, books, tuition—money for frills so you could pamper yourself. All I can see at this point is a greedy woman.

"And you Suzy ... I envied you. Your parents had all the money in the world. You always had beautiful clothes and everything you wanted. I would look at you sometimes and wish we could have traded places. I used to wonder what it would feel like to have everything handed to me, but in the end, I'm glad I didn't, because I see that by not earning what you possessed, you never learned to appreciate what you had and you never learned how to give. By killing that unborn fetus, the only message you send to me is selfish. You acted completely ungrateful and selfish. God blessed you with a child, even though it was a child conceived out of wedlock, and what did you do? You threw it back in His face like a spoiled rich kid who was not satisfied with a gift. Was Kash's baby not good enough for you?"

"Now just hold on there, Sister Rosa." Suzy was not willing to take abuse, not in her own home anyway. "Don't you dare come off as the almighty one. What kind of Holy Roller are you? You're supposed to be a nun. You drink like a fish, and you've been unfaithful to your vows. Doesn't that wedding ring on your finger symbolize a marriage to God? How can you be married to God and carry a torch for Kash at the same time? Isn't that adultery or some other kind of sin?"

"Oh Suzy, you're splitting hairs."

"I'm not splitting anything. I'm just trying to show you that nobody's perfect. We've all done things we wished we hadn't done."

Rosalee ignored Suzy's explanation. "I don't want to argue with you anymore. I've got a terrible headache, and I'm very tired. If I'm still welcome to stay the night, could you please show me to my room?"

Suzy shook her head and said, "Oh Rosalee you're impossible. Of course you're still welcome. I'm putting you in the guestroom. Come on, I'll show you where it is."

Lora knew it was going to be tough to convince Rosalee that Kash was not Prince Charming, but she had no idea Rosalee would spring to Kash's defense so readily or so boldly. She expected some fight out of her, but she never dreamed Rosa would be this stubborn. They had overcome one obstacle, though: Rosa now believed Kash was blackmailing them. Half the battle was over. If only they could make her understand how drastically Kash had changed.

Lora was shocked at Rosa's attitude and behavior, not just because she was a woman of religion but also because the Rosalee from Kanawha State had always been timid and shy—never outspoken or this forward about her feelings. Of course, they had never bad-mouthed Sam Kashette back then, either. There was no doubt that Rosa was still in love with him. If she had known that, Lora never would have asked her to come to their aid.

Suzy slipped into the kitchen. She looked at Lora through disappointed eyes. "Well I guess I blew that. You can't call the Pope an atheist and expect him to pray you into heaven."

Lora put a sympathetic arm around her friends shoulder. "It's not your fault. I don't think she was going to help us in any event."

"Maybe so, but insulting her didn't help matters," Suzy said. "She asked me to take her to church in the morning. I'll try apologizing. Do you want to come with us? We may need a referee."

"No, if you don't mind, I'll stay behind. Praying may not be a bad idea, but it's been so long since I've seen the inside of a church, I'm afraid it'll topple down on us all."

They laughed at the thought.

"I've put you in Tommy's room for the night. Is that okay?"

"That's fine. I'm about ready for bed now. Can I help you with anything before I go up?"

"No, everything's done that's going to get done tonight. Good night Lora."

"Good night Suzy."

Lora walked through the kitchen archway. She turned back and peeked around the corner. "And by the way, thanks for trusting my judgment. I'm not even sure I trust my instincts very much these days."

4

Sister Rosa attended noon Mass with Suzy. They sat in the third pew from the front. Normally Rosa liked to sit close to the altar, but today she felt uncomfortable, almost unwelcome. She knelt to pray.

The burning impulse she sensed from Kash's soul to hers always blazed in church, but today it could have scorched her dress. Her instinct told her to pray for Kash and pray diligently because the trouble he was into was just beginning, but she had a more critical issue to take care of first. She prayed, "Dear Jesus, I'm going to bypass Mary this one time and ask directly for Your support and assistance. I feel like a bit of a hypocrite soliciting You for help when my friends have asked for my help, and I've turned them down, but You've got one bewildered, guilt-ridden servant on Your hands. My feelings for Sam Kashette are genuine, as are my feelings for You and Your work, but I don't know how to make the choice. You know, sitting here looking at all the families sitting together makes me realize it was not so long ago that I attended Mass as a young adult with my family. I fantasized about hearing mine and Kash's name announced for the banns of matrimony. Did You know that? Of course You did. You know everything. It's very hard for me to admit this here, in Your house, but I have to get everything out into the open. I'm begging You to give Kash a second chance. If these things my friends say are true, then he needs Your help in a bad way, and please Jesus, give me a second chance as well. I've decided to put this whole affair in Your hands. Not only the situation with Kash or the favor asked by Lora and Suzy, but also my life—my entire life. You know what's best for all parties concerned. You'll guide me to do the right thing. I know You will. And Jesus, if You should decide that my life would be better spent as laity, would You consider giving me and Kash a second chance at love?"

Rosa sat back in the pew. Smiling at Suzy, she reached out for her hand and clutched it tightly in hers. *Let the cards fall where they may.*

5

The car ride back to Suzy's house after Mass was quiet. Suzy searched her mind for something to say—anything that would end the silence. Rosa had made the first move by grabbing her hand in church; now it was Suzy's turn to break the ice.

"This is the longest light," she said as they approached a busy intersection. She slowed for the stop light. "Look Rosa, I'm sorry for what I said last night. I didn't mean any of it. Will you forgive me?"

Rosa glanced her way, "I'm not the one to forgive you, Suzy. You need your forgiveness from God."

"You don't get it, do you Rosalee? I believe God has forgiven me. Not only did He forgive me, He challenged me to help others, so they don't make the same mistake as I did. I answered his challenge. I can only hope you'll answer the challenge you've been given."

"Don't start again. I don't want to think about any of this now. I called the airline last night and reserved an earlier flight for today."

"Why?"

"I just want to go back to West Virginia. I wish I had never made this trip. If the flight change insults you or Lora, it wasn't meant to, but by that same token, I don't want to be insulted by having to listen to any more nonsense about Kash. You have made him sound like a mad man, possessed by revenge and driven by the almighty buck." Rosa knew her words were true but was not ready to accept it as truth just yet.

The remainder of the ride was again silent. When they arrived at the house, Rosa and Suzy could see Lora, still in her nightshirt, through the kitchen window. She was fixing eggs. The clock on the stove showed 1:05. Her flight was scheduled to leave at 2:15. Rosa was sure Suzy and Lora had planned to use the rest of the day to sway her in their direction—to try and change her mind about talking to Kash. She hoped one of them would not be too upset with her to take her to the airport.

Lora poured two more cups of coffee when she saw Suzy and Rosa approach the kitchen door. "Just in time folks, the eggs are ready. I hope you don't mind Suz, but I made myself at home like you told me to do."

"No, I don't mind at all. I want you both to feel comfortable in my house."

But Rosa felt far from comfortable. In fact, she felt about as welcome as an ant at a picnic. The bickering had stopped, but it was still two against one. Even though Suzy apologized for the way she talked to Rosa last night, Rosalee remained uneasy. She suggested the late service, hoping she could keep to herself in the guestroom until it was time to leave. Suzy turned to Rosa. "Come on Rosa, Lora cooked the eggs over easy, just the way you like them."

Rosa smiled at Lora and pulled up a chair at the table. Lora finished buttering the toast before joining the other two.

"Look Lora, you might as well know," Rosa started, "I called the airline last night and got an earlier flight back home. Please don't take it personally."

"How much earlier?"

"2:15 this afternoon."

"Oh Rosa, that's just over an hour. You weren't supposed to leave until seven this evening. We've hardly had a chance to talk. I didn't want our reunion to turn out this way. We fought all day yesterday. Please, won't you reconsider? I'd really like to visit with you a bit longer."

"No, I'm sorry. I have to get back to my family. This is the first trip I've made home in several years, and I was only there a couple days when you asked me to come here."

"Are you sure we can't change you mind," Lora inquired.

Rosa shook her head. "No, I want to go home."

The three women chatted while they finished their brunch. Suzy turned the radio on to a classic rock station. They washed up the few soiled dishes, singing "Gimme Three Steps" along with Lynyrd Skynyrd. The mood had lightened somewhat. They talked about memories brought back by the old songs. A popular snappy tune from the early 70s came over the airwaves. Suzy turned the volume up while they accompanied Bette Midler in "Boogie-Woogie Bugle Boy from Company B." Soon the three could not resist moving their bodies and bobbing their heads until finally they formed a triangle and began to dance spiritedly. Lora was the better dancer of the group (dancing was free at old Pathetic Jokes, so she had lots of time to practice). She shuffled her feet and spun around and clapped her hands to the rhythm just like people used to do on "Bandstand." Suzy and Rosa attempted a little jitterbug step, holding hands and pulling each toward the other then back again. The moves were clumsy—they had trampled each other's feet several times—but it was fun nonetheless. They bellowed out the tune so loudly, poor old Bette could barely be heard. When the song ended, they huddled together, arms around each other and laughed breathlessly, only to be startled by a male standing in doorway of the elegant kitchen.

"Clayton, you scared us to death," Suzy said as she kissed her husband.

Clayton laughed, "Sorry if I spooked you, but I wasn't about to pass up the opportunity to get a 70s dance lesson."

Tommy came in carrying a string of three fish and some of the camping gear. Suzy took her two guys by the hand and led them to her guests.

"Clayton, you remember Lora, don't you?"

"Sure do. Good to see you again, Lora."

Suzy continued, "This is our other roommate, Rosalee. Rosalee, this is my husband, Clayton. And girls, this is my handsome son, Tommy. Tommy, this is Rosalee DeLucci and Lora Jordan. They were my roommates in college. I haven't seen them in 15 years."

Everyone shook hands and talked, but Tommy was not as friendly as he could have been. He excused himself and hurried off to his room. The others moved to the living room.

"So Lora, what's Alex been doing?" Clayton asked.

"Alex is playing executive banker this weekend. He's going to be a very busy fellow for the next few months. I'm sure you've heard about the merger between First National and Second National Banks."

"Yes I did," Clayton said.

"There's a lot of work with the merger, and Alex was asked to make a presentation to the new board of directors."

"Presentation!" Clayton exclaimed. He smacked his head with the palm of his hand indicating he had forgotten something. He turned to his wife sitting next to him on the couch. "It completely slipped my mind."

Suzy looked puzzled. "What slipped your mind Clayton?"

"Honey, I'm sorry to spring this on you, but I forgot to mention it before we left for the weekend. We've been asked to give a presentation on Tuesday afternoon. Are you free?"

"Yes, I think so."

"I'm sorry for the short notice, but I was concentrating on this weekend with Tommy and totally forgot about it. Can you prepare a lecture by then?"

"Well, I'll try. What's the subject?"

"Abortion." Clayton placed a loving hand on Suzy's knee. Talking to Rosa and Lora he continued, "No one takes a stronger stand on the abortion issue than my wife. If you've ever heard one of her speeches, you'd know what I mean. She's powerful and persuasive—really talks from the heart. She's so moving she can pull you right out of the pro-choice movement. No one understands the value of life better than Suzy. Every baby deserves the chance to be born, and no one says that better than my wife does. Right, Hon?"

Suzy remained speechless. She looked at Rosa and Lora, who looked back at her through sorrowful eyes. Suzy started to cry and ran directly upstairs. Within seconds, they heard the slam of the bedroom door.

Clayton watched the episode in astonishment. "What the hell was that about?"

Lora quickly jumped in to cover her friend's tracks.

"Clayton, don't take it personally. You know Suzy believes she's going through menopause. Being a doctor, I've seen some cases where women react emotionally for no reason at all."

"No disrespect Lora, but you're a neurologist, not a gynecologist. I think something else is troubling her."

"Nothing is troubling her. I do know about these things," she said in defense of her profession. "Menopause is not only physical, it's very much psychological. In an hour or so, she'll be fine. Take my professional advice on this one."

"All right, I'll take you at your word. I wasn't trying to say you didn't know medicine; I was only trying to say I know my wife better than you do, but apparently, I don't. This is not the first time something like this has happened. Sometimes I catch her crying and when I ask her what's wrong, she says nothing then she wants me to hold her. For the last few weeks, she's been insecure and nervous. Some days she's actually jumpy."

"That's all perfectly normal for what she's going through. Before long, this will all be over and she'll be the old Suzy again. I promise you."

"Do you think it's safe for me to go up and see how she's doing, or should I give her some privacy?"

"I think she would want you to be with her. Just hold her Clayton, and tell her you love her, and reassure her that you'll always be there for her no matter what."

"Okay."

With that, Clayton Whitmore ascended the steps to check on Suzy. Lora and Rosalee were left alone in the living room.

"Lora, what just happened here?" Rosa asked. "She was fine a few minutes ago. We talked about her abortion last night, and she didn't flip out like that."

"She's not threatened by us. We're not the one she's afraid of loosing. Do you see now why she's so frightened? Clayton would be the laughing stock of town if it were ever to come out that his wife had an abortion. Suzy is afraid Clayton would view it as an 18-year-old lie. Everything she has ever said about terminating a pregnancy will be thrown back at her. She would become an outcast in the press and in her women's groups. She'd never get through it. I'm worried about her, really worried. She could be headed for a breakdown. I've got to get these threats behind her and the only way I know to do that is to get back the evidence Kash has on her. You were our last hope."

Here we go again: two against one, Rosa thought, but said nothing. She sure could use a drink—maybe in the lounge at the airport, if she could dump whichever roommate would be taking her there. Instead, she went upstairs to get her overnight bag from the guestroom.

Upon her return, Rosa and Lora were preparing to leave for the airport when Suzy came down the steps. She stopped on the last one, just stood there, and held on to the banister. Her swollen red eyes appeared to be saying she was embarrassed about the episode. Suzy could always say so much with those big, dark eyes. She turned her attention toward Rosa. Without saying a word, Rosa knew what she was asking. She replied, "I'll think about it."

Suzy ran to Rosa and held her close. She whispered, "Thank you so much. If you can pull this off, you will have saved my marriage. I'll call you in a few days."

"No," Rosa said, "I'll call you. I only said I would think about it; I didn't say I would do it. I'll be in touch."

CHAPTER ELEVEN

Mind Games

1

Kash twisted his head from side to side; his sleep was very edgy despite the amount of vodka he had consumed last night. In his dream, he had been a little boy again, maybe three or four years old. He was in a very small space, but because it was totally dark, it felt even more like the walls were closing in. The little-boy Kash had been frightened because he was alone in there, even though he could hear music and voices from the rooms on the other side of the door. He whimpered, but quietly, because he knew what would happen if his sobs were to be heard. He began to explore the room; the more he turned his head the more disoriented he became. Darkness could play tricks on the mind—and also on the eyes. The blob hanging directly above him mirrored a great monster. It appeared to be moving in his direction. He started to cry harder and worse, louder. Even over the music, he could hear footsteps getting closer and closer. The doorknob squeaked as it was being turned from the outside. The young Kash was terrified, more so of what or who was outside of the door than of the blob inside hanging over him. He tried to hush his whine and wipe the tears from his face, but it was too late, the door had opened and ...

The young woman lying next to Kash did not so much as stir when Kash mumbled in his sleep. His eyes darted open. His body shot up stiff to a full sitting position. Still the young woman in Kash's bed remained immobile. His heart thumped rapidly against his bulky chest. Sweat covered his face and neck—he brushed it away with his hand. As he began to regain consciousness, he realized the need for coffee, not to mention a couple of aspirin. He had a bad hangover.

Kash stumbled clumsily to his feet. He looked at the Inferior sleeping soundly in his bed. Her blaze orange hair feathered across the white pillowcase looked like a sun setting over a snow-capped mountain. He tried to remember her name. It was different, sort of southern. Was it Trixie? Or perhaps Pixie? No, he remembered now, it was Dixie. He had finally done his redhead.

After slipping a pair of jeans over his nakedness, Kash went to the kitchen where he plugged in the percolator. He looked out the window to find the weather overcast and gloomy. Rain clouds looked like they would discharge any second, but he knew from prior experiences that although the day may start off looking like rain, the clouds would dissipate as quickly as they formed. No rain had reached the ground yet this summer. His disposition matched the current weather. He, too, felt gloomy in spite of his sudden wealth.

He had not spent all the money yet, but that was of no concern to Kash because he should be receiving another payment before too long. Money, however, seemed worthless without someone to share it with him. Dixie was not the kind of woman with whom he wanted a long-term relationship—neither was the Inferior he had brought home last night or the one the night before that—but she had served her purpose well. He figured money may not buy everything, but it would help him get by until the right woman finally came along.

When he opened the kitchen door, he discovered the outside air to be chilly for the first week of July. He watched Gabby walk through the yard toward his house. He poured two cups of coffee and greeted her with one when she reached the door.

"Hey Gabby. What brings you out so early this morning?"

"Early … it's eleven o'clock. I've been waiting all morning to see some signs of life over here. I'd like to borrow your power drill."

"Sure Gab. What are you into this morning?"

"I bought some vinyl blinds for the upstairs windows. I need to drill a few holes to set the brackets in place."

"Let me get my shoes. The drill's in the shed outside. I'll help you hang them if you want."

"Are you sure it's no trouble?"

"No trouble at all. You know I'd do anything for you, Gabby."

Kash sat at the kitchen table lacing his shoes when Dixie entered the room. She was wearing a tee shirt that came down barely far enough to cover her navel. The name of a local bar was stenciled on the shirt across her chest. She wore nothing else, save for thin white bikini underwear, through which a patch of bright red hair was visible. She smiled at him. He returned the gesture with a piercing glare that gave her cold chills.

"Go back upstairs," Kash said sternly. "I'll be up in a minute. And for God's sake, get some clothes on."

"What's wrong with the clothes … ?"

"Go … now!"

"But Kash, I just wanted to get …"

"Get out of here. Go back upstairs. Christ girl, I'm glad you're better at spreading your legs than you are at taking orders."

Dixie swung her head around and stomped up the steps.

"And make the bed while you're up there," he yelled to her as an afterthought.

Kash turned to Gabby. "Give me a few minutes. I'll bring the drill over and give you a hand."

"That's okay. I don't want to bother you."

"It's no bother, Gabby, just let me get rid of the whore first."

"Look Kash, you're obviously very busy with women these days. She's the third one you brought home this week."

"What do you do, stay up all night watching out the window? Maybe it's not such a good idea to put up blinds. I wouldn't want anything to obstruct your view."

"Kash!" Gabby was hurt by his sarcastic tone.

"Don't you have anything better to do than spy on me?"

"I've never spied on you. I care about you, is all. What's gotten into you?"

"Nothing's gotten into me. The number of women I bring into my house is none of your damn business."

"Don't you think your being a bit foolish by sleeping with so many different women? With all the venereal diseases out there and now AIDS … I hope your using protection."

"Please, I don't need a lecture from a washed-up, old school teacher like you. I'm 38- years-old. I think I know how to take care of myself."

"Not too well apparently. Look at you, your color is terrible. I know you're not eating right." She looked toward the corner where a garbage can was heaped with semi-crushed beer cans. "And how much are you drinking these days. I'll bet there are two cases of empties in the garbage."

"I have a few drinks at night before I go to bed. It's no big deal. I haven't been sleeping well. The beer helps me relax."

"It's no wonder you don't sleep well worrying about what disease you'll pick up from the women you bring into this house."

"It has nothing to do with women. It's the dream. A nightmare I guess you could say."

"What kind of nightmare?"

"A weird one. I'm a little kid, and I'm locked in some kind of small room. It's dark and I'm scared. Every time I start to cry someone opens the door, but instead of feeling comforted because someone is rescuing me, I become even more frightened."

Gabby instincts kicked in. She wondered what the dream meant and she was concerned it would eventually affect Kash's mental stability. "When the door opens, who's on the other side?" she asked.

"I don't know. I always wake up just before."

"Oh," Gabby said in a nonchalant manner.

She followed Kash outside to the shed in the back yard. Taking the drill in hand, she reassured Kash that she didn't need any help with her morning project and then proceeded toward her house.

Kash went back through his kitchen door and upstairs to the bedroom. Dixie was fully dressed now and in the process of making the bed. Rather than speak when he entered the room, she simply glared at him and busied herself with the bedding. Kash went to the nightstand and removed several bills from his wallet. He laid them on the bed in front of Dixie.

"What's that for?"

"Last night."

"Kiss my ass." Dixie threw a pillow at Kash—the one she was about to tuck under the spread—hitting his left shoulder. He snickered.

"Do you think I am some kind of whore?" she said. "I don't take money from any man. I came here last night because I wanted to have a good time, and I did, but this morning you're certainly not the same man I came home with last night."

"Sorry if I insulted you darlin'. I just didn't want you to think you weren't being compensated for your trouble."

"You're a pompous ass. How dare you humiliate me by thinking I would sleep with you for money. You're nothing but a beast—a worthless piece of shit. You may have to pay for sex Kash, but I don't."

Dixie flung her large purse over her arm. She wadded up the money in her hand and hurled it at Kash's face. When he started to chuckle, she shouted, "Bite me!" and swept herself through the door and out of the house.

"Bitch!" Kash muttered, "You're just like the Inferiors."

He remade the bed. Kash learned along time ago, if he wanted something done right, he should do it himself.

Gabby was in her upstairs window preparing to hang her new blinds. She watched as the voluptuous redhead emerged from Kash's house. She had never heard Kash talk to a young lady in the tone he took this morning. Kash was always a polite man. Why was he so cruel to this girl, and why had he become so defensive when Gabby questioned his relationships? He had never so much as raised his voice to her before today, much less call her *a washed-up old school teacher.* She was curious if he had taken this same attitude with other women as well. She wondered if there was a connection between his behavior this morning and the nightmare. Gabby tried to unconcern herself with Kash's dream, but the truth was, she was extremely interested in the nightmare. Could it be that his childhood was trying to unlock itself through his sleep world? *No,* she thought, *Kash is a good boy. He's just having a bad day is all. Maybe the redhead had provoked him somehow. It would explain why he talked to her the way he did. Yes, that had to be it.* She was sure her imagination was running wild again.

2

Rosalee brushed her hair in front of the bedroom mirror. Using a curling iron, she hoped to add a smidgen of body to her otherwise limp, lifeless hair. She was nervous about seeing Kash again after all these years. She had gone to see him last night, but when she reached his house, she saw Kash escorting a redhead inside. She really hoped the redhead wasn't the current Mrs. Sam Kashette. The thought of Kash being married never occurred to her, but surely, if he were married somebody would have told her when she called home or when one of them answered her letters. But then again, nobody bothered to tell her he had an accident, killed someone, and went off to jail. She wanted to ask Frankie about it, but she knew what his reaction would be. She did not want to spark any suspicion in case she did decide to help her old roommates, which would mean she would have to see Kash several times while she was home.

Glancing over her image in the mirror and being comfortable with the way she looked, she headed downstairs. Her mother and Frankie were in the living room.

"Come Rosa, sit with us and digest that big dinner," Mrs. DeLucci said.

"No, I can't right now, Mama. I'm going out for a walk."

Frankie looked at her skeptically. "You be careful walking by yourself. Try to be home by dark."

"Frankie, you worry too much. If I go somewhere and I'll be out past dark, I'll call you for a ride home, okay?"

God, she wished she had learned to drive.

Sam Kashette lived only a short distance from the DeLucci's house. Rosa walked briskly down the narrow streets of her small hometown. Up the hill on Water Street, down the other side, a shortcut through an empty field, two blocks on Sterling Avenue, and she was there. She slowed her pace as she approached the old white house.

She held her left hand out in front of her and stared at her ring finger. The presence of God in her life meant so much to her. The mind-boggling thoughts came back again. With unanswered feelings still pursuing, her conscience tugged and pulled her in different directions. She turned back toward the empty field and walked quickly through the overgrown grass almost as if someone were chasing her. Not being ready to face this dilemma was something Rosa expected. Filled with both guilt and anticipation, she continued to walk in the opposite direction of the Kashette house.

She made a left off Sterling onto Harrison. There she passed Gina Bartoni's old home place and paused a moment to remember how many times they had played in the front yard as children, and how many days they had sat on the porch talking as teenagers, and how many nights they had spent together in Gina's bedroom gossiping or looking at fashion magazines or fantasying about their dream houses and their dream lives with their dream husbands and children. Kash had always been the central character in Rosa's fantasy. She imagined herself and Kash as the perfect family, having plenty of love, money, friends, and plenty of kids, too. At least four of them, each named after one of their relatives. Teenage pipe dreams were just that—dreams. Recalling them as an adult, seemed corny compared to the way Rosa experienced real life.

She walked aimlessly now, not really sure where her feet would take her. On the other side of a small blind knoll at the end of Church Street, was Cottage Avenue, and the highlight of Cottage Avenue should have been Cole's Pool, but it was missing. In its place was a small housing development. All the summer days she had spent at that swimming pool and now, it was gone. She and her girlfriends would lay out towels in the grass—always in the sunniest spot—and grease themselves with oily suntan lotion to lay for hours and bake, hoping for the perfect shade of brown and no tan lines. She could almost smell coconut tanning lotion and the pungent smell of chlorine.

Back then, the pool had been enclosed within a nine-foot high chain-link fence. The boys who were not inside swimming would gather just outside the fence under shade trees to talk and smoke cigarettes and watch the girls. Rosa could all but see them now.

On the particular day Rosa remembered, Kash had been on the outside of the fence. Usually, he only came in to swim on really hot days. This day was a bit overcast and only moderately warm. It was mid-season and Rosa's tan was dark, which was an effortless achievement, given the natural hue of her olive skin. Emerging from the water at the deep end, she spotted Kash, who was leaning against the fence. His arms were raised level with his head, and his fingers were wrapped between the links. He looked so good Rosa could have fainted. Climbing the ladder out of the pool, she sucked in her tummy and pushed out her chest, shot a flirty smile his way, and waved.

"Hey Rosalee," he called to her.

She had not intended to go to him unless he had called, and since he did, she ran toward the fence where he stood.

"Hi Kash. You comin' in to swim today?"

"Maybe later," then he winked at her.

She could have dropped right there. For years through school, she had kept her feelings for him locked deep inside her heart. Only her best friend, Gina Bartoni, had known about her affections toward him. Could he finally be responding to all the hints and ogles shot in his direction? After all, he had winked at her. My God, he had winked! She could barely contain her emotions long enough to respond, but somehow she did.

"I'll probably be here till around six or so. Maybe I'll see you when you get in." She wanted to appear reserved but in reality, she thought she would pee herself if she did not get away from him soon.

He did come in to swim late that afternoon. By the time he had arrived, Gina had already gone home, so it was only the two of them together for the first time. Rosa had been about thirteen and already well developed for her age. She wore a two-piece suit; Kash was in cutoff jeans. They sat on her towel and talked for a while. They swam at bit, and finally they moved to an area of the pool where both of them stood in water up to their chests. Most everybody had left the pool by this time, Rosa remembered, because she and Kash had the huge pool to themselves. They had volleyed a beach ball back and forth until they got bored, then Kash swam underwater and pulled Rosa's feet out from under her. He had dunked her, and tickled her, and copped a few feels in the process, but Rosa didn't mind. She had finally gotten some long-fought attention from Kash. She was close enough to touch him, and he was touching her back. She would never forget the butterflies in her stomach that day, the sensation in her bones, and the rush of having been touched by someone she had wanted for such a long time. It was only after that day at the pool that Rosa began to feel the connection toward Kash, the draw of her soul to his, the same connection she feels today.

Now she drifted farther along Cottage Avenue. Just beyond where Cole's pool once sat, Rosa saw Keystone's Teen Dance Hall still where it belonged.

The ash-colored wooden structure had been covered with vinyl siding in chocolate brown so dark it almost looked black. The trim and doors were painted a pukey green, and the small particle board sign which used to identify Keystone's Dance Hall had been replaced by a huge gaudy neon sign giving Rosa the impression that the cliental it hoped to attract was skinheads who listened to head banging music, wore leather clothes, dyed their hair green or pink, and had more holes in their bodies from piercing in places where God had never intended holes to be.

In Rosa's day, Keystone's had catered to the 14 to 18-year-old age group. No one under 14 or over 18 had been permitted access. Driver's licenses or high school ID cards had to be shown at the door to enforce the rule. No alcohol had been allowed in the building either, but that never stopped the teens from drinking in their cars or outside in the parking lot. Bands played from 8:00 to 10:00; the doors opened at 7:30. Kids danced and paid 50 cents for a glass of fountain soda, 30 cents for a basket of chips or popcorn, $2.00 a head at the door, (the rubber stamp on the back of your hand that allowed you to go outside then come back in again without paying, was free) and, if the roller grill was working, you could get a hot dog with ketchup or mustard for a buck. The dances were packed with teens every weekend, new kids coming in all night long. The place cleared out by 10:30. Old Keystone had a nice little racket going. If you figured a half hour to set up and a half hour to clean up, Keystone made a tidy income for putting in no more than four hours each weekend night.

Rosa had been 15 on the night she and Gina Bartoni walked to Keystone's for the first time to hear a popular local group—the A2Z Band they had been called. It was late summer, just before the start of school, which motivated Rosa and Gina to have one last summer fling before the door was shut on fun.

The girls had gone to Keystone's without permission from their parents. Both families believed their respective daughters were at the bowling alley. Gina and Rosa's folks thought it was fine to spend a Saturday night at the bowling alley but not so fine to hang out in what they called a *nightclub*, even if the place was for teens only and no alcohol was served. Rosa's family—unlike Gina's folks, who thought nice girls had no business in a place like Keystone's, but who would not have totally flipped if they found out their daughter had been there—would have severely punished Rosa. Frankie would have seen to it, would have insisted on it because he was two years older and knew what kinds of things went on in the corners when the lights went down and in the parking lot and inside the cars parked there. Both girls took the chance anyway.

Kash had been sitting on the porch steps that night at Keystone's with some friends. A small paper bag containing cheap wine, Mad Dog 20/20 Rosa remembered, had been stashed in the bushes planted to either side of the porch steps. Rosa spoke first this time when she and Gina had come close to the group of boys.

"Hey Kash. How are ya?"

Gina had been anxious to get inside, just in case someone should drive by and recognize her. Small talk in a small town led to big trouble for teens caught doing something they ought not to be doing. Rosa wanted to talk with Kash a bit longer, so she grabbed for Gina's jacket to slow her down but came up with only a handful of air. Momentum and gravity took over from there, and a split second later Rosa missed the next step and found herself face down on hands and knees between the last step and the landing of the porch. The boys howled with laughter, even Kash, though not as hard as the others did. Chet Macey, a royal jerk, laughed so hard he had to stomp his feet as if running in place, to contain his energy. Another boy smeared spent tears across his cheekbone. Gina turned around to see what was so funny, but by that time, Rosa was already on her feet and pushing Gina inside the door. She was so embarrassed.

A while later, Kash had come inside along with the other boys. Thankfully, none of them had noticed Rosa. Some days it was a blessing to be plain and simple—the better to be invisible by. It was 8 o'clock. The lights had just dimmed, and the A2Z Band began to play. The group of boys who accompanied Kash had split up like a flock of vultures searching for possible prey. Gina was already on the dance floor when Kash made his way to Rosa.

"Wanna dance?" he asked.

"No thank you, maybe later."

"Did you hurt yourself or something when you fell?" He asked this with sincere concern. Not even the slightest smirk had turned up at either corner of his mouth.

"I'm so embarrassed about that. Sometimes I think I am the biggest klutz on earth."

"Hey, we all have our bad days. Since you don't feel like dancing, do you want to go outside and drink some wine?"

"No, I couldn't. I think I had better stay here and wait for Gina."

The A2Z Band opened with a fast song, which had ended. A slow one started now. Kash looked at the dancers, including Gina and her partner, then back to Rosalee.

"Gina looks like she'll be awhile," he said. "We could go out for a bit and come back when she's finished."

"It's still light outside," she said. "If someone sees me drinking and tells my parents, they'll kill me."

Rosa knew she overstated the kill thing, but she had made her point just the same.

"Oh come on Rosalee, live a little. We'll stay close to the porch, this way the bushes will cover us. Nobody will see us unless we want them to see us."

He stroked the left side of her face with the backside of his finger then turned his hand over and gently rubbed the right side of her face with the underside of his fingers. She looked into his bedroom eyes and smiled. He smiled back—only it was more of a bad boy grin than a smile—then he winked.

Sweet Jesus, Rosa thought, *there's that wink again!*

"If you promise no one will see us," she said with some reluctance, not able to resist that wink.

"I swear," he said.

They went out to the porch and slipped behind the bushes.

Two plastic milk crates had been neatly tucked away there along with a bottle of Mad Dog 20/20. At this stage of Rosa's life, she had put nothing stronger than chamomile tea though her system, so it took very little consumption for the effects of the Mad Dog to modify her personality. Before long, the bottle was empty, and she was feeling brave.

It was completely dark outside now; the only light came from a pole in the center of the parking lot to the left and a low wattage light bulb near the porch steps to the right. The A2Z Band had played one set, taken a break, and was now into a second set, but as far as Rosa could tell, they had played only a few songs. At first, she heard nothing but Kash and felt nothing but the Mad Dog buzz—and love. Rosalee had been moonstruck. Rosa thought it was the best night she had ever lived in her shallow 15 years of life. She was with the boy of her dreams, and she had figured out now how to keep his attention—drink with him! Finally, the sounds around her made their way to her ears. She heard a slow song playing from the band inside and said to Kash, "Let's dance."

"Here in the bushes?" he laughed at the thought of himself maneuvering a drunken girl around in the tight space between the bushes, bumping into one bush and then another. *Oh, excuse me Rhododendron, or so sorry for stepping on your branch Lilac, or beg pardon, Mums, I didn't mean to bump you.*

"Not here silly," Rosa said, now giggling too, "out there, in the parking lot."

And so they danced—one slow one, two fast ones, and a another slow one—before a car's squealing brakes and a pair of headlights startled both of them. The car was a '66 Chevy Nova SS, and the driver was Frankie.

Rosa didn't find out until the next day that Gina had called the DeLucci house when a search for her at the dance hall had turned up empty. Rosa, of course, had been in the bushes with Kash. Gina thought Rosa had gone home. She was afraid Rosa would be angry with her for dancing so much. Gina reluctantly told Frankie where she was calling from and within minutes, he was in Keystone's parking lot.

Frankie had never said a word to his parents about that night—or about the condition in which he had found his little sister—but he had said plenty to Kash. Rosa recalled how humiliated she had been for days after her brother's disruptive arrival at the parking lot. She remembered Frankie pushing Kash, and yelling at him to stay away from his sister, but when she had seen Kash a day or two later, she cringed when she saw the black eye, for fear her brother had done that too. She found out later that Kash had fought with another boy from school that night, and the black eye had been put there by Chet Macey—not Frankie.

Too bad Frankie couldn't ride up in his '66 Chevy Nova SS now and bail her out of this current scenario.

There had been rumors back then that Keystone ran high stakes poker games in the back room before, during, and after the dances. It was also rumored that the dance hall was built with money Keystone had won at other poker games. It mattered not to Rosa where the money came from, she was just glad it had been built back then, and she was grateful to see it standing there now. The sight of something that remained familiar took away the little stitch in her heart put there when she saw that Cole's pool had been replaced by townhouses.

Walking to the end of Cottage Avenue, she noticed a new playground had been erected. Nothing ever stays the same. Things change, times change, and people change. Could Kash have changed too? Could he be all the things Lora and Suzy said he was? Could he have turned into a monster, a blackmailer? Could he be evil? She could not put off the inevitable. She had to see him. Not realizing it, she had circled back and was now standing on the street where Kash lived.

Once again, she gazed at the ring finger of her left hand. Just the other day she had put her life in God's hands. She had left the outcome up to Him, asked Him to guide her. She had made the circle and ended up here again because this was where He wanted her to be. This was God's will. She removed the wedding band that signified her marriage to God. She had never taken the band off before today. She stuffed it into her pants pocket.

3

Kash sat in the living room watching the evening news on his newly purchased TV set when the doorbell rang. He looked out the window and saw a pudgy woman standing on the porch. When he opened the door and the woman smiled, he immediately recognized his visitor.

"Rosa. Rosalee DeLucci, is that you?"

"Yes Kash, it's me. I hope you don't mind me dropping by unannounced and all."

"Of course not. Come in, let's sit and talk."

Rosa could not help but smile when he looked at her. He was beautiful, just as handsome (if not more so) than she remembered. His body was firm, his blond hair full, his bedroom eyes were dreamy and on his breath, the faint odor of beer remained. Spandex shorts covered his legs just above the knee. His thighs rolled with muscle, his calves knotted with the same, so much so that Rosa wanted badly to touch them. In reality, she wanted to squeeze them the way she would squeeze a head of lettuce to check the firmness. She wanted to feel the thickness of his thigh all the way down to his calf. She believed Kash's leg must have been created on a Saturday because even the Good Lord Himself would need Sunday to admire them. He wore no shirt, which made Rosa's mouth hang open for a short time. Here she saw a perfectly flat stomach and a chest that puffed out two lumps like hard fist with a firm nipple in the center of each that were his breasts. His back was strong and formed too, she could tell, in that when he moved his arms to open the door, his shoulder blades worked the other muscles in his back like a well-oiled machine. The beard was new, but it could not disguise the square jaw that always made Rosalee think of the Marlboro man. My lord, she thought, he looks even better now than he did fifteen years ago. If Kash had winked at her, she surely would have fainted.

Sam Kashette was stunned by Rosa's sudden arrival. He had thought about her recently, hadn't he? Of course he had ... the other night when he found it hard to fall asleep.

He had only dated her from time to time when they were teenagers, usually when the girls on his A-list were unavailable. He remembered there had been something different about her, something special yet at the same time invasive. When he had been around her then, he believed she could see straight through him, like she could read his mind, like she knew his actions before he did. It sort of gave him a creepy feeling so he had kept his distance from her for the most part, but then in college at Kanawha State, he had changed his mind—or perhaps Rosa had changed it for him if she truly could get inside his head—and he started dating her again. She had mysteriously shown up at a couple parties. Since he and Rosa were only freshman then and had not made many new friends yet, the two of them kept each other company. They had drunk and partied and things were good, but then after awhile that creepy feeling came again, and he had backed off a second time. Yes, he remembered now … it had been before he started dating the Inferiors. They had been her roommates, but Rosa was not like them. She was different—not just that creepy different—but a gentle, somehow soothing different. He thought at the time that he could have made some kind of commitment to her if only he could have gotten past the creepy feeling, the *she-knows-me-inside-out* feeling. Not quite able to get a clear picture of her back then, he remembered her being sort of plain, never strikingly beautiful as the Inferiors had been, yet appealing in a fresh sort of way. He thought she still looked the same except for her hair. He remembered her hair being long, not short. Now as she came through his door, he looked her over. He noticed kindness and purity around her. She glowed with compassion from within.

Kash had never considered these features in a woman before. Kindness, purity, and compassion were never traits he gave notice to, yet today they were all he could see. After only a few minutes in her presence, he felt none of the things he had felt when he had known her before. There were no feelings of interference or intrusion coming from her. Instead, he felt a strange sense of security. He wanted to seize the feeling right away. He found an attraction to her, not an attraction of a physical nature but one of a spiritual nature, a mental connection. His shoulders seemed lighter when he was near her, as if she had thrown weight off of them, had lightened his load. He experienced a magnetic energy coming from inside her, something pulling him closer to her.

They went into the living room. Kash offered drinks, but Rosa declined saying she had eaten such a big dinner there was no room left in her stomach.

"Boy Rosalee," Kash started, "you look great."

"Oh, I don't know about great. I've gotten fat and sassy since you last saw me."

"How long has it been?"

"About 15 years."

"My God where did the time go? So what are you doing now? Are you living in Huntington?"

"No. Over the years, I've moved around a bit. Presently, I live up in the northern panhandle. I teach third grade."

"That's great. I'll bet you're a wonderful teacher and I'll bet the kids love you. You were always good with them, I remember. Are you married?"

"No. How about you? Is there a Mrs. Kashette?"

Rosa felt her face redden as she waited for the answer.

"No, I never married either."

Relief from that statement allowed her to ease up a bit. They reminisced about old times for a while before Rosalee brought up the subject which spawned her visit.

"Do you still keep in touch with Lora Cooper or Suzy Shaffer? It's been years since I've heard from them."

Kash's happy expression crumpled. Rosa could see all the muscles in his body begin to tense up. His eyes seemed to be dilating and his stare became cold. He picked up his beer can, took a long swig, and said casually, "No, I haven't kept in touch with either of them."

"Somebody told me awhile back that Lora got through medical school and married some guy from Boston."

"I wouldn't know."

"I'd like to see them again. Wouldn't that be fun? Maybe the four of us could put together a reunion."

"I wouldn't be interested."

Rosa sent a puzzled glance in Kash's direction. She could sense her interrogation was upsetting him.

Kash clarified, "I mean ... what reason would there be to have a happy little reunion with somebody who dumped me and made me look like a fool?"

The question took Rosa by surprise. After all, wasn't she doing the same thing? Wasn't she having a happy little reunion with someone who dumped her and made her look like a fool?

Not only could Rosa tell instinctively when something was wrong with Kash, she could also tell when he was lying. And right now, he was lying about Lora and Suzy. He immediately changed the subject to her family. She said nothing more about either of her old roommates.

After an hour or so of catching up, Rosa told Kash she'd better get back to the house.

"You know, I don't care how old I get, Frankie will always be older than me, and I don't think he'll ever stop worrying about me."

"Your brother never liked me much, did he?"

"Oh, I wouldn't say he didn't like you. I'd just say he didn't like any guy who paid too much attention to his little sister. Anyway, that was a long time ago."

"Yes, it was. I'm really glad you came here tonight. I've been feeling kind of lonely lately, and seeing you was just what I needed. Since you'll be in town awhile longer, would you like to have lunch tomorrow? I could fix something here, or we could go out."

"Sure, I'd like that."

They set a time and place to meet for lunch and then Rosalee headed for the front door.

"Wait here one minute," Kash said. "I have something that belongs to you; although I don't think you'll have much use for it now."

Kash was not a pack rat, unless you count the marbles, but something told him a long time ago to save this thing because one day he would be able to give it back to its rightful owner. He returned within moments holding in his hand a delicate hair ribbon, copper in color. Kash offered it to her.

As she fingered the satin hair tie, Kash asked, "Do you remember it?"

"Yes, I wore this with my tan jumpsuit. It was one of my favorites. I wondered what happen to it."

"I used to love to brush your hair, do you remember?"

"Yes, I do."

"Why did you cut it all off?"

Rosa analyzed the question then said, "It seemed like the right thing to do at the time." She ran her fingers through the short strands that covered her scalp. "But now I'm not so sure."

Whether or not she realized it, the decision to help her friends was made. Kash was hiding something, but she refused to believe he had turned into the monster Lora and Suzy depicted. Spending more time with him was the only way to get at the real truth.

Kash opened the door for his guest, but before he let her pass through it, he turned her body toward his and cupped her face into his large hands. He felt an unspoken bond between them. A bond he believed Rosa was already attuned to but one Kash had just discovered. He reacted to her warmth. He saw gentleness in her eyes and thoughtfulness in her face. He said, "I'll see you tomorrow," then he kissed her forehead with all the tenderness of someone cuddling a newborn puppy. Somehow, from his lips touching her forehead, he felt a force coming out from within her. Now he saw in her something he should have seen many years ago—peace, and order, and sanity.

Rosalee was like a schoolgirl. She almost had to remind herself that she was a grown woman, not a teen sporting pigtails and saddle shoes, chomping on piece of gum to drum up another wrapper for the chain. Butterflies squirmed in her belly, just like the day at the pool. Her breasts ached; her palms were moist from excitement. Her heart zoomed when she waved goodbye from the sidewalk below. It was such a simple thing, a friendly little kiss, yet it made Rosalee feel as though she was the only person in the world who had ever experienced such delight. She never gave a second thought to the gold band still in her pants pocket.

4

She made it back home before dark (much to Frankie's relief), stuck her head out the patio door where her family was outside sitting to let them know she was home, and then made a beeline for her bedroom.

She sat on the bed not able to get the thought of him out of her mind. Snuggled in her arms were the two stuffed animals Kash had won for her at the fair so many years ago.

Jesus had been beside her tonight and had guided her to Kash. He had placed her in Kash's living room like a pawn on a chessboard. He wanted her to be there; this was His will. Checkmate. How could Lora and Suzy expect her to believe that this gentle person could actually be an evil, sinister thief? The only way she could prove she was right and clear Kash's name was to help them, so she went to the phone in the hall and dialed Lora's number.

"Lora, it's Rosa."

"Hello Rosalee, I'm glad you called back."

Rosalee could tell by Lora's tone that Alex was in the room with her.

"Did you give anymore thought about the favor Suzy and I asked you?"

"Yes ... I did," Rosa answered. She waited for a response. When none came, she asked, "Is Alex in the room with you?"

"Yes."

"Okay then, I'll do all the talking. I went to see Kash tonight. He was just as sweet and gentle as he's ever been, but it doesn't mean I won't try to talk to him for you. When I mentioned your names tonight, he got defensive and annoyed. He definitely didn't want to talk about you."

"Well, you can understand why, can't you?"

"No I can't. But I'm going to find out what's going on between you three."

Lora whispered into the telephone, "You be careful around him, Rosa. He's a cruel and wicked man."

"He didn't seem cruel or wicked to me. I can understand this kind of thing coming from Suzy, but I thought you were different, Lora. I can't believe you two think that just because someone spends some time in jail he's automatically branded a cruel or wicked man. Do you really think he would stoop to blackmail in order to get money? If you do, I think you're both dead wrong about Kash. He's not like that at all."

Lora's ears perked up. Did she hear the statement accurately? Did Rosalee say jail?

Of course she did; some of this made sense now. Kash had been in jail and that's why he had no money and was unable to work. He was probably turned down for every job he applied. Who would want to hire an ex-con anyway, right? Yes, everything was all fitting together nicely. If she could find out the circumstances behind his sentence, she would have something to work with. Two could play this blackmail game. She dared not ask Rosalee for details. She was quite sure Rosa's mention of the jail thing was inadvertent. Lora had not heard a thing Rosa said after that. Rosa still rambled on.

"Do you understand what I'm saying Lora?"

"Yes ... yes I do," Lora said, not knowing what the hell she was agreeing to. "When is your next meeting?"

"Tomorrow. We're having lunch together. Haven't you been listening?"

"I'm sorry; I guess I didn't hear you. Should I call you tomorrow night?"

"No, I'll be in touch sometime next week. I can't just come out and ask him about the situation tomorrow. I'd like to spend a little more time with him first. You know, get to know him again, gain his trust."

"Okay then, I'll talk to you next week."

"Goodbye."

Rosalee hung up the phone then got ready for a shower. She let the fine mist drizzle over her entire body. She was so relaxed. She washed her hair and body, dried off, and dressed in her nightgown. She went to bed without even bothering to tell her family good night. She simply wanted to get into bed and think about Sam Kashette. Once tucked under the summer blanket, Rosalee tried to recapture the physical sensations she had felt earlier this evening. Then, she thought she would never forget it, now, she could hardly bring it back to life. She eagerly anticipated tomorrow's lunch. She remembered a trick from when she had been a child: if something nice were going to happen tomorrow, the earlier she would go to sleep tonight, the sooner tomorrow would come. With her lunch date in the back of her mind, she fell off to sleep.

5

Suzy and Clayton arrived at the rally only a few minutes before they were scheduled to speak. The sky was clear; the late morning air was moderate. It was a beautiful day in Massachusetts for outdoor activity.

The rally was being held in an open field next to the engineering building on the campus of Hinsdale University, Clayton's university. Five hundred students and adults were in attendance. A portable stage had been erected for the event. Clayton walked to the podium and tapped the microphone with the tip of his finger.

"Testing, one, two, testing." He gave a little nod to his wife who was sitting on the sideline waiting to be announced. When she walked across the stage, the audience applauded generously. The student body loved to hear Suzy Whitmore speak.

Suzy organized her papers at the podium and positioned the microphone to her mouth.

"Good afternoon Hinsdale University," she yelled. "I was overjoyed to be invited back again this year to your annual pro-life rally."

Again, the crowd clapped and whistled. Suzy glanced over at Clayton who was seated next to the podium on the stage. He too was applauding.

"I have a simple question for you today. Which is more valuable: an unborn eagle or an unborn child?"

The crowd screamed out their answer, "An unborn child!"

"You'd think so, but a person who kills, damages, or transports a bald eagle's egg or its nest is subject to fines of up to $5,000.00 or imprisonment for up to one year. A woman who aborts her unborn child has no consequences or penalties. In fact, they are protected by the laws of this country. Am I the only one who can see something wrong with this picture? I am convinced that abortion is unjust, inhumane, and a definite destruction of innocent human life. We, the people of this country, have allowed 30 million babies to be slaughtered since 1973 when abortion was legalized. That is one out of every four pregnancies. These killings must be stopped."

Suzy scanned the audience. She spotted a man in the back who looked a little like Sam Kashette. *No, it can't be him. If we paid, he said he would leave us alone.* She returned to her speech keeping an eye on the suspicious man.

"A clinic right outside this campus offers counseling to pregnant women. Now you and I know these clinics are not counseling for life. Most women considering abortion have two questions: Is it a real baby? And does it hurt? To both of these questions, the counselor will assertively answer NO! They tell them that the unborn baby is nothing but a glob of tissue and that the only pain they will suffer is a slight cramping, whereas, in reality, the abortion is very painful, not only physically, but emotionally as well. Why do these people lie to their patients? Money. We cannot let this go on."

A loud roar came from the crowd. Suzy took this pause to inspect the audience again. She glanced at the man in the back of the congregation. It was Kash. She was certain. Then she forced her attention to the front of the group. She saw the hat. Kash was there too. She surveyed the entire assembly of people and saw Sam Kashette everywhere. How could this be? Did he have people out there dressed like him? Was he trying to drive her out of her mind?

The crowd stopped applauding. They were silent, anticipating her next words. Suzy wiped her forehead with her fingers. She glanced at the papers in front of her and resumed where she had left off. She had to finish. Clayton would know something was wrong if she didn't.

"The director of the clinic just outside this campus gets $25.00 for ..."

She looked at all the Kash look-a-likes in the crowd. She was getting lightheaded. Her knees were weak, barely able to hold her up.

"... for ... for ..." She forced herself to continue, "... for every abortion performed. Last year the director pocketed $250,000. That's 10,000 abortions. Do you know how they get rid of an unborn fetus? They put it ..."

She saw two or three of the Kash look-a-likes laughing at her. Her eyes were watering. She could no longer focus on the papers on which her speech was written.

"... they put it down the ..."

A dozen of the Kashs laughed now.

"... down the garbage disposal."

The whole audience looked like Sam Kashette. They were all laughing hysterically. She broke out in a sweat. She stopped talking and turned to Clayton for support, but Clayton was not in his seat. Sam Kashette was sitting there, too. He smiled and tipped his Stetson hat at Suzy.

That was the last thing she remembered. She passed out at the foot of the podium.

6

Tommy was awakened by the sound of the neighbor's barking dog. Without looking at the alarm clock, he knew it must be close to 8AM. Mutley always announced the arrival of the mail carrier by barking sometime between 7:45 and 8:15. Sure enough, when he looked at the clock, it was five after eight.

He was teetering between getting up and rolling back over to catch a few more zees. Stretching and yawning, he debated. There was no law that said just because he was awake he had to get up. There was no school bus to catch, as it was still summer vacation. He and Jeff had made no definite plans for the day, and besides, he had the whole house to himself. He could do whatever he wanted.

Tommy checked the view through his bedroom window. What he saw was the most beautiful sky he had ever seen. Sunshine stung his eyes a little.

It poured through the window and blanketed his body in heat. The sky was a pale baby blue and the odd thing was this: it hardly looked like a sky at all. It looked more like one great big puffy pastel cloud that seemed to go on and on for as far as the eye could see.

The birds were waking up too, Tommy noticed. He listened to them sing and chirp for a few minutes then decided if the birds could start their day, he probably should too. Walking to the window, he took a better look at the new day outside. Man, could looks be deceiving. The view from his bed only allowed him to see the sky, but now looking down to the ground, he saw two acres of what should have been front lawn, that were, in reality, nothing more than burned grass that looked like brown sagebrush.

Still no rain after almost five months now. The Governor had declared a state of emergency, and all residents were ordered to cut their water usage by 25%. That meant no washing cars and no watering lawns. The Whitmore's yard was not the only one that looked dead. All the houses on the hill had sun-baked, parched yards, and shrubs that were wilted and lifeless. Nobody's plants or flowers had done well this year—if any had grown at all—except for Mrs. Ferguson that is, who lived two doors down on the opposite side of the street. She was an eccentric old lady in her eighties (and as healthy as a horse) who still wore old-fashioned silk stockings which she rolled down to her shoe tops. Tommy used to think it looked like she had two cake doughnuts wrapped around her ankles. Her only attire was an assortment of housedresses in really loud prints.

Mrs. Ferguson had worked and worked with the flowers in her yard until one day, frustration had gotten the best of her. Like a maniac, she pulled up all her plants. Big clumps of dry dirt scattered everywhere as she flung the uprooted remains to the left and to the right of the place where she was bent over. Tommy and Suzy had watched her from the living room window. Mrs. Ferguson had been yelling something too. They heard none of what she said, yet Tommy and Suzy both found themselves giggling. The view alone was enough to bring about laughter. Then old Mrs. Ferguson started on the bushes. She pulled and tugged on each one until it finally surrendered and then she gave it a toss to join the other disobedient plants that littered her yard. The bushes had barely grown, so there was never any danger of Mrs. Ferguson hurting herself when she commenced to give the next one what for.

The Whitmores had gone somewhere that afternoon and they retuned to find the Ferguson's yard in full bloom: brilliantly colored flowers of purple, yellow, gold, along with rich shiny shrubs—all artificial, of course—and brown dead grass. What a sight.

Tommy snickered at the memory while he got dressed then went downstairs to fix some breakfast. He was his own boss today as he had been yesterday and as he would be until Sunday. Suzy and Clayton had taken an unexpected vacation to the mountains. Before they left, Clayton explained to Tommy how his mother was having some "female trouble," and he believed a getaway would be good for her, but Tommy did not buy one word of his dad's explanation. He knew the real reason for his mother's weird behavior, and it had nothing to do with the change of life as his dad had told him. He knew it was the other man in her life … Kash. Tommy remained mystified as to what his mother saw in this man.

In the kitchen, he put a few strips of bacon in a pan to fry while he went out to the front porch to collect the mail. Walking back to the kitchen, he separated the junk mail from the rest. Leafing thorough the envelopes, he found five bills—all from different utility companies—an insurance premium, and his mother's bank statement. He never realized how many different bills his mom and dad paid out to keep their household running. He reckoned he had better learn fast because he would be out on his own in just a couple of years and maybe before then if his parents split up.

When the bacon fried to his liking, he carefully dropped two eggs in the hot grease. With the help of a pancake turner, he put the sunny side up eggs on a plate, grabbed the loaf of bread, and sat down to start his meal. Before he could take a bite, the phone rang.

"It's your dime, but my time." Tommy spoke into the mouthpiece.

"Hello?" the other voice inquired, "Is this the Whitmores?"

"Yes it is. May I ask who's calling."

"This is Lora Jordan. Is Suzy at home?"

"No she isn't, Dr. Jordan. My dad took her out of town for a few days." Tommy took the opportunity to see what she knew.

"Oh, I didn't know that. Is she feeling better?"

"Not really. She was in the middle of a talk at a pro-life rally yesterday, and I guess she really flipped out. My dad said she passed out cold at the podium and when she came to, she was telling my dad to 'get him out of here', and saying things like 'please don't let him get me.' We never did find out who she was talking about. You wouldn't have any idea, would you?"

"No Tommy, I'm afraid I don't have a clue," Lora said, trying not to sound like she was lying. "When do you expect them back?"

"Sunday. Mom's got another doctor's appointment on Monday."

"What kind of doctor is she seeing?"

"Gynecologist, I think."

"Can you leave word when your mother gets back to call me? I'd like to know how she's doing."

"Sure will, Dr. Jordan. See you later."

Tommy sat back down at the table. He was sure Dr. Jordan knew more than she was letting on. Although his breakfast was in front of him, he seemed to have a taste for the stack of mail instead. He examined the pile again. When he picked up the bank statement, it almost jumped out at him.

He scoffed at himself for being so stupid. It was right under his nose all the time. If she had written a check to Kash, she should have a copy of the cancelled check."

He carefully opened the re-sealable envelope intending to reseal it after he was done snooping. After shuffling through a dozen checks, he saw the one made payable to Samuel Kirkland on June 17. His peered over to the amount box. "Jesus Christ, $5000 dollars."

A voice sounded from just outside the screened-in kitchen door. "What's $5000 dollars?"

Tommy lurched in the chair. "Shit Jeff, you scared the hell out of me."

Jeff let himself in and pulled up a chair. "What are you doing?" he questioned.

"I opened my mom's bank statement. I found the check she wrote to Kash that day in the park. Look at the amount—$5000.00 dollars. What do you think she paid him for?"

"It must have been one really fine roll in the hay to be worth that kind of dough."

"Jeff, this isn't funny, it's serous."

"I'm sorry, Tom, but I don't know what to tell you. Is that the only one she wrote?"

"Yeah, I think so. I looked through the rest of the checks, and I didn't find any others."

"No, I mean did she write one to him last month or any other time before that?"

"I don't know, but I know where to look. All her bank statements are in the desk drawer."

Tommy got to his feet and went directly to the den. The drawer was locked, but Tommy knew where the key was hidden. He removed the picture of his grandparents from the wall and exposed a silver key hanging on the nail. Inserting the key into the hole, he opened the desk drawer. He and Jeff looked diligently through twelve months of bank statements but found nothing more written to Samuel Kirkland. At least he had some new information. He now had a last name ... *Kirkland.* He wondered why his mother had called him Kash. Must be some kind of nickname, he guessed. After putting the den back to it original order, they returned to the kitchen.

"I wish this check had an address on it," Tommy said holding the note in his hand. "I'd love to know where he lives."

"Look at the cleared stamp on the back."

"What's a cleared stamp?"

"Shit Tommy, haven't you ever had a checking account?"

"No."

"The cleared stamp on the back shows what bank he used to cash the check. Most people bank in their hometown, so wherever the bank is located is probably where he lives."

Tommy flipped the check over. He saw Kash's signature and a whole lot of numbers and stamps. "Which one is it?"

Jeff examined the check. "Well this is your mom's bank here in town, so the purple stamp must be his bank."

Tommy took the note and inspected the address. "It says National Bank of Kentucky, Ashland, Kentucky. Do you think that's where he's from?"

"Probably. You know his last name now, so call the operator and see if you can get a phone listing for him."

Tommy dialed directory assistance after getting the area code for Kentucky from the phone book. The operator found no listing for Samuel Kirkland.

Tommy was so frustrated. He wanted all this to be over. He wanted results, and he wanted them now, but nothing seemed to be going in his favor. He could not put his plan into motion without first knowing where to find Kash. His hands were tied and in the meantime, he was forced to watch his mother slowly lose her sanity, not to mention her good reputation. So many people in the community admired her for her loyalty and compassion. If only they knew.

He felt he lacked the proper skills to be his mothers protector, but he knew where he could find help.

"Hey Jeff, do you have anymore pot?"

"Why? Do you wanna catch a buzz?"

"Yeah, I do."

7

Rosalee thanked her brother for taking the time to drop her off at the restaurant on his lunch break. Ruby Tuesday, which was located on the outskirts of Huntington, happened to be on Frankie's way back to the police station. She told Frankie she was meeting a couple of friends from high school for lunch and someone would bring her home later on. She hated fibbing to him, but he would never have consented to her seeing Sam Kashette.

Rosalee's lunch date was punctual; in fact, he was already inside the restaurant awaiting her entrance. She was impressed by his promptness. She took it to imply that he too was eager for the arrival of their meeting time. The hostess escorted them to a booth along the wall.

Kash ordered for both of them. Roast Beef and gravy, mashed potatoes, no gravy on the potatoes, and corn with extra butter. Rosa was amazed.

"My, you're full of surprises Kash. You remembered all my favorite foods."

"Yes Rosa, I seem to be remembering a lot these days."

They chatted idly about things of little importance, while they ate the complimentary appetizers.

When the entree arrived, Rosa took her fork and gently moved the kernels of corn away from the mashed potatoes one by one. She then proceeded to slide the mound of mashed potatoes away from the roast beef and gravy. Very methodically, she ate each food group one variety at a time. Kash stared in amazement. He tried to remember if she had done this sort of thing when he knew her before. Then he concluded that he probably would have paid no attention to it back then because he did none of these quirky little things 15 years ago, and he was certain he wouldn't have noticed if anybody else did. He viewed this act as a sign that sanctioned Rosalee DeLucci to be part of The Order.

When he was with her, he wanted to remember his past. He wanted to relive the time when he was not different. She rekindled in him feelings of normalcy. He would have referred to her as his soul mate, if he believed he had a soul. Instead, he thought of her as his destiny, someone to share his life, someone with whom he would feel no shame about The Order or the Bad Thoughts or the marbles. She would understand; she would not think of him as odd.

With their meal winding down, Rosa felt the time was right to ask Kash about the accident.

"How did it happen, Kash?"

"I was driving for Ziegler Trucking, hauling steel coils from Pittsburgh. It was one of those days, you know, when nothing was going the way it was supposed to go. Anyway, I was held up at the loading docks, so I had gotten a late start and before I realized it, 9PM had rolled around and my stomach was growling. I stopped for dinner at a bar in an old mill town just south of Ashland, Kentucky. The place was known for its home cooking. That was my only intention: dinner and couple of beers—until I met this girl. We danced half the night, and I drank a bit more than I had planned. When the bar closed at 2AM, I thought I could handle the rig, but I couldn't."

Kash bit his lower lip in an attempt to hold back his emotions. He focused on the table and swirled his fork through the mashed potatoes as if he were making a bizarre mountain peak.

"When I came off the entrance ramp to merge with the interstate traffic, I crossed over two lanes and hit a Volvo that was traveling in the passing lane. By the time I realized the car was there, my truck was already pushing it."

"My God, were you hurt?"

"No," Kash said finally looking at Rosa. "Not in that rig, but it flattened the Volvo. I tried to avoid him once I knew he was there, but I had built up too much momentum. My reactions were slowed from the booze. I couldn't stop. They told me the driver was in real bad shape."

Kash's eyes filled with tears. He really wasn't an ogre or a lunatic. His heart had truly grieved for the boy. He certainly took no pleasure in killing him either. He had a great deal of regret for getting into his rig after having had too much to drink. His voice quivered as he spoke. He continued to play with the mound of mashed potatoes.

"The driver was only seventeen, Rosa—just a kid. Three days after the accident he died."

Kash covered his face with those same large hands which had caressed Rosa's face so tenderly last night. He was comfortable talking to Rosa about the accident. He was comfortable simply being in Rosa's company. When he was with her, he felt normal, like his life had some meaning. He had The Order to stabilize his daily activities, and he was learning how to suppress the Bad Thoughts by using the Healing Rhymes. She was the final piece to finish the puzzle. He was whole again.

She reached across the booth and gently pulled his hands away. "There's nothing to be ashamed of Kash. There's no disgrace in crying. It was an accident. A horrible accident."

"I felt so helpless. There was nothing I could do to help the kid, Rosa."

"I wish I had known. I could have prayed for him."

"Pray? To whom?"

"God. Jesus Christ."

"There is no God, and I'm not convinced that Jesus Christ is anything more than a stupid man who got Himself crucified with a couple of thieves."

Rosa's first thought was of the young girl, Tina, at St. Christopher. She too held no faith, but Rosa had brought her around, and like Kash, she too was misunderstood, but Rosa understood her completely. Once again, she was pulled by doubts. Kash needed her very much, but so did God. She wondered if this was a test to prove her devotion. Maybe God was reminding her that she did His work in a very unique way.

Like a loving confidant, she moved to his side of the booth so she could be near him. She took his hand in hers.

"Oh Kash, I know you don't believe that. I never remembered you being a radical Christian, but I know you believed in God."

"I used to believe in God but no more. God didn't do a damn thing to help me. Praying is a joke ... just a way for your God to keep you in line, to make you believe He's watching and listening. You think your prayers are being answered, when in reality, it's fate that plays a convenient role. It would have done no good to pray for the kid's life. He would have stood a better chance of surviving if I had wished on a star. We have to influence our own fate in this life."

"What about the next life?"

"This is it Rosa. There is no more. We live and then we die—the end. Ashes to ashes, dust to dust. We have no soul, just a body. Once we're dead and the decaying process is complete, we are nothing, just the way we started. We make our mark while we're here and then we're gone. Period. I've learned to protect myself, to put my guard up, and I will never let it down again."

"Satan is stalking your soul Kash. Don't you see he's feeding you the deception that God doesn't exist? He wants to make you comfortable performing deeds for which God will punish you."

"Are you telling me God is waiting in the wings to punish me for killing the boy with my rig?"

"Maybe, maybe not. The boy's death was an accident—granted one that could have been avoided. But the one thing I am sure of is He will punish you for not believing, for turning your back on faith, for denying Jesus Christ. You must ask His forgiveness. Jesus accepts all of His children into His kingdom. He makes it easy; all you have to do is ask. Believe with your heart. It's as simple as opening a door. Let Jesus into your life and ask His forgiveness for your skepticism."

"You're full of shit, Rosa." Kash listened for an interruption by the little organ keeper; he waited for the Bad Thoughts, but both failed to come, so he continued. "Get it through your head. I'm not being skeptical. I don't believe a god has ever existed. I've seen no evidence to prove otherwise."

"What about the Bible? Are you telling me it's all a lie? That the prophets and gospel writers made everything up? All the stories and parables are inaccurate? The Bible is the real deal ... a story of our Savior. Every page is full of His life and His teachings passed down from heaven by the Father."

"Look Rosa, things don't merely exist because someone writes a book about them. Have you never heard of fiction? And a person doesn't exist because someone tells a story about him, either. We all know who Santa Claus is, don't we? We know what he looks like, where he lives, what he drives. But that still doesn't mean Santa exists. Everyone can relate to the meaning of Santa Clause just like everyone can relate to the meaning of God. People talk about Santa Claus every Christmas, but it doesn't mean the fat man actually climbs down the damn chimney and leaves us all presents, now does it?"

My God, Rosa thought. What has happened in this man's life to make him think this way? He acts as if life has no purpose, and he lives his life as though nobody is watching over him. She had to make him understand that he needs a Savior. He cannot save himself.

"Kash, I'd like to tell you about Pascal's Wager. It goes something like this: if you believe in God and turn out to be incorrect, you have lost nothing. But if you don't believe in God and turn out to be incorrect, you could burn in hell forever. You don't want to burn. Do you, Kash? Don't be a foolish man."

"You may think of me as foolish, but I'm done with faith, I tell you. They tried to preach that garbage to me in prison. I would no sooner go back to God than I would go back to prison. They both restricted my everyday life. From now on, I live for me. I do what I want, when I want. I answer to nobody, and I'm confident there are no consequences for my action."

"You can't do that. There will be consequences, and one day you will have to answer to God."

Kash was at ease talking about religion and God with Rosa. He was shocked with the way he calmly discussed the subject. Usually when he debated religion with someone, especially with someone of the opposite sex, his emotions would run amuck. He would become angry and frustrated by the arguments. Those people had no tolerance for is way of thinking. They were right, and he was wrong. Then the Bad Thoughts would come; but not today, not with Rosa. He was in control of his emotions, and he was controlling the Bad Thoughts too. All these changes came about because of Rosa's companionship. He could finally be himself with someone.

Rosa was fighting hard now, after all this was Kash's soul she was trying to whip back into shape. She had no idea he was this spiritually depressed. Compelled to protect him at all costs, she continued to elaborate on faith and religion, but Kash was not budging an inch from his original opinion. He asked that they change the subject. She did so only because she had not wanted to spark any suspicion about her current lifestyle.

When she asked about the prison sentence, he was hesitant about sharing his feelings at first, but eventually he opened up.

"When I was in Kentucky, I couldn't take the confinement. I'm a very routine person, and you can't mess with The Order. Prison messed with everything. I was literally a caged animal. My whole routine was turned upside down. I couldn't eat when I was hungry, couldn't shower when I felt dirty, couldn't sleep when I was tired. Everything had to be done on their timeline, not mine. For a while I thought I would go crazy. Everything in my head was in disarray. Nothing was in order anymore. Sure, there was *their* order, but that wasn't *my* order. I needed my order.

"I tried to keep my cell as neat and organized as possible, but the bed was on the wrong side of the room, and the commode certainly didn't belong there. Those were things I couldn't control, so I tried to control the things I could. It was very hard for me to adjust."

Kash considered telling Rosa about The Order and about the Bad Thoughts but then he decided there was plenty of time to share the other aspects of himself with her. After all, they had they rest of their lives.

"How did you deal with the other criminals?"

"It was a minimum-security prison, so there weren't any hard-core criminals. Mostly they were white collar criminal: some accountants who were in for embezzling, a couple of judges, a few drug dealers. It may have been a minimum-security prison, but it was no country club, like people think. It was still jail. The inmates themselves weren't what made the time hard, it was the control factor. I don't take kindly to being told what to do and when to do it. I don't like to be bossed, and I don't like bosses. Inside prison, all there were was bosses. The guards boss you; the inmates who think they're somebody, boss you; the office personnel boss you. I hated that place. I couldn't wait to get home and sleep in my own bed, to get back to my comfortable, warm, familiar surroundings. The place was cold and damp all the time. It was dimly lit, really dreary. Every day inside was like an overcast, gloomy day outside, ready to pour rain 24/7."

"How long were you there?"

"Eighteen months. I could have been out in 12, but good behavior didn't apply to me. One of the inmates who thought he was somebody special caught me on a really bad day. I started pounding on him, and I couldn't quit. It took four guards to get me off him. Later on, I found out that one of the guards told another inmate he had never seen anybody with as much strength as I had that day. He said I was possessed. The next day the warden scheduled me an appointment with the resident shrink. He helped me to cope a little, but the time was still hard. I spent the rest of those months looking over my shoulder, afraid someone would come up behind me to retaliate for what I had done to the other inmate. I was stressed out and wrapped with tension the whole time. I never relaxed for one minute. Even when I slept, I kept one eye open. "Every sound, no matter how slight, echoed in that place, every noise shrieked in my head. To another person's ear, it probably didn't sound like anything more than an irritating echo, but I'm different Rosa—to me the echo screamed. It squealed like tires on pavement."

In his face, she could see fear as he spoke of being locked up. She could also see determination in his eyes that said he would never go back there again, no matter what.

When they finished dessert, Kash suggested they go back to his place for a drink. Rosalee accepted the invitation. Country roads took them back to Kash's house. He pulled over to let Rosa pick a bunch of wild daisies. He watched as she tenderly plucked each stem, wary not to break the delicate flower. He thought how wonderful it was to have her back in his life if only for a short time.

Unlike yesterday, today was a beautiful day to sit on the porch. The sun, shielded by a few cirrus clouds, shined mutely over Kash's back yard. Rosalee sat down with her legs crossed on a swing hanging from the porch ceiling. Kash handed her a glass of wine and sat down next to her. He rested his full arm on the swing's backrest behind Rosa. Although he never touched her, Rosa believed that soon he would expect something in return for his amenities. She faced him and smiled. His eyes focused on her face and mouth, his hand reached over her shoulder, his slanting head moved closer and closer. Rosa grew edgy. She squeezed the wine glass between herself and Kash.

"Could I please have some ice for my wine?"

"You're not supposed to put ice in wine."

"I do."

Kash took her glass and started for the door but then stopped in route. "Is there a problem?" he asked.

"No ... no problem, unless your ice maker's broken."

When Kash returned with the iced wine, Rosa talked about the children she had taught last year. Kash listened intently. He was interested in what she had to say. He wanted to hear her views on every topic. The connection to her was growing stronger. He could feel the invisible magnet, the force that tugged his heart closer to hers. It was contagious. She was making him love her, and the funny thing was he didn't care that she was managing him. He wondered if these new feelings could be the other side of the Bad Thoughts—a flip-flop he could call the Good Thoughts. These days, the flashes in his mind portrayed only one picture. Rosa was simple and plain, yet the picture in his mind was beautiful. He had to keep her in his life. She was becoming part of The Order. He wanted to know everything about her. She told him more about the joy the children gave her and that she could not wait to see them again next year.

"You know," she said, "that's not too far off. School will be back in session before you know it. I only have three more weeks left to visit with my family. It seems like I only arrived."

"Well then," Kash said, "we'll just have to spend more time together before you go."

"Oh Kash, I don't know if that's such a good idea. It's going to be hard enough for me to go back to the con … my job. I really enjoyed your company, but I think it would be better if we didn't see each other anymore."

"Why? I haven't laughed and smiled so much in months. You always had that effect on me."

"Yes, I remember," she said, and then added, "but you lost interest."

"I did Rosa, and I made a huge mistake. I had found my perfect mate, and I didn't even know it." He cupped her face into hands, just as he had done last night. "I've missed you Rosalee; I simply never realized you were the one I missed."

When their lips touched, she felt dizzy. He pulled her close to him. She wrapped her arms around his neck and removed his gray hat so she could stroke the back of his sandy hair. His kiss was familiar, yet it was different. It had passion, power. Her eyes were closed. She wished she could have seen what the two of them looked like entwined in each other's arms. He parted her lips with his tongue and dotingly forced it into her mouth. She felt tingles clear down to her toes. It was hard to tell whether the swing was bouncing or if her heart was pounding so hard it caused the swing to jump up and down. When he tightened his hold on her, she felt safe, almost shielded from harm. And then … reality took a firm grip. She pulled away from his embrace.

"No Kash. This is wrong."

"Why Rosa? Why is this wrong? We're both consenting adults. We have no other ties. What makes it wrong? I know you're going to think this is weird, but somehow I sense you've always been there for me, you've always been looking out for my wellbeing. Until a night a few weeks ago, I hadn't thought about you in years. I even struggled to come up with your last name, but when I remembered it, I knew you had been thinking about me for many years, that you had been taking care of me in some strange way, that you had been encouraging me from some faraway place. I've felt it all my life; I just never realized it. It's as if time stood still since I saw you last. When we talked earlier, I felt as though I was talking to my best friend again. I can talk to you about things I could never talk about with anyone else. I need you Rosa."

Rosalee knew she needed him too, but she was cautious to reveal her true feelings. She preferred not to deal with this right now. She needed to get out of there.

Her walk through life, thus far, resembled a walk through a maze. No matter which path she took, she still found no exit. Unfortunately, if she strolled down the wrong path, she could very well corner herself into a dead end from which she could never turn back.

She stood up, leaving the swing lopsided with only Kash's body to weigh it down. She scooped up her purse and hurried out of the yard to the sidewalk in front of Kash's house. Soon he followed behind calling for her over and over.

"Rosa ... Rosa, wait. Come back Rosalee!"

She ignored his cries walking swiftly in the direction of the open field that would take her home. Kash watched her silhouette get smaller and smaller until finally it dissolved into the horizon.

Rosalee reduced her momentum only after she discovered that she was out of Kash's sight and that he had not followed her. She was angry with herself for accepting his kiss so willingly. Her conscience-stricken mind was flustered. Could she be confusing the need of a man's touch with the feeling of love? Was it possible she was coloring her emotions for Kash because he was the only man who had ever shown any real interest in her? Maybe she felt nothing for him at all. Maybe the only reason she believes she feels these things is because, like her, Kash had never married either. Maybe she wouldn't feel this way if Kash were unavailable, if he had married someone else. And, if that did happen, would she finally be able to let go once she knew he was out of reach? Panic began to set in as the gap between the Kashette and the DeLucci houses widened.

Reaching her parent's home, Rosalee found the house to be empty. She could not imagine where her mother and *Nonna* had gone. Before she could get upstairs to check the second floor, Frankie came in the front door from work. He greeted his sister while he removed his gun from the holster and locked it in the drawer of the china closet. The key made a slight *ting* when Frankie put it back into one of the china cups. He took off his badge and tie, unbuttoned his shirt, and sat in the living room recliner ready to read the afternoon paper.

"Where did Mama go?" Rosa asked.

"She told you this morning that she and *Nonna* were going in to town for the afternoon. *Nonna* wanted to visit a friend, and Mama had some errands to run."

"That's right. I remember now."

"Boy, you must have been really excited to see your girlfriends today." Frankie looked at her suspiciously. "They were girlfriends you met for lunch, weren't they?"

She hesitated, not sure how she should answer.

"Well were they?" he repeated.

"No Frankie, I had lunch with Kash today."

His first impression implied sarcasm, or a joke—albeit a bad one—on Rosa's part, but after a moment, he realized she was being serious.

She didn't know what possessed her to tell her brother with whom she had spent the afternoon, but she did. He was not going to take the news well, yet she had a need to confide in someone. She assumed if she could talk this out, she would have a better understanding of her emotions and maybe reach the critical decision that had been plaguing her for some time now. She also knew that nothing she told Frankie would go any farther than his ears. He was a very good confidant.

Frankie's gaping eyes were riveted on his sister. Rosa saw both confusion and bewilderment in his glare.

"Who?" he questioned. "You had lunch with Sam Kashette?"

"Yes. I went to see him yesterday. We had a lovely visit, and he invited me to lunch today."

His glare hardened; his face reddened.

"Don't look at me that way, Frankie. I did what I felt I had to do."

"And what was that?"

"I had to see him. Please try to understand. He's always been a part of my life, just like you and Mama ..."

"Don't you ever compare him to me or to Mama. He's scum, Rosa, nothing but trouble. Ever since I've known him, it's been one woman after another, and none of those women has anything nice to say about him. He's a manipulator Rosa. He uses women as play toys, somebody to crave his sexual appetite. When he's had his fill, he throws them away. He's nothing but a whoremonger."

"Stop it Frank. I can't stand it when you talk like that. You don't even know Kash. You're so quick to make judgment that you don't try to understand. Did you ever think that perhaps the reason Kash has been with so many women is because he's searching for love? Maybe he needs a woman's touch to feel secure or safe. Maybe it's the only way he knows to get affection, or for that matter, to show it. Maybe he knows no another way to love. All he needs is to find a woman with whom he could remain faithful. A good woman, Frankie. Then he'll settle down and be a family man."

"Oh he's probably a family man all right. It wouldn't surprise me to hear he has kids scattered out in five states. Hey, if that's the kind of company you want to keep, go ahead. You're a grown woman—as you keep reminding me—you can make your own decisions. To be perfectly honest with you, I'll be glad when your vacation is over and you go back to the convent where Sam Kashette can no longer influence you."

"What if I don't go back to the convent?"

"What are you saying? Are you going to leave the church, revoke your vows? No, please Rosa—not for Kash. He's not worth it. You've worked too hard to make the life you have."

"Yes, and what kind of a life do I have? I have nothing I genuinely want. I want love, Frankie. Love from a man. I want to share his joys and help him heal his pains. I want him to tell me his innermost thoughts and I want to tell him my thoughts and opinions. I'd like to be able to experience real love—physical love—to feel his touch, to take part in making love, in joining together to create life. These things are important to me now. When I entered the convent, I thought I had made a good decision, when in fact I had not made a decision at all. I acted on impulse. It simply seemed like a good thing to do, a good place to hide from my broken heart—a last resort."

"Isn't Kash a last resort, too? Okay, I can accept the fact that maybe you're having second thoughts about your vows. Personally, I didn't think you'd stay at the convent this long. If you feel the need to be a wife and a mother, I can understand that too, but think hard about what you want from your life. Do you really think Kash can supply you with all the passion you just described? I don't think he can."

"I do Frankie. He's not the terrible person you think he is. Take for example the accident he had. He explained it all to me. He was overcome with sorrow for that boy when he died. He cried just telling me about it."

"Sure, I'd cry too if I knew I was going to prison for killing someone."

"Oh Frankie! You're impossible. I don't know why I even brought this up?"

"Hey, don't look to me for sympathy where Kash is concerned. You should know me better."

"I just thought you'd be a little more compassionate toward *my* feelings."

"I am. I don't want you to screw up your life because of him. I don't want you to leave the church either."

"This isn't about you Frankie. It's about me and what I want."

"You belong there, Rosa. You have a special ability. You touch people's lives every day. They need you."

"Don't look for something that's not there. I never had a calling, per se. I explained to you how I used the convent as a safe haven, a place where my heart would be protected. I'm no longer afraid of getting hurt. I think I know where my place is now. As far as leaving the church, I'm not actually leaving it; I just don't want to be a nun anymore. I want to be a wife and a mother. I want to be sexy and sensuous. I can't be these things in the convent. And yes, Kash needs me too."

"I think you're making a terrible mistake."

Rosa's mother pushed open the front door and pulled the bulky wheelchair in behind her. *Nonna* held a pizza box on her lap.

"Hey kids," their mother exclaimed, "we tried a new pizza shop on 8th Street today. The pizza there was almost as good as my homemade. We brought one home for your dinner. I hope you kids are hungry. I've got a large with everything."

"I'm starved, Mama," Frankie said.

"What were you two discussing? It looked pretty intent."

"Nothing Mama, nothing important," Frankie said, shooting a glance at his sister.

Rosa kissed her *Nonna* and took the box from her lap. The pizza smelled good, but food wasn't on her mind. She wanted to get away somewhere private to phone Kash and apologize for her abrupt behavior this afternoon.

She made the call from the phone in the hall upstairs—the call that would change her life forever. She was certain she had found a path to lead her out of the maze.

CHAPTER TWELVE

Schemes and Themes

1

Both Rosalee and her Mama were exhausted from the housework they had done this morning. They got up at the crack of dawn to begin the tedious chore of washing down the walls in the rooms on the first floor.

Rosa's Mama was grateful for her daughter's help. It was a big job for her to do alone. If she had asked Frankie to help, he would have done so, but Mama always felt that taking care of the house was woman's work.

Frankie sat on the couch, a sandwich of pastrami and provolone in one hand and a big glass of soda in the other. He still had thirty minutes of his lunch break left before he had to restart his patrol. Although a week had passed since he and Rosa had quarreled, Frankie remained somewhat cold toward her. He had said hardly anything—short of small talk—since the incident.

Rosalee, in contrast, felt better about herself and her life than she had in many years. During the past week, she spent a portion of every day with Kash, undisclosed to her family, of course. She and Kash explored different places each day and enjoyed one another's company very much.

At first, Rosalee was worried about getting into another intimate situation with Kash but much to her surprise when the second romantic interlude occurred, she felt no guilt, no pressure at all. She felt nothing but pleasure and satisfaction from the kissing and cuddling that took place. This was God's will, God's work. She had asked for His guidance and He allowed her to be with Kash. In her heart, she was still doing God's work because Kash was in great need of spiritual counseling. Rosa had appointed herself his personal advisor.

She had something special planned tonight for her and Kash, but before she could think about her plans, she would have to concentrate on finishing the walls.

Frankie jumped to get the phone when it rang. Distant babbles could be heard from the kitchen.

"It's for you Rosa. Someone named Lora."

Rosa could tell by his callous tone that he was still upset with her. She hoped he would come around before she had to leave.

When Rosa answered the phone, Lora explained that the reason for her call was to check on any progress she had made with Kash. Rosa told her that she had nothing new to report yet.

"Did you ask him about our situation?" Lora demanded.

"No I haven't."

"When do you plan to do that? He's expecting another payment this week."

"I'm afraid you're going to have to deal with it. I'm trying to play this wisely. I need to gain his trust before I run interference for you. Do you understand?" Rosa was trying to be casual with the dialogue, due to the fact that Frankie had fixed his attention on her phone conversation.

"Yes, I understand, but we're running out of time here. You only have a couple weeks left before vacation is over."

"I'll have plenty of time to take care of everything. How's Suzy doing?"

"I don't know. She was supposed to return my call Sunday when she got back, but I haven't heard from her yet. If she doesn't call by tomorrow, I'll try her again."

"Give her my love when you talk to her and tell her not to worry. Everything is going to be fine. I have never been more sure of anything. You'll see."

While Rosalee and Lora wound up their conversation, Mama DeLucci nudged Frankie's arm. "Hey Frank, you notice a change in our Rosa these day? She seems to be so happy and carefree. She likes herself again. I think this trip home has done wonders for her. Don't you think?"

"Yeah Mama, it's done wonders all right." And under his breath he mumbled, "Wonders that still amaze me."

2

Rosalee entered Kash's house through the back door. From what Kash told her during a conversation he and Rosa had earlier this afternoon, Rosa knew that Kash would not be home between six and seven this evening. She prayed he would leave a key under the mat when he left. He did. She slipped in though the kitchen door, went up the steps, and into the bathroom. Checking the view from the window there, she had a clear picture of the back yard and the area where Kash parked his car. She would wait until she saw his car pull in before she put her plan into motion.

Fifteen years ago, Rosalee made a hasty decision, which had drastically altered her life. Today, she was about to make another hasty one which would again drastically alter her life.

3

A short while later, Kash slipped the truck into his spot in the back yard and seized the two bags of groceries from the passenger seat. Tucked inside the paper sacks were all the ingredients needed to make tacos and homemade marguerites. Rosalee was not expected until seven o'clock, which left him plenty of time to start preparing refreshments.

Tacos were one of Kash's favorite foods. It was in prison that he first tasted a taco, the only good thing that came out of his time in the hellhole. When the crunchy Mexican shell was introduced to him, the thought of all those different foods mixing together—the meat, the tomatoes, the lettuce, the cheese—was revolting, but after one bite, he was hooked. They were quick and easy to make and much of it could be prepared ahead of time, leaving only the assembly to take care of before he served. He had fixed tacos so often, he could practically do it in his sleep which left his mind open to wondering while he put away the groceries and started the ground meat browning on the stove.

Kash's mind drifted toward Rosa. He was thrilled she was back in his life. The time he had spent with her these past few weeks seemed to speed by. He wondered how he would fill the days when her vacation was over. The Bad Thoughts had entirely slipped from his mind and in its place, the Good Thoughts had slipped in. She was changing him, controlling him, and he had no problem with it—not once did he have a desire to fight it. He had not so much as looked at another woman in days. The urges and needs that used to motivate him were non-existent. His wild lifestyle and his appetite for stimulation seemed like something from a time in a past life.

His thoughts drifted even farther back into the past now, to a time when Kash was a young teen. At this time, The Order and the Bad Thoughts had not yet made an entrance in his life. It was a time when commotion and chaos commanded Kash's day. Back then, the rowdier his daily activities were, the more he wanted to live. He had no order or continuity in his life, but at the time, it really didn't matter. He seemed to have a fascination with the boisterous side of living—the riskier the better. He lived for today, he answered to nobody, he believed there was no tomorrow. There was a reason for his unruly lifestyle: it was the only way he knew to live, the only way he had even been taught.

It was in his late teen years when he would stay out all night drinking, that the Bad Thoughts made their debut. At first, it was just a whisper of the awful organ music and a quick flash of the pictures, only one picture at first. Kash was dumbfounded by the picture, not knowing what his mind was trying to broadcast. Then more pictures flashed, and more, then quicker, and quicker, until eventually the pictures resembled an old time reel-to-reel movie. It was not until Kash had begun to act out the scenes from the movie he watched in his head and felt the satisfying pleasure afterwards, did he understand what his mind's eye had been trying to tell him. Into his adult years, the urges escalated. His cravings for women and liquor were growing. The excitement they provided was just as gratifying as living on the edge. His work, driving over the road, left him bored and annoyed, so he tried to create his own thrills. If he found a convoy en route to one of his drops, you could bet the farm Sam Kashette was in it. If he had a police unit chasing his rig, he was happy, but if three units were trailing him, he was utterly delighted. He had to be in the middle of the action, and he had to be the center of attention.

It took only a short time for all those thrills to become trivial. Because it seemed when all the booze bottles had been emptied, and all the women had been done, and all the dances had been danced, he was still very much alone at the end of the day. It was at this point that Kash had established The Order as a way to structure his life and repair his sanity. His life had been empty, so he filled it with organization and order.

Now Rosa filled that void. She understood him, all of him. With unspoken words, he knew she accepted him and the fact that he was different, that The Order was part of his life and that she was part of The Order. The signals she sent to him were strong. The magnet sucked him in even now. These feeling were foreign to Kash. He was almost normal again. He wanted to settle down, plant some roots, and share some of his love. All these newfound priorities were the direct result of his being reacquainted with an old friend. He had something he could plan on now, something he could look forward to when the time came. Rosalee gave him a future.

The ground meat for the tacos had browned up nicely. It lay draining on a paper towel. Cheese and lettuce had been shredded; the tomatoes and onions had been chopped. He could prepare tacos in his sleep. The frozen juices for the drinks were thawing nicely, the taco shells were arranged on a tray with individual cups set up for each topping, and the small mess he made in the kitchen had been cleaned.

Kash climbed the stairs to get himself ready for his guest. When he reached the top step, he heard an unfamiliar distinct sound coming from the bathroom—sloshing sounds. The door was not completely opened either, the way he always left it. He grabbed a baseball bat from the hall closet and held it ready to swing before he nudged the door open with his foot.

He was flabbergasted to find Rosalee in his tub covered in bubbles up to her neck.

4

Tommy worried too much for a boy his age. The weight of the world rested upon his teenage shoulders. Growing up turned out to be tougher than it sounded. Thus far, Tommy had taken a nonchalant attitude toward the transition. He took one day at a time and took care of tomorrow when tomorrow came. The problem now was he had to forecast tomorrow and handle it today. This way was new to him, and he was unsure of the proper procedure. He focused on the main objective, the one thing he knew had to be done: remove Kash from the confines of his happy little family, untwist everything that Kash had twisted, and put the Whitmore's day-to-day life back the way it used to be. To succeed, he would have to mature very quickly.

He always thought growing up would be a perfectly natural process. He figured he would go to bed one night a boy and when his time had come, he would wake up the next morning a man. What he didn't realize is that he had done none of the normal things that preempt this transformation. He had no real responsibilities to speak of. He had never been required to work. He was never obligated to take care of anybody or anything—not even a pet—and in most respects, he never took care of himself either. His mother saw to each and every one of his needs. She bought his clothes and laid out an entire outfit each morning. She reminded him when it was time to eat, told him when to do his homework, when to get a haircut, when to go to bed. She had the forethought to know when he needed things, too. These things were always there waiting for him. He had never run out of his favorite shampoo, deodorant, or his cologne. She knew before he did when he needed new shoes, or school supplies, or even the latest video game. He never realized just how much he depended on her to survive everyday life.

Kash was disrupting this flow. He would have to be dealt with; he would have to be stopped. Tommy would make his move soon. He could feel it in his bones. He was not afraid of Kash, at least he didn't think so; he merely hated him.

Tommy had been cooped up in the house for several days now watching over his mother. Between him and his dad, Suzy had not been left unattended since the incident at the pro-life rally last week. This morning, Suzy had coaxed Tommy to go over to Jeff's house for a visit today. She told him she was fine and that she hated being babied this way. Jeff lived only a short distance away, and she promised him she would call if anything bad happened. He decided to go for a short while. Tommy was no doctor, but he believed his mother did look much better these past few days.

When she had come home after the rally, Tommy wasn't sure Suzy was even his mother. Her face was puffy from crying, her breathing was staggered so badly that it took all her energy to speak in-between the whimpers—that is to say when she was able to speak. She shivered like a wet animal, and her eyes had lost that sparkle, that glow. Instead, they looked milky, and Tommy was sure the view would have been foggy if seen through his mother's eyes. What did Kash do to her that day to cause a breakdown? What happened to his mother's usually stable mind? Kash was to blame and he would have to be held accountable.

Tommy accepted his first responsibility as an adult, and it was a whopper. He would save his mother from this terrible man. With the thought lingering in his mind, Tommy left the house to visit Jeff. He needed some more of the courage which Jeff kept stashed in a little baggie.

5

"Hi Kash." Rosalee said in a most lively voice. She was sexy and playful lying there in Kash's bathtub. *Let the cards fall where the may.*

Kash released the bat he had clutched tightly in his right hand. It hit the hallway floor with a decided thump. He had never seen this side of Rosalee, but he liked it. He rested his body against the bathroom doorframe, his hands cupped in front of him, admiring the beautiful woman in his tub. He was turned on by the sight of her naked, but this time the turn on was different. The images he saw were not those of the Bad Thoughts. The feelings were in no way dirty or lusty; they were beautiful. His wish was not to be greedily satisfied *by* her; instead, he wanted to share himself *with* her, to satisfy her.

"Need any help?" he offered. "I could wash your back."

"Sure," she replied.

When she straightened her posture in the water, she exposed her beautifully shaped breasts partially covered with suds. Kash knelt down outside the bathtub and ran the sponge lightly over Rosalee's back, noticing for the first time the lovely olive color of her skin. Water dripped from the ends of her hair. It ran effortlessly over her shoulders and down her arms to make a soundless ping when it joined the pool of bathwater.

She kept an attentive eye on her admirer as he maneuvered the sponge from her back to her chest. When he reached her breasts, she twisted her body to face his. Rosa took the sponge from Kash's hand and put it aside. When he touched her, she rippled like the water in the tub. He touched every part of Rosalee's upper body; his lips followed close behind, kissing and suckling every section with true respect and devotion.

Her heart longed for his touch—her body ached for it.

When she reached for the bulge in his faded jeans, the silent connection told him she was ready to give herself. He scooped her from the water and carried her into the bedroom. A trail of water drops speckled the floors from one room, through the hallway, and to the other room. Under normal circumstances, Kash would have cleaned the floors immediately or better yet, the mess would have been avoided all together, but these were not normal circumstances. Kash could have cared less about water on the floors or damp bedding from where he laid down Rosa's wet body.

Their smacking lips and heavy breathing seemed to be amplified within Rosa's mind. She could faintly smell the musk of him over the lilac bath oil she had applied to the tub water. Jesus was so kind to allow her finally to feel—finally to encounter love in the ultimate way. They fondled and caressed one another until she was able to remove each article of his clothing. He lay on top of her, his body slipping and sliding when he made contact with her still lathery skin. He entered her unspoiled territory with all the gentleness of a man who knew this was his partner's first time. She flinched at the sudden burning sensation, but only for a second; Kash never noticed. They made passionate love for what seemed like hours. When the sensations of climax began, Rosa imagined her soul slipping away from within herself, her skin dancing openly, free from the rest of her body. She trembled uncontrollably as they reached the height of affection together. Then they laid collectively, joined as one, entwined in true ecstasy.

When the episode ended, Kash rolled over on his side to face his lover. "It was beautiful, Rosa. I felt so right inside you."

"I know. It felt right to me too."

Kash threw back the covers to get out of bed. Before Rosalee could explain her virginity, he noticed the spot of blood on the sheets.

"Rosa, you're bleeding. Did I hurt you?"

"No, I'm fine. It's just that I've never done this before. I've never been with a man."

"Are you telling me you're a virgin?"

"Yes, Kash ... I am. You were the first."

6

Suzy Whitmore was sick of being mollycoddled like some kind of psychotic on a suicide watch. Since returning from the mountains two days ago, she had had little time to herself. If it wasn't Clayton hovering over her, then Tommy was following her around. She had not been able to get away long enough—even for a few moments—to return Lora's call until now. Clayton had gone down to the campus, and she had persuaded Tommy to go to Jeff's house.

To bother Lora at the hospital was something she hated to do, but she had no other option. It was now or maybe never. Annie transferred her call to Dr. Jordan's office.

"Hey Lora, it's me."

"Suzy ... I've been worried sick about you. How are feeling?"

"I'm feeling fine, despite what my family thinks."

"What happened at the rally? Tommy said you fainted."

"Yeah, that's an understatement. I'm told I was out for 20 minutes. I could have sworn I saw Kash in the crowd."

"Are you sure? Did you get a good look at him?"

"Yes, I got a good look, but it wasn't Kash. When I started my speech, one fellow in the back looked like him. I tried to put it out of my mind and continue on, but as I surveyed the crowd further, everyone in the audience started to look like Kash. At one point, I glanced over to Clayton, and I thought he was Kash too. I've got to tell you Lora, I was never so scared in my whole life. I thought I was going insane."

"Are you all right now? I mean, have you had any more hallucinations?"

"No, thank God. Clayton forced me to see a doctor, though. He still thinks my problems stem from menopause. I'm not telling him anything different."

"Keep your chin up, kid. This thing could be over sooner than we expect."

"Really, is Rosa making headway with Kash?"

"No. I'm sure she's stalling. She says she needs more time, but I don't think she ever intended to talk to him about the money. But that doesn't matter any more."

"What do you mean it doesn't matter?" Suzy's pitch was getting louder and her voice started to quiver. "It matters a great deal." Now she was talking faster—all her words ran together. "She was our only link to talking Kash out of this mess." Her tone intensified. "Are you crazy or something, Lora?"

"Calm down Suzy."

"Calm down! I can't get any calmer. I'm eating valium five times a day. If I calm down any more you'll have to talk to me from my vegetable crisper."

"Okay, okay. Hear me out. When I spoke to Rosa a week ago, she let something slip. She said that Kash had been in prison. I did some checking through a friend, and it's true. He spent a year and half at the State Penitentiary in Kentucky. When Rosa told us Kash had been involved in an accident, she failed to mention that he was drunk and killed a teenage boy."

"So what? How does that help us?"

"He wasn't released from prison until Easter Sunday. He's still on parole. Don't you see Suz, if we can get him to come back up here—to Massachusetts, I mean—we can trap him in violation of his parole orders. He's not allowed to leave West Virginia."

"That's great, but how do you plan to get him up here?"

"I'm still working on that, but if we can get him to come here, all of our problems will be solved. There will be no more free cash for Mr. Kashette."

"What about this month? Should we send the checks or let him come up here after it? That's one way to get him in the state."

"No, we'll have to pay him this time. I don't want to take a chance on his going to see Alex or Clayton again. If all goes as planned, it should be the last check he'll ever see from us."

7

It was a gorgeous, sunny day in West Virginia. Rosa and Kash had driven a few miles into the mountains. The place where Kash chose to take Rosa today was called Farley's Falls. The woman who owned the property was a friend of Gabby's.

The land known as Farley's Falls consisted of three water falls—two small ones at the upper end, a larger one at the lower end—with a swimming hole beyond the big falls that was large enough to accommodate several dozen swimmers. Because of the lack of rain this summer, the two smaller falls barely trickled, and the big falls ran with no more force than a kitchen faucet running at half its intensity. Woods surrounded the area and Rosa imagined how beautiful it would have looked if all the trees would have been in full bloom. She especially liked the dozens of pink and white dogwoods. Although the swimming hole did look shallow, Rosa guessed there was still water enough to swim anyway.

At one time, Mrs. Farley had opened up her property to the public. People would come from all around to enjoy the waterfalls. As word about Farley's Falls spread, the place became infested with bikers and even criminals hiding from the law. Fights and trouble became an everyday occurrence—the local police were forced to put it on their hourly patrol—until one day a young woman had been stabbed. That was when Mrs. Farley put a stop to everyone and anyone taking advantage of the natural beauty of her land. Kash, however, was always welcome.

Rosa was awestruck by the majestic view. She and Kash stood atop a bridge which overlooked the two smaller waterfalls and a shallow area of rock and water. Huge boulder and cliffs encased the entire lot. It was truly splendid.

"This place is great," Rosa said. "How deep is the swimming hole?"

"About six feet when it rains. Today, probably half that. Are you ready to swim?"

"Yeah."

Fifteen years had passed since Rosalee DeLucci bought her last bathing suit. The one she selected this week was a fashionable, but conservative, one-piece suit. She was a bit embarrassed by her chubby appearance when she disrobed, but Kash quickly swept those self-conscience thoughts from her mind.

They played in the water like teenagers. For almost an hour, they dunked each other, played chase in the water, had splashing contests, and a few times Rosa climbed on top of Kash's shoulders to jump into the water. They were having a ball, but they were 38 years old after all, and their bodies were quickly tiring. Rosa was the first to suggest they go back to the blanket. They dried off and afterwards Kash pulled out a bottle of white wine and two glasses from a cooler. He also set out cheese and fruit packed in plastic containers.

"My," Rosa said, "I'm impressed. You didn't forget anything."

"Well maybe the candles," he replied as he poured wine.

They sipped their drinks in silence, occasionally glancing and smiling at each other. Rosa leaned across the blanket to get a piece of cheese. In one nimble move, Kash swiftly laid her on her back. He kissed her lips passionately. She returned his gesture equally. He pulled her close as they fondled each other, working hard to remove the other's wet suit. They made love two times that afternoon beneath the hot West Virginia sun. The tranquil sounds made by the rolling water of the falls made it the most romantic moment Rosa had ever experienced. She was falling in love.

When their romantic interlude ended, Kash and Rosa laid side-by-side—completely quiet—thinking about each other. Rosa was first to break the silence.

"Do you ever dream, Kash?"

"Not until I met you. I used to think dreaming was for the fool hearted who couldn't make things happen in their lives. I used to think only weak people dreamed, but now I know that's not true."

"I've always been a dreamer."

"Was I ever in your dream?"

"Only every day; you were my superstar. I dreamed about a life with you. You and I together, married, doing things, going places, even making love."

"I never knew, ya know?"

"I know you didn't. Let me show you how to live my dream."

He gazed into her eyes and said, "You make me so happy, Rosa."

"And you make me happy, too."

"You know … I think it's so much more than happiness. You do something to me. I'm drawn to you. I can't get enough of you. But somehow, you already know what I'm feeling, don't you? You know about the attachment, about the connection. Unless I've missed my guess, you've felt it for a long time." He nibbled on a piece of pepper-jack cheese and a wedge of apple before adding—almost as an afterthought, "You make me a better person. You make me feel young and alive, you give me spark; excitement."

"Oh Kash, that's so romantic."

"I'm not trying to be romantic, Rosa, I'm finally being honest. I was scrapping bottom before you came into my life. I was on my way to becoming an alcoholic, not to mention a few other things, before my involvement with you. You turned my life around. You've made me a whole person again."

He sipped his wine, never taking his eyes off her.

"I've learned from you, too," he continued. "You've taught me how to give, how to trust, and most importantly, how to be loved. You've taken a tiny pinhole in my heart and opened it up, letting in all these emotions I've never experienced—emotions I was too afraid to feel because I was afraid of getting hurt again."

Nobody had ever said such wonderful things about her before. Rosa could do nothing but stare. She was speechless to the point that she was afraid to open her mouth for fear something stupid would come out or worse, she would say the wrong thing and spoil a beautiful moment.

"Let's skinny dip," Kash said. Leave it to Kash to ruin a tender moment. "It'll be fun. We're already naked anyhow."

"That's like saying, 'let's jump off the bridge since we're driving across it anyway.' No, I'd be too embarrassed to swim naked."

"I've seen and touched every part of you—both inside and out. What is there to be embarrassed about? "

"This body," she said gesturing her to nakedness covered up by one end of the blanket. The only skin exposed was her feet and ankles, her arms, and her neck and head.

"Stop this egoistic bullshit right now, Rosalee! There is nothing wrong with your body. It could not look more perfect or more beautiful to me. Now come on, let's live a little."

My Lord, Rosa thought, *let's live a little.* Those were the same words, the exact phrase he said to her roughly 25 years ago at Keystone's. The night he wanted her to go outside and drink wine with him. Deja vu swept over her. She inspected the grounds for any signs of Frankie or his '66 Chevy Nova SS. Thankfully, he was nowhere in sight. Before she could think of another excuse, Kash had gripped her hand and pulled her from the ground, stripping her of the security blanket that had been shielding her.

"See," he said, "nothing to be ashamed of—two arms, two legs, five fingers, five toes, and all the essential parts in between."

Then he led her to the waterhole.

Once in the pool, Rosa felt better. The water covered all of her essential parts, as Kash had put it, up to her breasts. For this, she was grateful. If anything had to stick out, let it be the upper parts since she carried most of her excess weight in the lower belly, hips, butt, and thighs.

When they swam, the free feeling of water flowing over parts normally covered by clothing was a turn on for both Rosa and Kash. Rosa especially liked the feel of her skin rubbing against his. The way her body would slither and glide over Kash's rippled, hard body with only a thin layer of water between them when they cuddled in each other's embrace. This time it was Rosa who played the seductress. She had to have him again. In the water, she straddled his body, wrapping her legs around his waist. Then she raised her arm high above her head and forced a large breast toward his mouth. Her hard nipples ached for the suckle of his soft warm lips and his moist strong tongue. She could not get enough.

They moved from the water back to the blanket again where Rosa held Kash tightly. They coiled their naked bodies to make love once again. Rosa was falling for Kash faster than the water was spilling over the rain-deprived falls.

8

In her living room this evening, Gabby skimmed through some old photo albums. Her house was full of antiques, but to Gabby, these were just things she'd had for years. She looked at the pile of albums. With six children and eleven grandchildren, it was no wonder the pictures had stacked up over the years. She grabbed one of the older albums and leafed through it until she found the picture for which she was looking. She stared at the graduation picture of her eldest son, Larry.

Larry's photo did not accompany the other graduation pictures hanging on the wall, nor was there any evidence of Larry anywhere visible around the house. Gabby kept the memories of her son locked tightly inside her mind and heart. Some days she missed Larry very much. He was her first born after all. She remembered vividly the day he had come into this world. She and Larry Sr. had been so happy with the new addition to their family, and a baby boy was the gender they had both wanted. Larry Jr. died when he was just nineteen years old. Even though she had five other children over the years to occupy her heart, she still felt the loss of her first-born.

Gabby heard a vehicle pull in next door. She looked out the window. Dusk had just settled in, so there was enough light to see movement, but not enough light to distinguish faces. She knew the man getting out of the truck was Kash. She watched as he opened the truck's passenger side door for a young lady.

In some ways, Kash reminded Gabby of Larry. Some of his features resembled Larry's, and she believed they even had the same walk. As long as Kash was next door, she would always be close to Larry.

She squinted to get a closer look at the girl. She was sure this girl was the same girl whom Kash had been bringing home for the last couple of weeks. Gabby was glad to finally see someone steady in Kash's life. His reckless ways worried her terribly.

When the couple walked under the street lamp, Gabby was able to get a good look at Kash's date. She looked a great deal like Rosalee DeLucci.

But that can't be her; Rosalee DeLucci is a nun.

9

The days had passed swiftly for Kash since he began his romantic involvement with Rosalee. These were the last few days of her vacation. He could not remember being happier than he was right now. In the short time since their first encounter, Rosa and Kash shared each other's flesh a total five times. Kash was filled with new life. His outlook for the future was no longer bleak and lonely, but instead he viewed the coming days, months, and years as a welcomed opportunity. Rosa was his new adventure, his new stimulus. She aroused emotions in him he had lost sight of—not only emotions of a sexual nature but mental emotions as well. The Bad Thoughts were all but gone now; he no longer needed the Healing Rhymes. He still had The Order but from his perspective, The Order was just part of life. It would always be there. He was at peace with himself. Before she had come into his life, he was at a constant defense when in the company of women—always watching his backside—but with Rosalee, he could be himself. With other women, he needed to have the upper hand, had to be in control, but with Rosa, it was different. By giving himself freely and sharing his body with her, he came to realize the difference between having sex and making love with someone for whom he truly cared. With Rosa, there was no urge for him to be forceful or domineering, no requisite for selfishness. He wanted to be her partner, wanted the two of them to be a team.

Rosa and Kash planned to revisit the old campus at Kanawha State today. They decided on a picnic because, as usual, the weather forecasters predicted another dry day. Rosa was to make potato salad and baked beans. Kash was in charge of hamburgers, buns, and the hibachi. Kash chose today to ask Rosa where their relationship was going. For his sanity's sake, he had to keep her in his life. She would be leaving her hometown soon, and Kash wanted very much to go with her. He wanted to marry her one day soon, but first he had to know how she felt about him.

He made a mental list of the places he wanted to take Rosa. First stop would be The Jug, a regular hangout in their day. Next, they would have a picnic lunch then take a stroll through the campus. He'd purchased two tickets for *Oklahoma* at the University's summer playhouse. He planned to surprise her with the tickets.

Gabby pecked on the kitchen door.

"Hi Kash. I thought I'd better return your drill before you reported it stolen."

"It's no problem, Gab. Would you like a glass of iced tea? I just made it."

"No thank you." Gabby was thrilled to see Kash in such high spirits and was shocked by the offer of ice tea instead of a beer. She watched as he unwrapped a package of ground meat and began to form hamburger patties. Her eyes roamed the room. She spotted a dishwasher under the counter that she was certain had not been there before. In the dining room, she noticed a new dinette set.

"I see you've bought some new things?"

"Yeah, I got tired of sticking my hands in dishwater, so I bought a dishwasher. I got a good bargain on the table and chairs, and I couldn't pass it up."

"That's great Kash. I also noticed the lawn furniture and a big gas grill on the porch. Are they new too?"

"Yes, they are. And that reminds me ... I'd like to invite you over for a cookout tomorrow. I want you to meet someone who's very special to me. Can you make it?"

"Sure, I'll be here."

"About noon. I bought some nice porterhouse steaks, so don't eat a big breakfast."

"Look, I know this is none of my business, but where are you getting all your money? You haven't worked since you came home, and I know what was in your bank account."

Kash avoided answering the question. Instead, he offered, "You know Gabby, I'm thinking about fixing up this old house a little. Try to make it more of a home. I thought maybe I would install central air and put siding on the outside. And around front, I'd like to build some planter boxes and fill them with some kind of flowers. That would make this place real homey, don't you think? I hope to have someone to share my life and to share this place with me in the very near future."

"Is this special someone the same person you want me to meet tomorrow?"

"Yes Gabby, it is. She makes me so happy, and I feel wonderful when I'm with her. I'm not afraid of anything anymore. She keeps me from being scared."

"What could you possibly be scared of?"

"I'm scared of loosing, of dreaming, of growing old. Sometimes, I'm even scared to feel. She's opened my eyes to a whole new future. For the first time ever I think I can love."

"I see that, and I think it's great. Any woman who can make you this content about your life has got my vote. I can't wait to meet her."

"Well, actually, you already know her, but it was a long time ago. I dated her for a while in high school."

Thoughts of the silhouette ran through Gabby's mind. She pictured Rosalee DeLucci getting out of Kash's truck. She turned to Kash and saw him smiling while he continued to patty burgers. *Surely, he couldn't be talking about her.*

She asked, "You're not talking about Rosalee DeLucci, are you?"

"I swear you have a sixth sense, Gab. How did you know?"

"I saw you with her last night."

"You did? I'm not surprised. We've spent almost every day together since she's come to town. Today I'm going to ask her to spend the rest of her life with me."

"You are joking, aren't you?"

"No, I couldn't be more serious. I know everything happened really fast. There was no way to slow it down. It was like a snowball rolling downhill, only the faster it rolled the more she consumed my heart. I know the Rosa you remember was shy, backwards and even dull at times, but she's different now, more open and fun to be with. It's like she was this sleeping volcano and now all of a sudden it's erupted, and her lava is covering me with new passions, feelings, and joy."

"Do you know what you're doing Kash? I think there's a minor detail about her life that Rosalee has conveniently left out. I don't know how to tell you this, except to just come right out and say it. Rosalee DeLucci is a nun."

"A what?"

"A nun, as in Sister Rosa. You know … a religious woman. One who has taken vows."

"I know the definition of a nun Gabby, and I think the idea is crazy. You've been listening to too much of your lady friend's gossip."

"It's not gossip, Kash and it's not an idea—it's a fact. I remember when she left. Her family was not very vocal about the whole thing. I think it took them by surprise, too. I always believed you were the reason she left. You know she loved you very much back then. That's why I never asked you about her. I assumed you knew where she had gone and why she chose to leave."

"No Gab, you've got to be mistaken."

"Look Kash, I don't want to see you get hurt, but you're packing a romantic picnic for a nun. If you don't believe me, ask her. Where did she tell you she's been all these years? Did she explain to you what it is she does for a living? Ask her about her job, ask her why she never married, ask her if she'll stay here with you or better yet, ask her if you can come to visit her. I'll bet my next pension check that she can't give you a straight answer to even one of those questions without squirming around and stuttering. Just think about it Kash. Look into it, that's all I'm asking."

Kash leaned against the cabinets and stared at the ceiling. Gabby kissed his cheek and stroked his face in a motherly fashion. "You know I'll always be here if you want to talk. Thanks for the drill," she said before leaving.

From his kitchen window, Kash watched Gabby walk through the yard. He dug his hand deep into the package of cold ground meat. After rolling a handful of burger into a ball, he began to pat it down. Fury spread through him. He crushed the newly formed patty with his hand. Meat crowded out in-between his fingers. He produced another ball. Shuffling the ball from one hand to the other, then pressing it between his palms, he pulverized the meat. Kash could think of nothing but Rosa. This was absurd … Rosa a nun. Wherever could Gabby get such a notion? He continued to work the same ball of meat. What if Gabby were right? What if Rosa were a nun? What if Rosa had been lying to him?

Anger bubbled in Kash the same way hot tar bubbled on a newly laid surface. The little organ keeper inside his head pressed out one or two chords before stopping. It sort of teased him a bit, just to remind Kash that the organ keeper was still very much a part of him, and that he would not go away easily. Kash flattened the ball of hamburger against the countertop until the meat was paper-thin. He scrapped the meat back up, formed a ball with it, and threw it at the wall.

Kash packed the basket with all the ingredients for the picnic then he packed a cooler of drinks. Rosa would never lie to him. If she were a religious woman, as Gabby had said, then she would never have let him touch her, much less make love to her. They had a connection; he would have been able to tell. Her feelings were sincere, as were her action. Gabby had gotten some bad information, that's all there was to it.

Rosalee appeared at the door. She announced herself before walking into the house.

"Hello Kash. Are we ready to go?"

Kash pulled himself out of the sullen mood. "Yes, I'm definitely ready to go. I need to get out of here for a while."

"Then let's get going. I'm looking forward to seeing some of the old hangouts again, aren't you?"

"Yeah, I guess so."

The route leading to Charleston took them through downtown Huntington. Rosa slouched down a bit in the passenger side of Kash's pickup. Gossip in a small town was bad news. He could feel her tensing up from his seat on the driver's side. The feeling that she wanted to avoid being seen with him inched slowly into his mind but soon he attributed his paranoia to the earlier conversation with Gabby and quickly dismissed it.

Once out on the country roads, Rosa moved closer to Kash. She sat in the middle of the bench seat with her left hand resting on his right leg. All of the questions Gabby had posed this morning kept replaying.

Where did she tell you she's been all these years? How did she explain to you what it is she does for a living? Why did she never marry? Will she stay here with you? Or will you go to visit her?

Instead, he settled for a question of his own. "Why did you decide to scoot over just now? You were hugging the door all the way through town," he said.

"I thought I cleared that up for you last time we were in your truck. I don't want my brother to see us together. Not yet. He still has a few reservations about you. I don't doubt he'll come around, but it'll take some time. You said you understood."

"I do, but I don't. You're a grown woman. Why do you let your brother run your life?"

"He doesn't run my life. I just don't want to upset him right now."

"Is that the reason why I can't come to your house and why I can't call you?"

"Yes, what other reason could there be?"

"I don't know. I just wish I could show you off a little bit, I guess. Sometimes you act like you're hiding something."

"Oh Kash, you're imagining things. What could I possibly have to hide? Do you think I'm a wanted criminal or something?"

Kash made no response. The something part certainly applied. His mind raced with different theories and doubts. Could Gabby be right? Could the something part be that Rosa is a nun?

"Tell me more about the school where you teach," he said.

"It's a wonderful school. The children I taught last year were so disciplined. And you talk about bright kids. Our class scored third in the nation on tests given each year to students in the parochial school system. I don't mean to brag but those kids ..."

"Woo, woo," Kash interrupted. "Parochial school ... isn't that a Catholic school?"

"Yes. So what. You're looking at me like I told you I was teaching lepers."

"I'm just shocked you didn't mention it before."

"I didn't think it was important."

After a short pause, Kash continued with the interrogation. "What's it like to be around all those nuns?"

"It's okay, I guess. But you know Kash, nuns are people too."

"Do they have to wear those penguin suits all the time?"

"No, they don't wear those stuffy vestments anymore. Most of them wear regular clothes. Sometimes people feel intimidated when they see the habits. They become uncomfortable in the presence of a nun and that shouldn't be. Nuns are no different from regular people, with the exception of their vows to serve the Lord. Religious figures are often secluded from the rest of the world. People tense up around them, so they tend to stay away from them. And believe me that happens more often than you'd think."

The couple was mostly quiet during the remainder of the drive. Kash tried to block out the realization which kept turning over in his mind, but it was virtually impossible. There were too many coincidences to suit The Order. First, he recalled Rosa's vague response when he asked her about her life during their first visit. Second, he remembered how comfortably she defended God when they debated the topic at Ruby Tuesday. Third, she was certainly well informed about the life of religious figures judging from her comments mere moments ago. Lastly, she always turned the conversation to different subject matter when he tried to talk about her. Then there were all the unanswered questions: Where had she been all these years? Why was she so mysterious about her private affairs? Why was she was trying to conceal their relationship from her family? He knew Frankie never liked him much, but he refused to accept this fact as the reason why Rosa dispensed with telling the DeLucci family about their romance. Why did she choose to visit him now, after all these years? And more importantly, why did she come to see him at all if she knew her family would disapprove? No, there was something else going on here, something she was keeping from him. But what? Unless ...

Kash pulled the vehicle into a parking place near the front door of The Jug. The Jug was a quaint bar frequented by the circle of friends Rosa and Kash had run around with in college. It was located off the beaten path of Kanawha State. Named and known for its vast variety of jugs collected from the West Virginia moonshine days, the pub was a favorite gathering spot for students of the University even today. Positioned in a valley near Charleston, The Jug was secluded from the rest of town, which was a good thing because the bar could get rather noisy late at night. Rosa and Kash had spent many nights in this bar drinking, and talking, and laughing with friends.

When they got out of the car, Rosa could hear the tinkling of a fishing stream that ran behind the pub. She expected to find someone there fishing on a beautiful day like this, but the banks of the stream were empty. Only a scant ooze of water flowed along the bed. Oh, how she wished it would rain.

A weekday afternoon was not a busy time for The Jug, so Kash and Rosa had a variety of choice seats. Rosa chose a booth near the back, which overlooked the skinny stream. For the most part, the place looked the same as she remembered it, with the exception of a few minor renovations the owners had made to keep up with the times. Kash stopped at the bar, ordered two beers, and brought them back to the table. They sipped the draft beer served in mason jars. Neither spoke.

Rosa was concerned with Kash's sudden silence. He had been chatty since the first night they had gotten reacquainted.

"You're quiet today," she said finally. "Is something bothering you?"

"No. I mean ... yes ... sort of. I'm just a little stunned about our relationship."

"To be honest with you, so am I. It all happened so quickly."

"Yeah, I know. Why is that? Why didn't you ever visit me before? What made you think about me this time?"

"Well, for starters, I don't get a chance to come home very often. I was looking through some memorabilia, and I got to wondering about you. I took a chance one day and walked over to your house. You know the rest."

"Do I? Do I **really** know the rest? What about you? Where have you been all these years? You never really said. You told me you've traveled around. Where did you go?"

"All over. What's the big deal?"

"No big deal. You don't seem willing to talk about yourself, is all. I figured the only way I would get some answers is to ask some questions. Where do you live? Earlier you said the panhandle of West Virginia. That covers a lot of ground. What's the name of the town?"

"Wellsburg. Why all the questions?"

Kash sensed Rosa's nervousness. He caught her squirming around on her side of the booth. She avoided any eye contact with him. Gabby was right: Rosa was incapable of giving him a straight answer. His heart began to crumble; his pulse quickened. The awful organ music played softly in his mind. When he felt the Bad Thoughts returning, he fought back tears.

"Do you have a boyfriend back there? Is there anyone special waiting for you?"

"No. Is that why you're asking all these questions? Do you think I have a boyfriend?"

"Are you a lesbian?"

"What! Why would you even ask me that?"

"I find it hard to believe that a bright, nice looking woman like you has never had sex. You said I was the first. You said you had never been with a man. Does that mean you'd never been with a women either?"

"Kash, you were the first. I've never had sex with anyone, man or woman, because I wanted it to be perfect. I wanted it to be with someone I loved. Is that so hard to understand?"

"Do you love me Rosa?"

She hesitated a bit before answering. Her eyes looked in his direction, but not really at him. She sort of looked through him.

"Yes Kash, I do love you. I can't believe you're grilling me this way. What's the point?"

"The point is, darlin', you're a bit too secretive. I want to know you, Rosa. I want to know everything about you. I don't understand why you're so reluctant to talk to me."

"I don't think I'm secretive. I'm just a private person. What do you want to know?"

"Okay, for instance, what do you do in your spare time?"

"Not much. I'm afraid I'm rather boring."

"Are you telling me you don't go out with your friends after work? You don't have dates or go to parties?"

"No … not very often. I don't have many friends; I stay to myself."

"Why is that Rosa? Is it because you spend so much time with all the nuns, you have become secluded too?"

"No. What are you im …"

"Do you live in an apartment or a house?"

"A house, why?"

"Do you own it, or do you rent it?"

"I rent it. What's with all …"

"How many rooms does it have? What color is it? Is it a big house or a little house? Do you have a yard?"

"It's a big house?"

"How big?"

"I don't know, big. What does that have to do with …"

"How big Rosa? Does it have lots of rooms? Do you live alone? Or do you share the house with someone? Perhaps with several people?" He fired the questions fast and furious, wanting to trip her up. And he succeeded. Her cheeks glowed a bright pink now; the rest of her face was ashen. She was lying—or so the little organ keeper inside Kash's head believed. He pounded out a few heartbreaking cords just to let Kash know he was back. Time to play the trump card.

"I'll bet the house you live in is white. I'll bet there's a cross on the roof and a white statue of the alleged pure Blessed Mother in the front yard. Am I painting a pretty accurate picture?"

Rosalee swallowed hard. "Oh Kash," she said as she closed her eyes and dropped her head. "I never wanted you to find out this way. I wanted to tell you from the start, but things got so complicated, and everything happened so fast. I didn't know how to start. So help me God, I wanted to tell you, but I couldn't bring myself to do it. Not after …"

"Not after what? Not after we talked. Not after we kissed. Not after we made love. Not after what?"

"Not after I realized how much I still love you. I couldn't Kash. I would have told you eventually, if you had given me the chance."

"And when would that have been? Tomorrow? When you were ready to go back to the convent?"

"No, I'm not going back. My place is here with you. I'm leaving the convent. I want to spend the rest of my life with you Kash. Can't you understand that?"

"I understand that you lied to me, Sister Rosa. You were deceitful and misleading. I trusted you and you used me."

"No, I never used …"

Kash slapped his hand on the table. "Shut up, bitch. You crossed me, and I'm not interested in hearing any of your excuses right now. Just know this: you will pay your dues to me. One day you will pay dearly. I'm leaving now before I do something I will regret later."

The awful organ whispered in the background. The Bad Thoughts were coming on like gangbusters. He just wanted to get out of there so his darkness would pass. He stood up and marched out of The Jug.

Rosa could feel the room shake with each heavy step he took toward the exit. He was angry with her, and she was scared. Not scared of what he could possibly do to her—nothing he could do now could hurt more—but scared of loosing him. Her secret was out in the open, the worst of it being over. She would simply have to patch things up with him so they could get on with their life together. She ran out of the bar after him.

From the porch of The Jug, Rosa scanned the parking lot. She saw no signs of Kash. His truck was parked where they had left it. There was only one other car in the lot, most likely belonging to the bartender. She walked down the front step and started to call out his name while she worked her way around to the back of the bar. She had to find him and explain. Just as she was about to turn back, she spotted him standing near the entrance of the woods at the edge of the stream.

10

Kash stood on the banks of the water behind The Jug. He watched a fish slink upstream in the narrow slice of water. One by one, he threw rocks at the harmless fish. Kash wanted to hurt something. He didn't have the energy to fight the Bad Thoughts—not this time. His heart was crushed, his future plans ruined, his spirit, defeated. Rosa had destroyed what little love and dreams Kash was beginning to bring back to life. Hatred for this woman overwhelmed him when he saw her approach.

"Kash," she said softly. "Please talk to me. We can get past this."

"There is no we, Rosa, and I'm through talking."

She grabbed his shirt. He turned around with his fist drawn, but he backed off. The little organ player turned up the volume. "I'm warning you Rosa, get away from me."

She loosened her grasp on him, fully aware that she had his attention now. "Listen to me Kash, you want answers to all your questions, and I'll give them to you. I'll tell you truth, if you'll just talk to me. I swear Kash, no more lies."

"This whole affair has been a lie. Why should I believe anything you tell me now?"

"Because the truth is what I have left. All the lies are used up." She paused to catch her breath before starting again. "I came to see you the first night because Lora and Suzy asked me to talk to you."

"Lora and Suzy? How the hell did they ..."

"Please Kash. Let me finish. They flew me to Boston to tell me you had found out some dirty little secret they had been keeping, and that you were blackmailing them for money each month to keep quiet. I didn't believe it, but I told them I would talk to you anyway. I wanted to see what I could find out. I figured the only way I would be able to clear things up would be to get your side of the story. As the days went on and we saw more and more of each other, the less I wanted to be involved in their problems. I was growing more attached to you with each passing day, and I didn't care what you had done to them. I only wanted to be with you always. So when Lora called to ask how I was making out with you, I stalled her and when she calls back again, I had every intention of telling her I want to forget about all of it. I didn't think you were capable of doing anything as dirty as blackmail, however, now I can see that everything they told me was true. But it's okay Kash. I forgive you. You can leave them alone. We can get on with our life together. If I can find it in my heart to forgive you for what you've done to them, why can't you forgive me?"

"Because you tricked me. You toyed with my affections. I will never forgive you for that. Anyway, I don't see where I did anything that needs forgiving. I have no idea why those two crazy bitches concocted such an outlandish story about me, but there's not a word of truth to it. Let them try and prove it. I don't want anything to do with them, and I don't want anything to do with you."

"Oh Kash, you don't mean that. You can't give up on us. We have something special. We're connected to each other. We have something few couples ever get to experience."

"You're right, we do. Not every man gets seduced by a nun."

Rosalee raised her arm, aiming an open hand at his cheek. He seized her wrist with his left hand and pulled it snugly behind her. Then he repositioned himself, by pressing his belly and chest against her back. At the same time, he twisted her arm upwards in the direction of her head. Rosa felt fiery pain shoot through her shoulder—Kash heard a pop—as he forced her arm farther toward her head. He administered two solid punches to her right kidney after missing his target with the first punch and hitting her squarely in the tailbone. Keeping her wrist safely in his grasp, he twirled her around, much the same way he would have spun her around had they been on a dance floor, only this dance could be fatal. Still holding her wrist, he pulled her toward him next, and at the same time, drilled his fist into her stomach solidly, knocking the wind right out of her lungs. She coughed and gagged for a couple moments before he used the back of his right hand to swipe her face bringing blood to the corner of her mouth. After releasing her arm, he used his left hand to reverse the strike and backhanded the other side of her face.

He truly had no real yearning to hit her, even though she had deceived him. She must be punished; she had dues to pay. Now she was linked with the Inferiors. He could no longer trust her.

She stumbled to the ground, tried to crawl out of his reach, all the while weeping as the reality of the blows set in. Two giant steps were all that separated her from Kash. He quickly caught up to her and forcefully picked her up by the front of her shirt. The sleeve's cotton material cut into her underarms and at the same time, the collar was forced to pinch itself taut around her neck. His strong arms easily supported her total body weight. He had the strength of six men. He held her there within inches of his face. She could smell beer on his breath, almost feel the roughness of his parched lips, and see a glassy twinkle in his eyes. She could hear him breathing heavily as his nostrils flared in and out sucking up air. She could all but smell his temper emitting from every pore of his skin. Rosalee trembled in his clutch as she prepared for another whack.

Now the music in Kash's head blared. The pictures flashed rapidly, one after another after another. The Healing Rhymes were never even considered. The pictures, which supplied visual aid for his actions, overpowered him. They consumed him totally.

Rosa watched the window of the bar with the slim hope that somebody would see them and help her.

Kash jabbed at her face this time connecting with her left eye. He hit her again and again. After a poke in the nose, Rosa's eyes swam in tears. She literally saw stars. Blood quickly gushed from the right nostril, running over her upper lip and into her open mouth. She still labored to breathe and now her eyes watered so badly, she could not see either. Tasting her own blood put her on the verge of throwing up.

He was helpless to stop the violence. The Bad Thoughts guided his actions, forcing him to do whatever he viewed. She tried to fight him, but it had no effect. He punched her in the stomach again and when she doubled over in pain, he drove his knee through her face knocking her on her back a few feet into the woods. She never really screamed. The only things that came out were muffled, whispered screeches and hushed moans of pain.

The Bad Thoughts overshadowed Kash's self-control. He never tried to block it; he knew it was useless.

Rosa lay on the ground between the stream bank and the border leading to a wooded area. Kash hiked her up by her underarms and threw her deeper into the woods. Her head banged against a fallen tree branch when she landed on her back once again. He climbed on top of her, straddling his legs over her thighs. Rosa tried madly to free herself by thrashing her legs and pushing his upper body in wild protest with all the strength she had left in her arms. The struggle only excited Kash more until he could no longer contain his urges. Pulling up her shirt and ripping at her bra, he rampantly groped at her breasts. With the same mouth that had tenderly suckled her nipples earlier this week, he now sucked and bit at them with sadistic disrespect. Unzipping his pants and tearing at her underwear simultaneously, he was utterly out of control. He couldn't wait another second.

He entered her violently, thrusting himself in her with great force. Inside her now, she felt no different to him at all. She was just another one of the women who were put on this earth to serve man's needs—another Inferior.

His needs were served in a short time.

When Kash finished using Rosa, he removed himself from atop her. He fixed his pants and replaced the hat that had fallen off his head during the episode. He picked Rosa up by the strands of her short hair and kissed her full on the mouth, biting her lower lip hard enough to draw fresh blood. He then threw her shaking body to the ground. Just for fun, he dug the toe of his boot into the ground near her head, and kicked dirt into her face.

"Ashes to ashes, dust to dust." His voice was stern when he spoke. He walked away casually, his body satisfied, his mind content.

Within seconds, his truck could be heard speeding down the main road. Rosalee sat in the dirt near the edge of the woods, her legs gathered in her arms, her knees tucked snugly to her chest. She wept softly, at first, and then she cried madly, once again for the man who had broken her heart so many times before.

CHAPTER THIRTEEN

Coming to Terms

1

Kash sat in his favorite chair staring at a blank television screen; his reflection stared back at him. He was still tired this morning. His sleep had been interrupted once more last night by the dream about the little boy.

Kash was befuddled by the nightmare that depicted him as a little boy, a terribly frightened little boy. He had been trapped in a small, dark space. There was a door. After repeatedly jiggling the knob, the young Kash realized he was not trapped at all but instead, he had been locked in. A blob hung over his head. It scared the child to the point of practically wetting his pants. He was alone and afraid. The blob was going to get him. When someone approached the door, the boy should have felt relief because he was going to be rescued, but instead the young Kash's fear only worsened. As with the other occurrences, Kash woke up just short of the door being opened, so he never got to see who opened it or why the young Kash had been so afraid.

The dream seemed to start up again every time Kash experienced a drastic change in his lifestyle or an incident traumatic enough to alter The Order. The first time he had the dream was shortly after he went to Kentucky. He remembered it well now. It was during the first week he'd spent in jail. Although it was October and the prison was usually cold, this particular night had been warm and muggy. He had fallen asleep that night wearing only his underwear. Within a few hours of slumber, he had been awakened by the bad dream. His entire body had been chilled, yet perspiration oozed from the pores in his face and neck. After waking himself, he had examined his surrounding (the dark cell) only to find he still had the same horrible feeling of solitude and fear that he had been subjected to in his sleep. Then the dreadful ringing in his ears had begun. It sounded like a mild buzz at the onset, but the more attention he had given to it, the louder the buzzing became.

The second occurrence of the weird dream happened the first night after he had been released from prison. In the little shack at the football field in Kentucky, he had again been wakened abruptly by the nightmare and the disturbing ringing noises in his head.

The third time was the night the redhead Inferior had stayed over, and last night the dream came to him for the fourth time.

This morning, the ringing within Kash's ears gave way to an echoing voice. It was not the Bad Thoughts or the little organ keeper—it was the voice of Rosalee DeLucci. She repeated over and over again: *I wanted to tell you Kash. I never wanted you to find out this way.* Then Gabby's voice attempted to overpower Rosa's: *She a nun Kash, a religious woman.* Rosa's voice took over: *I love you Kash.* Then Gabby's voice again: *You're packing a picnic for a nun.* Then the two voices jumbled together, each saying their own lines. The noise got louder and louder, and the pitch of their voices got higher and faster. Kash heard both voices, one on top of the other, then the ringing sounds in his ears took the lead, and the little organ keeper chimed in softly in the background—his darkness had begun.

He could no longer handle the confusion, the utter disarray of thoughts and sounds. He needed to restore The Order. Jumping up from the chair, he stood in the middle of the living room with both hands pressed tightly over his ears and then he started to sing at the top of his lungs,

> *One little, two little, three little Indians.*
> *Four little, five little, six little Indians.*

"*NO!*" Kash screamed. He paced the room, slowly at first, and then his speed increased to a trot. His hands which had been covering his ears were now clenched taut to his head as if his head would crumble if he let go. His mind dashed with thoughts of Rosa.

> *Seven little, eight little, nine little Indians.*
> *Ten little Indian boys.*

He had given his heart to a servant of the Lord. He had shared his body, his mind, and his thoughts with a traitor. He had been used and conned; his body felt dirty. He had allowed himself to take part in a physical union with one of God's disciple. He had been cheated and double-crossed, his character soiled. He felt he would never be clean again.

He concentrated harder on the Healing Rhymes. Even though the sounds and thoughts were fading, it was still very much there. He reversed the Healing Rhyme, still chanting loudly,

Ten little, nine little, eight little Indians.

He had literally been sleeping with the enemy. This God of hers had betrayed him for the last time. He would never again permit a woman to take control of his life.

Seven little, six little, five little Indians.

Rosalee had taken him to the edge. She had shown him what lay below and he had fallen over. He blamed himself for that. Rosa had robbed him of several precious weeks of his life. In the end though, she had paid her dues. Kash always got what was due him. Lora and Suzy had paid with their money; Rosa had paid with her body.

Four little, three little, two little Indians.
One little Indian boy.

He started to pull books from the shelf then he ripped the pages from their binding. He hurled them across the room shouting out another rhyme,

One for sorrow, two for joy,

With one sweep of his forearm, he cleared the coffee table and both end tables, sending everything to the floor.

Three for a girl, four for a boy.

Although the Healing Rhymes were beginning to have an effect, he slammed his fist repeatedly into the wall anyway, until the paneling finally collapsed, leaving a softball size hole.

Five for silver, six for gold.

Kash crumbled to his knees in the middle of the clutter and rocked his body back and forth. There, he released a frantic wail and wept without restraint for the first time since his childhood.

Seven for a secret never to be told.

He focused on the Healing Rhymes until his order was restored at last—his darkness had passed. He must not think about Rosa anymore. It was plainly too destructive.

And so, he turned his attention to the task of cleaning up the mess he'd made. Rosa had distracted him so much this past month that he had gotten his priorities out of order. The checks from the Inferiors had been sitting in the post office box for several days waiting to be collected. Yesterday, after he had put Rosalee in her place, Kash drove into Kentucky to pick up his mail. The Kentucky state line was only a few miles from Charleston. Now he searched through the rummage on the carpet until he found the envelopes addressed to Sam Kirkland. He gathered himself up off the floor and put some order back into his life. His main concern right now ought to be the two Inferiors in Massachusetts. After all, it was because of them Rosa had made her way back into his life. For that, he would require extra compensation. He had deposited the checks in the bank yesterday, but just now remembered that there had been a note attached to Lora's check. Picking up the envelope, he read the note again.

Please call me as soon as possible.
We may have trouble with Suzy.
Lora

Below, she listed her office number at Boston General. Kash reclined in his chair, not quite able to understand the urgency of the note. What kind of trouble? Was this another trick? He was not comfortable letting his guard down especially since the two Inferiors had been the ones who convinced Rosa into helping them. How foolish to think she could possibly discourage him from making them pay their dues.

He was not happy with the fact that Rosa knew about the checks, either. After all, her brother was a cop, and he feared Rosa might confide in Frankie about the ordeal—she always was the righteous type—not to mention Frankie would surely ask about her injuries. She may think going to the police would be the best way of helping her old roomies, but that would be the biggest mistake of her life. After what he had done to Rosa yesterday, he was confident she would think twice before she messed with him again, yet there was no way to be certain. Today Rosa would wake up bruised and sore, but if she tried to make him pay for the beating, tomorrow she would wake up dead.

He wished he could get enough money ahead so he could leave for a while. He wished he could just pack up everything and take off for a year or so. Maybe by the time he returned, everything would be settled down. He knew his wish was just that, a fantasy.

Kash reached for the phone and dialed the number of the hospital in Boston. After a few minutes, Dr. Lora Jordan answered the call. Kash identified himself as the friendly, neighborhood blackmailer. Lora found nothing amusing about the greeting. Kash asked about the note.

"The trouble is Suzy," Lora answered. "She's considering telling Clayton about you and about the money. She's convinced she can tell him the truth without causing any damage to her marriage. You've got to talk to her."

"Why don't you talk to her?"

"I tried."

"What makes you think I can do any good? She would be more likely to listen to you than she would to me."

"Maybe you could threaten her. Tell her you'll go public with everything. Make her see that she'll be responsible for ruining Clayton's career when the press gets hold of the story."

"Hold on here darlin'. Are you saying you *want* me to threaten Suzy?"

"Yes, that's exactly what I'm saying."

"Why all of a sudden are you protecting my interests?"

"Because ... if word gets out about your business dealings with Suzy, chances are good that my name is going to be dropped with it. I, unlike Suzy, do not think my husband will be quite so understanding toward my affairs. Not to mention, I may never be allowed to practice medicine again. I'll be lucky to stay out of jail. Do you understand the predicament?"

"Yes ... I understand completely. You've backed yourself into one tight corner, haven't you, and now you want me to widen that corner. Does that just about describe it?"

"Perfectly. I promise, if you get this hurdle behind me, you'll never hear another word from Suzy or me, except of course, when you cash our monthly payments. Will you help me?"

"That just depends. Do you have a spare thousand you would be willing to part with?"

"Come on Kash. Don't get greedy. You owe me something. If you'll remember correctly, it was me who convinced Suzy to keep quiet about this whole matter to begin with. You would have been exposed from the start, which means you wouldn't have the ten grand you've gotten from us thus far."

"Yes you're right, but by that same token, you would have been exposed along with me, and you would no longer have your career or your husband. Are you starting to get the picture? If you want me to play, you've got to pay."

"Fine, a thousand dollars it is. If that's what you want, that's what you'll get. Do you want the check mailed to the same box number?"

"No darlin'. You can transfer the money directly to my account. Once the transfer has been made, then I'll call Suzy."

"Call her. No, you can't call her." Lora had not considered the possibility of Kash wanting to phone Suzy. "You've got to see her face to face. The effects of a threat would not be the same if she hears it over the telephone. She could just hang up on you. You've got to come to Boston. I'll arrange for her to be here when you arrive."

"Wow," Kash said in a sarcastic tone, "that means I'll need travel expenses, motel fare and …"

"How much?" Lora interrupted.

"Another five hundred should do it."

"Fine, I'll wire fifteen hundred into your account. When can I expect you?"

Kash took some time to explore his options. Because a prisoner had escaped from the county jail recently, he could not fly out this time. There would be too many cops on stakeout at the airport to risk being recognized or having his ID checked. No, he would have to drive up this time.

"I'll be there day after tomorrow."

"Why so long? Can't you fly out today or even tomorrow morning?"

"No, it's out of the question. I have some business to attend to tomorrow. Day after is the best I can do."

"Well, I guess I'll have to live with that. You'll get in touch with me when you arrive?"

"No, that won't be necessary. Just have her meet me at the same park where we met last time, around one o'clock. And just for the record, it was pretty foolish of you to get Rosalee involved in this. What did you hope to accomplish? Did you really think she could stop me?"

Oh no, Lora thought, Rosa's attempt to penetrate the surface of the Kash-Demon had been unsuccessful. If a nun was incapable of getting through, she and Suzy were screwed for sure.

"I suppose it was foolish, but I couldn't stand by and let you win without some kind of a fight. What did you say to Rosa when you figured it out? Did you tell her the truth?"

"It's not what I said to her Lora, it's what I did to her."

"What did you do? Please tell me you didn't hurt her?"

"She's not hurt." Then he added, "Badly."

"Go to hell Kash!"

"Hey darlin', don't bite the hand that feeds you. You do still need my help. You'd better hope your dark-eyed Suzy doesn't do anything stupid before I get there. Remember, if I go down, you go down with me."

"How can I forget?"

After getting Kash's bank account number so she could wire the money, Dr. Lora Jordan replaced the receiver on the phone base.

Her cupped hands hugged her face, much the same way the virtual, dire hope within her cupped her heart. Hope that this latest scheme would work. If things went sour and Kash figured out he was being set up, he could turn on Suzy; perhaps hurt her too. He had hurt Rosalee after all. She hated to put another long-time friend in this position. Even more, she hated having to suck up to him for help, even though the entire situation was fabricated and the telephone conversation was nothing more than an act.

The thought of his grins and smirks on the other end of the line caused a rancid taste in her mouth. Bile was backing up in her throat. Darting from her desk, she ran to the small bathroom attached to her office just in time to throw up in the toilet. Tears ran down her cheeks, mascara trailed behind in brown streaks; she sniffled.

"Dear God Lora, I hope you know what you're doing!" she said to her pitiful looking reflection in the mirror.

2

Suzy Whitmore stood at the dresser in the guest room arranging silk flowers in a wicker basket for the third time. She couldn't get the flowers to lie properly. No matter which way she positioned them, they just didn't look right. Her mind was too distracted to be creative. Since talking to Lora a few days ago, she finally felt good about things and wanted to do something constructive, but she wished Lora would call back to let her know how Kash had reacted to the note. If things went as smoothly as Lora believed they would, this entire mess could soon be over.

Tommy entered the kitchen just as the telephone rang. He answered it on the first ring. "Hello?"

"Tommy, is your mother there?"

Tommy recognized the voice of Lora Jordan. Whenever she showed up, trouble almost certainly followed close behind.

"Yeah, she's upstairs. Hold on please."

Suzy responded to her son's beckon. "I've got it."

"Suzy?"

"Lora, you sound shaken. Is everything all right?"

"Yes ... nothing to worry about. Kash called a little while ago. It took some fast-talking, but he has agreed to meet with you. Can you be here day after tomorrow?"

"Two days from now? Why isn't he leaving sooner? I need to talk to him now. I have to get this whole affair behind me."

"I know you do. He said he had some kind of business to take care of. I had no choice but to accept his terms."

"I understand."

"Will you have any trouble getting away?"

"No. I've already informed Clayton that I will be making a trip up there to visit with you. Did you brief Kash on the contents of the meeting?"

"Yes, but Suzy you must be convincing. Are you sure you'll be able to manage all this?"

"Oh yes. I will do whatever is necessary to get Kash out of my life for good."

"Fine then. I'll see you in a couple days. Come to the hospital. He wants to meet you in Sadler Park again at one o'clock. You may want to get here early. It wouldn't surprise me if he shows up a bit ahead of schedule."

"Okay. I'll plan to be at Boston General by, say 11AM."

"That's perfect. I've already trimmed my schedule for the day, so I can be available if any trouble arises."

"Lora, thanks for being so interested in the way my life turns out. I don't know how I would have dealt with everything if you hadn't been strong enough for both of us."

"It's my job, kiddo. I'll be seeing you soon."

"Bye."

Tommy remained silent and cautious, waiting a few extra seconds before hanging up the kitchen extension. He wanted to be absolutely sure his mother was unaware of his listening in on her conversation. He could ill-afford any mistakes to tip off his mother—not at this point.

The time had come. This was it. He was ready to make sure that cowboy Kash never bothered his mother again. He walked directly to his bedroom and shut the door. He did not turn on the stereo, nor did he turn on the television. He pulled out the chair from the desk and sank into thought. He had waited so long for this time to come; it seemed he was already prepared. He simply needed to organize his schedule, to get a good feel for the sequence of events.

Tommy reviewed the mental list as he puffed a marijuana cigarette. He supposed he was finally growing up.

3

It was two in the morning at the DeLucci home in West Virginia. Rosalee heard the sounds of crickets through her open bedroom window. The air was muggy, the night was as still as death.

The back of her legs ached not only from the beating but because she had walked almost two miles to the bus station in Charleston yesterday when Kash had deserted her. She had called home from Charleston, saying that she would be late and there was no need for her mother to wait up. Nobody was awake when Rosa arrived home last night.

Where Kash had hit her, her face was red in some places, black and blue in others. Her lower lip was torn open from his bite in one spot and split open from his fist in another. Her left eye was purple and swollen nearly shut now. Her nose had finally quit bleeding only a few hours ago. Her outer wound, however, in no way compared to her inner wounds. Her legs and stomach were sore from the punches, her back ached a lot, and she had noticed a pink tint in her urine when she had used the bathroom. She was queasy inside and bruised outside. Her breasts and private parts throbbed from the brutality administered to them. Her grit had been beaten down; she didn't want to live. Kash had violated her both internally and externally.

No one in her family had seen her in her current condition and no one ever would.

She glanced around the room taking note of everything. She even wanted to remember the tiny cobweb that occupied one of the corners near the ceiling. Frankie would have to help Mama wash down the upstairs walls. She would never be able to come back here again. Once everything was out in the open, she knew her family would not understand. She was sure Kash would take great pleasure in letting the whole town know how Sister Rosa DeLucci had broken her vows—how he had done a nun. She wanted to believe he wouldn't do it deliberately, but even a slip of the tongue during one of his drunken binges in a local bar would be enough to get the town buzzing. She was certain a juicy piece of gossip like this would travel pretty fast.

The lamp on the nightstand sprayed a dim light over part of Rosa's bedroom. She picked up the small cedar box that used to sit atop her dresser. She gently rubbed her fingers over the smooth wood, debating whether to open it. She knew what was inside—mementoes of Kash. Not mementoes like the ones her Mama had put in the dresser drawer. Those were good memories. The ones in the cedar box were the bad memories, the ones she went to the convent to forget. Contained there, were secrets about Kash she never told anyone.

Tonight, she felt she was ready, so she opened the box. Inside, she picked up three caps from bottles of cheap wine she and Kash had drank together. Each one held a story, an episode in which Kash had reduced Rosa's self-esteem to a pile of nothing. Either by cruel words or by hostile behavior, he had put Rosa down, had let her know that she was nobody in his book. Kash never could hold his liquor, she remembered. She had kept the bottle caps only because they represented time she had spent with him and time with him was something she wanted to remember and relish back then.

Shuffling deeper into the box, she uncovered two marbles that she had taken from his basement during two nights she spent at his house. She had told him upfront that she was not ready for sex, and he respected her wishes—at first. However, when the kissing and touching started, he became excited and that led to agitation. He forced Rosa to do despicable things to him in order to quench his urges. Rosa may have comprised her morals but she never comprised her virginity. After the first episode, Rosa could not believe she had been stupid enough to go back yet another time for the same treatment. There was no way to explain it except to say she was addicted to his attention. Aside from drinking with him, now she found another way to hold his interest. These little sex acts seemed to be the way to keep him coming back. Looking at each marble, she recounted the incidents of destruction, violence, and arrogance that surrounded each memory. Again, when she packed them into the box, the memories were something she truly cherished.

Next, she picked out stubs from a pair of concert tickets that she and Kash had attended nearly twenty years ago. She remembered the day so vividly. She had been 17 and so happy about Kash taking her to a concert. When the concert was over, Kash had talked her into going parking. He promised her he wouldn't let things get too far, but when things started to heat up for Rosa, she backed away from him. Not wanting to go all the way and not wanting to do the *other* things to him—the things that satisfied his revolting desire—she asked Kash to take her home. When physical force and considerable bickering didn't get him what he wanted, finally, he did take Rosa home, but only after he had insulted her appearance and put down her character the entire five miles back to town. Twice that night he had slapped her face with his open hand and twice he had tried to force himself on her. The next day at school, all the boys had called her a cock teaser. Kash had told everyone.

Lastly, she produced a sheet of age-yellowed paper folded in half and then folded in half again. She unfolded the paper and stared at Kash's own secret displayed there in black and white from the Huntington Library copy machine back in '71. Tears came to her eyes again when she whispered, "I hate you. Even though I know it's not your fault, I still hate you." Then she tore the brittle paper into tiny pieces and sprinkled them back into the box.

The cedar box was filled with memories of this nature. She had seen the dark side of Kash years ago, the side Lora and Suzy just recently discovered, and she only wanted to forget. She had simply locked all those memories into this tiny box and had forgotten all about the dark side of Sam Kashette. She was so sure he would change—so sure all the years of prayers would have changed him. How could she have let him do this to her again?

She dumped the entire contents of the box into the trashcan. With this effortless gesture, Rosa severed the tie between herself and Kash as clearly as if she had sliced the invisible thread—the same thread, which connected her soul to his—with a knife. There was nothing left. She had failed in her mission to light his darkness.

She placed the empty box into her suitcase and zipped it up. The faint scent of cedar still hung in the air.

Taking a piece of paper from the nightstand she began to write, *Dear Frankie,* and by the time she had written, *Love you always, Rosa,* an hour had passed. She had poured out all the hurt, all the shame, all the mistakes onto four sheets of paper. It was time to go now. Her *Nonna* and Mama would be getting up shortly. She turned off the light and quietly left her bedroom behind her.

Creeping noiselessly into her brother's room, she laid the letter on his bureau. She waited at the door for only a few seconds to listen to Frankie's loud snoring. She wondered sometimes, how after spending all day in the chaos of the force, he could come home at night and sleep so well. He had always slept like a rock.

She tiptoed down the stairs and paused in the kitchen to take one last look at the place where she had eaten so many wonderful meals. She savored the memories of family gathered around the huge kitchen table, snacking on homemade pastries and drinking freshly ground coffee. Her mental nose picked up all the wonderful aromas. Now the room was silent except for the minor creeks made by all old houses, and the almost silent tick, tick, tick, of the wall clock. She walked into the dining room, set down the suitcase, and opened the top door of the antique china cabinet belonging to her *Nonna*. The dishes and cups were neatly displayed there. She reached into one of the hanging cups and removed a silver key that unlocked the bottom drawer. She pulled out the heavy blue-steel object and fingered it, before placing it in her purse. She detected an unpleasant smell of metal and gun oil lingering on her hands. She seized a clip from the drawer and slipped it into her purse as well, before locking the cabinet and replacing the key. There was nothing else to do here, so Rosalee opened the front door and ventured outside into the darkness.

4

The day Tommy waited for was finally here. He walked the short distance to the Baker's house. If he ever needed a friend, the time was now. Mrs. Baker told Tommy that Jeff was in his room. She also informed him that Jeff was not allowed to leave the house for a week because the grass had not been mowed yesterday after his father had told him to cut it.

Tommy found his friend sulking on the bed. He didn't want to appear insensitive towards Jeff's feelings, but Tommy concluded that his problem was more important right now. He came straight to the point.

"Hey Jeff, I need a favor."

"Yeah, and people who are grounded need a town pass, too. I'm afraid I can't be much help."

"It's a bummer you're grounded, but the favor I need doesn't require you to leave the house."

"What do you need?"

"Will you cover for me tonight? I'm going to tell my parents that I'm spending the night over here."

"Where are you going?"

"My mom is meeting Kash tomorrow afternoon. I'm going to try to head him off before she gets a chance to talk to him. I overheard her talking on the phone to her friend from college, and I got the impression that Kash is pressuring mom again. I think she's trying to tell him to get lost, but he's ignoring her."

"Why don't you just let your mom talk to him? She can probably handle this guy. She's going to be real pissed when she finds out you were messing in her business."

"She won't find out, if I can get to him first. You're the only person who knows what I'm doing. You wouldn't rat me out would you?"

"No, of course not."

"I didn't think you would, so you see, she'll never find out. I'll be back before tomorrow evening, so nobody will know I was even gone."

"How are you going to find Kash?"

"I took a chance and called the motel where he stayed last time, and it paid off. Sam Kirkland is registered there. The clerk said he'd made the reservation yesterday, and he should be checking in sometime late tonight. I told the clerk that I was a relative and I wanted to surprise him, so the clerk said he wouldn't mention my call."

"Wow man, you're really serious about this, aren't you?"

"Damn straight. I've never been more serious. I've got to stop this thing before it separates the two people I love more than anybody. I've got everything planned out. If all goes well, Sam 'Kash' Kirkland will be out of our lives forever."

"Where's the motel?"

"In a little town between here and Boston, a place called Gilbertville. It's about a 45-minute drive. Lora, my mom's old college roommate, is helping her set up the meeting. She lives in Boston. I'd sure like to know what's in it for her."

"Okay Tom. I'll cover for you from here, but if you get busted, I don't know anything about all this, okay? I'm in enough trouble around here. I'd like to be ungrounded before my eighteenth birthday, if you know what I mean?"

"Yeah, I got ya covered. You're a good friend, Jeff."

Tommy got up to leave then he remembered the other reason for the visit. "Oh by the way, do you have any more pot I can buy? I smoked the last joint yesterday."

"No I don't."

"None! Can you sell me some out of your bag?"

"I'm tapped out."

"Shit Jeff. I need a buzz if I'm going to get through the next two days. You sure you can't find any?"

"I'm sure. I've been looking for myself. There's just none around. When the college students get back from summer vacation, the town will be polluted with it."

"That's too late. I can't wait another month. I need the marijuana today." Tommy started for the door in a huff.

Jeff yelled, "Good luck tonight."

Tommy never answered.

When Jeff heard the front door slam, he reached into his dresser drawer and pulled out a wrinkled baggy that was tucked between two socks. He unwrapped it and inspected the contents. Jeff lit the marijuana cigarette.

"Sorry pal, but if I've got to be cooped up in this room for seven days, I'm going to need this more than you."

Jeff didn't know how wrong he was.

CHAPTER FOURTEEN

Get Off of My Cloud

1

Kash checked into the Sleep-Over Inn in Gilbertville, Massachusetts at a quarter to three in the morning. He arrived in a nasty mood. About 25 miles into his trip, he had a flat tire. The lug nuts were stripped, so he had to hitch a ride to the nearest town to buy new ones. As if that wasn't bad enough, within 30 miles of the end of his journey, the water pump had come out of his pickup. He had to get a tow to a gas station, where an all-night mechanic on duty fixed the truck. The mechanic was old and he worked at one speed and one speed only—slow. The tow bill cost twice as much as the repair bill. Having to put out big money for something that provided him no pleasure made Kash angrier than breaking down in the first place.

He checked in with the clerk at the desk, got his key, and headed for room 85. All he wanted to do was sleep. He didn't want to shower, even though he could have used one; he didn't want to eat, even though he was hungry. He was back in the driver's seat where control over life was concerned. He could do whatever he wanted to do, whenever he wanted to do it. Never again would anyone else run his life. At this moment, he just wanted to clear his mind and get some rest. He was so uptight about the meeting with the stupid Inferior tomorrow. This had better be the last time either of them caused him any trouble. Considering the mood he was in, if the meeting were to be right now, he probably would have decked both of them for making him come all the way up here.

He turned the key to open room 85's door and flipped on the light switch. This motel was the same one he had used for his previous stays. Not the same room, although it was hard to tell since every room looked the same: flowered print polyester bed spread with matching curtains, shaggy wall to wall carpeting that was matted flat from too much foot traffic and not enough vacuum sweepings, and we can't forget the noisy air condition unit. Every room had one—no extra charge. How was anyone expected to sleep with the unit humming all night long?

He threw his suitcase on the stand near the bathroom before removing his shoes and shirt. When he used the remote control to power on the television set, nothing but snow showed up on the screen. He flipped through a few channels but only snow appeared on each station. *Great*, he thought, *the television doesn't work*. The perfect end to a perfect day. Kash liked to sleep with the TV on when he was in a strange place. He would probably not even be able to fall asleep now.

He had one hand on the bedspread, ready to fold down the covers and climb in, when there was a knock at the door. He assumed it was the clerk letting him know that the TV set didn't work. He opened the door.

"Yeah I know, the TV doesn't work," he said to the tall blond boy who stood outside his room. The boy made no reply. He simply stared at Kash. "What do you want kid? It's late and I need to get some sleep."

"I need to get some sleep too," the boy finally said, "but first I want to talk to you Mr. Kirkland. May I come in?"

Kash wondered how this boy knew his fictitious name. He marked something familiar about his voice although he couldn't remember what. The face, too, was familiar, but he was unable to put a name to it. Then he spotted the jet black BMW in the parking lot.

Jesus Christ, it's Suzy's kid.

He invited him inside.

Tommy was not quite sure what he should do next. He had a plan all mapped out in his head, but it soon went out the window when he found himself face to face with Kash. He didn't know exactly how he should approach the subject burning in his mind. His heart raced; adrenaline coursed through him. The time had finally come. This was his chance to prove he had grown up and that he really could handle confrontations and conflicts. He wished he had a joint though, as he caught himself sinking below the confidence he had mentally just built up. He could do nothing but gawk at the man who held his family's future in his hands.

Kash decided to play dumb with Tommy. "Come on boy, state your business. It's three o'clock in the morning. I'd like to get some shut eye."

Tommy's voice quivered when he spoke. "I'd like to talk to you about my mother. I believe you know her."

"Yeah, I know a lot of women. What's her name?"

"Suzy Whitmore."

Kash pondered on the name, having fun toying with this kid. "Suzy Whitmore ... Whitmore ... Suzy ... Suzy ... nope, I don't believe I know her."

"I wouldn't think you'd forget the name of a woman who paid you $5000." As Tommy said this, he pulled out a canceled check from his shirt pocket.

Kash grabbed the check and then looked sternly at Tommy.

"You know kid, you shouldn't go snooping around in your mother's business. It's not good for *her* health."

"I want you to leave our family alone. I want you to terminate this affair you're having with my mother."

"Affair, what are you talking about?"

"Don't play games with me. I know everything. I know you and my mom are lovers, and I know she's keeping you."

Kash's amusement escaped through his mouth. He laughed out loud at the thought of a woman keeping him.

"Look kid, you don't know anything. I've never had a woman keep me, and I'm not about to start now. You have no idea of what's going on here."

"I followed her to Boston the last time she met with you, and I saw the two of you at the park. She was sitting with you on the bench acting all lovey-dovey. She's been upset ever since. I want my mother back, and I want you to let her go."

"Your mother is free to go anywhere she pleases. I'm not stopping her from that."

"I heard her on the phone. She said she has to get this affair behind her. She said she has to get you out of her life."

"Well, you certainly are a good little detective, aren't you?"

"Don't talk to me like a child. I'm a teenager, almost an adult, and I can handle anything you have to say."

"All right Mr. Whitmore," Kash mocked him with a business like tone. "Do you know why your mother gave me that check? She paid me to keep quiet about something. Something she didn't want your father to find out about."

"I'm sure ... probably your affair."

"Wrong again, Sherlock. You see, a long time ago, the good Suzy Shaffer wasn't such a good little girl. As a matter of fact, she wasn't much older than you are now. What she did back then is what she's trying to keep from your father."

"I can't believe my mother would ever get mixed up with anything that she couldn't tell my father about."

"Oh it wasn't illegal or anything like that, but it was very unethical. Even more unethical for her now than it was then."

"Could we please quit playing games? Will you level with me and tell me what going on here?"

"Sure kid. I'd love to. Maybe if I tell you what your mother did she won't be so quick to send you here next time."

"My mother has no idea I've come. I followed you here after you left my mom at Sadler Park last month. I took a chance that you would stay here again. Now what's going on between you and my mother?"

"I was you're mother's lover, as you put it, but it was a long time ago, back in our college days. We were a hot item for a while. I even thought about marrying her. Then one day she broke off our happy relationship with no warning whatsoever. I said to her, 'Suzy, what about the baby?' Yeah kid, you heard me right. I said baby. Then she said to me, 'Kash, I had an abortion. I didn't want to have your baby.' Well she didn't say it in exactly those words, but that's what she did. She lied to me at first and told me she'd had a miscarriage but later I found the truth—she had aborted our baby. Now, what would a news flash like that do to your daddy?"

Tommy ignored the question. "You're crazy. My mom never had an abortion. She loves kids, and even more, she loves life. She and my dad are always giving talks at pro-life rallies and …" Tommy realized where this conversation was going. This man was not his mother's lover; this man was his mother blackmailer.

"You gettin' the picture now, Sherlock? Hell, if the truth were known, your mom probably didn't want to bring you into the world you either. She probably figured getting knocked up was the best way to keep your rich daddy and his money."

"You son-of-a-bitch!" Tommy exclaimed before he made one giant leap in Kash's direction. Tommy was a good three inches taller than his opponent was and because Kash had not been prepared for a lanky body being thrust against him, he fell to the floor with Tommy landing on top of him. Tommy tried to strike out with his fists, but his swing was rigid and each time he attempted it, Kash clutched his wrists. Making one forceful movement with his body, Kash flipped Tommy around on his back. Then with all the strength he had, Kash landed a blow to the side of Tommy's head.

Tommy laid motionless on the floor of room 85, knocked out cold.

2

Suzy and Lora sat on a bench at Sadler Park waiting for Kash. They were a bit early, but neither seemed bothered by the wait. Rays from the late morning sun warmed their bodies. The weather forecasters predicted a chance of rain today for the first time this summer. The ladies were relaxed and confident that this nightmare—as well as the drought—would soon end.

Lora explained to Suzy the importance of her performance. If Lora's plan was to work, Suzy must fully convince Kash that she was willing to put her marriage on the line. She had to keep Kash engrossed in her act until Lora could get Detective Kenyon to the park. In reality, the detective was already here, but Lora decided not to tell Suzy. She was afraid Suzy would involuntarily glance toward Detective Kenyon one too many times, and it would be enough to tip off Kash. Lora gave a slight nod to a man sitting on a bench maybe 20 yards away.

Brian Kenyon, who started his career as a security guard at Boston General before joining the Boston Police Force, pointed out to Lora that in order for him to make contact with Kash, he would need probable cause. He simply could not walk up to Kash, ask to see his ID, and run a check on him. That would be invading his privacy. He needed a reason to approach him. Lora instructed Suzy to make a scene with Kash that would attract Detective Kenyon's attention. If the detective saw Suzy in a vulnerable position, it would be reason enough for him to approach Kash and run a check on him.

Suzy understood the part she was cast to play. She sat quietly for some time acting out the scenes in her mind. Her daily dose of Valium kept her moods quite serene. She was not the least bit anxious about the job at hand. She checked her watch frequently.

"It's getting on one thirty. Do you think he's going to show up?" Suzy asked.

"He'll be here. He knows if he wants his money, he'll have to do this."

Suzy agreed but still she wondered what could be keeping Sam Kashette.

3

The little boy in Kash's dream trembled. He sat in the middle of a small space. There was sufficient room to move, yet he remained still. Every time he moved around, he bumped into the thing hanging overhead. He was very scared. Bugs could be in here, or mice, or worse, rats! The pitch-black darkness added to the boy's disorientation. He was able to tell, though, that he faced front now, from the little slice of light that crept in underneath the door. Every once in a while, the ray of light would break as if someone had walked past. He could not understand who was out there and why he was in here.

The place smelled musty, and it was stuffy in his space. He could hear laughter and music coming from the other side of the door. There was a party out there. People were talking and popping snaps on aluminum cans. The young boy was thirsty—and hungry too. He had eaten his favorite sandwich for lunch, peanut butter and bananas, but that had been around noon. It must be much later than that now.

His little legs started to cramp and ache from sitting all bunched up for too long. He wanted to straighten them, but he was afraid he would bump into the thing again.

Swallowing hard, not only to produce saliva but also to produce courage, he stood up. He did not like being a coward, but after all, he was just a little boy. Once in a vertical position, he stretched his legs out and his arms upward. The blob brushed against his elbow. A soft screech came out and almost immediately, he was back on the floor again with his knees tucked tightly to his chest. The blob was directly above his head; he could tell it was there without being able to see it. It appeared to be swinging. He could feel the slight movement of air as it moved. It made a sort of scraping sound when it swayed back and forth.

Meanwhile on the other side of the door, the party was breaking up. People were saying goodbye, the music had been lowered, he could hear the screen door bang as people left, and he could hear car doors shutting and engines rumbling to life.

Panic began to build in his frail body. What if everyone was leaving? He would be left alone in here with the *thing*. While he sure hoped someone would remember he was still in there, the thought of being rescued was anything but a comforting notion. Then he heard footsteps approaching. He was going to be saved. Somebody was coming to get him. Then why didn't he feel relief? Why did the panicky feeling only worsen? The footsteps stopped at the door. The little slice of light coming from the crack disappeared. The knob squeaked when turned. The door opened, and light filled his little space.

The young child's heart pounded vigorously in his tiny chest. He squinted against the flood of light. He didn't know why he was still so scared. After all, someone was coming to take him away from the thing, but he found no trust in his rescuer. The rush of cool air coming from the other side of the door, provided some relief for his breathing, but it provided no relief from his fear. His eyes had not adjusted to the light yet, so it was hard for him to see who stood there. He smiled, nonetheless, blinked a few times, and then rubbed his eyes to help his vision focus on the figure in front of him. The face was blurred, but finally he was able to bring about an image. It was …

Kash was suddenly brought back from his slumber by the muffled sound of something romping around in the room. He tried to ignore the ruckus.

Although he was feeling scared, and beads of sweat covered his upper body, he wanted to go back to his dream. With the other occurrences of the nightmare, Kash had always woken up before the door had been opened. Not so this time—the door had been opened. Kash wanted to go back to sleep so he could see who had opened the door and what fate awaited the young boy Kash.

He tossed back and forth in bed punching the pillow, trying to overcome the noise in the room. Finally, a restless Sam Kashette opened his eyes and sat up in the bed.

He had almost forgotten about the Whitmore kid. The noise he had heard came from Tommy struggling to get loose from the chair in which Kash had tied him. His mouth was stuffed with a washrag and was held there by a terry cloth belt from a robe left in the bathroom by the previous occupant.

Kash tried to think. He paced the floor reviewing his options. This kid already knew too much, so it wasn't a matter of simply letting him go. He could call Suzy and tell her where to find him. He was sure Suzy would keep him quiet. *Shit, Suzy!* He looked at the clock; it was one thirty. He overslept, and now he was late for the meeting. Knowing that he could not make it to the park in time, he continued to ponder. The situation was getting out of hand. First, the Inferiors had told Rosalee about the money, and now this little Sherlock Holmes had come up with some evidence of his own. Too many people knew his business. He didn't like it one bit either, but he had no solution to the problem.

Although Tommy's voice was muted by the gag, the stifled grunts he attempted to make were getting on Kash's nerves. Tommy rocked back and forth in the chair making a thumping impact on the carpet.

"Shut up kid. I'm trying to think."

Tommy thrashed about wildly. The belt which held the gag started to give way.

Kash considered his next move. If Suzy were unable to silence her son about their arrangement, Kash was sure to end up back in prison. He absolutely would not let that happen. He knew he would never make it though another term inside. If only he could get his hands on a lump of quick cash, he would be free to retire wherever he wanted. In 60 days, his probation would be up, and he could go anywhere he damn well pleased, but he needed money in order to do that.

"Help ... *HELP ME!*" Tommy screamed using every element of his vocal cords. He had spit the washrag from his mouth. It fell to his lap, the terry cloth belt hung loosely around his neck.

Kash slapped Tommy's face then took the opportunity to backhand him three more times for disturbing his meditation. Tommy's screams turned into soft whimpers. Kash grabbed the washrag and reinserted it into Tommy's open mouth. He tied the belt again. He had to get this kid out of the way so he could bury himself in thought.

Kash went to the car, opened the glove box, and searched for the roll of silver duct tape he always kept there. He would use the tape to cover Tommy's mouth and prevent another outburst like the one that had just happened. When he pulled out the roll, the handgun fell to the floor. He slipped it in the front of his pants before returning to room 85.

Back in the room, Tommy worked diligently at loosening the rope that bound his hands. His ankles were tied to the legs of the chair, but he could remedy that problem if he could only get his hands free. He wondered if anyone had heard him scream. He hoped the police were on their way, but judging from the few cars parked in the lot last night, his chances of anyone being around to hear his cry for help was pretty slim.

When Kash came through the door, Tommy stiffened up immediately. His eyes followed Kash as he removed a pistol from under his shirt and loaded it. He waved the gun at Tommy and smiled before he placed the weapon on top of the dresser.

All at once, Tommy came to realize just how big a mess he was mixed up in. This crazy man with the cowboy hat could very easily kill him any time he wanted. He knew he should have gone to his father. The courage given to him by the pot was nowhere to be found now, and Tommy knew he was in way over his head.

Kash sat down on the bed and faced Tommy. "I'm going to untie your legs now. I don't want you to give me any trouble when I do. Understand?"

Tommy shook his head up and down.

"When I untie you, I want you to take off your clothes."

Tommy shifted his head in rapid sprits from side to side. He had heard about things like this happening, men abducting teenage boys for sex. No way was something like that going to happen to Tommy. Again, he started to thrash about in the chair.

Kash reached for the gun on the dresser. He released the safety and pointed it in the vicinity of Tommy's head. Tommy quit fidgeting. Kash cut the ropes that harnessed Tommy's legs and hands. With the gun now pressed firmly against Tommy's temple, Kash told him to strip.

Tommy obeyed.

Next, Tommy was forced by Kash's strong arms, into the bathroom where Kash directed him to sit on the commode. He pushed Tommy forward and fastened his hands together with the duct tape. He then coupled Tommy with the commode by wrapping tape around the tank and Tommy's chest. This would restrict any movement of his upper body. He strapped Tommy's ankles together in the same manner then secured his lap, stomach, and thighs by overlapping tape around Tommy's midsection and the base of the commode, sort of the same way a seat belt secured its occupant in a car, only much, much tighter. His post-pubescent penis lay on his lap, nestled in the crease of his thighs. When Kash was finished, he stood back to examine his work. He shook the boy's shoulders and was satisfied that Tommy wasn't going anywhere.

Kash removed the terry cloth belt from Tommy's mouth. He shoved the washrag deeper into his oral cavity and held it in place with a generous piece of duct tape.

The last thing he did was give Tommy's penis a little push between his taped thighs so that if Tommy had the urge to urinate, there would be no mess.

Kash locked the bathroom door and started to pace around the main room once more. At least now he could think. The boy was nowhere in sight and the room was quiet at last, without all the noise made by his romping around in the chair. It seemed to Kash that his only option was to call Suzy. He glanced at the clock. It was 2PM. He was sure that even if he left now, Suzy would be gone by the time he arrived at the park. He decided to wait until later this afternoon and place a call to her house. He wondered where she thought Tommy had been all this time. He hoped she hadn't done anything stupid, like call the police and report Tommy missing. He was amused by the thought of telling her that he had Tommy tied up in the bathroom. Her first thought would most likely be that he had kidnapped the boy.

Then, with a sudden bolt of energy, Kash registered what his mind was saying.

"Kidnap! That's it. The kid's worth a fortune."

4

Suzy and Lora waited for Kash at Sadler Park until three o'clock, well beyond the one o'clock meeting time. He never showed up. Detective Kenyon had waited too, unbeknownst to Suzy. Lora told Suzy there was nothing else she could do expect go home and wait for him to call. Lora was certain Kash would be in touch with her sometime today. The girls would stay in touch until the call came.

Suzy had the feeling it was going to be a long day, so she decided to refill her prescription for Valium on the way home. When she arrived in Dalton, she found a parking place directly in front of McPhearson's Drug Store.

While she waited for her prescription to be processed, she looked at the merchandise near the pharmacy area. A light touch on her back caused her to jump.

"I'm sorry Suzy. I didn't mean to startle you." The voice was that of Sherry Baker, Jeff's mom. "How are you feeling? I understand you're having some female problems. I hope it's nothing too serious."

"No, it's nothing serious. I've been on a menopausal rollercoaster for a while, and it's been a little rough on my nerves," Suzy lied to her neighbor. "I hope Tommy wasn't any trouble for you and Dan last night."

"Tommy?" Mrs. Baker looked puzzled.

"Yes, I know how rowdy he and Jeff can get sometimes when they spend the night together. I hope that wasn't the case last night."

"Tommy wasn't at our house last night. Jeff's grounded. He's not permitted to leave the house or have anybody stay over for the rest of this week."

"I don't understand. Tommy distinctly told me he was spending the night with Jeff."

"No, he wasn't with us."

The pharmacist called Suzy's name, announcing her filled order. She left Mrs. Baker standing there. Suzy hung her head low. She was so embarrassed she could have crawled out of the store. When she got home, she was going to do more than ground Tommy; she was going to ring his neck.

As soon as she reached the house, she called Tommy's name. There was no answer. She checked the carport out back but Tommy's car was gone. Her mind raced with images of things that could have happened to her baby boy. Why would he want to keep his whereabouts from her? Had he gone someplace where she or Clayton would not have him permitted to go? Could it be that Tommy had a girlfriend, and perhaps he had spent the night with her? He certainly would not want her or Clayton to know about that. Then she suddenly realized how little she knew about her son's life.

She puttered about the house for a while, straightening things, unloading the dishwasher, checking out the window every time she heard a car pass by. After about an hour, she started to get worried. Maybe there had been an accident. It was not the first time a thought of this nature had entered Suzy's mind. This fear had been inside her from the day Clayton brought home a fast car for Tommy. How could Tommy add new worries to her already overburdened shoulders? She had enough to think about with Kash and his damn money.

Her mood switched from worry to anger. Her son was going to suffer a long time over this little escapade.

5

Jeff sat in the middle of his bed puffing on a pipe. He had enough pot left for a few more good buzzes. He felt badly about lying to Tommy when he had asked him for a joint, but Jeff knew he would need something to smoke to keep from going insane until his parents revoked his grounding.

His room was a mess. Clothes were strewn around the floor and over the back of the chair. The bed was unmade. The room had a basic lived-in look. His mother had warned him to clean it up yesterday. Big deal ... what was she going to do, ground him. Her threats didn't excite him too much these days. On the other hand, he took his dad's threats to heart.

A Rolling Stones tune blasted from the stereo. Jeff sang along, "Hey, you ... get off of my cloud. Hey, you ... get off of my cloud. Don't hang around 'cause two is a crowd. Go on."

Smoking pot gave Jeff a better understanding to the meaning of the words behind certain songs. He guessed this one to mean that when you're high, you're on a cloud, and when someone tried to mess with your buzz, they were invading your cloud, so get off. Don't hang around 'cause two is a crowd. He figured the Stones were trying to tell everyone to leave him alone.

Mrs. Baker tried to open Jeff's bedroom door, but it was locked. She pounded on the door and told Jeff to come downstairs. She said Mrs. Whitmore wanted to talk to him.

"Shit," Jeff whispered, "don't tell me that asshole got busted." Then he yelled over the music, "I'll be right down."

Hey, you, get off of my cloud!

Sherry Baker and Suzy talked about their teenage boys until Jeff came downstairs. Suzy started to question him as soon as he was in plain sight.

"No I don't know where Tommy is," Jeff said, remembering the promise he had made to his friend.

"Please Jeff," Suzy pleaded, "Try to think of anything he said that may give me an idea as to where he could be. Has he mentioned a girlfriend?"

"No, he doesn't have a girl."

Mrs. Baker could tell when her son was holding something back, and she felt this was one of those times. She cut in on the conversation.

"Jeff, if there's something you know that you're not telling Mrs. Whitmore, I'll be forced to talk to your father about your involvement, and I'm sure you will not be permitted to get your driver's license next month. Now, is there anything you want to say?"

Jeff thought for a moment. He hated breaking a promise, but he also remembered telling Tommy that if he got busted, he was on his own. *Sorry Tom ole boy*, he thought, *I can't give up the driver's license for you.* Then, he spoke up.

"I know where Tommy is."
Suzy sighed with relief. "Where?"
"He went to see that man."
"What man, Jeff?"
"Kash, the guy with the cowboy hat from the 7-Eleven."

Suzy was lost for words. The color drained from her face, her heart pounded frantically. How did Tommy find out Kash's name? How much did Tommy know? It was clear that Suzy was beginning to unravel. The valium had lost its punch. She had to get home. She had to try and find her son.

Surprisingly, this time she didn't cry. Her beloved Tommy was in trouble—there was no time to cry.

Like a relay racer taking the baton, she left Sherry Baker standing there without any explanation for a second time today. She walked briskly down the Baker's sidewalk, and then once on the road and out of the Baker's sight, she began to trot. The Jenson's rosebush must have jumped out in front of her because she didn't see it now nor did she remember it being there on her walk to the Bakers. Her feet tangled in the bush and down she went on all fours. The tiny brush burn on her knee was nothing compared to the crushing heart within her chest.

She brushed herself off and started to jog. She had lost precious seconds with the stupid bush.

Suzy Whitmore ran at top speed the rest of the way to her house. When she threw open the kitchen door, the phone was stilling ringing. Completely out of breath, she snatched the receiver from the wall and answered, "Tommy?"

She heard the old familiar voice on the other end say, "No, not Tommy. Sorry darlin', it's just me."

6

Dr. Lora Jordan had just prepared a romantic dinner for two. She hoped this would be a secret celebration dinner for herself, but since Kash had not shown up at the park today, she turned it into a special dinner for Alex. He had lost a few more pounds this month, so she allowed him a little splurge.

It was 15 minutes after five when Lora looked at the clock. Alex was late, and it was unusual for him not to call when he was running behind schedule. She was so thankful she had him to help distract her attention from Kash and his threats. She wondered how Suzy was making out at home without Clayton. Suzy had told Lora that Clayton would be gone until the weekend. Lora was grateful that Alex only had to take one or two business trip a year. She couldn't bear to be apart from him any longer than that.

She ripped lettuce and cut vegetables for the salad. She always waited until the last minute to fix it. A soggy or rusty looking salad could ruin a beautiful dinner. As she sliced a cucumber and tossed the salad, she tossed around a few thoughts in her head as well. What could have happened to Kash? Was it possible the police had picked him up for another violation? Not that it would have bothered her if that were the case. If not that, why hadn't he kept his meeting at the park? If he wasn't in jail somewhere, why didn't he call her or Suzy to set up another meeting? He said he understood the importance of talking to Suzy, so where in the hell was he? The primary goal remained the same: get him to Massachusetts so Lora's plan could be set in motion.

Lora put the remaining cucumber and the knife on the counter top. She stared up at the ceiling in deep meditation. An idea occurred to her which she had never taken into consideration before. What if Kash had never intended to show up at the park in the first place? What if he was growing tired of the *games*, as he put it, and decided to tell Alex and Clayton the whole story? Kash would figure the men would keep the checks coming, because they wouldn't want their wives' stories made public. It would be too much of an embarrassment for them. Yet by Kash revealing Lora and Suzy's secrets, he would call in at least part of his threat: he would ruin the girls' marriages. Splitting up Lora's and Suzy's otherwise happy homes was most likely one of his objectives all along. *My God,* Lora thought. *Would he really risk doing that? Where was Alex? What if Kash was talking to Alex right now?* Again, it was very unlike Alex not to call and say he would be late.

The phone rang. She knew it was Alex so she was surprised to hear Suzy's hysterical voice on the other end.

"Slow down Suzy," Lora said, "start again and tell me what's happened."

After Suzy explained how Kash had contacted her to say he was holding Tommy and he wanted one million dollars before the weekend for his safe return, Lora was relieved. She should be ashamed for feeling that way, but she wasn't. Suzy's son was in danger, but at least Kash had not gotten to Alex.

Lora was selfish. There, she admitted it. She justified it by remembering that she had to protect herself and her interests. When it came down to it, there was nobody else to do it for her. Unlike Suzy, who had always had Lora to lean on, Lora had no one to rely on except herself.

She turned the gas burners on the stove from low to off and sat down with a pen and paper to write Alex a lengthy note.

Within twenty minutes of Suzy's call, Lora was in her car traveling west to Dalton.

7

Suzy Whitmore tore her house apart looking for any clues which might lead her to her son. In the den, she looked through papers on the desk. Her bank statement was there. On it was the entry for Kash's first check was, but the canceled check was missing. She guessed Tommy had found the check and construed a name from it.

She searched his bedroom for signs of a trail, but the only thing she found was a map of Massachusetts lying open on the bureau. *He could be anywhere*, she thought. She dug deep down into his sock drawer. She knew he always kept a stash of money there. It was gone. Under the bed, she found an ashtray but no cigarette butts were snuffed out in it. She saw three roaches—the remains of the joints he had smoked—and the clip which had held the marijuana cigarettes.

She began to cry. How could she not have known her son was smoking dope? What kind of a mother was she? Had her seclusion from the family forced Tommy to get involved with drugs? Had she been abandoning her son's needs and attention? Had she let Sam Kashette take such total control of her life that she was unaware of things happening in her own home?

She curled herself up on the floor and wept with sincere shame.

A loud call came from the first floor. "Suzy ... Suzy, where are you?"

Lora gazed at the cluttered living room. She ran to the lavishly decorated den and found that it too had been left in shambles. "Suzy?" she called again.

She darted up the steps to the second floor. She saw light coming from Tommy's bedroom, so she headed in that direction. She picked up the pace when she heard weeping from within the room.

Lora gathered Suzy up in her arms. Between fits of bawling, Suzy told her closest friend everything she knew.

"Did you ask Jeff where Tommy had gone to meet Kash?" Lora asked.

"No. I went out of my mind when Jeff told me Tommy knew about Kash. I stormed out of the house like a mad woman and ran all the way home."

"Okay, I think we need to talk to Jeff Baker again," Lora said calmly. "From what you've told me about Tommy, I don't think he would be able to keep something like this to himself. He'd have to talk to someone, and Jeff is his closest friend. I think he knows more than he's letting on."

"So do I. I think his mother sensed he was holding back too. It was after a few words from her that Jeff finally told me Tommy had gone to see Kash."

"Come on then, let's go," Lora said, getting Suzy to her feet. "Do the Bakers live far from here?"

"No. Just three blocks down."

The pair of friends departed the Whitmore's house.

8

At six o'clock on a weekday evening, there was little excitement in Barboursville, West Virginia. Most of the businesses close up shop at five, even the restaurants were not opened much past six. This being the one bad thing about small town West Virginia: the sidewalks get rolled up when the sun goes down. The only places booming at this time of day were bars. People stopped by their regular watering hole to unwind from the daily chaos of the office and other places of work.

Buck's Place was one of those taverns where working folks lined the bar trying to de-stress from the day's affairs. It took but one look for Rosa to figure out that this place was definitely geared toward male patrons. Deer mounts, both buck and doe, covered the walls, along with other animals' heads. Some of the animals had their mouths open, bearing huge sharp teeth; some looked sort of docile, almost like they had posed for the mount. On shelves here and there, whole animals (presumably stuffed) were displayed. There was opossum, raccoon, a couple of squirrels, fox, and the biggest rabbit Rosa had ever seen. Now this was not a typical white fluffy rabbit like the Easter Bunny. Instead, it was a huge gray rabbit with pointed ears that stood straight up. There were no fuzzy, floppy ears on this bunny. Its mouth was open wide too, giving Rosa a full view of all of its teeth. The nose was turned upward and the eyes were squinted. Rosa believed it could lunge off the shelf and eat her alive at any time. This place gave Rosa the creeps.

When she walked in, everybody stopped what he or she was doing to gawk at her. Rosa could see a look of caution in the eyes of the patrons. *Hey, this is our bar. How dare you just walk in here without being invited?* Everyone knew everyone in these local establishments, so on the rare occasion when a stranger did show up in their conclave, people were curious to know who she was. The most logical person to grill a stranger for answer to the patrons' inquest was the bartender.

Rosa took the only seat left at the bar counter. On the backs of each of the bar stools, someone had nailed antlers belonging to male deer, long since dead. Each stool's rack was different, a 10-point rack on one stool, a 4-point on another, a spike on yet another. Rosa wondered if the racks represented some kind of seniority system. Maybe the more years you spent drinking in the seat, the more points you got on your stool. Or maybe people were ranked by how much they drank. Someone nursing a drink would get the spike stool, a casual drinker would get the 4-point stools, and the alcoholics got the really big racks—the 8, 10, or 12-point seats. Rosa found herself sitting in an 8-point stool.

She looked directly to her left at the wall near the far end of the bar. She laughed at what she saw. Among the assorted deer heads, was a mount of a deer's backside. There it was, nailed to a board and hanging on the wall, just like the heads, only it was the rear end of a deer. Unlike the head mount, which contained the neck (and shoulders, in some cases) the rear mount was done without any part of the legs. It displayed, in a bold and blunt exhibit, the split of a deer's butt and its tail.

What an odd place this was.

She ordered a draft beer and a shot of Lord Calvert. The bartender opened the conversation as he poured her shot, hoping to get some answers for his customers. *Always keep the regulars happy*—that was his motto. He noticed Rosa's fascination with the buck's bottom.

"You like the deer's ass? It's a real conversation piece for newcomers. I haven't seen you around here before, mind if I ask your name. Mine's Mike."

The woman looked blankly at him as though the question deeply perplexed her. The bartender extended his hand to shake hers and repeated. "My name is Michael, but everyone calls me Mike."

The woman shook his hand and said, "I'm Rosalee, but everyone calls me Rosa."

"Pleased to meet you, Rosa. Do you live nearby?"

"For the time being. I'm just passing through."

"On your way to where?"

Rosa shrugged her shoulders and giggled again, this time not because of the buck's bottom on the wall, but because of the question. "You know Mike, I'm not sure. I'm still trying to sort that one out."

Oh great, Mike thought, *just what I need. Time to put on my psychoanalysis hat.*

Mike had been Buck's primary bartender for the last three years. He cleaned, he cooked, he served up drinks like a professional, and he was well underpaid. So far, his day had been going pretty smoothly: all the chores were done, the regulars who took their supper with their alcohol were fed, and everybody's glasses were full. Things were going smooth right down the line. He had listened to old Oscar complain about his little aches and pains, he had listened while Peggy bragged again about how her two boys made the honor roll last year. That made three years in a row now for Peggy's boys. Mike kind of wished they would screw up just one time so Peggy would have something different to say. He listened to Kurt whine about his wife leaving him for a second time this summer. Kurt asked Mike if he could tell him how to make lasagna because Kurt claimed it was the only thing he'd truly missed about his wife's absence. Mike wrote it down for him and then followed up with verbal instructions. He wouldn't want Kurt to go another day without his lasagna. Mike lived to please his customers and his tip jars confirmed his effort—two large jars stuffed full on both ends of the bar.

With all the bullshit he'd listened to thus far, he thought he had already earned his money today, yet now he had a new customer to pacify, another chick crying in her beer over a broken romance. From the looks of the woman, the break-up must have been a violent one. Her eye was purple and swollen shut. She had several bruises and cuts on her face. Her lip was busted open in two places, and unless she was in dire need of a nose job, Mike figured her nose was broken, too, since it sat sideways on her face. He also noticed she favored her right arm, which meant that her left one must have been hurting her in a bad way. Yes sir, Mike was underpaid. Even a crappy psychiatrist would soak you for $50 an hour. Mike on the other hand, listened to everyone's problems for a dollar over minimum wage.

He was hesitant to ask the big question, but he did so out of shear kindness for this frail lady. "Do you want to talk about it?" Mike asked.

"No, it doesn't matter anymore." Rosa answered.

Wow, this one doesn't want to talk about it. What a refreshing change.

Rosa drank her first shot and beer back quickly then nursed the second set. She lied when she said her affair with Kash didn't matter. It mattered a great deal, but it was over now. She was finally free of Sam Kashette. All the cares, all the worries, all the burdens were gone. They had simply evaporated. It took a physical beating and a brutally sexual encounter for her to get the ultimate wake-up call, but it had finally happened. She had been so stupid to think she could make a life with him and even more stupid to let things escalate to the point of violence before she had put a stop to it.

She was being frank when she told Mike she didn't know where she was going. She had no idea what she would do about her life now. As though 18 years had never passed, Rosalee DeLucci was faced with the same quagmire: what should she do with her life? And like 18 years ago, Sam Kashette motivated her decision. She could not go back to the convent, and she definitely could not go back home. She was stuck between the preverbal rock and a hard place.

She needed some time alone to take stock before she could make any intelligent decision. This time she would give more thought to whatever she decided to do. She would need Jesus' assistance and guidance, if He would still have her. Reacquainting herself with the Lord would take center stage in her deliberation—not the kind of Lord with which she was currently reacquainting herself. Her days as a nun were over now. She could accept that, but she could not accept life itself without Jesus Christ in it.

She flagged Mike down and asked for another shot. Still soul searching, she wondered about life as layperson. She would have to get this little drinking problem under control soon but not tonight. She had relied on The Twelve Step Program once; she only hoped it would work again. In the past six weeks, she had consumed more alcohol than she had in the 18 years she spent in the convent. Again, she would need God's guidance, yet she was unnknowing in the ways to ask for this kind of forgiveness. Jesus Christ was her virtual husband and in reality, she had been unfaithful. While she was sorry for what she had done, she was in no position to ask Him for anything. She was afraid of turning to the Blessed Mother right now, as well. She was far too ashamed to speak her name even. Rosa's reverence for the Mother of Jesus was still as strong as the day she had decorated her statue at the church when she had been a young girl. She was afraid now that The Mother would not be as forgiving as The Son. Guilt weighed heavy in Rosa's heart. She would have to make amends with Jesus and the Blessed Mother. She wondered if a million Hail Marys would be enough to wipe away her sins.

She would love to call Suzy or Lora and talk to one them, but she already knew what they would say—I told you so—and hearing that was the last thing she needed now.

Rosa liked Barboursville. It was a small, quiet town like Huntington, but unlike Huntington, nobody knew her here, and Kash was 50 miles away. During her walk to the bar, she noticed that Barboursville had a beautiful Catholic Church. She could get herself established there, make a good confession and receive Holy Communion, and get absolution for her sins. Maybe she could do some volunteer work there and make some new friends. She could check with the school board and apply for a teaching position.

She was finally ready to put Kash out of her mind and get on with her life. He had hurt her badly yesterday. The hurt was physical and sexual. Emotionally, however, something was different this time. Usually, after a conflict with Kash—it didn't matter if it was a physical attack or one of a psychological nature—she would be upset for a while, perhaps sulk around and pout for a short time then she would go back to chasing after him again like nothing bad had ever happened between them. Yesterday, Kash had physically beaten and raped her, but today her mental state was in tact, her heart was not breaking. She had no desire to sulk or to pout because the affair had ended. Her heart instead boiled with resentment and anger—

anger aimed toward herself because she let him do this to her after she swore she would never let it happen again—and resentment meant for Kash. She feared him, she loathed him, she surrendered to him.

Rosalee was ready to start over again, and she would like to get that fresh start here, in Barboursville.

The television set above the bar was on and turned to everyone's new favorite station: the Weather Channel. The man on the set stood to the right of a radar screen which displayed a massive green area of precipitation just south of West Virginia. The green gob crawled up from the gulf like the legs of a huge spider. This system, the man said, was headed due north and had the potential to dump a significant amount of drenching rain to much of the drought stricken east coast. Rosa knew that other systems of this kind had developed and never made it to West Virginia, but this system was powerful thus, it would not stall out, so the man said. At this time, Rosa could see that it was already raining in the southern most part of the state. The man said the rainfall would bring new life to the east coast, if, that is, the damage hadn't already been done.

Yes, Rosa thought, *the damage has already been done.*

Rosa had a hard time focusing on Mike the bartender when he appeared to ask if she wanted another drink. Mike didn't find it odd when she asked for a double shot of Lord this time with her beer, but he found it most peculiar when next she asked where she could find the nearest AA group meeting.

9

The walk to the Baker's house took only a few minutes. Lora saw evidence of the spot where Suzy took out the Jenson's rosebush. Neither Suzy nor Lora knew what to expect from Jeff, but something told Lora there was more to learn.

Jeff answered the door after the third ring of the doorbell. He explained his mother's absence by saying that she had gone into town to pick up his father. Lora was relieved to know they were alone in the house. She felt they had a much better chance of getting Jeff to open up if his parents were not there to influence him.

Suzy immediately took the boy by the shoulders and shouted demands at him. Jeff was stunned and confused. Lora gawked at Jeff. She could tell instantly that he was high after one look at his appearance, his manner, and the glassy tint in his eyes. She could smell the moldy residue that clung to his clothes. A stoned kid was not going to tell anybody anything if he was frightened, and Lora could see this boy was scared to death. She persuaded Suzy to back off.

Jeff walked to the couch and sat down. Lora sat next to him. Suzy paced the Oriental rug in front of the dormant fireplace. Speaking calmly, Lora asked Jeff what he knew about Tommy's disappearance. Jeff denied knowing anything about anything at first. After a few rounds of questions without answers, Suzy got into the conversation.

"Jeff, you know whatever you tell us will stay just between us—me, you, and Dr. Jordan, I mean. We have no intention of bringing your parents into this."

Jeff looked at her as if he didn't trust her. *Hey, you, get off of my cloud.*

"Suzy's right," Lora said, "we only want your help. We don't want to cause you any trouble with your family. Tommy's life could be in danger. You wouldn't want to be responsible for that, would you?"

Jeff turned his glance to Lora this time. She seemed more trusting. Finally, he shook his head and answered, "No ma'am."

"I didn't think so." Lora responded. "Now let's try again. Do you know where Tommy went?"

"I told Mrs. Whitmore, he went to talk to that cowboy guy we saw at the 7-Eleven."

"Where did he go to talk to the man? It's very important."

Jeff did not respond right away. *Get off of my cloud!*

Suzy became impatient. "Please Jeff, tell us."

He looked angrily at Suzy. "You should have thought about that before you took up with that guy. If you weren't having an affair with him, Tommy wouldn't be in this spot."

"What are you talking about? I'm not having an affair with anybody. Where did you get an idea like that?"

"Don't deny it. Tommy found the canceled check you wrote to him. He even saw you give it to him the day you met him at Sadler Park. He followed you. You didn't know that, did you?"

Suzy sat down on the bottom step of the stairway and hugged the banister. She was left speechless by the outrageous accusations of a 16-year-old. "No Jeff, you've got it all wrong."

"He saw you, Mrs. Whitmore. He saw you kiss Kash, and it nearly tore him apart. He was convinced his family was going to split up, and he was trying to stop it. He went to tell Sam Kirkland to stay away from you."

Suzy's mind was idle, but as usual, Lora's mind was busily active. Things were starting to make sense to Lora now. With all the facts Tommy *thought* he knew, an affair would be the most logical conclusion at which a teenage boy would arrive.

Suzy cupped her face in her hand and started to cry. This time Lora was against the clock; she had no time to console her. She continued questioning Jeff Baker trying to gain his trust and acquire more pieces to the puzzle.

Lora put her arm around Jeff. He was shaking now. She told him to settle down. She told him Tommy would be fine if only they could find him.

"I tried to talk him out of it," Jeff started. "I told him his mother could handle this thing better than he could. I even told him it was none of his business, but he was determined to try. He said he was going to stakeout the motel where Kash stayed the last time he was in town."

"How did he know where Kash was staying?"

"After Mrs. Whitmore left the park that day, Tommy followed him to a motel, but he didn't talk to him. He just watched him."

"What's the name of the motel?"

"I don't know, Tommy never said."

"Where is the motel located? Is it nearby?"

"No. It's something like 30 minute away."

"Where Jeff? Did he ever tell you the name of the town?"

"Yeah, but I can't remember."

"How much pot have you smoked today?"

Jeff was shocked by the abrupt question. Was it that obvious? He remembered that Mrs. Whitmore called her Dr. Jordan, so he knew it would be useless to lie. "I smoked a couple of bowls. What's that got to do with anything?"

"It has everything to do with it. Marijuana kills the cells in your brain. Your memory isn't as good as it would be if you were straight. Were you stoned when you talked to Jeff?"

"I'd smoked some earlier that day. What difference does it make?"

"Plenty. Sometimes if we can relate to a certain frame of mind, we can more easily recall a particular situation. It's called mood association." She did not have time to explain to a stoned teenager what she had learned in Psychology 101. Lora proceeded, "Try to think back, Jeff. What kind of mood were you in when Tommy came yesterday?"

"I don't know."

"Were you happy or sad? Were you angry? Did you have an attitude? Were you feeling cocky yesterday? Think Jeff, think."

"I was happy I guess 'cause I had a buzz. No wait ... I was pissed off. My dad grounded me in the morning. I was mad."

"Good Jeff. Now think about your conversation with Tommy. Do you remember how it started?"

"Yeah, a little." Jeff squinted his eyes, straining to think. Little wrinkles formed on his forehead just above his brows. "He started laying all this stuff on me about his mom going to meet Kash. He said he wanted to get to him before his mother had a chance to talk to him. I was pissed, because I thought he was being insensitive to my problem. Then he asked me to cover for him. He said he was going to tell his mom he was spending the night with me."

"Is that when he told you he was going to the motel?"

"Yeah, somewhere in there. He said he was going to wait for him at the motel."

"Then he told you where the motel was."

"Yes." Jeff's eyes opened wide. Things were starting to come back to him. "He said it was a 30 minute drive—no wait, a 45 minute drive to ... to ..." He closed his eyes in an effort to recall, "I'm sorry, I can't remember. The name of the town was a man's name though. I'm sure of that."

Lora ran down an imaginary map in her head. She started naming off towns that were within an hour's drive of Dalton. "Was the name Warren?"

"No."

"How about Dwight? Or Hermon?"

"No. It ended in *town* or *street* or *ville* or something."

"Was it Bradstreet?"

Jeff shook his head negatively.

"Phillipstown?" Lora said with some excitement.

Again, Jeff said, "No."

Suzy let go of the banister she had been hugging and looked up from the stairway. She offered without much emotion, "Gilbertville?"

Jeff sprang to his feet. "That's it. Gilbertville! That's the name of the town."

10

Meanwhile, at Buck's Bar in Barboursville, West Virginia, Rosalee DeLucci continued to review her life. The deeper she thought about the catch-22 situation she was in, the more she drank. And the more inebriated she became, the faster her sense of depression grew. She had really made a mess of things this time. Tears swelled up in Rosa's eyes. The overflow spilled out and trickled down her cheeks until they dropped off the edge of her chin and landed on the bar top for Mike the super-bartender to clean up later.

She stumbled off the bar stool, careful not to put too much pressure on her left arm. She had been drinking for nearly three hours. It was her duty to stay until she had drank enough to earn the privilege of sitting in the stool with an 8-point rack on the back. She was on a mission when she staggered to the phone booth to place a collect call to Dalton, Massachusetts. In need of a friendly voice, she debated between calling Suzy and calling Lora, and then decided, ironically, to call Suzy. Rosa thought Suzy would be more considerate of her feelings. She was sure Lora, with her brazen, strong makeup, would be short with her and probably point out the fact that Rosa was a weak, drunk fool, where as Suzy would only throw a few smart remarks her way and be done with it. She would not attack Rosa's current emotional state nearly as badly as Lora would.

After seven rings, Rosa hung up; Suzy was still not home. This was the third call she had made trying to reach her. Each trip to the phone booth was a new adventure since Rosa had put down several shots and beers between calls. Not wanting to go back to the 8-point stool just yet, she sat in the phone booth awhile longer. She hesitated before finally making another collect call, this time to Boston, Massachusetts. At this stage, she couldn't care less what Lora had to say. She needed to talk to someone. She tried to straighten her posture on the little piece of wood that was supposed to be the seat, as if sitting up properly would keep her, in some way, from slurring her words together when she spoke. Yeah right.

Alex answered the phone at the Jordan residence. He sounded somewhat disappointed when he heard Rosa's voice on the other end and not Lora's. He accepted the charges for the call and asked Rosa if anything was wrong.

When she asked if she could please speak with Lora, it came out something like, "Can I *spleak* to Lora?"

Alex explained the situation in Dalton to Rosa. "Lora said that Suzy was trying to keep Tommy's disappearance quiet. Clayton is off on a business trip, so Lora went there to help."

"Do they know who Tommy's holding?" is what came out, but Alex knew she meant to say *do they know who's holding Tommy?*

Rosa did not have to hear the response. She already knew the answer.

"No, at least they didn't when Lora left for Dalton. I'd like to call, but I don't want to tie up the line. I'm sure when there's something to report, Lora will get back to me."

Rosa could hear static in the telephone connection. She assumed it must have been storming on the other end of the line. If Buck's Place had windows, she would have been able to see that the storm was on her end, not Alex's. The sky had quickly turned from a wicked gray to an ominous black. It was raining hard outside, but the jukebox inside muffled the sounds expect for a loud clap of thunder which had suddenly made its presence known now. Rosa flinched a little in the phone booth when she heard the noise outside in one ear and the crackle on the line in the other ear.

A tiny puddle of drool had accumulated in the corner of the telephone receiver's mouthpiece. Rosa's chin brushed through it. She was miserable and worse, she was going to be sick.

"I'll call Lora back later," Rosa quickly blurted out. "Sorry I bothered you."

Before Alex could say it was no bother, Rosalee had hung up. Her head spun from all the whiskey she had consumed. The contents of her stomach sloshed around and crept ever so slowly up her esophagus and into her throat. She had to go now before the Lord spewed out all over the floor of the phone booth.

When she stood up her knees were rubbery, like Gumby, the little green man that you could stretch in every direction. Rosa had one of those as a kid, she remembered. She swayed a little before she got her balance by holding on to the corner of the phone booth. When her eye caught sight of the Buck's ass on the wall again, she laughed a little. It was just enough movement to churn the Lord in her stomach to the top of her throat. She took a swift walk to the restroom.

In a bar such as this one, it was not surprising to find the head of a female deer hanging over the entrance to the ladies' room. It was not surprising either to find a sign that read 'Doe' instead of ladies. The men's room was laid out on the opposite side of the bar. A deer head hung there too, but over the entrance to it was that of a male deer and the sign on this door read 'Bucks' instead of men.

Inside the door marked 'Doe', Rosa knelt over the toilet. She was not really kneeling over it, but more like hugging it, hugging the old porcelain throne. It had been a long time since she had been this drunk. With one tiny gag, Rosalee emptied her stomach.

Where did all this stuff come from?

She felt like she had thrown up her entire intestinal tract. She checked the goop in the toilet just to make sure.

What makes people do that, she wondered. *Why is it that people always look at whatever comes out of their bodies' orifices? Whether it's something coming from their nose, or their mouth, or their butt—they always look.* Nevertheless, Rosa found no intestines.

By ridding herself of some of the booze, she became more aware of the pain in her body. Her eye thumped, her lip had split open again, her muscles ached, her shoulder burned, her nose and lower back were sore, and then reality made its way back into her mind: she had been raped. She had seen Kash's darkness, his utter blackness, and now he had Tommy.

Just then, thunder boomed—two, three, maybe four times, in quick succession. The storm was directly overhead. Rosa could hear rain pounding on the roof, even over the jukebox now; the pellets that were hail pinged against the building and off of the cars that were parked in the lot. Then came another loud bang. The lights flickered off ... on ... off ... and then back on again.

She started to retch once more; the Lord wanted out. Her stomach, which was still sore from Kash's blows, hurt her even more by the act of regurgitation. She coughed then flushed when she had finished. At the sink, she splashed water on her face then shoveled several handfuls of water into her mouth. She would have sold her soul for a big bottle of Listerine.

Once the alcohol had been discharged from her system, Rosa felt a bit better. She was still hurting, still drunk, and things were still spinning, but not as badly.

She made her way back to the stool with the 8-point rack. She wanted nothing more to drink. If puking up your guts were not enough to deserve the honor of sitting in an 8-point stool, then so be it. She left Mike a generous tip and then gathered up the change from the bar top. After a second thought, she threw the handful of change into the tip jar as well.

The building had emptied out. Most of the patrons who had been inside drinking were now outside looking at the rain. She found it hard to believe that something as simple as water falling from the sky would be intriguing enough to clear out a bar. Then again, there had been no rain in five months, so she guessed it really was a big deal.

The residents of West Virginia had always believed that the rugged mountain terrain would prevent a tornado from ever touching the ground here. Tonight, that theory would prove to be only a myth. When Rosa looked out the door of Buck's Place to see what exciting activity out there had captured everybody's attention, she heard a muffled roar in the distance that grew louder and sharper. Suddenly, she saw a snake-like form of swirling mist take shape. The end of the funnel was laced with brilliant lightning. It was a rare event for all of the meteorological ingredients to come together to form a tornado in this climate, but tonight the conditions were just right. Not even West Virginia's highest mountain could deter the super-cell from circulating. Rosa watched the swirling mist stagger and twist a path alongside the bar. Beer cans, and debris, and small gravel stones from the parking lot were sucked up into the whirlwind like a giant vacuum cleaner. Some of the debris was spit back out and hurled at buildings or toward the cars in the lot.

The patrons who were outside raced back to the shelter of the bar. By the time they had made their way inside again, the swirling mist outside was gone. It had dissipated as quickly as it had formed.

She would not find out until morning when she read the newspaper that the tornado was a F1 on the Fujita Scale. She would also read about a coop of twenty chickens on a farm just around the corner from Buck's Place. The chickens there had been plucked clean of every feather from the circulation of wind which fed the storm.

Rosa fumbled in her purse for the little folding Totes umbrella that she kept there. Her hand brushed the cold metal of Frankie's gun she had taken from *Nonna's* china closet at home.

If Kash did kidnap Tommy, which she was sure he did, she simply could not stand by and watch. She had to do something. Yes, she knew exactly what she had to do.

CHAPTER FIFTEEN

Just Believe With Your Heart

1

Suzy sped down the interstate following close behind Lora's sporty car. They took both cars so they could cover a wider territory in their search for Tommy. They presumed Kash would not use his own name to register at a motel, so they did not waste time calling ahead to the different establishments. However, they never considered he would use the name Sam Kirkland either. If they did, they could have found Kash as quickly as Tommy had.

They pulled off the interstate and drove only a short way before they saw the sign, *Welcome to Gilbertville*. Lora pulled into the first gas station she came upon. She jumped out of the car, ran to the phone booth, and grabbed the telephone book. Leafing quickly through the yellow pages, she found the section for motels. She tore out two pages. Surprisingly, there were six motels or hotels in the small town of Gilbertville. Lora ran to Suzy's car and handed her one page from the phone book.

"Here, you cover these three places, and I'll check the other three. We shouldn't have too much trouble finding him. The town isn't that big."

"How do we go about looking for him?"

"First off, check the parking lot for any West Virginia plates. I don't know if he came by plane, but he certainly had enough time to drive up. If you don't see any WV plates, go in and talk to the clerk. Ask them if they registered anybody giving a WV home address, or if they remember anybody with a southern accent, or anybody with a Stetson hat. The creep doesn't go anywhere without his stupid hat. Tell them you're a doctor and you have to get medication to this person. Most of the time they won't even question it; they'll just check their records."

"Okay, that's fine," Suzy said. "But what happens when we find him. What then?"

"We'll cross that bridge when we come to it."

Lora took a pen and wrote her car phone number in the margin of the yellow page. "If you find him before I do, call me and let me know where you are. What's your number? I'll call you if I find him first."

Lora jotted Suzy's number on her page before the two women left in different directions.

The first place on Suzy's list was a high-class joint called The New England Regency. She really did not expect to find him there, but she searched the parking lot anyway. There were no WV plates in the parking lot. She didn't even check with the clerk because she knew this was not Sam Kashette's kind of place.

The second motel was about four miles away heading out of town. It was a small motel, maybe a hundred rooms, that sat off by itself down a little country road. *Yeah*, she thought, *this is Kash's kind of place*.

She pulled into the parking lot and started hunting for the Mountain State license plate. She saw many plates from different states, but so far, no WV. Keeping a slow steady speed, she checked the second row of parked cars. Her heart began to race when she spotted the beat up old pickup bearing the plates for which she searched. She moved to a higher speed, eager to talk to the desk clerk. When she reached the office door, she threw the car into park and hurried inside.

The desk clerk at The Sleep-Over Inn confirmed that he had indeed registered a gentleman from West Virginia. He checked the register and gave Sam Kirkland's name and room number to Suzy. Kash and her baby boy were in room 85.

Suzy bolted back to her car and looked for the room number. Once she found it, she pulled the car around the corner to get out of sight until she could reach Lora. She dialed the number that Lora had written on top of the yellow page listing, but after six rings, she hung up. Lora must have been inside one of the motels checking with a clerk. She wished Lora would hurry back.

Inside her Lincoln Town Car, Suzy was fidgety. She fiddled with this and that, adjusted the seat then the rearview mirror, and in between, she bit her nails. The sky became increasingly darker as clouds that looked like puffs of dirty smoke emitted from a smoke stack, inched its way over the horizon. Up above, thunder bellowed from a distance, rattling and rumbling like a lawn mower resistant to start. She could see faint flickers in the sky from lightening still far away. The humidity was 97% with a 72-degree dew point today. The weather forecasters had been calling for thunderstorms for the last three days, but they never formed. Tonight, though, it looked like they could get some doozies.

Suzy ran the air conditioner for a while to get some relief from the heat, but the humming and the vibration coming from the unit made her uneasy. She feared she would not hear Tommy if he needed her, so she rolled down the electric windows instead, before turning off the motor. Even though the outside air was sticky, the fresh breeze made her feel better.

Suzy could hear someone quarreling, but she was unable to see who it was. She checked the area around her and saw no one, yet she could still hear two people bickering. She listened more closely for a familiar voice, maybe Kash's or even Tommy's, but neither voice was familiar. It came from just around the corner. A couple there seemed to be arguing over the woman's car, which was apparently in need of repair. The man told her he would fix it for her, and she insisted that she could do it herself. "I don't want or need your help, Bruce. Just leave me alone." Suzy heard the woman say.

Directly, she heard a car door clap shut and the man pulled away in his car leaving the young woman alone.

Suzy hit the re-dial button on the car phone—still no answer. Suzy was eager to rescue her son. She tried to put herself in Lora's shoes. What would Lora would do if Lora were here? Lora would have a plan, that's what Lora would do. Suddenly an idea came to Suzy. She got out of the car and approached the young woman.

"Excuse me," Suzy said, "but I couldn't help overhearing your conversation with your boyfriend."

"He's not my boyfriend; he's my ex-husband," the girl replied.

She was short, blond, and busty, and appeared to be a bit of a scatterbrain, Suzy thought. She chomped swiftly on a piece of bubblegum, cracking it loudly as she chewed.

"He can't accept the fact that we aren't married anymore. He still thinks he needs to take care of me and he doesn't."

"Yes," Suzy shook her head acknowledging the problem. "I have a similar problem. You see my ex-husband is staying in this motel. He's in room 85."

"Wow, does he have woman in there with him?"

"No, but he does have something in there that belongs to me. He stole it when he was getting his things after the divorce. I was going to break into his room when he left and take it back, but he hasn't come out all day."

"That's a bummer. How long do you plan to wait?"

"That's my problem. I can't stay much longer. I have a teenager at home that I really need to get back to."

Suzy snapped her fingers as if to say an idea had just come to her. "You know, I think you could help me. Your car is not running, right? Well, my Kash knows everything there is to know about cars. I'll bet if you knocked on his door and told him your car wouldn't start, he'd come out and look at it for you. Then, while he was fixing your car, I could sneak into his room and get what belongs to me. I know it's a lot to ask, but do you think you could do this for me?"

"Well, I can't see any harm." The girl pondered the idea not yet agreeing to anything. "After all, I do need to get my car started, and we women have to stick together, don't we? Which room did you say?"

"Eighty-five ... it's about halfway down this row. I'll wait around the other corner until I see him leave."

"I'll be glad to do this for you. I can't stand to see innocent women like us get stepped on. I'll give you a few minutes to hide before I knock on the door."

"Thanks so much. You're a life saver."

Suzy made her way to the other end of the building walking between two rows of parked cars. She was careful not to be seen by the occupants in room 85.

The clouds were beginning to thicken; a few drops of rain dotted the ground, as well as Suzy's clothes. A chill ran though her body, not one that was generated by the cooling spots of rain, but rather one that was generated by the fear of something unknown, as if to say that maybe this little idea of hers was not such a good idea after all. Maybe she should have waited for Lora. Suzy usually didn't do well when left to her own devices.

The wind had picked up now. It blew discarded candy wrappers around the parking lot. Empty soda and beer cans clanged when they brushed against the pavement.

When Suzy was safely hidden around the corner, she watched the busty, blond girl approach Kash's door. She said a prayer for this little plan of hers to work.

2

Inside room number 85, Kash stood by the sink in the bathroom holding a piece of Kentucky Fried Chicken in front of Tommy's mouth. Tommy nibbled as best he could without actually being able to hold the chicken himself. Kash had removed Tommy's gag so he could eat with the promise that there would be no more outbursts. So far, Tommy was holding up to his end of the bargain. He was very hungry. Kash was in the process of feeding him a spoonful of mashed potatoes when a knock came at the door. Kash pointed the .44 toward Tommy.

"Not a peep out of you, kid. Got it?" He stuffed the washcloth back into his mouth and taped it securely in place.

When he reached the door, Kash peeked out the peephole. He did not recognize the blond girl but pulled back the curtain at the window anyway to get a better look. An almost silent whistle escaped him when he checked the fine body of his visitor. She looked like a typical dizzy broad though, and since he didn't know who she was, he had no intention of answering the door, yet the knocking persisted all the same.

"What do you want?" Kash yelled though the closed door.

"My car won't start. Could you please take a look at it for me?"

"No. I don't have time."

"Please mister, it's getting dark out here and it's going to storm any second. I don't have enough money to stay another night. Please!"

Kash open the door but left the chain hooked. "What's wrong with your car?"

"I don't know. If I knew, I'd fix it!"

Kash laughed, realizing how stupid his question had been. This Inferior would think that a piston was a tin you took a piss in.

"Please mister. I've knocked on every door in this row. Nobody will help me."

"Just a second. I'll take a look at it."

Suzy's instincts were right: Kash could not pass up the chance to be the macho man when a busty bimbo was in need of help. The young woman was saying thank you when Kash shut the door. He went to the back of the room and closed the bathroom door.

He did not lock it because he assumed he would be back in a few minutes. Before he opened the front door, he pulled the gun from the back of his pants and laid it on the dresser. He threw a copy of today's newspaper over top of it. Kash left room 85 to assist the helpless damsel in distress.

As they walked in the direction of her car, the blond turned and winked at Suzy just before Suzy opened the door and entered Kash's room.

Once inside, she expected to find Tommy somewhere out in plain sight. She panicked when she didn't see him anywhere. She quietly whispered, "Tommy? Tommy, are you here?" Never once did she consider that maybe Kash had taken Tommy elsewhere. She heard a soft mutter coming from the bathroom. She opened the door and found Tommy.

She was horrified at the sight of her son wrapped like a naked mummy and connected to the toilet with silver tape.

"Tommy, oh my sweet Tommy," she said as she moved closer to him. Not knowing how long the blond could keep Kash occupied, she knew she must move quickly. She removed the tape from his mouth and pulled out the washcloth. He gagged on the bit of chicken that was still in his mouth when Kash stuffed the washrag back in. She tried to pull the tape around his chest loose but could not get a hold on it.

"There's a penknife in the pocket of my jean." Tommy informed his mother.

Suzy scurried to the outer room, returning with his clothes; the pocketknife was already out and opened. She started the process of cutting Tommy loose.

Each time Suzy pulled off a section of tape, hair from Tommy's chest—and hair from other more tender body parts as well—were yanked out by the roots from deep beneath his skin. The pain was tremendous, but Tommy believed he could withstand any amount of suffering to get out of this mess. When he had been a child, he remembered how his mother would remove a band-aid from a scraped knee or elbow. She would always rip it fast, so it would hurt less. She seemed to be using this same technique now, only Tommy knew pain was not what she tried to spare him this time. This time she was trying to spare his life.

Within minutes of entering the room, Suzy had detached her son from the bonds which had held him there for the last ten hours. When Tommy tried to stand up, his legs were weak. He could feel pins and needles pinching from his toes to the cheeks of his buttock. Quickly Suzy helped her son get dressed. Walking was almost impossible, but with the aid of his mother, he struggled to his feet and began what seemed like an endless journey toward the door. Suzy wrestled vigorously with Tommy's weight rested against her body. She struggled to hold him up. Her grip on him weakened, and before long, Tommy was on the floor.

"I can't do it mom. My legs are numb ... my knees won't work."

"You have to do it Tommy. Kash will be back soon. Now get up, we've got to get you out of here."

Once again, Tommy rose to a standing position. They were approximately four feet from the entrance, when the door flew open and the large frame of Sam Kashette blocked the entry way. Behind him, the heavens displayed a spectacular light show. Bolts of energy sparked one after another, illuminating the dark, cloud-filled sky. The bursts of light were so bright, Suzy found herself squinting, as if looking at it would give her flash burn. Thunder exploded in unison with its partner.

Without saying a word, Suzy charged Kash, dragging Tommy's limp body along with her. The futile attempt perturbed Kash. He lashed out at Tommy, easily knocking him to the floor at the foot of the bed.

Suzy lunged toward Kash again, this time sticking him in the stomach with the small penknife she had used to cut Tommy free. The knife pierced his belly just to the right of his bellybutton. She twisted the knife a half turn and then used all her strength to drive it upward.

Kash felt the stinging twinge as the knife penetrated his stomach. His darkness was back; the Bad Thoughts filled his being. They had never really left since the episode with Rosa at The Jug. His mind was crammed with the Bad Thoughts, with the pictures—the little scenes of a play, miming his forthcoming actions. He struck Suzy with a closed fist lifting her off her feet. He was emulating the scenes in his mind.

She landed three feet away on top the bed near the footboard. Directly below the place where she lay, Tommy was positioned face down on the floor, his nose pressed into the shag carpet which, by the way, was in dire need of vacuuming. She could only pray that he would not move.

Tommy exerted an effort to crawl on his belly toward his abductor. He stopped moving on the spot when Kash grabbed the gun and pointed it in his direction. The newspaper that covered the weapon had not even hit the floor yet.

To Suzy, Kash said, "You stupid lunatic, you cut me! I can't believe you were foolish enough to bring a knife to a gunfight. You are one crazy bitch."

Kash kept the gun pointed at Tommy. He held his wounded side with his free hand. Blood trickled out between his fingers. The pain was tremendous. His vision was clouded by the Bad Thoughts. His darkness had blocked out everything else, had blinded reality. He could only do what the pictures told him to do now. In a final attempt to restore sanity, he recited a Healing Rhyme. Whether or not he it realized it, he was talking out loud.

> *One I love thee, two I love thee,*
> *Three I love I say.*
> *Four I love with all my heart,*
> *Five I cast away.*

Just as Kash suspected, the Kentucky doctor's rhymes proved inept this time. The Healing Rhymes were no longer functional. The Bad Thoughts had taken over totally. This time, his darkness would not pass.

Suzy Whitmore looked into the face of a madman. What was he trying to say with the poem? His eyes were opened wide. They appeared to be wild when he pulled back the bolt of the pistol. Taking two steps in Tommy's direction, he said to Suzy, "An eye for an eye, a tooth for a tooth. You took my child's life from me, now I'll take your child's life from you."

With those words, Sam Kashette took aim at Tommy with the .44 caliber pistol.

To Suzy, what took place next felt like it was going in slow motion. First, she screamed one word, "*NO!*" Then, giving no thought whatsoever to her actions, she rolled off the bed and hurled herself on top of her son, just a split second before the gun was fired. She would not be held accountable for the killing of another child. She would rather be dead first.

Outside, the roar of thunder so distant not all that long ago, was directly above Gilbertville. The sky had opened up, and Suzy heard rain thumping down on the roof. The wind howled; little hailstones struck the window. Angry outbursts from the sky should have sent shivers up her spine, but instead, Suzy felt nothing—her body was numb.

The bullet entered her in the middle of her back. She knew her spinal cord had been severed because she had no feeling throughout her body. She was helpless to move her arms or her legs. The shallow breathing sent signals of a punctured lung as well. She knew her time was limited. She wondered if the bullet had traveled clear through her body and into Tommy's. She tried to speak, but no words came out.

She had heard somewhere that when you die, your life flashes in front of you. For Suzy it was like watching a home movie. She saw her wedding day, the day Tommy was born, and the ceremony which had made Clayton president of the University. She saw bad memories too—the day she laid on the table at the abortion clinic, the day she and Clayton had fought, and the day she saw her father lying in the coffin. *Oh daddy*, she thought, and then she saw him. He stood in the center of a puffy white cloud with a great bright beam radiating around him.

"Suzy," he said, and stretched out his arms for her. She knew her time had come. She tried to hold on a little longer before reaching for her father's embrace.

Kash stared in disbelief at the two bodies heaped like a pile of dirty clothes on the floor. He was unaware his anger had turned into rage, and rage had turned into the demise of two lives. The Bad Thoughts had been controlling his actions. The killing was easy now. If he had known just how easy, he would have killed many times before. The conclusion was simple: if someone got in the way of The Order, remove the obstacle. He had to kill again. He had to do away with Lora before she had a chance to talk. With both of them out of the way, the connection between himself and his old flames would never surface. Then he remembered Rosalee. Yes, Rosa would have to be taken care of as well. He must hurry.

He tossed the pistol in his overnight case. Using his handkerchief, he swiftly swabbed the exterior of everything he remembered touching. His side stung and burned at the puncture site. The more he moved, the more defined the stream of blood from his stomach flowed. The rain came down in sheets now, mixing with hail that sounded larger than it probably was. The rumble on the roof matched the rhythm kept by a hundred bass drums playing in unison. The sound of thunder echoed within minutes of each other. Kash was about to wipe clean the knob on the front door when he looked up to find a woman standing there—a gun held out in front of her. It was too dark to see a face, but he knew it was a woman. Her hands were too small and her body too petite to be that of a man.

Behind the woman, Kash could see Mother Nature's fury and could hear her anger. A dark mass of clouds covered the sky. At first, Kash thought he was looking at a really big patch of fog in the distance, but as it drew closer, he saw it was actually a rotating cloud, a cloud which brought with it a wall of flying debris.

The woman stood at the door amidst the rain and hailstorm. She wore a yellow rain coat, the hood pulled over her head. She pulled the trigger. Sam Kashette saw the white flash coming at him. He heard the deafening bang of the pistol. Outside the unearthly roar grew steadily louder. The red circle in the middle of the flash struck him in the center of his bulky chest. Warm sticky liquid sprayed out of the wound with each of the last flutters made by his heart.

Kash closed his eyes expecting to see a white light, or a tunnel, or a bunch of angels, or some other ridiculous thing people claimed they experienced before being brought back to life—or perhaps before cheating death. At first, he saw nothing but darkness then slowly a picture began to emerge. It was a picture of a deck of playing cards, two decks to be exact—one blue back and one red back. Suddenly the cards were thrown to the floor. The two decks jumbled up and mixed together as if the card handler wanted to play 52-pickup. Some of the cards lay face up; some were face down. The blue back cards were mingled in with the red backs, and all the cards were lying at different angles: long-ways, side-ways, kitty-corner. Kash was notably agitated by the vision. If this was what awaited him on the other side, he wanted no part of it.

Kash could feel life draining from his body. He fought hard against it. Then he felt something else too. A pull on his heart, only now he realized it was not pulling his heart, but instead his soul—he really did have one—and Rosalee was tugging hard. Rosa's likeness crossed over the threshold of his mind. His stomach hurt from the puncture, his chest hurt from the gunshot wound, but his heart hurt from Rosalee. Her face appeared over the cards, sort of like a transparency. He was still able see the cards through her face. He could feel her gathering, yanking with all her might so hard that Kash thought his soul—now that he knew he had one—would be ripped from his body.

In his mind, he saw her as she was the day at Ruby Tuesday. He listened again to the words she spoke. *"Believe with your heart, Kash. Jesus makes it easy. All you have to do is ask. It's as simple as opening a door."*

Below Rosa's face and the playing cards was a plate of food, the same meal he had ordered for her that day. He could see her hands separating the food with a fork just as she had done at the restaurant. She had no body now, only a transparent face and a pair of transparent hands.

How could he have been so shallow to believe only in things he could hear, feel, see, taste, or touch? How could he have been so foolish and so quick to dismiss the theory of the other side—a side where he was sure there would be no place for him now? His shirt became quickly saturated.

The plate of food had gone away, and Kash could see Rosalee's hand again. She started to separate the playing cards by color.

As his last minutes in this life expired, Kash asked Jesus to be his Savior. He asked forgiveness for his sins and accepted Christ into his heart. *How did that prayer go?* Kash thought. The one Gabby had taught him when he was a boy. *Oh my God, I am ever so … no, that wasn't the right word. Heartly … that was the word. Oh my God, I am heartly sorry for having offended Thee …*

Rosalee's hands made two stacks from the jumbled playing cards—one blue stack and one red stack.

… and I detest all my sins because of Thy just punishment …

Rosa organized the blue deck by suit—clubs first, then spades, diamonds, and hearts last.

… but most of all because they offend Thee my God …

… then the red deck—clubs first, then spades, diamonds, and hearts last.

… who art all good and deserving of all my love.

Next Rosa arranged each suit in the blue deck by numerical order from ace to king …

I firmly resolve, with the help of Thy grace …

… then the red deck, each suit from ace to king.

… to sin, no more and to avoid the near occasion of sin. Amen.

Rosa's hands fanned out the cards in perfect order so Kash could see it.

Yes, what he saw now was much better. Rosa was trying to tell him there would be order where he was going.

Rosa's prayers had finally been answered.

If for only a mere second, Sam Kashette was at peace but not before lightning filled the sky and lit up the face of the woman who was wearing the yellow rain coat—a woman who had spent her lifetime loving him.

3

Lora heard sirens blare when she pulled into The Sleep-Over Inn. She had known there was trouble here whenever a stranger answered Suzy's car phone. The woman told Lora that Suzy never came out of her ex-husband's room. The woman was worried.

The windshield wipers on Lora's car thump, thump, thumped against the glass as they cleared the windshield. The rain poured down with great force. Pea-sized hailstones hammered her car.

She panicked when she heard a shot from a nearby room. She was sure Suzy didn't have a gun; therefore, the shot must have been fired by Kash. She hurried to find a place to park the car. As she got out of the car, she heard a second shot from the same direction. At least she thought it was a gunshot. It was hard to tell over the thunderous roar of the storm. She ran toward the sound. She never gave a second glance to the woman wearing the yellow hooded rain gear trotting in the opposite direction.

Lora saw the same rotating cloud Kash had seen. Only now, it had changed from misty white to a solid brown mass. A powerful jet of air flowing into it picked up debris and loose earth as it slinked along. Lora watched as a thirty-year-old cottonwood tree behind the motel began to snap. She would not find out until later that the tree had landed a block away in the parking lot of a Kentucky Fried Chicken, the same Kentucky Fried Chicken where Kash had bought Tommy's dinner, and the same Kentucky Fried Chicken where Kash had hidden Tommy's car. The cottonwood tree came to rest on Tommy's jet black BMW, flattening Tommy's Bimmer.

Lora spotted an opened door. When she entered room 85, three bodies were crumpled on the floor. Kash's body was just inside the doorway, Suzy's body on the floor at the foot of the bed face down, and under her body laid Tommy's. Lora saw the gaping wound in Suzy's back.

She knelt down beside her dear friend to check for vital signs. Her pulse was very weak, but nonetheless, she was alive. Outside, the high-pitched shrill of sirens told Lora help was close by.

"Lora," Suzy said, her eyes barely open.

"I'm here baby. The police and ambulance are on their way," Lora said looking into the slits that used to be Suzy's beautiful dark eyes. She gathered her old roommate up into her arms.

"No more secrets," Suzy whispered through staggered breaths. "I have to make peace. Please explain everything to Clayton. No more secrets."

Suzy's breathing had all but stopped; her heart barely made any movement at all. Life sustaining blood crawled in her veins with no force to push it through her body effectively. She hurt nowhere—then again she could not feel anything either—yet she hurt everywhere. Her neck moved. That was good but none of her other parts worked.

She closed her eyes, and she was a littler girl again, maybe seven or eight years old. It was bedtime back at the house in which she had grown up. Dressed in a little satin nightgown, she knelt beside her bed, her hands folded and resting on top of the quilt. The bed had been turned down and Suzy had been recently bathed. She could tell because her hair was still wet, and she could see the pink tint from hot bath water on the bottom of her feet where she knelt.

Now I lay me down to sleep, I pray the Lord my soul to keep. If I should die before I wake, I pray the Lord my soul to take. Amen.

She made the sign of the cross and got up off her knees. When she turned around, she saw her daddy standing in the doorway. A huge smile covered his face. She returned the smile. Her heart burst with love for him.

"My little angel," he said.

Back in room 85 at the Sleep-Over Inn, Suzy opened her eyes and blinked. When she closed them again, she saw her daddy, but this time he was back in the middle of the clouds surrounded by the great light. Suzy reached out for her father's hand. Prentis Shaffer extended his arms to receive his little angel. He embraced his daughter and guided her into the light.

Then, Suzy Whitmore drew her last breath.

Lora Jordan pressed her face to Suzy's cheek. Emotion that had been held back for many weeks, flowed easily now in the form of tears. From the first day Lora had met her, Suzy had been the one who was always running late. For once in her life, she had been on time, and Lora was the one who was late. The result was fatal.

All of a sudden, Lora rolled Suzy onto her back. She ripped her blouse open and began pounding on Suzy's chest.

"You're not going to do this to me," she yelled angrily. "You're not going to leave me in this tight spot."

Even now, Lora was still taking care of Suzy and her problems. She vigorously performed CPR on her friend.

"Damn you Suzy don't die. You can't leave me here alone to explain this mess."

When she realized the efforts were hopeless, she stopped CPR and laid her head on Suzy's chest. Then she mourned.

Within seconds of Lora's grieving, the police bolted through the door, their drawn weapons pointed at Lora. Between sobs, she tried to explain that she was a doctor and a friend of the dead woman, but the officers were not convinced. They barged in and surrounded Lora. One of the patrol officers held Lora by the arm, while another one forced her into a spread eagle position to frisk her. As the officer in charge checked her ID, another trooper appeared at the door.

"Hey Sarg, you'd better come out here."

"What's up?" the Sergeant replied casually. He had been looking over Lora's identification.

"A lady turned herself in to Mollohan—right out here in the parking lot. We took a look in her car and found a 9mm Berretta. Looks like a police issue. She says she killed the guy. She keeps saying 'he had to die … he had to die.'"

"Does this woman have a name?"

"Yeah. Gabbert … Sarah Gabbert."

CHAPTER SIXTEEN

Gabby's Chronicle

1

Captain Brad Neely was unaccustomed to all the chaos going on in the small building which served as the police station in Gilbertville. The last time anyone had been murdered in this town, Brad was on vacation, and that was seven years ago. He had no indication when he started his shift at 5pm that the night was going to turn out to be this crazy, but now at 5am he had two dead bodies—one male and one female—a teenage boy nearly in shock, a husband of the female victim in tears, a fairly hysterical doctor, and a 75-year-old lady who confessed to one of the killings. An F2 tornado had swept through Gilbertville. The last time that had happened was 1937 when Hurricane Alfa came through leaving a trail of small tornados behind. It had been steadily raining now for the past six hours and although the ground was totally dehydrated, flashflood warning had been posted for the entire county. Rain was falling at the rate of two inches an hour causing many small streams and creeks to overflow their banks. Could it get any worse?

With Tommy's help, Lora had managed to track down Clayton. Tommy told his father about Suzy's death. He was completely devastated by the time he arrived at police headquarters a few hours later. He turned to Lora for some answers. She complied by telling him every detail of the last three months. Only after explaining to Clayton the particulars about the blackmail and their past relationship with Sam Kashette, did Lora tell him Suzy's story and one of the reasons for the extortion.

Lora had earlier revealed her own secret as the reason for the blackmail to the middle-aged Captain Neely.

Tommy was questioned as well about the incident. He told the police captain how Kash had knocked him out and tied him up in the bathroom. He said he heard Kash make the call asking his mother for money in exchange for Tommy's safe return. Tears filled the boy's eyes when he recounted the part where Kash had intended to fire his weapon at Tommy, before his mother had thrown her body on top of his to shield him from the bullet. After making his statement, Tommy had nothing left to say; he sort of stayed to himself.

Lora on the other hand was full of questions. She asked Captain Neely, "How is Kash's next door neighbor involved in this mess?"

"Do you know Sarah Gabbert?"

"No ... not personally. I remember meeting her at the funeral when Kash's parents were killed. Kash spoke of her many times back then."

"My deputy's gone downstairs to holding. He'll be bringing her up to my office in a few minutes. She insisted on telling all of you everything in person. Why don't you go in and wait with the others."

Reluctantly, Lora followed the captain's instructions and opened the door to his office. She took a seat in a straight back chair.

Lora had not seen Sarah Gabbert since their initial introduction nearly twenty years ago; however, she recognized her as soon as Gabby was escorted through the door. Although she wore orange coveralls, provided by the Gilbertville PD, every strand of Gabby's silver hair was neatly in place. Her hands were cuffed in the front, but because her nails were groomed and polished, the cuffs simply looked like a pair of silver bracelets. *My God, she's America's grandma*, Lora thought. *Why in the world would she want to kill Kash?*

Brad Neely entered his office, sat down at his large but cluttered desk, and took control of the conference. He took a moment to get his papers in order, and as he did, he glanced at the visitors sitting around the room. Tommy stared straight-ahead, unaware of the goings-on around him. Clayton sat next to him on the couch. Although he consoled his son, he too was in need of consoling. He dabbed his eyes and blew his nose again. Brad hated like hell to put this ragged man though this, but it had to be done, and there was no time like the present. His eyes turned to Lora next, who was sitting in one of the chairs directly in front of his desk. She seemed to have settled down somewhat, Brad thought. Sarah Gabbert was waiting impatiently in the other chair. She rubbed the palms of her hand along the front of her pants; she appeared to be apprehensive.

"May I start now, Captain Neely?" Gabby asked.

Brad removed his wire-rimmed reading glasses and straightened the stack of papers on his desk. He was ready to give this story his full attention.

"You may begin, Mrs. Gabbert, as soon as you're ready."

"I'm ready. I've been ready for the last 38 years."

With those words, she searched her memory for a place to start. Everyone listened attentively as she spoke.

"I don't quite know where to start, but I reckon the best place to begin is at the beginning.

"Kash's mother's name was Katy Johnson. As you know, Kash now lives in the house where he was raised by Katy, but what you may not know is that Katy was raised in that same house as well—the house next door to mine. She grew up with my children. I was her teacher when she was in the fifth grade, as well as her neighbor. Katy was a delightful child. When she was in her early teens, her father was killed in the Korean War. She was devastated. She and her father were very close.

"As Katy matured into her high school years, she became interested in boys and dating, as did the other young girls her age, but even though Katy was very attractive and carried a lovely figure, she had few steady boyfriends. One young man, Howard Kashette, tried to date her for several years, but she continually put him off. She said he wasn't good enough for her. She told me once that since her father's death, she had come to realize that life was very short, and it could be taken away in a snap, so she wasn't about to waste her life dating boys she wasn't really interested in being with. She said she would wait until the right one knocked on her door, and then she would jump in with both feet. You see, she had her sights set on the perfect man. She wanted a jock, but he also had to be intelligent, funny, and at the same time, romantic enough to sweep her off her feet. I hated to tell her, but men of that caliber were few and far between. Katy was convinced Howard was not that type.

"One day early in the summer, 39 years ago, Katy was lying on a blanket in the back yard. She was wearing a swimsuit. Her mother had been working on that particular Saturday. She, Mrs. Johnson, would have died if she had seen her daughter lying out there half-naked. In those days, women didn't sun themselves the way they do today, but there was Katy, all greased up in her two-piece suit working on a tan. I had taken my three younger children for their dental appointments that afternoon, and my two older girls were visiting friends, so after lunchtime, my house was empty except for my oldest son, Larry. He watched Katy from the kitchen window.

"When Larry was sure everyone had gone, he slipped through the back door of our house and moved quietly across the yard. He raped Katy Johnson, violently tearing the swimsuit from her shapely figure. He attacked her with great force, leaving marks on her newly browned skin. Katy never told her mother about the episode. She came to me instead. When I confronted Larry, he seemed to be very pleased with himself for what he had done. He said she deserved it. He said she should not have been exposing herself to him that way. Larry said Katy wanted it as badly as he did. I knew at that moment there was something mentally wrong with my son.

"One week after the rape, I put Larry into an institution. He was diagnosed with Borderline Personality Disorder, a mental illness that affects your mood and your self-image. The doctors never knew about the incident with Katy Johnson, although it would have come as no surprise. Unusual and sometimes violent sexual misconduct is part of the illness. You have to understand, his disturbance was the reason for the attack—he wasn't a bad kid. People suffering from Personality Disorders often act out their anger, and for Larry, seeing Katy lying there for the taking, made him very angry. Don't get me wrong, I am in no way condoning my son's actions, but I have come to understand that he was not himself when he violated her."

"Where is your son now?" Captain Neely inquired.

"My son is dead. Three months after he was put in the hospital, he killed himself. He couldn't take being confined to one place. He hung himself with the bed sheets. I only wish I had known at the time that suicidal threats and self-destructive acts were symptoms of Larry's disease. I would have kept a better eye on him.

"The other thing I didn't know about Borderline Personality Disorder is that the disorder is biologically inherited. So when Katy approached me shortly after Larry's death and told me she was pregnant, I became worried. She told me Howard Kashette had asked her to marry him knowing the baby was not his. He would take full responsibility for raising Kash and supporting Katy. Shortly after Kash was born, Katy's mother died. She and Howard moved into the family house along with Kash. I was glad to have my grandchild near me, even if he would never know I was his grandmother. I never told Katy about the genetic connection until Kash was in college and seemed to be a normal young man. That day, we sat at the kitchen table and talked. The window overlooked the same backyard in which she had been raped. When she asked a favor of me then, I felt obliged to grant her request. I believed I owed her for the life my son had taken from her. She asked me to promise that if anything ever happened to her, and if I ever saw Kash showing any signs of Larry's illness, I would have him put away forever. She did not want Kash to do to anyone what Larry had done to her. I gave her my word. A few days after our conversation, she and Howard were killed in a car accident."

"But why did you kill him? Wouldn't it have been easier to do what you promised? To have him hospitalized as you had done with your son," Brad Neely inquired.

"No. I knew what Kash had gone through in prison. You see, like his biological father, he couldn't handle confinement either. Eventually, he would have done the same thing Larry had done—he would have killed himself anyway—only he would have suffered every day until he had the opportunity to take his life. I felt my way was the most humane approach. He never knew what hit him."

"When did you notice the first signs that Kash had this personality disorder?"

"When he came back from serving his prison term. He hardly ever came out of the house. He always had the drapes pulled. It was as if he felt safe inside the house where nobody could see him. I noticed he seemed very insecure. He mentioned one time that he felt inferior to other people, like he didn't stack up or fit in anywhere. I told him it wasn't true, but I knew these were the first signs of personality change. God knows I had read enough about it over the years. So I started to keep a close watch on him. I noticed that sometimes he would become preoccupied with himself. He would act as if nothing could harm him. He had no fear of anything. He didn't believe in God, so there was never any limit toward his principles or his way of living. He thought he was entitled, special. Then at other times, he would act emotionally shallow. He would say things like: *I don't care if I die today, and I don't know who I am or what my real purpose is*. He carried feelings of emptiness and loneliness. Sometimes he would get very depressed. On those days, he would drink heavily.

"Kash was always the kind of person who thought things out well before acting on them. As a matter of fact, he was meticulous to a tee. He had his Order and he lived by that Order. Even his food had to be placed on his plate in a certain fashion—no two foods could touch each other. If it did, he became extremely agitated. I believe his time in prison produced some higher plane of obsessive-compulsive tendencies. His Order had been so screwed up he didn't know how to handle it all. About a month ago, he began to act impulsively no matter what he was doing, and he displayed highly unpredictable behavior. I knew Kash was frequenting the local brothels, but lately he would bring five or six different women home in one week. His then current relationships were usually temporary and brief. I talked to him one day about his sexual promiscuousness, and he became angry. In his life, he had never said a mean word to me until that day. I had walked in on him and a lady friend the morning after, and he was very critical of the young woman. He was mean and degrading when he spoke to her. He even called her a slut. I didn't take too lightly to that. His voice was cold and the words he spoke were bitter and sarcastic, not only to the woman, but to me also.

He called me a nosey old lady, a washed up old school teacher. I had never seen that side of him before. He showed a great lack of respect or regard to both this girl and me. He was revealing all the signals of his father's illness. From the time my son Larry was a small child, he felt other people, especially women, were second-rate, and on that day, I could see Kash was taking the same attitude as his father's.

"That day he also told me about a reoccurring dream he had been having. There was a frightened little boy in the dream, who was locked in a small room. When the little boy heard footsteps outside the door, he wanted to feel relieved, because someone was coming to let him out, but instead the little boy in the dream became more frightened. Kash told me he always woke up before he could see who had opened the door. That person was his father.

"Both Katy and Howard had paid little attention to Kash when he was a small child. They were too involved with their friends to give him much notice. They frequently had people over and threw parties until all hours of the night. I tried to keep Kash at my house on those nights, but sometimes I just couldn't. When he was left with his parents, they would lock him in the hall closet until their friends had left. The two bedrooms were being used by people taking hard drugs or for other couples to have sex. When Kash reached an age where he would be able to remember the things his parents were doing to him, they backed off somewhat. At this point, they would just leave him behind when they wanted to do something or go somewhere. Those first four years had to be a nightmare for poor Kash—a nightmare that was beginning to resurface. The hall closet was the setting for Kash's dream. The blob that had frightened the boy in the dream was nothing more than winter coats hanging there in storage. He had been too young to remember being locked in the closet. He'd blocked out those memories of his childhood for years, but now he was starting to remember. I was horrified at the thought of how he would react when he realized his parents had treated him so terribly.

"About a week ago, I watched Kash from the outside of his living room window. He didn't know I was there. When I first started to watch him, he had been sitting in his chair staring at a blank TV screen. Then, for no apparent reason, he became disturbingly angry. I looked on with considerable sadness as he completely demolished his sitting room. He threw things across the room, ripped pages from the books in his bookshelf, knocked over tables, even punched a hole in one of the walls.

"One time many years ago, Kash had confided in me about some feelings he had been having. He called them the Bad Thoughts—his darkness. He told me he would see little movies inside his mind, sort of like a daydream, and these Bad Thoughts would urge him to act on what he had seen. I had all but forgotten about the conversation until the day I watched him trash his living room. I knew it was too late. He had inherited Borderline Personality Disorder. The time had come; he had to be stopped."

Lora's hatred for Sam Kashette had suddenly turned into pity. She had listened to everything Gabby said but still could not believe all she had just heard. She was disappointed in herself. She had seen the changes in Kash, and being a doctor, she should have been able to distinguish that Kash had a mental problem, but she didn't. She was a neurologist; she should have seen it coming.

Captain Neely was about to ask another question, but Lora beat him to it. "Gabby … did you know Kash was blackmailing Suzy and me? Did you know he had kidnapped Tommy?"

"No, not until last night. Rosalee DeLucci paid me a visit. At first, I didn't know whether to believe her story, but after giving it a little thought, I knew she was telling the truth. You see, she was very drunk, not to mention she had been beaten badly. She told me Kash had done that to her. I knew history was repeating itself. She said that she had spoken with your husband, Alex, and he told her of Tommy disappearance. She knew immediately that Kash had taken the boy. She wanted me to go with her to try to convince Kash to let the boy go. Rosa told me Kash had been taking money from the two of you. She explained in detail the nightmare through which you and Suzy had lived. I told her I would go along. I went into the kitchen to make some coffee in an attempt to sober her up, but when I returned, she was passed out cold on the couch. Her purse was lying on the floor next to her. Sticking half out of it was the butt of a gun. I took the pistol with me and decided to make the trip alone."

"How did you know where to find him?" Brad probed.

"Before I left, I went to Kash's house. I've always had a key. I searched for something that would indicate his whereabouts. Among some bills on his desk, I found two receipts for the Sleep-Over Inn. When I saw the address was in Massachusetts, I knew that's where he would be. He was a creature of habit. I took the first available flight, which happened to be within the hour. I had no luggage with me. I guess airport security didn't believe a little old lady carrying only a purse would have anything to hide. My pocketbook was never checked. I boarded the plane with the gun. As soon as I arrived in the state, I rented a car, got directions to Gilbertville, found the motel, and you know the rest."

"You understand, Mrs. Gabbert, that you're under arrest for the murder of Sam Kashette, and you're being held over for …"

"*No!*" Tommy jumped to his feet, "Why should she be punished for killing that son-of-a-bitch? She did us all a favor. That man killed my mother. He deserved to die."

Tears streamed down Tommy's cheeks. He turned his body away from the others. Clayton stood up to comfort his son—it would just be the two of them now.

Gabby approached the grieving pair. She placed her bound hands on Tommy's shoulder in a consoling manner. "I'm sorry for the trouble Kash has put your family through. I'm sure your mother was a fine woman, and I'm so, so sorry he took her from you." To Clayton she added, "Please accept my condolences and my apology on behalf of my grandson."

With tear-filled eyes, she told Captain Neely she was ready to go.

After Brad adjourned the meeting, Lora left his office. Alex and his lawyer were waiting for her in the outer room. He extended his arms to Lora, but she could tell from his touch that he had no sympathy for her involvement with Sam Kashette. Alex told her that he had briefed the lawyer of the situation. A sudden sense of hopelessness came over her.

"Dr. Jordan, the police in Huntington are searching Mr. Kashette's house for the evidence you told the captain about," the lawyer informed Lora. "You'll have to remain here until they have finished."

"Am I being charged with anything?"

"Not as of yet," the lawyer replied.

Lora glanced at Alex. Their marriage was dwindling. She could tell from the disillusioned look in his eyes. After a wait of about an hour, word came from the Huntington Police. Captain Neely brought the news.

"The Huntington police called. They found nothing to link Lora or Suzy to the dead man. They found no papers from a clinic in Kentucky nor did they find a cassette tape or any tickets tying Lora to a drug swindle. The only thing they did find was a few deposit slips for large sums of money."

"Those were the checks Suzy and I had sent to Kash," Lora explained to Captain Neely.

Alex's lawyer stood up. "Well as I see it, there's simply no evidence to hold my client any longer."

"That's correct counselor," Captain Neely said. "If you'll come with me we can get the papers signed and Dr. Jordan is free to go."

Lora mumbled a thank you. She and Alex were now alone. Lora was shocked about the findings.

"I saw those papers Alex, and I heard the tape," she said. "Kash must have hidden them somewhere else. I don't want any more secrets."

"I know you don't," he replied.

Alex was shattered; nevertheless, he held his wife tightly.

"I thought I knew you Lora. I thought I knew the woman I married, but I don't know who you are at all. Everything you stood for has been wiped away by your past. Even after you explained why you took the drugs and sold them, I still can't accept your logic. When Kash came after you, why didn't you come to me? Don't you trust me?"

"Of course I trust you. I didn't think you would understand. You always put me on a pedestal, Alex. You told me I was special; you thought I was perfect, for God's sake. I didn't think I could count on you."

"If you can't count on love, what can you count on?"

"Yourself," she answered.

Lora fought back the tears. She felt like Alex now viewed her as a self-centered woman who only looked out for herself. As long as she got what she wanted, it simply didn't matter who she hurt in the process. What brought out the tears was that she knew Alex was right. She was selfish, but she could change. She could do anything to save her marriage.

Alex was lost for words. Lora looked into his dazed eyes. "Can you ever forgive me Alex?"

Alex took a second to think before he sighed and said, "It will take some time, Lora. But I think we can get through this."

Lora now cried and smiled at the same time. She kissed her husband and held him firmly. She never, ever wanted to let go.

CHAPTER SEVENTEEN

The Simple Thing in Life

1

Lora sat on the couch totally engrossed in the dancing flames at the fireplace. The fire snapped and crackled. With every orange flicker, tiny explosions of cherry aroma filled the air. This October evening in 1994 was a cool one, but Lora was toasty, not only because the fireplace generated heat, but also because her life with Alex was finally back to normal. Fifteen months had passed since that dreadful day in Gilbertville.

She picked up an apple from the basket on the coffee table and began to buff the fruit. *Wow,* she thought, *so much has happened, and so many things have changed since that night at the Gilbertville Police Department.*

After the shooting, Lora and Alex had spent the next two days in Gilbertville. Trees were down everywhere from the storm. A major bridge that connected the main artery leading out of town was totally under water. Many roads had been washed out. Basically, they had been stranded there.

When the electricity and television cable service had been restored in the tiny town of Gilbertville, Lora and Alex watched the reports of the storm on the Weather Channel. Tornados had touched down in both West Virginia and Massachusetts—two states not commonly plagued by such weather events. The experts on TV said the entire storm system seemed to have a great number of oddities associated with it.

In Gilbertville, the south wall of The General Store had been blown down and shattered; while a shelf of can goods, which stood against that same wall, were unmoved. The cancelled check with which Tommy had confronted Kash had traveled 80 miles to the northeast. The founder turned the check over to the Gilbertville PD.

In Dalton, where the Whitmores lived, a tornado had brushed through

Suzy and Clayton's bedroom, clearing the contents. Clayton's necktie rack was carried 40 miles. The 10 ties were still attached. A four-page love letter from Clayton to Suzy written 15 years ago ended up 30 miles past that. The four pages never separated throughout its journey.

Near the campus of Kanawha State in West Virginia, an iron jug which sat outside a bar called The Jug was blown inside out; a rooster was blown into the jug. Only its head stuck out of the neck of the jug.

In Rosa's hometown, a bag of mail was found in the DeLucci's front yard. The mailbag belonged to a postal worker from a town 110 miles southwest of Huntington.

Lora could relate to the queer events. When she and Alex had finally made it back to Boston, they found the kitchen of their house setting three feet away from the rest of the structure. The kitchen's inside had been completely destroyed, yet the shell of the room remained intact. It looked like someone had just picked up the room and moved it. The other 11 houses on Kelsey Circle were untouched.

Lora believed the destruction caused by the storm and the strange happenings that surrounded it were easy to explain. She was sure Satan had been welcoming Kash back into the lair. She was certain he was celebrating the return of one of his servants. While she and Rosa agreed the destruction was the work of the devil, they could not have been farther apart on the reasoning. Rosa believed the devil was expressing his anger because Kash had accepted Jesus. Rosa's theory was simple: the devil was a sore looser.

It rained day and night for the next eleven days.

Suzy had been buried four days after the shooting. Even though Lora had not kept in touch with Suzy for many years prior to the Kash incident, she was still crushed by Suzy's death. Clayton took it extremely hard, and Tommy was completely devastated. Lora's heart went out to them. Rosalee came to Massachusetts for the funeral. Lora was happy to have her by her side. She needed someone to lean on. Even though Alex had been sympathetic toward Lora's feelings, Lora and Suzy and Rosalee had been through so much together, the two surviving roommates needed each other more.

Rosa left on the evening of the burial service. She told Lora she would go back to the Mother House and try to correct all the wrong that had been done. Her intention was to leave the convent, and she wanted to get the paperwork started as soon as possible so she could make peace with her fellow sisters and with God. She also needed to make it a quick transition so she could make peace with herself and start a new life.

A few days after Rosa left, Alex accompanied Lora back to West Virginia. They searched Sam Kashette's house from top to bottom. The dispensing tickets, Suzy's records from the clinic, and the cassette tape were nowhere to be found. They found no keys for a safe deposit box or any other records which may have lead them to search elsewhere. Lora was very scared. She needed to find the papers and destroy them before they turned up in the wrong hands or before she ended up in jail.

As the weeks went by, however, Lora pushed the thought of the papers to the back of her mind. She and Alex had been working out their problems, and of course, her work at the hospital kept her mind occupied. Her PET scan had arrived just before Thanksgiving. The staff at Boston General was quite proud of their Chief of Neurology.

Lora called the Whitmores regularly, (about twice a month), to check on them and to see if there was anything they needed or anything she could do for them. Subconsciously, she assumed she did this because she felt partially responsible for what happened. Besides, she did not have Suzy to take care of any longer, so she transferred that care to the remainder of Suzy's family. During one call, Clayton politely asked her not to phone again. He explained that he and Tommy were trying to get on with their life and that Lora was a reminder of something about Suzy they were trying to forget. Clayton did not want his memories of Suzy tarnished by that part of her life. Lora never called again.

By Christmas, Alex had lost the last pesky 15 pounds that Lora thought would never come off. Her worries about his health had diminished, and she and Alex had recaptured the marriage they had had before Sam Kashette came back into Lora's life. She believed the reunion with her husband was the best Christmas present that she ever could have received, but on Christmas Eve, the true Saint Nicholas brought news which overjoyed both her and Alex. She had no way of knowing when she opened the front door one night that their lives were going to change forever.

When the doorbell rang on Christmas Eve, Lora opened the door to find Rosalee standing on the porch, suitcase in hand. She had been to Huntington with the hope of spending the holiday with her family, but they had turned her away. They said they were reluctant to see her again, and they told her she was no longer welcome there. She could not bear spending Christmas alone; she had nowhere else to go. The Jordans welcomed her into their home. That evening, as they watched the lights on the Christmas tree and listened to Perry Como sing Christmas carols, Rosa told them she was pregnant. The seed Kash planted had been growing inside her for five months. She told them about the time she had spent with Kash. Lora remembered the look on her face that night. It was the look of a woman in love. She described, in great detail, the love she had felt for him at one time.

Then she told them about the day at The Jug, and about the rape. She said she could not determine whether the baby had been conceived in love or in violence. The timetable between the two emotions had been too close to call. Either way, she could not keep the baby. Rosa cried as she explained the reasons why she could never accept this child. She was finally free of her connection to Kash, finally over any feelings she had felt for him. She was convinced that each time she would look at the child it would be a constant reminder of her failures and of her ever-scorned heart. She told them she was going to give the baby up for adoption. Lora remembered how the adrenaline ran through her veins as she listened. She was sure she knew why Rosa had showed up at their doorstep, and she was correct. Rosa asked Lora and Alex to take her baby. They discussed the consequences of bringing up another man's child, but neither Alex nor Lora gave it much thought. They agreed to raise Sam Kashette's baby.

Both Lora and Alex had done extensive research on Borderline Personality Disorder. Lora had spent all her free time in the hospital library. They learned that their adoptive child had a 50/50 chance of inheriting its father's disorder. They decided to take the chance. After all, the baby would not have all of Kash's genes—it would have some of Rosalee's genes too. They wanted this baby badly. Lora was aware of all the symptoms of the disease. They would monitor the child closely and if any symptoms occurred, they would seek immediate help. Lora prayed that maybe a treatment would be found before they ever needed it.

Rosalee had moved into the guest room of the Jordan's home. She had no money and nowhere else to go. She would not be able to get a job until after the baby was born, so she really had no way of supporting herself.

Lora tried to make Rosa's pregnancy as comfortable as possible, but Rosa simply could not wait until the whole gestation period was over. Ironically, Rosa's wish came true on Easter Sunday, for at 1:10 AM Rosalee DeLucci had given birth to a beautiful 6-pound baby girl. On Easter Sunday, one year from the day that Kash had been released from prison, another life had been freed, thanks to her adoptive parents. Lora and Alex were delighted with the family's new addition, but Rosalee opted not to share in their delight. She became steadily more depressed. She cared less about holding the baby or even seeing it for that matter.

Two days after she had given birth, Lora had gone to Rosa's room to bring her breakfast, but Rosa was gone—no note, no nothing, just an empty, silent room.

Currently, a crying baby in the crib on the second floor brought Lora back from her daydream. She looked at the apple which she had begun to polish a short time ago and was surprised to find that she had not only polished it but had eaten it as well. The core was clutched tightly between her thumb and forefinger. It must have been there for a while given the dark brown tint of the core.

Lora went to her baby, changed her diaper, and carried her downstairs to prepare a bottle. Suzana Lee Jordan was now six months old. When they passed through the living room, Lora heard the distinctive sound of the garage door closing.

"Listen sweetie," Lora said to the bundle in her arms, "you're daddy's home."

The baby giggled and cooed.

Lora and Suzana greeted Alex at the door. He kissed Lora and took little Suzana into his arms. While father and daughter played, Lora leafed through the mail Alex had carried in from the box. She recognized the handwriting on the clasp envelope at once. It was a letter from Rosa. She tore open the envelope.

> *Dear Lora,*
> *I didn't intend to wait so long to write, but it's taken longer than I expected to get my life on track. I've finally gotten settled in a quaint apartment in a town on the eastern coast. It's a small town, but it's quiet, and its residences are country people and really nice. I registered at a new Catholic Church here, and I attend Mass every Sunday. I volunteer as a "little sister" three nights a week, working directly with the nuns in the parish. We do a lot of good work in the community. I am also attending AA meetings on a regular basis.*
>
> *I hope you will understand when I say that after I have written this letter I will no longer be able to keep in touch with you. It eases my mind to know that the baby will always be taken care of, and I have you and Alex to thank for that. The two of you rescued me from a virtually impossible situation. I had nowhere to turn until you gave me hope.*
>
> *However, I must insist on one detail that concerns the child. I don't ever want her to know about me. As far as the baby is concerned, you are her mother, and Alex is her father. You must never tell her about me. Please promise me that. In return for your silence, I have enclosed something of great value to you.*

Lora pulled the remaining contents from the clasp envelope. What she found brought tears to her eyes. Inside were the dispensing tickets from Charleston Memorial and the tape Kash had made of Rob Parker. Lora whispered to herself, "My God Rosa, how did you get these things?" She read on …

> That night at Gabby's, after I sobered up, I realized Gabby had gone on to Boston without me. I discovered Frankie's gun was missing from my purse too, and I knew what she had gone to do. You see, I had known all along that Gabby was Kash's grandmother. Twenty-two years ago when Kash and I were in high school, we worked on a project together for one of our classes. We were assigned the task of tracing our family tree. We were supposed to swap ideas and help each other with research, but as with anything Kash and I did together, I did all the work and Kash got all the credit. When I began investigating Kash's family background, I discovered that Howard Kashette was not listed as the birth father on any of Kash's records. The father was registered as unknown. After some deliberating, I confided in my Nonna about the findings. She told me that I should think twice before I revealed any of my findings to Kash. She said if the family had wanted him to know about his birthright, they would have told him. Then she told me the story about Larry Gabbert and the alleged rape. She also told me that Katy Johnson left town shortly after the incident and returned a few years later with a husband and a baby. I checked into the story and verified everything my Nonna had recounted. The papers had run a couple of pieces on the rape, and although the rape victim's name was never made known, I knew in my heart it was Katy Johnson—things were just too coincidental. The dates all matched, and there was no mistaking the facts.
> When Kash's parents were killed, I assumed the secret had died with them, until that night at Gabby's house. When I learned the gun was missing, I knew that Gabby knew what I knew, and I was sure she had gone to stop him.
> Since I was alone next door to Kash's house, I used the opportunity to go there and look for the incriminating evidence he was holding over you and Suzy's head. I found the dispensing tickets in his bedroom under one of the ceiling tiles, and I found the tape in the basement buried in a jar of marbles. I never found Suzy's records from the clinic. Apparently, he didn't have them to begin with. He had been bluffing all along. I can't tell you how it saddens me to know that Suzy lost her life over threats of evidence Kash never had. I cannot bring Suzy back, but I hope these papers and this tape will lessen your feelings of worry. I owe you so much.

Lora was crying now. Alex put the baby in the playpen and came to the hearth to sit next to his wife. She handed the first page of Rosa's letter to her husband.

Lora's fear of loosing her career and of going to jail had overwhelmed her for over a year. For the first time in Lora's life, she felt as though her hands had been tied—she was helpless. Without knowing the whereabouts of the papers, the worry had grown each day. She needed someone to bail her out this time and someone had been there for her. Just as Lora had protected Suzy Shaffer and the grown woman Suzy Whitmore, Rosalee DeLucci had protected Lora and her interests. The feeling she was experiencing now was indeed a new one, and it was a genuinely good feeling. Lora turned her attention back to the conclusion of the letter.

> *I have not tried to get in touch with my parents since I left Boston. I did, however, write to Frankie via the police department. I knew he would not get the letter if I mailed it to my parent's house. He answered my letter within days and wants to correspond regularly. You see Lora, I've come to understand that time heals all. Eventually, I believe the rest of my family will contact me just as Frankie has.*
>
> *Remember Lora, God is forgiving—He has forgiven me and He has forgiven you. Just believe with your heart. You must put the past where it belongs.*
>
> *In closing, I would like to wish good health and happiness to you, and Alex, and your new baby. You have been a wonderful friend. You will be in my prayers, my thoughts, and in my heart always.*
>
> *All My Love,*
> *Rosalee*

Lora looked up from the letter. Because of her greed, some 15 years ago, she lost two very good and loyal friends. Until now, Lora never realized what true friendship was all about. Until now, she never understood that the important things in life were not about money, or material things, or social status, but about people. She watched as little Suzana sucked on a bottle in the playpen. Things began to fall in place. Alex and Suzana were important to her; her family was important. Their future, their well-being, and their good name were the things that mattered now. Kindness toward others would be rewarded three fold in the end. It took 39 years, but life finally made sense to Lora.

Alex put a loving arm around his wife. In his hand were the dispensing tickets from the hospital and the cassette tape.

"What do we do with these?" he asked.

Lora wiped the tears from her eyes. She took the handful of papers from her husband and walked to the fireplace. She dropped them into the fire one by one. Alex followed suit by tossing the tape of Rob Parker into the fiery pit. As they watched the contents turned to ash, both Alex and Lora reflected their own thoughts. Maybe they were thinking about the second chance they had been given at a life together, maybe they were thinking about the happiness and joy Suzana brought them, maybe they were thinking about the love they felt for each other, or maybe they were thinking about secrets that brought nothing but destruction into their lives. But probably they were thinking about faith—faith in friends and people and, most importantly, faith in God. If you just believe with your heart.

The End

Printed in the United States
126742LV00002B/94-249/P